SUN RISING IN THE WEST

Does Japan Buy California?

Tom H. Richardson

tomhr1954@yahoo.com

Ὑπό Τῷ Ἥλιῷ

HYPO TO HELIO BOOKS

Houston

School/Library ISBN: 978-1-49298920-2
Bookstore ISBN: 978-1-938293-00-9
Ebook ISBN: 978-1-938293-06-1

Second edition, first printing
First edition, 2000 (private printing)

Front-cover and back-cover art by Tom H. Richardson

The "Hariuddo Sign" was photoshopped from a photo by Getty Images (David McNew, photographer)

Contact Tom H. Richardson at:
tomhr1954 AT yahoo DOT com

HYPO TO HELIO BOOKS
2427 Clearbrook Drive
Missouri City, Texas 77489-6061

Author's Note—
Sun Rising in the West

In 2005, the Senate receives a treaty that sells California to Japan. Senate wife Barbara objects to the treaty. Barbara's Japanese mother Takeko objects to Barbara objecting. What's worse, Barbara's husband, California's junior senator, is pushing <u>for</u> California to be sold. Matt's secret reason: He arm-twisted Japan's ambassador into promising a huge bribe.

So sue me, I like to read the tabloids. In 1991 or 1992, the *Weekly World News* ran an article claiming that "top Japanese businessmen" were pressing the U.S. government to cede California to Japan because of the trade deficit between the two countries. I read the article, thought "This is [nonsense]," turned the page, and forgot about what I'd read. Or so I thought.

In January 1993, I had a dream that Japan had bought California, and I was touring the new Japanese colony three years after the transfer. I woke up with the thought, "This would make a bestselling book!" The next morning, I started researching the novel.

I completed the first draft in February 1994. But I'd never written a novel before, and I needed to learn the craft and then rewrite. Actually, I needed to do a *lot* of rewriting. Worse, this novel required a godawful amount of spot research, and often the results of my spot research themselves forced rewriting. All in all, it was 2000 before my commercial novel was written well enough to be placed with an agent and publisher.

That's when I discovered that there was no market for my story. Japan was by then just emerging from a long and crushing recession, while the United States during those same years had enjoyed unbroken prosperity. In the 1980s, Americans were afraid of the Japan juggernaut; in 2000 Americans saw Japan as a has-been nation economically. American readers in 2000 would not spend cash on a book asking if Japan would buy up an American state; therefore no American publisher was interested in my story. I found out the hard way, that a commercial novel can be destroyed by commercial forces, regardless of the quality of its writing.

Then to add to my joys, in February 2000 Japan's Diet (legislature) passed a bill eliminating twenty proportional-representation seats in its Lower House. You probably don't understand (or care!) what that means, but accept that this news killed one of my major plot points.

So in 2000 I quit trying to sell the novel, and began my next writing project. The decision to quit hurt like hell, because in 2000 I was finally satisfied with the writing in the manuscript.

Experienced authors can write and revise a novel in six months to a year. Had I been able to do that, had I finished and sold the manuscript in 1994, now I would be hailed as a prophet. Because so many fictional elements of my first draft of February 1994 happened later in real life: an intelligent young Washington beauty in a menial position lures a politician through her knowledge of a sexual specialty, later there is talk of impeaching that politician, there are allegations made that this Washington politician was bribed by an Asian power, and a presidential election hinges on a close election in a populous state. Well, I didn't write the novel in six months, so I'm not being hailed as a prophet—instead, I seem like another ripped-from-yesterday's-headlines hack. "Winds and snows."

So that's the story about the story. Why should you read my novel? It's gripping, it's unique, it's funny, it's thought-provoking, it's sexy, and—it's damned cheap.

Enjoy.

Author's Note II

Suppose Japan had trillions of dollars to spare. Also suppose, the USA desperately needed that money. Ah, the possibilities. . .

Hello

You've never read a book like this before. Where on the planet is a book about Japan buying California?

But that unique premise isn't the only goody you'll find in this book. My villain lives out his favorite sex fantasy, while both the Mafia and the yakuza make big trouble for my heroine. I blended into the story 1-1/2 romantic subplots. You'll smile at a TV comedian's jokes, and then there's—

Sorry, I don't want to spoil any more surprises. You'll just have to read the book.

Now, I know what you're feeling. "Japan buying California? Can't happen."

True. My story is a fantasy, and perhaps a warning. What my story is *not* is some dire prophecy.

Could California be really sold to Japan? Let's see, Japan needs elbow room, raw materials, and a frontier for its young people—bad news for Californians. More bad news: I believe selling off California is possible under the U.S. Constitution (he casually mentions). The good news: such a sale is extremely unlikely politically. And *if* the U.S. government were to negotiate unloading California, Washington's asking price would be so impossible that Tokyo very likely would walk away.

So Japan *might* buy California, but probably won't. Then there's the third possibility: California might be spared when Japan realizes Rhode Island is affordable.

Enough. You don't want to read about probably-won't-happen political scenarios, you want a hell of a ride between the covers. This book delivers. I've worked hard to make this imaginary world seem utterly real and completely entertaining.

Information Overload, and How I Worked to Prevent it

I began with a wild idea (Japan buying California), and I took it seriously. The result is that this book presents a lot of information in such a way that you enjoy the story instead of becoming confused (or bored). I've inserted the most essential information into the story itself, briefly, or else into this Author's Note.

For diehard wonks, at the end of the book are three appendices. But for everyone else, remember you're not in Literature class anymore; the appendices aren't required reading.

Family Names—Before or After Given Names?

When someone who is speaking or writing Japanese refers to a Japanese by both family name and given name, the family name is given first. This order is the opposite of the Western custom. To prevent confusion, the first time I give both names of a Japanese character in a Japanese context, I put the family name first, in all caps. (ex: MIFUNE Toshiroh).

Japanese refer to Westerners, including those with Japanese surnames, by family name second.

Japanese 101

Americans, when listing a range of numbers, count up from the lowest, while Japanese count down from the highest. Americans say *two or three*, but Japanese say *three or two*. Americans say *southwest, northeast*, while Japanese say *west-south, east-north*. When answering a negative question ("You didn't commit the murder?"), *yes* in English means *But I did,* whereas *yes* in Japanese means *That's true, I didn't.*

When writing in English that's actually Japanese, I've followed Japanese forms of addressing people, appropriate to their status as compared with the status of the speaker.

Japanese has more words and grammar to distinguish the addressed person's status, with regards to the speaker, than does English. This greater status-vocabulary allows flattery or insult, from using the wrong form of address, that an English translation cannot render.

Japanese address higher-status people, and lower-status people in very formal situations, by name and title ("Clerk Smith"), or just title ("Clerk"), rather than "Mister," "Mrs.," etc. (To save beginners from needing to master a huge vocabulary of Japanese job-title words, beginning Japanese-language books oversimplify and tell the beginners to call everyone "X-*san.*" Though still polite, this is not always most proper.) All the conversations between Japanese in my novel, except when clearly between friends, I've written as following the title-rule. Senator Nakamura addresses Japan's ambassador in English as "Excellency," in Japanese as "Ambassador Fujima."

In Japanese, a person always introduces himself without a title ("I'm Smith," rather than "I'm Smith-

san," or "I'm Clerk Smith.") Someone within a group refers to others within the group without titles, when talking to someone outside the group.

Elvis started to walk away. "Wait, Presley-*san,*" John Lennon said. "McCartney, Harrison, and Starr will go with you. Is Jagger-*san* also coming?"

Note that I've used -*sama,* -*san,* and -*kun* (explained below) when I haven't used a title. Any of the three may be translated as "Mister" or "Miss," but this blurs the distinctions in respect of the three terms.

(Warning: If you don't want to know more about Japanese address, skip the rest of this section.)

Sama is used when the speaker is being very respectful, *san* is everyday-polite, and *kun* is familiar. The word *kun* is used by a man to address another man of equal or lesser status, or by a boss to address a subordinate of either sex. Please note that a difference of only one year, in starting school or in starting a job, creates a very real status difference in Japan. Neither *san* nor *sama* is gender-specific.

Friends in Japan who are older than college age when socializing address each other only by family name, with *san* or *kun* at the end, and even friends use no given name.

Lovers in Japanese, as in English, address each other by given name. Unlike in English, they append -*san* ("John-*san*").

Older family members in Japanese are referred to and addressed by their relation to the speaker (such as "Father," "Mother," "Older Sister"). Younger family members are referred to and addressed by their given name then -*san* (or in the case of children, their given name then -*chan*).

Scholars: I've Fudged Some Facts to Make a Better Story

American and Japanese economic numbers.

I've made Japan of 2005 much richer than she's ever actually been, while I've made the United States more messed up economically than we were in the late Seventies. Don't take my story as prophecy.

Senate procedures.

It is a truth universally acknowledged, that Senate committee bill-markup sessions and Senate floor debate both are boring to listen to. Thus transcripts of such are boring to read. I had to confront this problem to write a gripping novel.

My Senate procedures are correct where it matters. However, I've skipped much real-Senate procedural minutiae and parliamentary gamesmanship that would be boring without a great deal of my explanation. (And probably even with it.)

Timing of the ordinary session of the Diet.

A Diet ordinary session is 150 days. I've convoked the Diet on January 20, 2005, and I've counted the days at the rate of five days/week. I've stopped the count during five Japanese holidays. Thus my Diet ordinary session ends on August 24, 2005. (Since 1947 Diet ordinary sessions have run for 150 calendar days, and so end in June.)

Politics in Japan.

Realizing that American readers know zero about Japanese politics, I've oversimplified such. The informed reader will notice only bare mention of factions within the LDP, no mention of the JCP as a spoiler party, and no mention of intraparty power struggles among the leaders within each party. I've simplified the leadership of Japanese political parties.

Conflict between Japanese characters.

Wakoku wa wa o kizuku kuni desu (Japan is the land aware of harmony). In any disagreement, Japanese culture values keeping harmony, not "being right." Thus Japanese are soft-spoken and act calmly in conflicts where Americans are grandly histrionic. To a novelist, of course, calm and quiet equals boring. So I compromised culturally with Superficial Politeness: Japanese characters in opposition observe the forms of politeness, yet their conflict is clear.

Characterization of politicians.

Respect for politicians got erased in 1998. In the U.S., 1998 began with Zippergate and ended with Republican voter-deafness. Japan in 1998 endured Diet politicians who took no action except blaming while Japan's economy rotted; Japan in 1998 also was rocked by bribery scandals galore. But cynicism is a tiring emotion. So except where the plot demanded it, I made the politicians in my story concerned about the greater good, statesmen who rose above kneejerk partisan game-playing and cynical vote-pandering. My naïveté was deliberate.

In short, the fictional economies of both countries are fanciful, my Senate procedures are wrong, my Japanese politics is oversimplified, and Japanese characters act somewhat American, and I don't characterize all politicians as rascals. Yet despite these distortions (or perhaps because of them), I say you will enjoy this book. And if my story disturbs you, remember it's only fantasy.

For the Law People

All characters in this book are fictional. Any resemblance to actual persons, living or dead, American or Japanese, is entirely coincidental and not to be inferred. The book refers to famous real persons, including present and deceased members of Japan's Imperial Family. The book refers to real businesses, and to their products, in the United States and Japan. Trademarks referred to in the book (Godzilla, McDonald's restaurants, Malibu Barbie, the "Dummy" books, etc.) are the property of their respective owners.

The fictional California Treaty has minimal precedent in American law, based on my own examination of the Constitution and its amendments, the *United States Code Annotated*, and the *U.S. Supreme Court Digest, Lawyers' Edition, Vols. 5, 5A, 12A and 13*. All constitutional interpretations are mine alone. (That "whoosh" you just heard was the collective sigh of relief of the entire American Bar Association.)

Who Deserves Credit and Thanks

I thank Senator Kay Bailey Hutchison, and her staff, for answering my Senate-procedure questions and my questions about layout of senators' offices.

Heartfelt thanks likewise to the Japan Information and Culture Center in Washington, for answering twenty letters' worth of questions.

A very special "thank you" to Senate Parliamentarian Bob Dove, for personally answering a googol of my Senate-procedure questions, for reviewing the Senate portions of the manuscript, and—at least as important—for passing on "insider" info about how the Senate *really* works. (Although his "war stories" were only about departed senators, never currently sitting senators, darntheluck.) He and I also had several enjoyable deep disputes on the constitutionality of my little premise, and Appendix 2 gained much from his challenges.

Special thanks to the local university reference librarians, for answering a zillion fell-between-the-cracks research questions.

Also providing major help: the U.S. Embassy in Tokyo; Doctor Richard Francaviglia, for answering my questions on the Treaty of Guadalupe Hidalgo and the Gadsden Purchase; Charles Goggans and Don Andrews of the North Richland Hills (Texas) Bomb Disposal Team, Warren Hurlock of the District of Columbia Police Bomb Disposal Unit, and Gilman Udell of the Hazardous Devices Section of the U.S. Capitol Police, for these men's necessarily closemouthed technical critiques of my bomb-disposal write-up in Chapter 12; Professor Yumiko Keitges of Texas Christian University in Fort Worth; SETO Takeshi of the Ministry of Justice; TSUKIYAMA Nobuhiko of the "Congressional Affairs" Department of the Embassy of Japan, for answering my questions about when a Diet lower-house member resigns, and about the timing of lower-house ordinary sessions; Steve Hawes of Media Marketing International, and Linda Buzzalini of World Media TV; Vaughan P. Simmons, publisher of *Mangajin*; and Rod T. Beaman, D.O., for his medical critique of the knife-fight scene in Chapter 14.

I wish to thank other experts providing assistance: the White House Social Office and the White House Curator's Office; the consulates of Japan in Houston and Los Angeles; Pete Frias of John C. Formant Real Estate in Washington, D.C.; Hugh Hunton at the Federal Aviation Administration office in Fort Worth; Robert Woolson of the *Los Angeles Times* pressroom; Robert Chatterton Dickson, press officer of the Embassy of the United Kingdom in Washington, D.C.; and Fred Doka at the Sacramento area office of the Bureau of Indian Affairs. Information on *ikebana* (flower arranging) graciously was provided by Joan Pasek, trained in the Sensho Ikenobo school.

Notwithstanding the help of the people who helped me in the research for the novel, I assume all blame for any errors of fact or of translation in the novel.

The conversation between Barry Goldwater and John F. Kennedy referred to on page 33, is found on page 137 of *With No Apologies* by Barry M. Goldwater, William Morrow and Company, Inc., New York, New York, 1979.

I've written Barbara's reply at the end of Chapter 12 to obnoxious Representative Kada, by starting with suggestions from *Doing Business with Japanese Men: A*

Woman's Handbook by Christalyn Brannen and Tracey Wilen, Stone Bridge Press, Berkeley, California, 1993.

I Dedicate This Book. . .

—To my late father Thomas R. Richardson, Jr., who gave me encouragement and support to write this novel. My father taught me by example that clear writing is an important goal.

—To the three best teachers I've ever had. No coincidence, all three taught at the USAF's Johnson High School within Iruma ASDF Base, Saitama Prefecture (west of Tokyo). The trio:

- (the late) Henry Matsumoto, Mathematics
- Joseph J. Prasil, English
- Millard "Bud" Brewer, U.S. History/Government.

Matsumoto Robotics is named after Henry Matsumoto, as a small repayment of *tsukiai* (social debt).

PROLOGUE
Friday, May 20, 2005

Barbara Nakamura was enjoying the day as she pushed her groceries to her car. For good reasons was Barbara contented: The late afternoon temperature was balmy, the sky over Alexandria, Virginia was blue mixed with fluffy white clouds, and birds were singing.

When smiling Barbara reached her car, she idly noted a faded red pickup was parked next to it. The truck's hood was up, and she heard two men talking. She turned to unlock her driver's door.

Her left arm was seized from behind, and something hard and cold was jammed into her side.

"Barbara, I have a gun." Now she recognized Joe's voice. Joe then said, "Unlock the back door."

"No. You won't shoot me in front of witnesses."

"You sure?" The gun poked her. "Unlock the back door."

Be calm, Barbara told herself. "You got it, Joe."

Barbara swallowed when the second man at the truck turned out to be Bernoulli, who got into the back seat of Barbara's car.

His eyes were eager. "Boy, will we have fun today."

Her mouth went dry. Joe had the muscles to blend in at Venice Beach, while Bernoulli looked like a regular at comic-book conventions—but Bernoulli she judged more dangerous.

Joe was still standing behind Barbara. He said, "Now load the groceries into your car like you would normal. I'll help you, but don't try to run." She transferred the bags, putting the food on the back seat next to Bernoulli. Joe said, "Passenger door unlocked?"

"No."

"Unlock it."

She obeyed, while Joe shut the hood on the pickup. He came around her car and climbed into the passenger seat. Immediately he dug into her purse, found her digital phone, and pocketed it. "You'll get this back when we're done."

In her rear-view mirror, Bernoulli smiled at her. "You'll *probably* be alive to use it. Good news, huh?"

They had her drive a block north, then pull over. Joe said, "Switch places with Bernoulli." As Bernoulli pulled her car back into traffic, Joe told her, "Get down and stay down."

From her huddled position in the back seat, she called to her kidnappers, "Did Matt put you up to this?"

Bernoulli's laugh was like the bark of a seal. "Do we look like guys who'd hang out with a senator?"

"Besides," Joe said, "your husband is a hero."

"For selling out California?" Barbara's laugh was sour. "My husband's a snake, and this is too convenient for him."

"You're way off," Joe said. "Our people have a plan, but you keep messing up the plan, so you and us are taking a trip."

Barbara snorted. "I can guess the plan: When those trillions of dollars filter down to Joe Blow, *your people* plan to show him how fun gambling can be—for a killer percentage in return."

Bernoulli said, "Still, you're working to starve hardworking casinos, you bad girl. And bad girls become good girls, else they're punished."

"Killing me won't sell California to Japan. The California Treaty is unconstitutional."

"Not what your husband says on TV," said Joe. "Says some Supreme Court case long ago means the president can sell California."

Bernoulli reached over the seat to Barbara behind him, groped for her hair, then pulled it. Her scalp felt like it was on fire. As Barbara gasped, he said, "Lady, you don't gotta worry about no Constitution. All you need to worry about are hamstringing and permanent scarring—dying too, if you really piss me off. Those, I'd worry *big* about, if I was you."

Ten minutes later, Joe called to huddled-down Barbara, "Sit up."

They were pulling into a motel. The place needed painting, several doors had their numbers missing, grass grew untrimmed through cracks in the pavement, and empty bottles and other trash were everywhere. Barbara spotted too many local tags among the cars— clearly she'd get no help from her new neighbors. Bernoulli pressed his switchblade against her while Joe unlocked the door to Room 31. But as Bernoulli was covering her with his right hand, he also was digging through her groceries with his left hand. She heard a plastic bag rustle.

Bernoulli force-marched her into Room 31. Joe eyed the onion that Bernoulli held in his left hand. "What is that for?"

Bernoulli smiled with delight. "We're gonna make her sad that she keeps bothering the treaty."

Part I
Afternoon

Gogo

CHAPTER 1
Six Weeks Earlier
Thursday, April 7, 2005

Alexandria, Virginia was only minutes south of Washington, D.C. That is, except during rush hour—then the trip took years.

But being a senator's wife meant that Barbara never suffered through rush hour. *Like all souls in hell are safe from frostbite*, she long ago had realized.

The Nakamuras' house, in Alexandria's Old Town, was another supposed perk. Trim-landscaped, three-bedroom, two-story, with two full baths and a den, the house was painted forest green with cream trim. But inside this mansion, Barbara was hand-washing the dishes from supper for *one*. Her digital phone, which was lying on the kitchen counter, started playing "California, Here I Come."

At the same time, upstairs in the home office, Matthew "Bomber" Nakamura picked up his own phone to make a call. Matt's home-office line was paid for with public money—but Matt hoped this call would be for his decidedly personal benefit.

Barbara dried her wet hands, then picked up the digital phone. "Barbara. Hello."

"Stop the presses! New banner headline: `Senator Nakamura is a rotten husband.'" The voice of Carol Parks held a smile.

Barbara returned to her everyday voice. "Hi, Carol, great you called. But from work? Tsk."

"No, this is news-related. Consider this an interview."

"Got an American Red Cross story, or is it flower arranging?"

"No, the treaty. You're the ideal person for the *Union-Tribune* to interview about it."

Barbara frowned. "Which treaty?"

As Matt touch-toned the Northern California phone number, he thought, *Gary seems like a ripe one.* Ten seconds later, Matt switched to Tone of Voice One (Friendly): "Gary, this is Senator Nakamura. I'm giving you my full attention about bill S.556."

"Thanks, Senator. Bill S.556, is that the one—?"

"About timber harvesting in national forests. Sherry tells me that you're worried that this bill hurts the timber industry."

"*Hurts*? Try *screws*. Those ivory-tower bunny and birdy lovers—"

"Can be unreasonable, I agree," Matt said, in sympathetic Tone of Voice Five. "Still, they do make a strong case for this bill. Besides, we Democrats have a proud tradition of saving the environ—"

"Dammit, *monthly* environmental impact reports? Those regs will ruin my mill—we'll produce *paperwork* instead of *paper*. Please, Senator, stop this bill."

Matt just *loved* a man who was rich and desperate. Commence Operation Shakedown.

Carol was laughing into Barbara's ear. "Which treaty? The one that sells California to Japan, silly."

"*What?*"

"My god, this came over the wire three hours ago. Doesn't Matt talk to you?"

"You kidding? He walked in fifteen minutes ago, kissed me on the cheek, grabbed a beer, and dashed straight upstairs."

"Still, any *caring* husband would've made time to say, `Honey, you won't believe what happened today.' But no-o-o—"

"Enough, Carol! Tell me about the treaty."

"Japan gets California, our whole state, and in return they have to pay three trillion dollars a year for twenty years."

Barbara blinked. "That's a price tag of. . .sixty million million dollars."

"Right. The rest of the treaty is the details."

"I'm floored—what a ridiculous and unnecessary treaty. Anyway, you're calling from work because you want my response?"

"Yeah. I assigned myself you and Matt, editor's privilege. Two minutes ago, did you hear the phone ring upstairs? That was me."

Barbara sighed. *Even by Carol, Matt gets called first. No matter the journalist, a senator's wife is the afterthought.* "What did Matt say?"

"Treaty has no chance; forget it."

". . .Please, Senator, stop this bill," Gary said.

Matt's voice was warm, caring; Dale Carnegie would have smiled approval. "Hey, relax. Since Forestry Committee is evenly split but for me, I can help you."

"Thanks, Senator, I really appre—"

"Trouble is, constituent messages to me likewise divide out fifty-fifty."

"But the polls say Californians think this bill is psycho, way too extreme."

"My mail is running even, believe me. Anyhow, Gary, I haven't decided how my vote will go—I'm open to `persuasion.'"

"And how can I persuade you, Senator?" Gary's voice held no wariness; clearly he'd missed Matt's hint.

Matt took a breath to calm himself, for he needed his next words to sound ordinary. "A contribution now to my re-election campaign would leave me deeply moved by your trust and regard. A contribution of at least. . .ten grand is a nice, round number."

Gary neither slammed down the phone nor started swearing. Instead, he fell silent. Matt had learned to keep quiet himself.

Matt had counted to thirty-seven when Gary sighed over the phone. "Whose name do I write on the overnight envelope?"

I love my life. "I or Sherry Adams may sign for it. Address it to me, and write `Personal and Confidential' on the outside, several places, in big letters."

Now on to Step Two: getting the money as cash. Matt switched to Tone of Voice Six (Casual): "Oh, Gary? You might want to deliver it by courier."

"By *courier* for a *check*?"

"It would be better to send me cash, since my campaign petty-cash fund is always low. I would be really grateful."

"Oh. I'll need a receipt, for tax purposes."

Matt shook his head at the man's denseness. "Sorry, my staff can be really casual about record-keeping—likely your donation won't be written down anywhere." Before Gary could speak, Matt said, "But hey, even though your money won't be recorded, *doesn't* mean I won't remember you. Besides, I've yet to find even *one* endangered species that can vote."

"You mother, you," Gary said. "Okay, *Bomber,* you'll have your *bribe* by Tuesday. Small, unmarked bills are still traditional?" Gary didn't wait for Matt to answer before slamming down the phone. Matt shrugged.

The way Matt saw it, he was way underpaid as a senator: For his responsibilities, a million tax-free dollars a month wouldn't be enough. So why not use his Senate seat to harvest as much as he could?

"I just love a man who's rich and desperate," a satisfied Matt said aloud.

Barbara told Carol, "I'm sure Matt brought the treaty home with him. Let me read it and I'll call you with my reaction."

Seconds later, Barbara was climbing the stairs. She heard Matt hang up the phone in the home office, then remark aloud. She knocked; "Okay to come in?" When he didn't object, she opened the door.

Matt had the nervous eyes of a boy who'd just hidden a *Playboy* under the bed—though at fifty-one, Matt was no boy. He ran a hand through his salt-and-pepper hair; obviously he was bothered by her surprising him. "Hi, what's up?" he asked.

Were you talking to a woman, Matt? "Carol just called me about the California treaty. Do you have a copy of it?"

Matt opened his briefcase, found the treaty, and handed it to her. With fake casualness he shut the briefcase before she could do more than glance inside.

Rather than comment on that, she said instead, "Carol was amazed you didn't tell me about this."

"I had a Forestry bill on my mind when I walked in, didn't have time to talk."

She held his eye. "These days you never have time to talk."

"Does the word *swamped* mean anything to you?"

"No free minute in your entire day?"

"What's the deal? It's a joke treaty."

"We *shared* jokes, once."

He made a face of impatience.

Sighing, she turned her attention to the pages she was holding. She noted his handwriting in the top margin of the first page. "'REASONS TO SELL CALIFORNIA,' 'REASONS TO KEEP CALIFORNIA,' what are these?"

"Got a call from the White House just before I left the office. No way could I buy what Charlie told me, but it so amazed me, I wrote it down."

"I guess Charlie remembered what subcommittee you chair, besides what state you represent."

"Yeah, the president knows I have both motive and opportunity to shut down his treaty. Anyway, Charlie's talking like this treaty is so vital to America's future."

"How could he possibly say that?"

"He called our monstrous national debt `a termite colony that nobody heeds.' Look there, Charlie gave me four reasons why he claims America needs this treaty."

REASONS TO SELL CALIFORNIA
1. Lots of money in treasury, for either new projects or debt elimination, or both.
2. Pays for START III ("Nickels-for-Nukes") Treaty.
3. Japan hobbled for twenty years, which is great for USA in international competition.
4. Many businesses would move from California—reduces unemployment in rest of United States.

Barbara pointed to Reason Two. "Evidently America's president plans to pay for Russia's missiles with Japan's money."

Then Barbara's eyes drifted across the margin, and she laughed out loud.

REASON TO KEEP CALIFORNIA
1. If California goes, I'll lose my job.

Matt smiled. "My list's shorter than Charlie's, but more persuasive."

"So why'd Charlie call you? How can he expect you to vote for this?"

"He wants me to not sabotage the treaty. As if there were danger of it passing in spite of me."

"And you told Charlie no."

"DeGarcia told Charlie no. Charlie told me Hector screamed at him, `I campaigned hard for you last November, and now you betray me?'"

"Did you scream, too? Five years ago, it was you and I stumping with Charlie."

"No, I just cut a deal. I don't break my back to kill the treaty, and the president keeps his veto pen in the drawer for a while."

"I *see.*"

He grinned at her disapproving tone. "Other senators practice pork-barrel politics; *I* am stimulating California's economy."

Barbara frowned. Rather than argue, she picked up the cable-TV remote. "I wonder what the news is saying?" She turned on the computer monitor, set it to TV mode, then pumped American Satellite News into it.

Senate Minority Leader Steve Leaird was smiling and joking for the cameras: ". . .But folks, when Charles Swensen was a boy, did somebody beat his head in with a cornstalk? This treaty is the biggest waste of the Senate's time since the quorum call was invented. It should be *Comedy Central* that televises the hearings. And if the treaty gets two votes when the joint committee votes, I'll watch the sun rise in the west the next morning."

Matt's hand shot forward to stab the monitor's Power button. "It's bad enough, my suffering that hyena at work."

As Barbara was turning off the cable box, she asked, "What's this about a joint committee? Treaties are supposed to be referred only to CFR," the Committee on Foreign Relations.

"Yeah, *supposed to.* But Dick Thompson asked unanimous consent for a joint referral. So Armed Services could study treaty parts about California military bases, he said. Also to lay down a precedent, *which* he forgot to mention."

"Nobody objected? Joe Bob Saunders didn't object?"

"You know *I* wanted to, but it was Farmboy Saunders's place to speak up. He almost didn't—it was as if he didn't care. But he looked back and saw me glaring at him: `Dammit, start acting like the chairman you are!' So he stood up and reminded Dave, `Any treaty goes only to Foreign Relations.'"

"How odd that Dave even needed to be told. You can't become majority leader without knowing something so basic."

"*Knowing* and *honoring* aren't the same," Matt said, hammering his knee with his fist. "Right after Saunders sat down, Dave himself stood up and said, `I know a treaty hasn't been jointly referred in the Senate in my memory. However, this treaty vitally impacts our national defense. I beg Mister Saunders to reconsider.'"

"That's trouble." Barbara laid her hand on Matt's.

Matt, gesturing as he told his story, pulled his hand out from under Barbara's. "Saunders turned and looked at me, then he turned and looked at Dave and Dick. `Okay, fine,' he said. `But I insist, Mister Nakamura still chairs the hearings.'"

"Poor Joe Bob had to decide who to make mad at him. And Dave and Dick had you both outnumbered and outpowered."

"For sure."

"At least you're still the hearings chair." Barbara squeezed Matt's arm.

He shrugged. "But now I'm stuck with Armed Services' ranking minority member, whose clever wit you just heard."

Barbara made a wry smile. "If it will make you feel better, I know Steve Leaird is just as upset to be working with you." She squeezed Matt's arm again.

That's when Barbara's eye was caught by a bird flying outside the window. The bird landed in the back yard and began hopping around in the long shadows. Daylight still? A glance at the clock showed not yet seven. Matt usually wasn't home until long after dark—but for now she refused to worry about that.

She turned back to him. "What are your plans for tonight?"

He blinked at her change of topic. "Hm, I finished everything I need to do tonight. I guess massage some legislation, then watch TV. Why?"

"I was thinking of catching a movie." She waved the treaty. "After I call Carol back, why don't you join me?"

"A movie? Maybe *Wanted: James Bond*?"

She smiled, amused. "No, *Endless Circle*. I enjoyed the book."

"A mystery, I hope."

"No, it's about a middle-aged woman and her troubled relationships with men. At forty-seven, I relate. I'll bring tissues in my purse."

"Mm, sounds delightful." His face disagreed. "Violent?"

"Only one death, natural causes."

He smiled. "This is a problem, and I see nothing but torrid sex to hope for. Let's do it."

She blinked. "Are you ill? You haven't been this easy since our third anniversary."

"Back in San Diego I didn't value how carefree my life was. I need a break. Tomorrow we'll go to the Canadian ambassador's party, and I'll play senator—but tonight I want an ordinary life. Ordinary people go to movies."

"You're agreeing to do something with me that *I* want to do?"

"For my own reasons, but yes. Plan on it."

She strutted to Matt still in his chair, and caressed his stomach ("Mmm, flat") and his pecs ("Mmm, firm.") She picked up the treaty and walked to the door—but with hip-swing enough to grind pepper. At the door she turned and, using the treaty pages, covered her face below the eyes like the geisha of Old Japan did with their fans. "Okay, tiger," she said, "I promise you `ordinary' tonight. Until bedtime, or until we find a *conference table*."

Downstairs, Barbara plopped herself into the papa-*san* chair and began to read the treaty.

The treaty contained thirty-eight articles, covering everything from what made a legal name, to how the prisons and jails would be transferred. Most of the treaty was boring—but a few parts would keep editorialists across America scribbling for weeks, besides causing a meltdown on the Internet.

One of the boring, workhorse articles decreed that for a while afterward, California traffic laws would still be enforced and California drivers' licenses required. This meant Japanese pioneers would have to learn how to drive on the right and would be required to learn American traffic signs.

No easy task, that. Barbara had learned at age five how different California traffic laws were from Japan's. She recalled the traffic signs in the books that *Ojii-san* (Grandfather), *Obaa-san*, Aunt Makiko, and Aunt Chieko had sent Barbara when she'd been a child.

The books had had pictures and Japanese writing. Sometimes a picture had shown a road sign Barbara didn't know. So she had asked Mother what the sign said. Mother had told her how people drive in Japan. One time Mother had been teaching Barbara about a road sign in a book, when suddenly Mother had looked sad. Mother had told little Barbara, "I miss the traffic signs. They're part of Japan that I miss."

Later, Barbara had been fifteen, and her father had been stationed in Japan the second time. Had her *gaijin* classmates been impressed that she spoke fluent Japanese? *So what*, they thought. That she could read and write Japanese at the sixth-grade level? *Big deal*, they thought. But some kids had tripped out that a girl their age, who wasn't a math brain, already could work mile-kilometer conversions—

Quit daydreaming, Barbara told herself in present time.

Barbara now forced her thoughts back to evaluating the treaty. The whole idea was outlandish, selling off California. Not to mention how many special interest groups were cleaning their weapons to battle the treaty. Barbara's conclusion: The California Treaty had no hope of approval.

Barbara's gaze was caught by the framed anniversary photograph on a nearby wall. Photograph-Matt gazed adoringly at photograph-Barbara. *Which proves that politicians are good actors.*

Then the other framed photograph in the living room caught her glance. Hand-dated December 2000, in that photo Charlie Swensen was pumping Matt's hand and grinning. On that photo the president-elect had scrawled with felt-tip pen, "Thanks, Matt, you won me California."

Barbara smiled, amused. "Gee, Mister President, don't you want to keep your prize?"

Then she pulled out her digital phone to call her mother, Takeko Morris, in San Diego.

She heard Matt's phone ring upstairs.

Downstairs, mother and daughter exchanged greetings in Japanese, then each shared her day with the other. Barbara asked Takeko if she'd heard about the treaty. No. Barbara explained it, then asked her mother, "So what do you think?"

"I don't need to move to Japan—now Japan moves to me? Wondrous. Don't you agree, Daughter?"

After a pause, Barbara said, "Agreement is difficult."

Had Barbara not been constrained by the rules of polite Japanese, she would have said instead, "Mother, are you *nuts?*"

Matt's upstairs office said much about him. Not all of it was flattering.

To his right hung a stolen government-issue clock. On the facing wall were three photographs. The first was of him giving an election-night victory speech back in San Diego, and the second was of him shaking hands with Russian President Dimitrov. The third photo was of Matt in 2000, nonchalant next to then-candidate Charlie Swensen. In both the victory-speech photo and the picture with Swensen, Matt was wearing the bomber jacket.

To Matt's left, just beyond his office desk, a window looked out onto the back yard. Decades earlier, one also could see the Potomac from that window. On the doorknob of the bedroom door hung his suit coat on a hanger, tie draped over the coat. A computer desk was behind him, its equipment now turned off. Near the computer monitor was the cable-TV box, its remote, and the Internet cable modem. The computer desk hosted eight empty beer bottles, and a copy of Dale Carnegie's *How to Win Friends and Influence People* that leaned against the monitor. Matt sat in a black executive chair, whose leather creaked whenever his weight shifted. The chair, too, was "borrowed" government property.

In a little frame on the far left corner of the office desk sat a clone of the downstairs twentieth-anniversary portrait of him and Barbara. The two-thousand-page *Black's Law Dictionary* blocked his view of most of the photo. Setting on the middle of the desk was his open briefcase, jammed with papers. A legal pad lay atop the desk, to the right of the briefcase. The ringing telephone sat to the briefcase's left.

Matt picked up the receiver. "This is Senator Nakamura."

"Hello, Matthew." Mela Jackson's voice dripped with sex.

He glanced at the door: shut. "Why have you called me at home?"

"Did you want me to call you at work? Suppose someone overheard me and told my boss?"

"If Gibson asked, I'd tell him it was his staffer who initiated the affair."

"Come now. After all the rumors about you?"

"Whatever. Why are you calling me here?"

"Remember Tuesday night? Wendall Harland? You introduced me to Secretary of State Harland, and I am *so* grateful."

Matt felt frustrated that he couldn't express his jealousy. "Harland's married."

"So are you."

"So now your ice-cube trick creates another addict."

"Nuh-uh, Matthew, remember Rule Four: `You may not ask about my other friends.' About Wendall Harland I'll neither confirm nor deny."

"Your attitude stinks. Plenty of women in Washington—"

"How many have tits my size? How many have kept up Kegel exercises for the past six years? You've seen my collection of sex manuals. Am I not the best lay you've ever imagined?"

Matt could not disagree, but agreeing would give Mela an edge later. Matt kept silent.

Mela broke the silence: "Meanwhile, I use my MBA every day, writing tax legislation for Senator Gibson. I'm no bimbo, I'm your equal—"

Matt's laugh was scornful. "How you figure that?"

"I have sexual power like few women, sexual power to match your power over appropriations and laws. But you wound me. I told you I'm grateful for Harland—and buster, I intend to prove that."

"How? Bake me an apple pie?"

"Matthew, have you ever made it with two women?"

Matt choked.

Mela chuckled. "I'll mark that as a no. Anyway, I was rear-ended at a stoplight today."

"Were you hurt?" *If she can't perform in bed, I'll have to look elsewhere for my fun.*

"A taillight broken, a corner dented a little. Three hundred total, we figure. But the driver doesn't want me to file a claim."

"Sure."

"We're working out how she's going to pay for it out of her own pocket, I ask her, small talk, what she does for a living. Turns out Shirley works for an escort service, and today's her day off."

"She admitted this to a total stranger?"

"She said she's an actress/model. In Washington, D.C.? I said, `You're a call girl.' `An escort,' she said, `I sleep only with men I like.'"

"So how does this lead to sex with two women?"

"She offered herself as my indentured servant until midnight, if I'd forgive the three hundred."

"Does she know the ice-cube trick?"

"Come over and I'll teach her." After Matt made no reply, Mela said, "Let me mention she's a blue-eyed blonde, with legs and tits out to here. Like me, but for hair and nails."

Matt smiled. "You two would look hot together—"

"Sorry, no lesbian—"

"But it's no go."

"Why? Your car in the shop?"

"No, you called too late. I'm taking Barbara to see *Endless Circle.*"

Now the scornful laugh was Mela's. "Aren't *you* the tame little hubby tonight."

"I haven't taken her anywhere in months."

"Then you best hope *she* thanks you with a threesome, or at least sucks you off on the drive home."

"She did promise something great, yes."

"This is absurd. I refuse to accept it. I'm offering you *two women.* Two nimble, big-breasted, unwrinkled beauties for your sexual delight—and you're turning us down for *Barbara.*"

His teeth were clenched: "I promised her."

"You're a politician, what's another broken promise? Imagine, two women."

"Barbara deserves a reward. Do you take my suit to the cleaners and pick it up an hour later?"

"Does she know the ice-cube trick? Is she twenty-seven? Two women, imagine."

"Goodbye, Mela."

"My grandmother told me once, `I don't regret the things I did, nearly so much as I regret the things I didn't do.' Two women."

He'd be damned if he let her know he was wavering. "What will you do if I turn down your offer?"

"Shirley still stays here, and I call someone else. Maybe Wendall Harland, hmm? Maybe I'll break out my little black book. But such a pity you'll miss out, when you have the unique advantage."

"What?"

"That jacket. Shirley says men in leather excite her."

Downstairs a few minutes later, Matt had fetched the bomber jacket from the hall closet. Now he was explaining to Barbara, ". . .That call I took was from some local electricians' union pooh-bah from San Jose. See, Mike's in town overnight and wants me to meet with him before he flies—"

"You'll be out late," Barbara said. "I won't wait up."

No argument, no calling me a liar? Matt's back muscles relaxed. Tone of Voice Four (Penitent/Regretful): "I'm really sorry about the movie. You know I love you, but I need to run."

———

A few seconds later, Barbara heard Matt shut the front door. Wherever he was going, it wasn't to meet with any man—Matt was almost dancing with excitement but trying to hide it.

Barbara realized she'd again played his game of "Let's Pretend." Let's pretend I value my marriage to Barbara. Let's pretend I'm not fooling around. Let's pretend that when I'm out late, I'm working. Barbara asked herself, *Am I devoted and patient, or just stupid?*

The hell with him, Barbara thought, *I'm going to the movie without him. Wonder if Tiffani's seen it?*

But before Barbara could leave for her movie, she'd promised to call Carol at the newspaper.

Barbara didn't tell Carol about Matt's latest stunt, because Barbara knew what Carol would say. Instead, Barbara said, "Before I forget: Call me Saturday for an update. The Canadian ambassador is throwing a party tomorrow night, and many joint-committee senators will be there."

Computer keys clacked, then Carol said, "Good, more column inches under my byline. Thanks. As for the treaty, what do you think?"

"My mother thinks it's wonderful. *Please* don't print that."

"No problem. But what do *you* think about it?"

"This treaty is *wrong*. It would overturn our lives, we Californians, but we didn't ask for it—that's wrong."

"May I quote you on that?"

"Why? Nobody wants to read what a senator's wife thinks. Besides, in a month this treaty will be trivia."

All this was fodder for the comedians. In Los Angeles, the Variety-Show Host joked—

> *The nation's unemployment rate is 9.6 percent this month, but some folks are still hiring. A lady in Laguna Beach added three people to her business, which prints cardboard "Will Work for Food" signs. One good part about this high unemployment: We'll save trees printing fewer income-tax forms next year.*
>
> *In other news, the president today handed to the Senate a treaty that would sell California to Japan. One change this would mean: Occidental*

Petroleum and Six Flags Magic Mountain would need to change their names.

California has earthquakes, it has smog, it has crowding and it has traffic jams. No wonder the Japanese want California—it reminds them of home.

CHAPTER 2
Friday, April 8, 2005

This morning called for celebrating, Matt decided, even if in secret. As he was shaving, he thought, *Wow, in bed with two women. Too bad I can't tell anybody.* He yawned; 7:30 came way too early this morning.

Barbara's reflection gave him a look. From the doorway behind him, she asked, "Matt, did you hear me? I read the treaty."

"Mm? Sorry, Barbara, I was thinking." *I'd better lose this grin before Barbara notices.*

"I still can't believe Charlie made this treaty."

"Mm," Matt said, barely listening. *That Shirley, what a wildcat. Which reminds me: I'd better make sure Barbara doesn't see those scratches on my back.* Matt tightened the belt of his robe.

Barbara's reflection looked puzzled. "Back on the campaign bus, Charlie always sounded so sensible."

"They say being president changes you," Matt said. *Ah, what a worldly woman like Mela could do with an electric massager.*

"It's scary: You talk to a man so much, you think you know him. Then it turns out, you don't know him at all." For some reason, Barbara's reflection was watching him.

"Scary, yeah, I guess so." When Matt had come home last night, Barbara had bought his story about "Mike, the union president from San Jose." She'd given Matt no hassles at all—it was the perfect end to a perfect evening.

"As for that silly treaty, after I read it and called Carol, I put it back in your briefcase."

Now she had his full attention. "Back in my briefcase?"

"You left it unlocked when you rushed out."

Then Barbara was grabbing a tissue and dabbing his face. "Goodness, you've nicked yourself."

Barbara sat in her kitchen an hour later, arguing with herself again.

Barbara, you're a coward. You should've called Matt the liar and cheat he is.

—*No, I'm being practical.*

When Matt had returned sometime between midnight and dawn, Barbara had pretended to listen to his story. She had nodded at all the right times and had made all the right noises. It still bothered her that she hadn't confronted him then.

Then forty-five minutes ago Matt, claiming a breakfast meeting with other Small Business Committee senators, had rushed out the door without sharing breakfast with her. She had locked up the empty house to take her morning walk earlier than usual.

Now it was 8:30 in the morning. She was spooning cornflakes in her kitchen, and was trying to distract her conscience with "The Today Show."

Coward!

—*But if I did confront him, what good would it do?*

". . .Later in this half hour, we'll talk with Lambert Carver and Christina Ricci, whose new movie, *Cameron's Terminator Four: Cyborg Slaughter*, opens today. Lambert and Christina play against a computer-replicated Arnold Schwarzenegger. Also, we'll have a story on John and Mary Garner, Americans living in Hong Kong, and how they're affected by the latest tensions between the Hong Kong region and the mainland government. Next hour, we'll have pediatrician Doctor Mary Withers discussing how to deal with a fussy eater, and we'll show you imaginative ways to cook with broccoli. But first, here's Donna Jamison with the news."

"Good morning, everyone. In our top story, President Swensen yesterday sent to the Senate a treaty with Japan. . .."

Barbara headed to the fridge for more orange juice. She'd heard all this before.

When she came back from the refrigerator, the television showed a man in his forties, who wore a light blue suit. ". . .A number of Democratic senators with whom I've spoken have told me they won't support the California Treaty. . .."

Matt's making a fool of me with his flings. I'm a laughingstock.

—But I don't know for certain he's cheating.

Oh, don't I?

Light Blue Suit glanced at a writing pad. "Under the Constitution, the two-thirds approval of the Senate present and voting is mandatory for the president to ratify a treaty."

Is it fair to Matt to hurt his political career by the stigma of divorce?

—Is it fair to me to be used only as a cook, laundress, and ornament? When's the last time he couldn't wait to get me naked?

Light Blue Suit then said, "The president has no way to override the Senate when they reject the treaty. Everyone to whom I've spoken, agrees that the president's lapse in judgment has cost him much prestige, right when he needs it in negotiating the purchase of Russian nuclear weapons. . .."

Carol's urged me for years to leave him.

—Mother's stayed married forty-nine years, and her marriage had problems tougher than mine. Barbara's father Ed, while stationed at Tachikawa Air Base in the mid-Fifties, had married local girl Takeko. Added to the in-law problems they both endured were friend, neighbor, co-worker, and even total-stranger problems.

Light Blue Suit now was wrapping up: "Donna, one more item. President Swensen will address the nation about the treaty, tonight at 9:00 p.m. Eastern time. This is Capitol Hill correspondent Richard Rush, live at the Senate for `Today.'"

—I'll give Matt time to straighten out. But this situation can't stay like this much longer.

"*I'll give Matt time.*" *Hasn't this been the plan for years?*

————

That evening in the living room, Matt tapped his fingers on the couch arm, as he waited for Barbara to dress for the Canadian ambassador's party. Matt filled the time by cursing the fates that had made him a United States senator from California.

A frustrated President Kennedy once had quipped to Barry Goldwater, "So you think you want this fucking job, do you?" That was what Matt wanted to scream at all those Golden-State glad-handers who were hot for his seat.

Earlier that day, Matt had met with the Foreign Relations committee, and the Agriculture, Nutrition, and Forestry committee. He'd attended six major and one minor subcommittee meetings, and chaired a Small Business committee meeting and an East Asian and

Pacific Affairs subcommittee meeting. Matt also had attended six caucus meetings.

His staff made his job merely exhausting instead of impossible. The whole day he flitted from one meeting to the next. In each meeting, he talked for a few minutes to the staffer who was attending the meeting in his place, perhaps made a comment himself, gave the staffer instructions of what to say or do, and then Matt dashed out to his next meeting.

Those demands on his time hadn't been the only ones. Visitors to the office all wanted a picture taken with him. If they brought kids, invariably they wanted a picture of their youngest child wearing the bomber jacket. Otherwise, they wanted Matt to be wearing it in the photo.

He hadn't been able to walk to the snack room without being jumped by lobbyists. Some of them knew information he needed, so he couldn't ignore them.

His staff handed him a big stack of letters and e-mail messages from voters. The writers all demanded something from him, running the gamut from his leaning on particular bureaucrats, to his proposing private bills.

In addition, amid all this bustle he somehow still was expected to propose, sponsor, debate, amend, and vote on floor legislation.

In short, this had been a typical day. Emergency-room doctors had it easier than he did.

Now Matt added his voice to the chatter of the TV. "I'm beat, and what the hell else is new? I hate my job. Maybe next year I'll say I won't run for re-election."

The idea delighted him as soon as he spoke it. "Yeah, I wanna spend time with my loving wife, return to my roots in the community, blah-blah-blah. Jesus, law firms would mud-wrestle to make me offers."

He slapped fist into palm. "I'll do it, I'll leave. Next year, I am not running for re-election."

A few minutes later, Barbara stroked her husband's lapel and smiled. "You know I enjoy seeing you in a tux." She turned around. "Zip me up?"

"Finally?" He zipped up her cocktail dress. "Chess tournaments have taken less time."

Be nice to him—I'm sure he's had a hard day. "Honey, I'm sorry, but it's important for me to look good. I don't want people to think less of you because I'm dressed poorly."

Two minutes later, after choosing suitable earrings, Barbara was ready. Her dress was lemon-yellow for spring, and complimented her Eurasian skin color and auburn-dyed hair. The dress was elegant and robot-tailored, perfect for the occasion. The dress also was slinky, to showcase her health-club physique and her height of 180 centimeters (5'11"). Complementing the dress were new green heels with matching bag, and a gold necklace.

She walked to the refrigerator, nabbed the host's gift (an expensive California chianti) and carried her purse and the cold gift-box into the living room.

A sitcom was on. Matt glanced at her and remoted the television off. "Look good," he said as he stood. "I've got the keys."

She gestured him to hold. The budding apple-tree branch in her flower arrangement was askew, so she walked over to the dining table and set the branch right within the vase.

Matt jangled the keys in his pocket. "Couldn't that have waited?"

"I'm sorry, honey. But see, it took only a moment."

––––––––

"So how's the Red Cross?" Matt asked during the drive to the party.

Barbara smiled. "Last week we scored a pallet of surgical dressing."

"Great," he said. Barbara wondered if he'd even heard her.

She let it pass. "How about you? What's new with you?"

Matt snorted. "Read a great letter today. The Park Service is secretly growing brain-eating alien plants in Yosemite, and would I please investigate?" Matt rolled his eyes.

"That poor person."

"Poor *me*, having to waste office time on a nutcase."

Barbara and Matt made only small talk, matters neither important nor personal, while he drove to the Canadian ambassador's official residence. The Nakamuras arrived to find two valets at the curb, one of whom was holding a clipboard. The other valet asked, "May we see your invitation, please?"

Matt presented it, and the man with the clipboard checked off their names.

A minute later, the valets were parking the car, while Barbara and Matt stood at the front door. Classical music wafted over from somewhere in the house, as Matt again presented the engraved invitation. "The Honorable Matthew Nakamura, United States Senator of California, and Mrs. Barbara Nakamura" they were announced.

Right inside the door was Ambassador McNeill in a tuxedo. "Welcome, Senator Nakamura, Mrs. Nakamura." He shook Matt's hand, and shook Barbara's when she offered it.

Standing next to the ambassador, begowned Yvonne McNeill offered her own hand to the Nakamuras. "Good to see you again. You're welcome to our home."

Barbara held out the tall, thin box she held. "Mister Ambassador, Mrs. McNeill, I'm sure you've already planned the wine tonight, but I know you'll enjoy this; 2002 was a very good year."

The ambassador showed a toothy smile. "Thank you very much. Trust Californians to know good wine, eh?"

Yvonne added her own smile. "Please enjoy the party. Your tuxedo is cut well, Senator Nakamura."

Matt murmured a thank-you.

Yvonne McNeill continued, "Your dress is so lovely, Mrs. Nakamura."

"*Merci beaucoup.*"

"*C'est un plaisir, madame! Parlez vous Francais?*"

"No, I'm afraid I've spoken all the French I know. Too bad, because French always sounds so beautiful."

"Oh, doesn't it? I know you can master it if you wish, since you speak two languages already. Then Quebec is even more wonderful to visit."

"Yes, I've heard Quebec is lovely—"

Matt said, "Thank you, Excellency, Mrs. McNeill, for inviting us tonight." Matt then marched Barbara to the food table.

Barbara thought, *For once, I was the one somebody wanted to talk to. You couldn't have waited a few more seconds?* She murmured through her smile, "Matt honey, Yvonne McNeill is the most well-mannered person I've ever met. We both could learn from her."

He shrugged, as he took a champagne glass from a passing tray. "She's not a somebody, only a somebody's wife. It's her *job* to act nice."

The McNeills hadn't skimped at the food table. To start, Barbara couldn't believe how many lobster tails she saw. All she had to do was gesture, and a steward would crack a tail open and put its meat on her plate. A second steward did nothing but core and slice apples, throwing away any laid-out slices that were starting to brown. A third steward was carving roast beef for sandwiches, then cutting the sandwiches to finger size. Platters of fish—smoked salmon, steamed trout, and baked halibut, according to a steward—tempted a fish lover. Cheese fondue, Swedish meatballs, devilled-chicken finger sandwiches, many kinds of crackers, and big cut-your-own blocks of cheese represented more familiar party food. Several trays contained carrot sticks, potato chips, and chip dip.

In one corner of the room, a string quartet was softly playing classical music.

Matt, with Barbara on leash, found Senator Lamont and her husband Paul. They were joined by Senator Wagner and Penny, and then by Senator Sheppard and Beverly. Barbara couldn't follow the senators' conversations, which were very "inside," so she put on a plastic smile. Whenever she tried to talk with another Senate spouse, Matt's smile was indulgent.

After a half hour, the Wagners left to chat with Senate Majority Leader Dave Fuller. Soon after, the remaining group broke up. Matt said to Barbara, "Enjoy the party," and walked away. She didn't need to be told the translation: *Get lost.*

By now most of the guests had arrived. Cocktail dresses, tuxedos, and dinner jackets were everywhere, along with a sprinkling of native costumes on both men and women. Barbara was near the door when the

Harlands arrived, and saw Secretary of State Wendall Harland look her over. She wondered why.

Across the room she saw Matt, his champagne glass already replaced by a shot glass. He was in an animated discussion with Senator Wagner and the Mexican ambassador. The Mexican ambassador's wife stood there, smiling and saying nothing.

"Barbara, you look right fine tonight." She turned to find Joe Bob Saunders beside her. Joe Bob added, "Your dress is the color of the sun shinin' through springtime dogwood trees."

Instead of tensing, she flirted back, for Joe Bob was safe. "Why sir, does Americus teach all its boys how to talk such sweet words? Be aware, sir, that my husband is right over there, ready to protect my honor."

"Yes, ma'am, Ah just spoke with him."

Barbara was no longer smiling. "I did enjoy your compliments, Joe Bob. They're more than *he's* said to me this evening."

Joe Bob quickly changed the subject. "Ain't this a great party? Ah know Marilyn would enjoy it."

"She's still in Georgia? Has Lizzie Ella gone into labor yet?"

"If not now, soon. Marilyn says Joe Tim is more jumpy than Lizzie Ella is."

Barbara glanced over to where two senators were talking with Ambassador Borzov, then she turned smiling back to Joe Bob. She said, "For me, yes, it's a great party. But for you Foreign Relations senators, it's just more work."

"Yes, ma'am. Tonight Ah've spoke with the Japanese ambassador, the Russian ambassador there, and the British ambassador." Then Joe Bob's lips and eyes both smiled. "But this work ain't nothin' like on a peanut farm."

"What did you and Ambassador Fujima talk about?"

"How the California Treaty will do in the Senate. Ah had no good news for him."

"Poor Kohzoh Fujima. As much as I don't want California sold, I feel sorry for him."

"Oh?"

"He's stuck with the job of making this treaty happen. It's easier to dig a swimming pool overnight with a spoon."

Two minutes later, Joe Bob had wandered over to the food table and filled his plate as he and Barbara talked. Now Barbara was asking him, ". . .So why didn't you object right off when Dick Thompson asked for a joint referral? Matt's sure this gives Armed Services a precedent to horn in on treaties."

"He told you that?" Joe Bob's eyes laughed. "This treaty is a special case. Ah'll be a long time with Jesus, the first time Armed Services finds a way to cash in their precedent."

Barbara leaned in close. "And when the joint committee votes whether to recommend the treaty, how say you?"

Joe Bob leaned toward her, and dropped his voice to a murmur: "Ain't no question how Ah'll vote—the only question is how Ah'll answer the reporters before then. Ah cain't tell them, `My President is crazy to think we need this.' But Ah cain't endorse his treaty, neither."

Barbara smiled. "I'm glad to hear that."

Joe Bob smiled back. "So Ah reckon Ah'll play word games with the press folks until the committee votes." He raised his voice to normal to say, "Excuse me, ma'am, Ah need to mingle. Hope you enjoy the party."

His smile was warm as he squeezed her arm and wandered off.

When Joe Bob left, Barbara spotted Tiffani Ingram, who was at the other end of the food table. Tiffani was eyeing the food, a fingertip mashing her lip.

"Love your dress, Barbara. Everything here looks so delicious."

"Love yours." Barbara looked at the table in mock dismay. "Too bad the food's so rich." To join Tiffani, Barbara had to walk past that food—clearly Canada had plotted to lure her off her diet.

Matt chose that moment to join the two women, a shot glass in his hand. He gave Tiffani an oily smile. "Tiffani, you have damned sexy shoulders. I'm sure Chris is very proud of how you look."

Tiffani glanced at Barbara. "Thanks, Matt, I try."

Matt said, in lounge-lizard tones, "Really, Tiffani, if Barbara and you host a fundraiser in these dresses, I guarantee the Red Cross will be drowned in donations."

"I'm glad you came over to join your wife, tiger." Barbara's smile didn't show her discomfort. To Tiffani she said, "Matt likes to see taut muscles poured into tight dresses."

"Actually, the tight was my idea. Chris thinks I should look all family-values, like a great-grandmother at thirty-eight. So my dress was picked to please both of us." The dress was cut to fit, with Tiffani's shoulders exposed; but it was also high-necklined, knee-length, and long-sleeved.

Matt gave Tiffani a smile surely meant as sexy and sophisticated. "Good, your dress leaves more to the imagination. Say, why aren't you with Chris?" His voice dripped with innuendo.

"Chris is talking with Ambassador Borzov and his wife, and some State Department guy. I got hungry, and what do *I* know about Russian nukes?"

"You'd better grab something and hurry back. Chris will think you're swapping looks with some young stud foreign attaché."

Tiffani smiled. "Chris distrustful? Not a bit. If I were found naked and smiling on an aircraft carrier, Chris would still believe in me."

A minute later, Matt had abandoned Barbara and Tiffani for the bar, where he downed another bourbon. A minute after that, he stood by the glass doors leading to the balcony, and thought happy thoughts. *It doesn't get any better than this. I've fantasized about sex with two women since I was sixteen, and last night, bingo. Tonight I can eat and drink all I want, and Canada picks up the tab—*

"Good evening suh, I'm afraid we haven't been introduced," said a bald man with a refined English accent. "I am Reginald Caldwell, Ambassador of the United Kingdom. I apologise for speaking in English, but my Japanese is quite poor."

Matt looked at him with amusement. "You think I'm Japanese?"

Caldwell's upper lip might have been stiff, but his lower lip twitched. "You aren't one of His Excellency Mister Fujima's staff?"

Tone of Voice Seven (Haughty Amusement): "I'm Senator Matthew Nakamura of California. I chair a Foreign Relations subcommittee." *Let's see him sweat.*

"Oh, dear. I'm pleased to meet you, Senator Nakamura." The two men shook hands. "Please accept my most abject apologies."

"I'm sorry I can't introduce you to my wife, but she's the tall lady in the greenish-yellow dress, over by the food table."

"You must be quite proud of her. She's quite attractive, and she carries herself with grace."

"Thanks." Another tray of champagne went by, and Matt again liberated a glass. He sipped, then turned to the ambassador. "Pardon me, Excellency, but what happened to His Excellency Sir Smithwick?"

"He's in hospital in London, I'm afraid. I presented my credentials a week ago."

"New in town, huh? Then let me introduce you to Chris." Chris Ingram at the moment was nearby, alone, and looked game. "Your Excellency, may I present you to Senator Christopher Ingram of Indiana? Treat him well, and not only because he's the ranking Republican on the Foreign Relations Committee."

"Why else then?"

Matt's smile and eyes both held mischief. "He's a licensed attorney besides a senator, which guarantees he's a rascal."

Chris laughed. "You're an attorney, too, Nakamura."

"This proves my point, right?"

"Oh my," Caldwell said. Then he turned toward Matt. "Pardon me for changing the subject, but may I put a question? Since you're from California, what are your thoughts on this treaty with Japan?"

"Tell London the treaty's a lost cause."

The ambassador eyed both senators. "That the president is mentally compromised has been suggested. What are your assessments?"

Chris looked worried. "Truthfully, I. . .I won't say."

"But I will," Matt said. "I've taken a good, long look at him up close, and he's not crazy."

Caldwell raised an eyebrow. "Please explain."

"Back in 2000, I was running for re-election. Once Swensen sewed up the nomination, whenever he wanted to campaign in California I'd arrange to be in California, too. Charlie, Hank Collins, and I, we'd stump a day or two, then leave. Yet while we were there, we rode throughout California on a campaign bus, from early in the morning until late at night. A week or two later, we'd fly back to California again. We spent a helluva lot of time in California."

"From so much time together, what did you learn about Charles Swensen?"

"He'll say what he thinks, do what he thinks, even when he knows he'll be whipped for it."

Chris raised a hand. "Whipped for good reason. Swensen raised Nebraska's sales tax by one-point-something percent back in '97—"

"Because he knew the state needed the money," Matt said.

"Anyway, Governor Swensen raised the sales tax in 1997, and in 1998 Nebraskans voted him out for a Republican. That's how Swensen wound up free to run for president."

Matt gave Chris a dirty look before turning back to the ambassador. "*But*, campaigning in 2000, Charlie turned the sales-tax increase into a political plus. He said, `You may not always like what I do, but you always can know I mean what I say.' Republicans were trying to label him a tax-and-spend Democrat—"

"Which he was, you must admit," Chris said.

Matt gave Chris an impatient look. "I admit no such thing. Anyway, Charlie's own campaign advisors were pushing him to avoid or recant the sales-tax increase.

Instead, he declared that the tax increase was the best bill he'd ever signed."

Caldwell's eyebrows went up. "I know of no British politician who'd make such a vigourous pronouncement, and especially about taxes."

"And nobody smart in America, either," Chris said. "Look what almost happened to Swensen."

At the ambassador's puzzlement, Matt shrugged. "Charlie won California in 2000 by only five hundred votes, out of millions. And it was *four hours* after the polls closed before they knew that."

The ambassador nodded. "Yes, I remember the *London Times* headline: `Who Won?'"

"When Charlie won California, he won the election. Now, if I may brag a little, I believe that my days and days campaigning with him brought him at least those five hundred California votes."

Now Chris gave Matt the dirty look. "Perhaps, but mainly Swensen won in 2000 because the American people admired his courage."

"Which he showed again his first month in office, when he and I fought the Religious Right over his Elementary School Curriculum and Standards Act."

"*Has* the president courage?" Caldwell asked Chris. "What sort of fellow is he?"

The Republican shrugged. "Sure, Swensen has courage—but hey, so did Don Quixote. I'll admit the president is hardworking and dedicated. Of course, so are all of us in public life, except for a warped few, but Swensen's the match of any of us."

So all of us in public life are hardworking and dedicated, except for a warped few? Matt struggled to keep a straight face at Chris's naiveté.

Twenty minutes later, Barbara remained at the food table, but Tiffani had left to rejoin Chris. Now Barbara and Inge Weihmüller, the wife of Germany's ambassador, grinned at each other as they argued which was the greater deathtrap: L.A.'s freeway system, or the Autobahn.

The debate stopped when Ambassador McNeill walked over to where the string quartet was playing, silenced the musicians with a gesture, and raised his hands and voice. "Ladies and gentlemen, a number of you have expressed an interest in seeing President Swensen's address about the treaty with Japan. My guest here, His Excellency Mister Fujima, was active and indispensable in the negotiations."

The Japanese ambassador snapped off a deep bow to the Canadian ambassador, as the guests made polite applause. Barbara, unsure whether to applaud, clapped three times.

Ambassador McNeill then said, "I've set up a television in my study for you to watch. The president will be on the air in five minutes. Please don't abuse my hospitality and explore my belongings, eh? Besides, I know you all are spies anyway, so I took the important papers out beforehand."

Barbara and the rest of the room laughed.

"My study's over there, or ask someone to direct you. Enjoy the party." Ambassador McNeill nodded to the lead violinist, and the music resumed.

Ambassador Weihmüller stopped by. After greeting Barbara, he spoke several sentences to Inge. Barbara couldn't understand German, but then Inge waved, and the ambassador left for McNeill's study.

Barbara turned to Inge. "That's where I'm going, too. Excuse me, please?"

"Of course." Inge looked at Barbara. "You have met the president, correct?"

"Yes, we spent many hours campaigning together."

"So what is he like, truly? I hear concern that he is—"

"He holds hands with his wife, even when he thinks nobody is looking. He's an *awful* singer. And he wasn't crazy five years ago."

Inge nodded. Barbara nodded back, stood, waved, and walked over to the study. Matt and Joe Bob, talking together, walked in ahead of her.

A few minutes earlier, Matt had left Chris, Tiffani, and Ambassador Caldwell to return to the bar. But almost there, Joe Bob Saunders had caught him. "You have a chance to talk to Ambassador Fujima yet?"

Matt snorted. "At any goddamn given moment, half the people here are quizzing him about how and why Japan wrote this treaty, and the other half are asking me what I think of the goddamn thing. How can I get near him?"

"Actually, another half are hitting on me. Too bad Marilyn isn't here to see all these high-hat diplomats seeking me out."

Matt's face didn't show his thoughts. *You can vote bills these days, Joe Bob, and you can confirm judges, but you're still a hillbilly.*

The music stopped, and the Canadian ambassador announced that a television was available to watch the speech. He also made a joke that Matt found stupid.

Now with drink in hand, and with Joe Bob still chattering, Matt and Joe Bob went to see the televised speech. Once in the study, Matt noticed the Japanese ambassador standing about two yards away.

———————

A minute later, Barbara stood at the back of the throng which had flooded into His Excellency's study.

Five years earlier, Barbara and Matt had spent hours with the Swensens (and with the Collinses) on the campaign bus trips that crisscrossed California. Barbara had seen the tie-loosened, scratch-where-it-itches Charlie Swensen. On the bus Charlie had expressed opinions, in a Vietnam-vet vocabulary, on everything from abortion to taxing Internet sales. The Swensens and Nakamuras had shared, joked, sang, and debated for hours on end.

Five years earlier on the bus, Charlie had not sounded crazy. The four "REASONS TO SELL CALIFORNIA" he'd given Matt yesterday did not sound crazy. But this treaty was a hopeless cause, Charlie had to know. Was he a visionary, or instead was he cut off from reality? More importantly, could Charlie make a good case tonight, so that the treaty might gain steam? Barbara needed to learn from the source.

A network news anchor was talking on TV: ". . .A just-released MSNBC/*Wall Street Journal* poll found only 2 percent of Americans support the treaty—"

Then the face of the news anchor was gone, to be replaced by the presidential seal. McNeill's study silenced. ". . .and gentlemen, the president of the United States," the TV said.

In the study, the foreigners' faces developed looks of total concentration. Next to Barbara, a man with an unfamiliar accent said, "Turn it up, please." Those were the only words in the room not spoken by Charles Arthur Swensen during his ten-minute address.

At fifty-four, the president was a powerful man, a balding former high-school linesman who still exercised often. But tonight on television he didn't look sexy or threatening, he looked thoughtful.

Swensen began by reciting several U.S. economic statistics, all dismal. He next noted that the national debt was out of control: 23 percent of the budget was allotted to interest on it. And, he reminded viewers, Washington had no control how the people who were paid this interest could spend it. "Americans, we have 23 percent taxation without representation today." Politicians in Washington would grin as they worsened this problem, Swensen predicted, as deficit spending bought votes. Meanwhile, Baby Boomers were close to retirement age, so Social Security was about to be bled white. Swensen's forecast: much more borrowing soon, much more interest. Which was imminent disaster: the president predicted that, left untreated, interest on the debt soon would be an inoperable tumor on the budget.

So what? The president answered that if nothing were done to stop such growth, he foresaw the day when the government would trample civil liberties in its desperation to collect taxes.

In the meantime, under negotiation with Russia was the START III treaty, the so-called "Nickels-for-Nukes Treaty." More money in the U.S. treasury ensured that START III would be ratified and proclaimed, and the most possible Russian and American nukes would be destroyed, "to calm the world's children from nuclear fear."

During this same time, Japan was trying to buy a colony. She already had secretly (and unsuccessfully) wooed China. Swensen felt that if the United States also had refused Japan, Japan would have persisted until she'd found a seller. Under a 1960 treaty with Japan, the United States then would be bound to defend the colony in addition to defending Japan itself. So by selling California, Swensen argued, the United States not only would be receiving money, the government also would be preventing an increase of defense spending.

Ten minutes after he began, the president said, ". . .For many Californians this treaty will create hardship. I regret this, but *America needs the money.* May God and Mister Lincoln forgive me. Good evening."

Barbara begrudged a grain of sense to the president's arguments. Yet her conclusion remained: Charlie was dead wrong. And say what you will about politicians, the Senate would not follow in folly. She could stop worrying.

After a few seconds of silence except for the voice of the news anchor, someone reached forward and turned off the TV. Everyone began to talk as they were leaving. Barbara heard snatches of conversation:

"Mister Minister, why did your government turn down Japan's offer?"

Joe Bob's voice, behind her: "The trade imbalance and those other numbers Swensen mentioned, they went by too fast for me."

Matt's voice, behind her: "What those numbers mean is that our economy's in awful shape."

A man with an accent: "I wish Japan had asked us—my country would welcome sixty trillion dollars." Laughter followed, and someone asked what the speaker would do with the money. He said, "We'd buy Russian missiles, too—but only for decoration." Barbara heard laughter again.

Barbara followed to the bar a knot of men who were in intense discussion. At the bar Barbara took a glass of diet soda and resumed talking with Inge Weihmüller. Soon Inge invited Barbara to join her in listening to the quartet. The women crossed the room together, as Inge preached on the genius of Mozart.

Joe Bob said to Matt, "The trade imbalance and those other numbers Swensen mentioned, they went by too fast for me."

Matt and Joe Bob were walking out of the ambassador's study. Matt wasn't surprised at Farmboy's remark—*The man's brain couldn't power a flashlight bulb.*

Matt gave Saunders an answer, but his attention was caught by Ambassador Fujima, who was standing beyond the doorway. "Excuse me, Joe Bob," Matt said over his shoulder as he homed in on the ambassador. A "Pardon me, suh" behind his back a second later told Matt that Joe Bob was tagging along. Damn.

When Matt (and Joe Bob) reached Fujima, the ambassador recited polite American greetings. Then Matt switched to Japanese: "*Fujima Taishi, komban wa.*" After Matt said this, he and the ambassador bowed to each other.

More polite pleasantries in Japanese followed. Then Ambassador Fujima said, "Senator, it is refreshing to again speak with you, who speaks Japanese with fluency and flair."

Matt wondered, *Is this mere standard politeness, or is he after something? Play modest, uncover his game.* "How I wish. Humble-I learned too little Japanese before my grandparents passed over, and often I regret

I cannot read Japanese at all. But you are always kind and ignore humble-I's mistakes."

Matt smiled as he changed the subject: "I've tried all night to talk to you. It took the president's speech to catch you."

The ambassador spoke carefully: "That speech was superb, wasn't it? President Swensen was very informed about Japan's situation, and he saw how the treaty would benefit the United States."

Shouldn't the ambassador save his gushing for the White House or for American reporters? Ah, he realizes that I can really hurt Japan, so he's trying to sway me. Talk about slim odds. Matt said, "That the treaty would benefit the United States even a little is a surprise to many people here." Matt was implying that he was smart enough to not be surprised, while modesty quieted him from stating such.

"Yes, so I have just heard them say. Senator, may I please bother you to ask what is your opinion of the treaty's chances?"

"The treaty will be sent to the mountain to play." Matt was quoting the Old Japan euphemism for abandoning babies on mountaintops.

"It is so."

"Nobody in the Senate wants to champion the treaty. Even if somebody did befriend the treaty, pushing passage would be difficult."

"I wonder if the treaty has such a friend."

Again Ambassador Fujima tries to sway me! He must be desperate. So squeeze him—though I'm sure he'll try to pass the problem to his bosses.

Matt smiled as he asked for the bribe with polite indirectness: "I know that if the Senate approved this treaty, that would be a huge gift to Japan."

The ambassador paused, and his eyes searched Matt's face. "Ah, would the prime minister and his cabinet agree?" Meaning: *I'm not agreeing to bribe you unless the cabinet reaches favorable consensus.*

Matt's wave dismissed that. "Certainly they'd agree"—this was pure bluff—"in a crane's lifetime." Japanese folklore said cranes lived a thousand years, so the cabinet's consent would come way too late to rescue the treaty.

The ambassador fell silent again. "This is a limited-time offer" is a Western selling tactic very offensive and alien to Japanese. "Taking charge"—making a decision by oneself that will affect other people, without gaining prior consensus with those affected people—is another un-Japanese concept. Yet if the ambassador didn't agree soon, he knew the treaty was doomed. Distaste warred with realism inside the ambassador's head, Matt was sure. Matt also was sure that Fujima had been given this job because he was adaptable to Washington ways—but was the ambassador adaptable enough? Silent Matt hoped so.

"*Sa*," Fujima said. Well, then. For many reasons—some cultural, some practical—the ambassador wished to avoid saying no; but if he said yes, he was leaving himself naked to criticism. Then too, *sa* was code: Fujima was hinting he was being pushed too hard. A polite Japanese speaker would back off.

But Matt was American. He gave Fujima a hard look and said, "I'm sorry, I didn't hear you."

Half a minute of silence passed before Fujima's eyes met Matt's. "I agree, if the Senate approved this treaty, that would be a huge gift to Japan."

He bought it, and without haggling price, I'll be damned. Seems I just agreed to sell out California.

The ambassador switched to English and asked, "What do the people in California think of the treaty, Senator Nakamura?"

Matt's smile showed teeth, as he noticed Saunders staring at him in amazement. *You have no idea what I just said, do you, Farmboy? Soon you'll find out.* Matt himself returned to English: "Nobody in California is worried, Excellency." *Little do they know.*

Outside three minutes later, Matt was leaning against the balcony railing, with a cold glass of champagne bubbling just beyond his right hand. Nobody was with him to see his face's gleeful glow as he inhaled the cool breeze. His attempted bear-hug of the moon missed by thousands of miles, but so what.

"Moon, both Fujima and I said, `If the Senate approved this treaty, that would be a huge gift to Japan.' What neither of us needed to mention is that, by Japanese etiquette, if I give a gift, the receiver *must* give me a gift just as good. Even if my gift is a political miracle, Japan is *blood-bound* to match that gift. Blood-bound, isn't that wonderful? But for poor Japan the web is even stickier. Because my gift is the type that can be enjoyed a long time, same as the `gift' of a parent's care or of a teacher's teachings. So? When someone receives a gift that keeps on giving, Japanese etiquette never marks his debt paid. Japanese call this eternal burden *tsukiai*, `social debt,' and oh, how they dread it. But it's so sweet to be owed it. Especially since Japan would be enjoying my gift for centuries—Japan's social debt to me would be monstrous.

"Understand, moon? Fujima locked Japan into *the bribe of the century* if I deliver the treaty—and that's only the *start*. Oh, *yes!*"

A second later, Matt grinned at the moon. "So what goodies will I get? Let's see, Japan must give me a gift equivalent in value and kind. Of course, Japan can't give me anything exactly equivalent in kind, although signing the island of Honshuu over to me could be a good start. Wouldn't that be great—Tokyo, Osaka, Kyoto, Nagoya, Yokohama, they're all mine?"

The idea of owning the priciest real estate on the planet, enabling him to collect billions each year in rent, made him dance with glee on the balcony.

"Or maybe `equivalent in kind' would make my gift something wonderful that I never could attain on my own. Maybe a week in bed with one of the Emperor's young nieces or cousins?"

Matt's grin was wicked. The moon didn't reply.

"Scratch that last; it's not going to happen. So that means that the huge gift to me will be money. *Real* money: forklift after forklift bringing me stacked pallets of cash!"

"Wait, what about a downside? Hm, if I work for the treaty, no matter what the vote, I'll lose my Senate seat. The only question is when."

Matt shrugged. "Big deal—didn't I decide to quit a few hours ago? Nothing stops me from working this."

The time was 10:25, and Barbara was talking to Yvonne McNeill and Tiffani. Matt, his walk unsteady, approached them. He burped, then announced, "Sorry, ladies, but it's time for us to go." Yvonne gave Barbara a look of sympathy.

Barbara hadn't moved. "*Well?*" Matt said. "You coming, or do I drive home without you?"

After saying their goodbyes, Barbara and Matt walked out to the valets at the curb. Rather, she walked and he staggered.

She gave him an angry look that said *I hope you're proud of yourself.* He gave her an angry look back, and belched besides.

When the valet brought the car around, Barbara told the young man to turn off the ignition and to give her the keys. Matt, braying what he thought of this, tried to grab those keys. Barbara outmaneuvered him and slid behind the wheel. Matt rolled in the other door, cursing unsubmissive women.

Good wives don't start arguments, Barbara had been taught, so she kept silent. But how she longed to shuck the whole "good wife" act for some rock-concert-loud catharsis.

Needing distraction, she turned on the car radio. ". . .In San Francisco, two Japanese businessmen were found murdered in their hotel room this afternoon. Police suspect gangsters based in Tokyo. The FBI—"

Barbara changed the station to one playing music.

They drove on for a few minutes in silence. Matt burped. Still looking forward, Barbara said, "If you need me to pull over for you to puke, tell me as soon as possible. I don't want to smell it in the car."

"Wow, Queen Barbara, don't you think *you're* special. You think I'm only a silly drunk?"

"Right now, yes."

"Then listen up: I plan to swing the treaty. *I*, Matt Nakamura. I talked with Ambassador Fujima, who started me thinking."

She only dared look away from the road for an instant. "What do you mean, `swing the treaty'?" *Surely he doesn't mean. . .*

"Make it approved by the Senate."

My god. "You can't do that. It's treason."

His head-shake was drunkenly exaggerated: "No, because we aren't at war with Japan. Besides, Charlie wrote the treaty, so I'm being a good party man."

"It's betraying the people who elected you! It's treason against them." Inside she was a maelstrom of anger, confusion, and horror. She had to make Matt see reason.

Matt gave her a taunting smile. "`Giving aid and comfort to the enemy,' *that's* treason. The Constitution says *nothing* about Japan, or the people of California."

"I'm not going to quibble about trifles with a drunken lawyer. *Yes* it's betrayal, pure and simple!"

She tried every argument she could devise, but he wouldn't listen. After several minutes of their arguing, Matt said, "No matter what you say, I still plan to push the treaty through."

He'll try, Barbara thought. *I know how determined he can be, especially now that I've challenged his pride.*

But of course he won't succeed.

Right?

—————

About which, the Variety-Show Host joked—

When President Swensen explained why he was selling California, he never promised not to pull this trick again. You states that went Republican last election, some advice: Act very nice to Charlie Swensen.

The president wants to buy and destroy Russian nuclear weapons. He has a great idea: If a country has something that disturbs Americans, then the U.S. government buys it and destroys it. Think we can persuade France to sell us its waiters?

CHAPTER 3
Saturday, April 9, 2005

"What do you think of this pair, Tiffani? I'm thinking my apricot suit." The mall had just opened, and Barbara and Tiffani were shopping for earrings.

Tiffani looked at Barbara's ears. "The apricot, that's what you're wearing for your Montgomery General pitch? Sure, those are lovely. I'm getting these for my navy-blue suit."

"Lemon? A good counterpoint."

"And a happy color, so those hospital administrators will happily donate medical supplies."

"How clever, earrings as subliminal suggestion. Of course, I could've used those lemon earrings last night."

"Barbara, you know you looked fine at the party. Um, which reminds me. . ."

"Yes?"

"Could you ask Matt not to act so. . .*friendly* around me?"

"He thought you looked hot, that's all. Consider it a compliment."

"If so, then tell him I said thanks, *but.*"

"Matt might be a bastard at times, Tiffani, but he won't proposition you." *Not when so many single women populate the world.*

Tiffani glanced sidelong. "Mm. If you want to talk about your marital problem, I won't blab to the other wives or Chris, I promise."

"What marital problem? I should leave him, but good wives stay with their husbands, but he's a real shit sometimes, but sometimes I still love him, but sometimes I feel like a whore."

"Is that all?"

"That isn't enough?"

"I sense you need to share something."

I need to share that my husband wants to sell out California. "There's nothing else to tell. Honestly."

Tiffani looked at the earrings on display for several heartbeats, then back to Barbara's face. "Our lives are so alike, it's spooky. We both have lawyer-senators as husbands, and they're close in age. You and I are both Red Cross fundraisers." Tiffani smiled and touched Barbara's hand. "Whatever's bothering you, I'm sure I'd understand and support you. But I won't push."

Barbara longed to tell Tiffani—Barbara sighed instead. "I wish that were true. But nobody on the planet can understand what I'm living through."

By noon, Barbara had bought her earrings, had enjoyed a light lunch with Tiffani, and had returned home to the usual empty house.

That afternoon at 3:30, Barbara just had shoved a wet swatch down the bore of the barrel when her digital phone chimed. It was Carol. "What are you up to?" Carol asked.

Barbara leaned back in her chair at the kitchen table. "This minute? Cleaning my nightstand pistol." Barbara's gun lay in pieces on newspapers covering the table. Mixed in with field-stripped gun parts were swatches of cloth, a can of cleaning solvent, a can of rustproofing oil, a wire brush, and a ramrod. At the moment the ramrod was sticking out the gun barrel.

"Cleaning your gun?" Carol made a schoolyard noise. "That sounds so girly-girl."

"Women clean, don't we? And it's been three months. Anyway, what's up? Bobby acting like a teenager again?"

"No, it's another work-related. I called to pump you about last night's party."

Barbara kept her voice light: "O Editor, be warned: The Code of the Capital requires me to evade answering and to bump you off the topic." Carol would think Barbara was kidding.

Carol laughed. "Hold on while I hook up the voice-stress analyzer. So how was the party?"

"Oodles of Canadian lobster."

"I hate you."

"I talked to lots of interesting people, and I received many compliments on my dress."

Carol asked what her outfit looked like. Barbara described it.

Barbara then said, "Some of the diplomats were wearing native costumes, and everyone else was semiformal, so everyone looked good. The Ingrams were there, and Matt complimented Tiffani on her dress."

"Which means she looked sexy. So who's there?"

"Foreign Relations Committee senators, State Department people, diplomats from all over—Japan, China, Germany, U.K., you name it."

"With the Japanese ambassador there, what did people say about the treaty?"

Barbara was silent, while she phrased her reply. *I wish I were sure that Matt didn't mean what he said.*

"Barbara? You still there?"

In a cheery tone, Barbara said, "Don't you remember my warning? I'm thinking how to evade answering." *I hate this: I'm keeping a secret from both my best friends.* "I think the other diplomats were amazed at Ambassador Fujima for what he achieved."

"Anybody talk about the treaty actually going through or not?"

Barbara again picked her words: "At the ambassador's party, all the senators were saying that the treaty had no chance."

I hate this lying. I'll get Carol talking instead. "So how are you and Larry? When I talked to you last week, you told—"

"I think I'm in love. I sing when I'm making breakfast."

"That's sweet."

"I love Love when it's new like this."

"Long-time love can be great, too. Joe Bob Saunders, last night I could tell he missed his wife Marilyn."

"The Foreign Relations Committee chairman? Sure, he'd have been at the party, too."

"Um, yeah."

"Oh, such different lives we lead: I'm going to work just as Bobby arrives home from school, I'm always racing the clock, while you fill your evenings wearing robot-tailored clothes, and eating free lobster in the company of important people."

"Carol, I always burn when people tell me I have it easy. *You* should know better by now."

"Yeah? Who of us has a teen-age son to feed and clothe? Who of us is divorced? I'm happy with my life, but compared to yours, I'm a slave breaking her back to build the pyramids."

"*You* aren't the pyramid slave, *I* am. All we Capital wives are pyramid slaves."

"Yeah, right. And sharks prefer Brussels sprouts."

"Think so? Anytime Matt asks, I clean the house for company, run to the liquor store, or run to the dry cleaner. *Anytime.* Because a senator who wants to be re-elected must entertain like he must breathe—but I'm who gets stuck with the details."

"That makes you at worst a servant."

"Then explain these: Never may I disagree in public with Matt's political views. I must dress sharply, every moment I'm in public. I must whip up tasty home-cooked meals for guests on short notice—but never may I put on weight. I can't take a job working for anyone else, not even part-time—"

"Still, your life has such glamour—"

"Always in public must I pretend that my marriage is perfect."

"My job has shark shit, too, and without the lobster. Speaking of my job, may I quote your remarks of a few minutes ago?"

Starting an argument, how's this for a diversion? "Fine, you're stuck with `shark shit.' But at least you're not *forced* to overlook your man's affairs. Is anything more degrading? Really, I know several Senate wives—"

"Matt's fooling around. I thought so."

"I didn't say that."

"Because I'm a journalist."

"For the record, I don't know that Matt is fooling around."

"But you suspect."

Barbara was silent.

"Do you *want* to know?"

Barbara stayed silent.

Carol sighed. "Okay, believe your mirage."

"How can you know it's a `mirage'? My parents suffered every marital problem imaginable. Yet they stayed married, and faithful to each other."

"But your father wasn't a senator."

"I have it easier at marriage than my parents had it. As long as I don't give up on Matt, I can hope."

"I gave up on Matt years ago. The signs are everywhere."

"Not true. You can't name even one `sign.'"

"Here's two. First, back when Matt was an attorney at. . .what was that firm?"

"Taylor, Finch, and Holmes."

"Back at Taylor, Finch, and Holmes, that day he told you court ran late. All the other lawyers were back at the office by five. Second, remember that campaign volunteer during Matt's first congressional campaign?"

"You mean the pug-nosed peroxide princess with cartoon-sized implants? The bimbo whom Santa had obviously filled her Christmas stocking with kohl?"

"Meow," Carol said. "I was covering Matt on election night, remember. Black leather and all, that slut was all over Matt, and he let her paw him."

The memory made Barbara wince. "True. But do you *know* Matt has cheated on me?"

"Isn't there only one way I'd *know* that? I've *suspected* since. . .well, since college. When Matt made a pass."

"Oh god," Barbara breathed.

Several seconds of Barbara's stunned silence passed. Then Carol said, "Barbara, I have two stories to write before deadline. May I quote your remarks of ten minutes ago?"

"Huh? About whether cleaning a pistol is unfeminine?"

"No, whacko, the treaty. I want to write, `A source close to Senator Nakamura said that he and other joint-committee members were heard discussing the treaty yesterday, and they agreed it had no chance.'"

"Okay, but add somewhere that the remarks were overheard at a diplomatic party."

"Who cares where they were said? Besides, if I become too specific, people can figure out who's the informed source."

"Under your byline? Gosh, who could Mystery Source be? The `where' part has to go in."

Carol gave a snort. "I'll print the story under the pseudonym of Albert Wilson. Listen, you're telling me how to do my job. Don't. I don't see where one little phrase can make a difference—"

Barbara sighed. *Because as soon as he left the party, he recanted what he said during it.*

"—and Barbara, it's my best judgment that it not go in. Let's drop it. Back to my original question: Okay to quote you as I said?"

"Sure, whatever you want, Carol."

"Something is shady about how you're acting."

"Nothing's wrong, everything's fi—"

"Gold-plated shark shit. I don't know why, but I think you *are* evading my questions."

"That's not tr—"

"And as I think back, somehow the conversation always wandered away from the treaty."

"Look, I'm sorry, but I've been on the phone a long time, and I need to run to the stores before they close. I'll talk to you another time, or you call me, okay?"

"Sure, whatever you want, Barbara. I enjoyed talking to you. No, I enjoyed *most of* talking to you." The line clicked.

Barbara was glum as she finished cleaning and oiling her weapon, and as she cleared away her gun-cleaning kit. In the bedroom, she sighed as she put the pistol back in the drawer of her nightstand.

"Carol could tell I'm holding back."

A second later, Barbara pulled out her digital phone and speed-dialed Matt's office number. *Of course I've worried over nothing. Surely he realizes the treaty is folly, right? I'll just confirm he's become sensible again.*

Melissa answered. After a minute of pleasantries, Barbara asked, "Is Matt in?"

"Boy, is he. At the moment, he's cooking the phone lines. Did he only drink coffee last night?"

"No, champagne and bour—why do you ask?"

"Because usually everyone here slows down on Saturdays, and we're gone by noon. But he's a *rocket* today—hold on, he's hung up."

The receiver clicked three seconds later. "Hello, Barbara." Matt sounded wary. "What can I do for you?"

Barbara knew she'd best act her nicest. "I was thinking about how I acted last night when I was driving home from the party. Maybe I was a bitch."

"Maybe you were."

"I called to say I was sorry, and find out how you felt today." She'd pass on Tiffani's cease-and-desist order some other time.

"I'm okay, mostly. Thanks for asking." His first word came out breathy, as if he'd been holding his breath.

"Everything's okay with you?"

"Got a headache, but I'm not letting it slow me down. I'm pushing to shrivel the backlog, clear the decks for action."

She made her voice light: "What kind of action?"

"What we argued over, last night—when you were `maybe' a bitch."

"No, please, I'd thought—I'd hoped that you'd changed your mind."

"I haven't."

"Have you discussed this with anyone else, told anyone else your plans?"

"Not yet."

"Then forget this. Don't worry about pride, because nobody will ever know. I haven't told Carol or Tiffani."

"Soon everyone will know."

"Does it mean nothing to you that your wife pleads this of you? Don't I mean *anything* to you at all?"

"It's decided, Barbara."

"California didn't ask for this. What you're doing is *wrong*, it's—"

"Barbara, I have a lot of work to do today." Matt spoke with the slow enunciation of a judge announcing a verdict. "If you'll excuse me, I'm going to hang up now. I'll see you later."

She sighed. "Goodbye, Matt." The receiver clicked in her ear.

Barbara was in the bedroom ten minutes later, sweating out her rage to an exercise dijvid (digital video) that she'd downloaded.

Her digital phone chimed. She lunged for it and snarled, "This is Barbara, and I don't want any!"

"*Barbara?* What's wrong, honey?" The caller was her father, Ed Morris.

She took a slow breath and exhaled, as she muted the TV. Panting, she said, "I was upset about something while I was working out. Then I thought you were a telemarketer, sorry."

Her father put on a jolly act: "I thought exercise was to rid you of anger, not to make it worse."

"The only way to rid me of anger right now, is to shove Matt naked out the space shuttle."

"Yeah, he can be hard to live with."

"Dad, you can't imagine what he did." She told her father about the party and Matt's heavy drinking. She mentioned that Matt and the Japanese ambassador had talked, but she hadn't heard them herself. ". . .So I'm driving us home, and he tells me he intends to make the California Treaty pass."

"He takes the grand prize this time."

"But part of me still clings to the thought, he *must* see how *wrong* it is."

"*Matt?* I'm not holding my breath. Lord, this is terrible."

In the background, Barbara could hear her mother's voice: "What is terrible? Something wrong with Barbara is?"

"It's not Barbara, it's Matt," Ed said. "Matt's done something very wrong."

"Let me speak to Barbara, please," Takeko said in the background. A second later, Takeko's voice, besides being clear, was speaking Japanese: "Good afternoon, *Baaba-chan.* How are you?"

"I'm calmer now, but when Father called I was really angry with Husband and myself."

"Why angry?"

Barbara again covered the previous night's events, including the argument on the drive home. Then Barbara told her mother about her recent phone conversation with Matt.

Takeko shocked Barbara with her reply: "*Baaba-chan,* I'm glad that our family isn't here to hear your shameful words. Our ancestors weep."

"Mother?"

"Nakamura-*san* is a good man, always polite to me. You ignore what I taught you, how to be a good wife."

Keep it polite. Keep harmony. Observe the forms. Be calm. "Mother, perhaps there are events of which you are not aware."

"Perhaps it is *you* who is not aware, of your *giri*," obligation to a benefactor, "to your husband. If he plans to do this, help him."

"No. I would feel ashamed."

"If you cannot, be a `silent flower,'" be someone who wisely keeps quiet. "In any case, you have a duty to give him a household filled with peace and harmony."

"Mother, he wants to sell California to Japan."

"And what is wrong with that?"

Take a breath. Calm yourself. "California is part of the United States, and has no wish to leave, but was never asked."

"Would it be worse off as part of Japan?"

"Yes! I commit a rudeness, but yes, I think California would be worse off."

"No. I don't think that, and I would be glad to see the change. I would be overjoyed if *you* helped to make this happen."

Barbara shook her head, again and again, though nobody could see. "I think if Husband sells California to Japan, he dishonors the people of California. Mother, I have no *giri* to help Husband in dishonor."

———

About which, the Variety-Show Host joked—

If the treaty is okayed, California schools will be run like Japan's. Do Japanese think stopping Godzilla was tough? Let them make California kids clean the school bathrooms.

A recent survey of a thousand adults found they all favored the U.S. ditching California. The thousand live in Oregon.

CHAPTER 4
Heisei 17-nen 4-gatsu 11-nichi, Getsuyohbi (Monday, April 11, 2005)

At last, today I prove I'm a full member of the Matsumoto Robotics team, Hiroshi thought.

Yokohama time was 10:25 in the morning when IWATA Hiroshi and his friend, KINOSHITA Ryuuji, stood at sinks in Sales Department's men's room. Hiroshi was combing his hair while Ryuuji was washing his hands.

Ryuuji looked at Hiroshi's reflection. "So, Iwata-*kun*, you've worked on those schematics for. . .is it four days this time?"

"Three days this time, four days last time. Section Manager Masumi sets high standards."

"Meaning, he's criticized everything you've put it front of him since you started here? I well understand. So good luck on today's presentation." At Hiroshi's look of surprise, Ryuuji said, "That's twice you've straightened your tie."

Sure enough. Embarrassed Hiroshi brought his hands down to his side. "Still, I think I've learned a lot since January about robotics and factory layout, and finally the section manager will see that."

"That's good, because Matsumoto Robotics can't afford—"

"Please, Kinoshita-*san*." Hiroshi made himself laugh. "Not you, too!"

"So then what?" Ryuuji asked Hiroshi an hour and a half later. The two young men were eating lunch in the Matsumoto Robotics company cafeteria.

Hiroshi tapped his tray with a chopstick. "After the section manager corrected my mistakes, he stopped me as I was gathering up my drawings. `Iwata-*kun*,' he said, `you know we can't afford the luxury of time to baby you that Nissan gave you. We have much competition in Japan, plus Deseret Robotics in America, so we must keep our costs down. Unlike Nissan, here you can't wait for someone else to teach you the knowledge you need.'"

"Ouch."

"Then he stared me down as he said, `We realized when you came here that you knew basically nothing about robotics, despite your degree from Tokyo University. You have learned quickly enough here, but some perhaps could say that you might be expected to learn even faster.'"

Ryuuji sucked air through his teeth in sympathy. "Then what?"

"Then he said, `A week and a half from now, when you go to that robotics conference in California, we don't want you to shame us.'" Hiroshi made a face. "What could I do? I bowed deeply and replied, `I shall try even harder to fulfill my *giri* to Matsumoto Robotics.' Oh, I miss Nissan."

Ryuuji sighed. "Same with me and Sony."

Back in January, Hiroshi had been a first-year trainee at Nissan's automobile-manufacturing plant in

Yokosuka. Hiroshi had been with Nissan for nine months, as had the plant's ten other trainees who were in Hiroshi's "year club." Every payday, Hiroshi put money in savings toward buying a Bluebird (Altima) at employee discount.

January 21, a Friday, started out a wonderful day. Fellow trainee KATOH Nobutaka bought his own car, a Maxima with ADS (automatic driving system). Hiroshi and the other Oppama Plant trainees rushed through lunch and then hurried outside to Nobutaka's new car. Using washable white paint, the trainees wrote their names and good wishes all over the glass.

Hiroshi was smiling when he returned to work, and kept smiling for the next half-hour. Then his boss walked up to him. The man's expression was odd.

"Iwata-*kun*, Personnel Department Manager Yanaga wants to see you." The man's voice was odd as well.

Hiroshi's expression changed to puzzlement.

At first Hiroshi and Department Manager Yanaga made small talk. Mister Yanaga learned Hiroshi was on Oppama Plant's sumo-wrestling team, because while Hiroshi wasn't heavy, he was fit. Hiroshi played racquetball to stay in shape, he told Mister Yanaga, and Hiroshi loved golf but couldn't afford to play it. Neither Hiroshi or Mister Yanaga mentioned Hiroshi's home town of Sendai; Hiroshi's Tohhoku regional accent went politely unmentioned.

Five minutes after they'd begun talking, Hiroshi was still puzzling over why he'd been summoned. That's when Mister Yanaga switched from small talk and ordinary politeness to full formality. "Trainee Iwata, you're familiar with the term *administrative guidance*?"

The question surprised Hiroshi. "Yes, it's the term for directives from the Economy and Industry Ministry. EIM has given Nissan administrative guidance on `voluntary' restriction of exports of our cars, on plant and equipment modernization, and on buying American car parts and building factories in America. Deregulation thankfully has reduced the amount of EIM's meddling." *What's this got to do with me?*

Mister Yanaga nodded. "Up until now, Nissan has received administrative guidance mainly from EIM and the Foreign Ministry. But last week, the Minister and Deputy Minister of Health, Welfare and Labor visited Nissan's corporate headquarters."

"Health, Welfare and Labor? Both ministers?"

"Yes. The Minister and Deputy Minister reminded Corporate that a large and still-swelling portion of Japan's population is over sixty, and the government can't afford to pay so many pensions. Soon Health, Welfare and Labor Ministry will bump up another year the eligibility age for retirement allowances. Before that day, the ministry `asks' us to raise our retirement age one year."

Then strangely, Mister Yanaga sucked air in through his teeth, and rubbed the back of his neck. Hiroshi felt alarmed: Either gesture signaled that Mister Yanaga felt pressured to say something unpleasant.

Mister Yanaga did so: "We're calling back the people we retired within this past year, but the trainees we've hired this year are being released. Trainee, I'm sorry."

Hiroshi stared in shock. "Th—these retirees, you're recalling them as *shokutaku*," retirees temporarily rehired, "right? They're gone in a few months, right? Then we trainees returning from furlough is the plan, right? My money will be scarce for a while, but if that's what Nissan needs from us, I can endure it."

Mister Yanaga was silent, but his eyes spoke: "It can't be helped."

Hiroshi refused to accept that. "What about waiting until next April? Nissan doesn't hire trainees next April, and lets the most senior year-club of employees not retire, hm?"

"Health, Welfare and Labor Ministry has asked us before, but we've resisted. Last week we were told, `Nissan is holding up the train.' We have no choice now; remember how much Nissan depends on the government's favor."

"Then let's try this: Nissan keeps us both, trainees and recalled retirees."

"Can't afford. We've already discussed this with Headquarters."

"Could we trainees become on-loan employees?" Perhaps the trainees could be loaned temporarily to Nissan's vendors.

"I'm sorry."

"Did you know Trainee Katoh bought a Maxima today? Now people will say to him, `You bought a car from Nissan, then that same day they *fired* you?' He will feel so ashamed."

"He told me. It can't be helped."

Hiroshi slumped in his chair. "But, we've done nothing—this is so *dorai*," insensitive. "Because that ministry asks it, it's done?"

"Many Nissan managers agreed with you. They asked what Health, Welfare and Labor Ministry could do to Nissan if we defy them."

"Directly? Little. *Indirectly*? Nothing. Everyone knows how intense the rivalry is among the ministries. Even if Health, Welfare and Labor Ministry is angry with us, that doesn't mean that EIM or the Foreign Ministry will oppose Nissan."

Mister Yanaga looked at Hiroshi in surprise. "You are politically informed."

Hiroshi made a quick head-bow of thanks. "I follow current events." Hiroshi's hand gesture dismissed that as unimportant. "Anyway, why must we lose our jobs for nothing we've done?"

"The defiance faction asked those questions, too. Yet cautious managers felt that Nissan dare not risk offending EIM or the Foreign Ministry, no matter how small the odds. The consensus plan became that we would both call back our latest retirees, and find jobs for our trainees."

Mister Yanaga dipped his head. "I've already spoken with the company union. I'm sorry."

"Thank you," Hiroshi made himself say.

Mister Yanaga managed a weak smile. "But your credentials impress Matsumoto Robotics in Yokohama, and they're eager to start you Monday. Maybe you won't even need to find a new apartment; they're close enough by train."

Hiroshi had pushed himself out of Mister Yanaga's chair to stand straight, like a warrior going to his beheading. "Now I understand the saying, `For a tiny leaf floating down the stream, it's senseless to fight against the flow of water.'" Hiroshi had been pleased that he could speak so calmly. He had bowed goodbye to Mister Yanaga. "Thank you for finding this other job for me."

————

Now Hiroshi glanced around the Matsumoto Robotics cafeteria. "Oh, I miss Nissan."

Ryuuji sighed. "Same with me and Sony. I loved working on those robot pets."

Then Ryuuji brightened. "But as you say, in a week and a half we're going to California. I wouldn't be doing that so soon at Sony."

Hiroshi smiled. "'We'? You're going, too?"

"Yes, I found out this morning. Section Manager Tsurumi from R&D Department also is going."

Hiroshi could have pretended he knew the name; instead, he asked, "Who's he?"

"He heads Arm Design Section. His team earned a patent for our company."

Hiroshi showed his puzzlement. "So it is. Matsumoto Robotics is sending a heavy hitter to this conference. Then why you and me?"

"Because my English is good enough, I was told." Ryuuji made a sour face. "We're all three engineers, though you and I are in Sales Department. Also, with you, the company wants an English expert." Ryuuji's face this time was even more sour. "I did alright in upper-secondary school English, but I'm glad the teacher wasn't my father, no offense. And your father made you *speak* English at home?" Ryuuji shuddered.

"My father believes the national curriculum doesn't emphasize spoken English enough." Now Hiroshi smiled with delight. "Can I complain about the result? I get a company-paid trip to California, and with you. I still can't believe our luck."

Ryuuji gave Hiroshi a look. "*Are* we lucky? I worry how Californians will treat us."

"You mean the treaty? The nightly news says Washington's senators will kill it. California will never be sold, so why should Californians be rude to two young Japanese?"

"I hope you're right. So what do you think of this treaty?"

"I'm surprised Foreign Minister Utsumi dared it. Some say the United States is an old and flabby lion, but still, it is a lion."

"While Japan is a declawed pussycat."

Hiroshi's smile was dreamy. "Japan buying California will never be, but how marvelous it would be for our company if it did happen."

"Because many factories in California will change owners, and the new Japanese owners will install Japanese robots?"

"Yes. Imagine if Matsumoto Robotics sent me, on expense account, to replace all the movie cameramen in Hollywood with MReiga 7000s."

Ryuuji looked dreamy, too. "Mm, nice."

Hiroshi bowed to an imaginary person. "Excuse me, Mister Director, but you must film a nude scene for me to calibrate the robot camera." Ryuuji laughed at Hiroshi's joke.

And then Hiroshi wasn't looking at Ryuuji anymore. "*Hariuddo wa. . .*" Speaking of Hollywood. . .

Ryuuji turned to look. "She is striking, isn't she?"

Both men watched a woman their age carrying a lunch tray to a distant table. The woman had a ready smile and stylishly cut shoulder-length hair, and she wore a lavender business suit.

Hiroshi wrenched his gaze away from her. "Beautiful, yes, and all I know about her is that she often wears hats to work."

"She is maintenance programmer HIGASHI Reiko. She started here last April, coming straight from Nagoya University."

"So she would be in R&D Department, along with Section Manager Tsurumi. Do you know if she's involved with anyone?"

"I've only talked to her once, and that was about work. But you're wise to want the Section Manager to introduce you."

"How so?"

"Approaching her without an introduction is vulgar, and she's a lady who can be choosy."

"Then I will figure out how to arrange an introduction." Somehow Hiroshi would find a way to meet Reiko.

Ten hours later, Washington time was after nine Monday morning when Matt hung up his suit jacket in his private office. Saturday he had told Barbara he was "clearing the decks for action" on the treaty. Finally he was set to start.

Matt picked up the phone and punched in Diane's extension. "Diane, the next ten minutes, I want Peace And Quiet."

"Even for the president?"

"Him, put through. For everyone else, standard drill."

"Yes sir," Diane said. Matt hung up.

Now to figure out how to sell the treaty. Matt unlocked and opened his briefcase, and took out the treaty and the keep/sell reasons that he and Charlie had listed.

At the top of the first page, he had written his smart-aleck "reason" to oppose the treaty: He'd lose his job if California went. Matt scratched through Reason One with a pencil. *Not a problem anymore.*

Matt reread the treaty, and realized many special-interest groups would scurry forth to oppose it. He needed to figure out ways to neutralize them all. And just how the hell could he—

Money!

Didn't senators always need money, to fill the pork barrel? Matt slapped a fist into a palm. Money would be the key, how to sell the treaty!

He reviewed his handwritten reasons to sell California. Selling California stuffed money into the treasury, financed nuclear disarmament, hobbled Japan, and moved businesses and jobs to the Remaining States. He had four reasons to sell, and every one was motherhood, apple pie, and the flag.

Matt made a plan. He'd remind everyone that he was throwing away his Senate seat for this. He'd say that he was acting solely to benefit his country, unlike his selfish opponents. Then he'd try to draw the general public behind him.

"While I *push* that sixty trillion." Matt grabbed the pencil again and circled the word *money* in Sell Reason number one.

After eleven minutes of Peace And Quiet, Matt touch-toned Diane again. "I'm back. Any visitors or messages I should know about?"

"A Mister Asakawa is hoping to speak with you, registered lobbyist for Japan. Send him away?"

Ambassador Fujima works fast, Matt thought. "No, I'll give him five minutes. Tell Melissa he can see me."

Once Diane had closed the door behind him, Asakawa switched to Japanese. "Senator Nakamura, I am deeply honored and flattered that you so graciously have consented to see me. Here's my *meishi.*" On one side, the business card looked like the regular English-language business card of "Mister Minoru Asakawa, Lobbyist for Japan." On the other side was Japanese hen-scratch.

Matt handed Asakawa one of his own business cards. Lower-status Asakawa bowed deeply, and higher-status Matt returned a part of that bow.

Matt said in Japanese, "Lobbyist Asakawa, please tell me why you are here."

"Fujima believes that you've become a friend of the treaty." Now Asakawa was watching Matt's face.

Matt's smile was meant to be disarming. "Yes, I'm not only a friend of the treaty, but right now I'm the only true friend the treaty has."

"Go on."

"Fuller is play-acting with the treaty only because he's majority leader. Nobody else pretends interest."

"That is most unfortunate—but we are greatly honored that we have your favor in this matter, Senator. I offer to help any way I can."

You can start by not contacting me so publicly next time, Matt thought. But how to phrase the message, without sounding critical so that Asakawa lost face? Matt tried hinting: "*Here* your help is not needed."

"Please excuse me if I have offended you, Senator," the lobbyist replied, stony-faced.

Great, Matt had still hurt his feelings. If Asakawa bailed out and Matt had to deal directly with the ambassador, that would be dangerous. "Lobbyist, please accept my apologies for my clumsiness in not making myself clear. We need to talk and plan, and so we will—but not here. I don't dare be connected to Japan." Matt picked up Asakawa's business card. "I'll call you to arrange places to meet. I'll tell your receptionist I am `Kawakita.'"

"Yes, thank you for your attentive consideration."

Matt looked sharply at Asakawa. "Again: Our relationship must be secret. Not even my staff may know."

"I see." Asakawa's eyes revealed nothing.

"I don't want anything leaked to the press, and I don't want to read any rumors. Do you understand?"

Mister Asakawa bowed. "Yes, I understand." What it was that he understood, he clearly had brains enough not to say.

Five minutes after Mister Asakawa had departed, Matt stood by the office's bathroom and called a meeting. Soon about twenty-five staffers not out on business were gathered around. His people looked attentive and curious.

But are they compliant? he wondered. Could he cow them into working for the treaty, or would everyone head for the exits? He was about to find out.

Matt stood straighter. "I'm late for a meeting, so I'll be brief. You all know about Swensen's treaty with Japan; several of you have told me jokes about it. . . ."

He took a breath, then plunged in: "I intend to push the treaty approved by the Senate. I require your help to achieve that."

Bonnie, who was from Long Beach and less than a year out of college, looked aghast. "Mister Senator, do you mean that? How can you support such a horror?"

"That's a good question, and a number of you are asking it yourselves." *But unlike Bonnie, you weren't foolish enough to ask aloud.* "I heard Charlie Swensen's speech Friday, then I reread the text of it. I'm convinced that this is the best choice for the country."

Matt went on to list and explain the four "Reasons to Sell California" that Charlie had listed.

Bonnie shrugged. "That's great, helping the country—but aren't you forgetting? Sell California, and *you* won't have a job and *we* won't have jobs."

Tone of Voice Nine (Humble): "I'm willing to sacrifice for the good of the USA. From time to time, a man in Washington does what he thinks is right, knowing it means political suicide."

Bonnie shook her head. "Myself, I'm not going to work to eliminate my own job. I ask you to please reassign me to other duties." Bonnie's tone of voice was that of someone being reasonable.

"Bonnie, I won't ask you to work on this Japan treaty if you don't want to."

She smiled with relief. "*Thank you*, Mister Senator."

Tone of Voice Three (Businesslike): "Instead, I'll fire you." Every face he saw showed shock. "Anyone else not with me?"

"Yeah!" yelled twenty-four-year-old Marty. "If the price of keeping my job is I must work on this *shit-for-brains* treaty, then I'm gone right now, this minute. Any man who stays has no *balls*, and the woman's a *whore*. And `Bomber,' I haven't the words to describe *you*."

The staffers all gasped. Marty looked around for support, saw none, and shrugged. "Excuse me, I have a desk to clean out." Marty spun on his heel, and the crowd parted to let him leave.

Matt's expression didn't change. "Anyone else?"

Silence.

Matt looked at still-shocked faces. "I'm glad we've settled that. Sherry, I want Bonnie out of here by noon. Marty has five minutes, under escort by Cliff."

Matt paused. "And to answer the unasked question: Should you lose your jobs when DeGarcia and I lose ours, I'll give you great referrals and help you find other jobs in Washington. Cross me though, and I'll cast you adrift amid the icebergs—as Marty will learn when he goes job hunting."

The room remained silent. Bonnie's chin was quivering, and she was blinking back tears.

Matt looked into each face in turn. "Put together a game plan. I want `Dear Colleague' letters to go out to other senators, so figure out what the letters will say and when we'll send them. I want to work with the White House on using the Internet to reach voters outside California. I want press coverage, however possible, whenever possible. I'll be chairing hearings on the treaty Thursday, so we have lots of work to do and too little time to do it in. Any questions?"

Nobody would meet his eye. "Good. I'll see you later," he said as he headed for the door.

Waiting for the elevator, out of his staffers' hearing, he sighed relief. "Lost only two. Terrific."

Matt arrived at the Senate dining room slightly after ten. It was too late for breakfast and too early for lunch, so the room was empty. Matt just had ordered lunch when Ken Gibson walked in.

A casino pit boss, as soon as he enters a room, glances into the eyes of every gambler there. He wants to see who's watching him, and he wants to see who's watching the dealer too closely. Nevada's Senator Gibson made that same sharp eye sweep, Matt noted.

Matt needed to turn senators around on the treaty. He'd start with Gibson. "Hey, Ken, care to join me?"

Gibson gave Matt a puzzled look, but sat down at his table. Gibson ordered from the waiter, then turned back to Matt. "I should be in a subcommittee meeting and a committee meeting now, but a man must eat."

How did Dale Carnegie say to make people like you? Encourage them to talk about themselves. Matt put on a face of caring interest and asked, "So what projects are you working on?"

Gibson summarized his struggles, describing them in terms of satisfying this voter or that bloc. To Matt, it all sounded like the same voter whinings as he himself had to endure.

Right after the waiter brought Gibson's food, Matt nodded. Matt shifted into Tone of Voice Five (Sympathetic): "You're busy, all right."

"Comes with the job. And you? Hm, Thursday you're chairing hearings on that Japan treaty."

"Thanks for remembering."

"So how short will you make the hearings before everyone shreds the treaty in markup? One day, or drag it out to two days?"

"Fact is, I'll give people as much time as they need." Matt leaned forward. "I'm going to bust my ass to push the treaty through."

Gibson blinked. His coffee cup stopped dead. "Why?"

"It's good for the country."

What's your real reason? Gibson's look asked. But Gibson said, "Perhaps. Good for the other forty-nine states, *maybe.*"

"More to the point, Ken, the treaty's good for Nevada. Look, California goes Japanese, a lot of businesses in California are going to flee. To where? The best bets will be the states next door."

"True, *if* the treaty ever went through, Nevada would get jobs."

"Then again, don't forget that a military buildup will occur along California's borders. The Japanese may be

America's good friends now, but the Pentagon will insist that the border with Japan be secure."

Gibson smiled. "Oh, the spending. . ."

"Meanwhile, every yen Japan can rake together will go to paying for the treaty. How easy will it be for businesses in Japan to borrow money?"

"It'll be impossible. Their expansion will come to a screeching halt, while we'll have so much money flowing in."

"Now one idea *you* should consider, Ken. This treaty would pay three trillion dollars a year for twenty years. Capitol Hill takes about a fourth of that, eight hundred billion, and applies it to the national debt. In twenty years the debt's gone. You know what that means?"

"Everybody here is a hero with the voters."

"But what do you do with the rest of that money? *Whatever you want.* Throw some pocket change at Swensen for his Russian nukes, then watch the Hill spend money like drunken sailors in port. You're heroes back home *again.*"

Gibson smiled. "Our re-elections are locked up." Then the smile disappeared. "But we fought a war to preserve the Union."

Matt leaned forward and eyed Gibson. "Right, and in 1868, the Supreme Court ruled secession was unconstitutional. Yet in the same decision, the Court wrote that a state could leave the Union at `the consent of the States.' The states give their consent when the Senate approves the California Treaty."

"`When'? The treaty has a snowball's chance, Matt."

Dale Carnegie said show respect for the other guy's opinion. "Right now it looks that way. But my point is, our Constitution and its amendments, our statutory law, and our Supreme Court decisions hold *nothing* to stop California from going to Japan."

"But you have to admit the whole idea is sick. It's like selling your sister to a brothel."

"Isn't this better than the sister remaining a virgin, but the whole family suffering ruin?"

"Then what's to stop Swensen from selling Nevada to Monaco?"

"For what he'll earn from California, he won't need to do that."

"Well, the idea *still* sounds sick to me."

"Of course. But if we don't act now, on this treaty, I'm rock-solid sure we'll have to act later—when the terms will be nowhere as good."

"Something I don't understand, though: Why are you doing this? You *want* to be unemployed?"

Careful, careful, Matt thought. Tone of Voice Nine (Humble): "I figure that after starting my political life looking out for my district, and going on to looking out for my state, I should end my political career looking out for my country."

"I see," Gibson said. His expression said *You're a lying sack of shit*, but he honored the Senate's *no name-calling* rule.

Gibson ate his cake and sipped on his coffee, not saying a word. When the cake was gone, Gibson put the dessert fork face-down on the cake plate, and shoved both away. "It still *feels* wrong, but I can't see any other plan that solves our debt problem better. You want to throw away your job, who am I to say no? I'm in."

———

Matt kept the joy he felt out of his smile. *Now to put Gibson on record endorsing the treaty.* "Great you're on the team, Ken. The president will appreciate your early endorsement of the treaty—"

"Whoa. I never said I'd endorse it publicly."

"True, but I presumed it."

"Fuller couldn't even recruit a co-sponsor. We're wasting time talking."

"Who's for the treaty? Dave Fuller, you, and me. Maybe some others who haven't declared yet. However many others Fuller can arm-twist into going along."

Gibson raised a hand to object. "Worse-case scenario: only we three. Starting from three, we'll have to recruit every Democrat, and also bring Republicans to our side."

"The Republicans *are* a problem." Matt's eyes stared into space, but then snapped back to Gibson's face as Matt grinned in triumph. "Point out that the treaty would enable tax cuts."

"Maybe even completely. Imagine, a twenty-year tax holiday." Gibson grinned back.

"So around the Republicans it's taxes, keep talking taxes." Matt lowered his voice and leaned closer. "Republicans cream when they cut taxes."

Gibson laughed. "Certainly the other arguments you used on me would also work on them. And I doubt that some Republican senator on the east coast would be so worried about Japanese troops invading *Nevada* that he'd kill *his* state's shot at part of sixty trillion."

Dale Carnegie wrote, let the other guy think the idea's his. "Gosh, you're right. When our Republican colleagues realize exactly what sixty trillion dollars means, the Senate will be one big bipartisan lovefest. So may I announce you're with the president and Fuller and me?"

"Not yet. Nevada knows what happens to people who bet on slim odds."

Not a yes—yet. But not a no. Matt clapped Gibson on the shoulder and looked him in the eye. "I'll be honest: I'm disappointed that you won't speak out yet."

"Since we're being honest, I'm not sure the political gains of that outweigh the costs."

"Yet I'm glad you're with us. You're helping your state, and you're helping your country. You can be proud of your support of this."

Gibson looked at his watch and stood up. "We'll see."

Five minutes later, Matt was in a good mood as he was walking back to his office. Now Gibson was on the team. Even better, if Matt recruited someone the first time he'd tried, how many more senators could he sway in the future?

He was smiling when he walked past Bonnie's cubicle—somebody else had already taken Bonnie's place. Soon Matt was walking up to the desk of his chief of staff. "Sherry, what do you have on the treaty project?" Matt gestured for her to follow into his office.

Sherry was an overweight divorcee in her late thirties. She had kids she was sending through college, Matt forgot how many. Bottom line: She couldn't afford to lose her job. Matt smiled; holding power was fun, even in the little things.

Now, as she answered Matt's question, Sherry's face was expressionless. "Jeff thrilled the White House when he told them you'd come to their side."

Matt laughed. "I'll bet Charlie fell on his ass in shock when they told him."

"Yes sir. It's my understanding that nobody but the majority leader has endorsed the treaty," she said in a flat voice. Sherry's disapproval of Matt's actions was likewise clear from the frown of her mouth.

Sherry briefed him on what his staff had accomplished in those few hours. She then said, ". . .You wanted press coverage. Carla arranged an interview with Glen Ferguson of American Satellite News on Wednesday."

As soon as she left, Matt picked up the phone and called Ken Gibson. Matt was eager to drop the Nevada senator's name in the interview. But Gibson was out. Matt left a message asking Gibson to call him.

"This is ASN Newsbreak, 3:00 p.m. Eastern time, Wednesday, April 13.

"The California Treaty has gained modest support among Americans outside California. According to today's American Satellite News survey, 13 percent of Americans in the forty-nine other states favor selling California. Before the president's speech Friday, support was paltry at only 2 percent. . . ."

"In international news, the leaders of Syria and Russia will meet soon, to discuss Syria's defenses. Beginning Monday, Russian President Dimitrov will host Prime Minister Al-Amin of Syria, Dimitrov's office announced today. The defense talks are at Al-Amin's request. The specific agenda has not been announced."

By 5:45 Wednesday afternoon, Matt had called Gibson's office several times more. Every time, the result was "Sorry, may I take a message?"

Now Matt's interview was in fifteen minutes. Matt couldn't take any more time to call, he had to head to the TV studio.

But Matt was lucky: Just as he stepped out of the elevator, he saw Gibson walking the hallway toward his own first-floor office. Matt waved as he followed. "Hey, Ken, hold on. I've been driving your receptionists crazy, leaving messages."

Gibson now was at the door of his outer office. "What's this batch about?" He gestured Matt inside.

"My chief of staff scored me an interview on American Satellite News. Ten minutes from now."

"At our studio?"

"Yeah. I only wanted to know if you'd given more thought to endorsing the treaty."

Gibson laughed. "Yeah, I thought about it. You can tell them I'm with my president."

"Great!"

"Senators don't back anything until they see other senators on board—you know how it is."

Matt relaxed. He glanced at his watch, which told him he could spare another minute. With idle curiosity, Matt looked around. Through the doorway of Gibson's reception area, Matt could see into a cubicle that was marked "Internet Station 1."

In front of the computer, Mela sat absorbed in her work. Her appearance was businesslike. Her hair was in a jogger's braid, and her makeup, viewed in profile, was low-key. She wore a tan suit with a light purple silk blouse and low-heeled, dark-purple shoes. Except for her talon-length nails, she looked nothing like the mistress of a senator—Matt's secret was safe.

Visible by Mela's keyboard were several printouts, a computer-disk holder, several scribbled-on legal-pad sheets, and an open thick tax manual. On top of the monitor sat a yellow-and-black book, *The Federal Budget for Dummies.* She truly was a tax specialist.

She looked around and met Matt's eye. Her gaze was steady for a second, the gaze of an equal. She held his look, then broke eye contact and returned to work.

Only a few seconds had passed since Gibson had spoken. Matt now turned back to face him. "Great, Ken, I owe you for joining my crusade."

"Yes, Matt, and I'll remember it, too." They both laughed, then Gibson glanced at his watch. "Don't smile prettier than the TV reporters. They turn rude."

Matt smiled pretty. "Do you realize you're the last person to talk to me before I become famous?"

Twenty minutes later, in the Senate television studio, Matt's voice was smooth for the microphone. ". . .Glen, President Swensen's treaty is of great benefit to the people of the USA, and I plan to nurture its Senate approval."

American Satellite News reporter Glen Ferguson stared open-mouthed for a second. Then he leaned forward in his chair and slashed down with his arm. "Dallas, *cut!*"

Ferguson's eyes on Matt were shocked. "You're endorsing the treaty? Your home state sold to Japan, and you're *endorsing* that treaty?"

Tone of Voice Eight (Patient): "Yes, Glen. And if you resume the interview, I'll tell you why."

The interview set contained comfortable matching blue chairs on either side of a low, white table beneath bright lights. In front of each man on the table was a water glass.

Ferguson was a tan, athletic, and handsome man in his thirties, with a receding hairline of sandy blond hair. Ferguson was also a low-seniority Capitol Hill correspondent. This fact, and the fact that ASN had sent only one cameraman, told Matt how unimportant his interview was rated.

Debbie, the site director's assistant, looked confused. "And *I* thought the treaty was only a crock."

Lights in Matt's eyes made it hard to see the cameraman's face, but he sounded puzzled as well. "If California is sold, won't this guy lose his job?"

Somewhere beyond the lights a digital phone played "William Tell Overture." The site director spoke in a low tone for a minute. Matt overheard him chuckle; "Hell, *yes*, this is news!"

After the call, the site director raised his voice to normal. "Senator, my apologies for any inconvenience we've caused—"

Matt waved that away and smiled. "It's no problem at all."

"Everyone, in a minute we'll resume the interview. My people, listen up: Dallas says we're the lead. And after Dallas runs it, I figure tomorrow our piece will be all over the goddamned *planet*. So do yourselves proud. Senator Nakamura, may we extend your interview to forty-five minutes?"

Matt put on an innocent expression to ask, "I'm not filler anymore?" He shaded his eyes, and turned to face the hidden voice. *Am I willing to sacrifice fifteen more minutes of my evening tonight, to be tomorrow's lead story worldwide?* "Yes, I can agree to that."

About which, the Variety-Show Host joked—

"Bomber" Nakamura, a senator from California, champions the California Treaty. He warns that if we don't ratify the treaty, a dire fate awaits America. Yeah—the U.S. taxpayers will have to pay "Bomber" for another two years.

If this treaty goes through, I feel sorry for Mattel. They'll need to rush out lots of little kimonos, to go with all their Malibu Barbie dolls.

CHAPTER 5
Thursday, April 14, 2005

"Hi, Barbara?" It was Tiffani calling. "You okay?"

"Sure, why?"

"Because it's after nine here at the office, and you're usually here by now."

Barbara was about to watch the treaty hearings, to learn something to stop Matt. She just had remoted-on the TV and changed the channel, when her digital phone had rung.

Now Barbara told Tiffani, "I'm fine, thanks for checking up. But I'm involved in work against the treaty that'll keep me away awhile."

"I understand," Tiffani said, but Barbara sensed her disapproval. "Guess I'll talk to you later," Tiffani said, then hung up.

Barbara returned her attention to the TV. Speaking to the camera was the news anchor, Sharon Hamilton, a serious redhead in her forties. "Good morning. In a few minutes, the Senate Foreign Relations and Armed Services committees begin joint hearings on the California Treaty. The hearings are chaired by Senator Nakamura of California, who amazed the world last night when he endorsed the treaty on American Satellite News. A joint NBC/*Los Angeles Times* survey this morning, taken of Americans aware of this new development, found support for the treaty at 18 percent, plus or minus 3 percent. This is a literally overnight jump of 5 percent."

Damn, the treaty made too big a jump. At least people in favor are still a small minority. Barbara opened the unused notebook in her lap and wrote inside, "After Matt endorsed: 13 percent to 18 percent overnight."

———————————

Several miles away in the large Senate Caucus hearing room, Matt turned to the other senators present and asked, "Is everyone ready?"

The chairman and the ranking minority member of the parent Foreign Relations committee, Senators Saunders and Ingram, told Matt they were ready. The chairman of the Armed Services committee and his idiot Republican counterpart, Senators Thompson and Leaird, also gave the go-ahead. Next, Matt polled the other attending senators of the joint committee.

This took an entire minute. Had the treaty been uncontroversial, only the eight other members of his subcommittee would have been in attendance. Or maybe even they'd be absent, replaced by staffer substitutes. As it was, of the fourteen members of the Foreign Relations committee, only Sheppard was absent. Likewise, nineteen out of the twenty members of the Armed Services committee were in attendance.

Almost every senator had one or two staff members standing behind him. Every senator but Matt was at the moment in conversation with a staffer or with a neighboring senator.

Television cameras, both homegrown and from Japan, were everywhere. The cameramen were tripping over still-photographers who sat all over the floor.

In the front of the room stood a train of long tables, placed end-to-end and covered with green tablecloths. Behind the super-long green table thus created were a dozen chairs, which all faced the senators. A bouquet of microphones sat in front of the fourth chair from Matt's right, the hot seat.

In the gallery in the back of the room sat a horde of spectators, as well as the day's witnesses waiting to be called. Plenty of people wanted to testify—many more than could speak today.

Matt took a drink of water, adjusted his desk microphone, cleared his throat, and took a breath. The hubbub quieted.

Matt eyed the room as he spoke: "This is a hearing to determine the facts relating to Treaty Document 109-3, `Treaty between Japan and the United States of America, on the Sale of California.' Many people wish to speak, so I'll dispense with making speeches, except to note that I endorse the treaty. Hostile witnesses will speak first." While Matt worked like a packhorse to blunt their testimony.

Leaird smiled. "Hostile first? Having trouble finding supporters, Mister Nakamura?"

Matt ignored that. "Miriam, call the first witness."

Foreign Relations committee staffer Miriam glanced at the cameras and gulped. "I call Derrick Russell of Santa Monica, California."

Quiet vanished at mention of Russell's name, and photographers sitting on the floor sprang to their feet. As the tall actor with the strong jaw rose from his seat and began to swagger forward, television lights and camera flashes marked his progress.

Matt recited, "Please stand and raise your right hand. Do you solemnly promise and declare that all the testimony that you shall give in this matter pending before the committee shall be the truth, the whole truth, and nothing but the truth, so help you God?"

"I do," Russell said. He sat.

What followed was a heated exchange among Matt, other senators, and the actor. Russell reminded the senators that the treaty required Californians to obey Japan's strict gun laws, six months after Japan took over. Japan's gun laws banned or severely restricted gun use. This meant that Californians would lose their "right to keep and bear arms" under Amendment Two of the United States Constitution.

That didn't bother Senator Dag Anderssen, who defended strong gun control in general, and Japan's laws in particular. That's when passionate arguing began over gun control.

Ernest Mooney, a metallurgical engineer with a Pennsylvania steel manufacturer, testified about the element boron. Boron was used in manufacturing high-temperature steel, like for jet-engine parts. Boron was needed for proper plant growth, and boron 10 was used in nuclear-reactor control rods. The United States needed boron, and all the boron in the U.S. was mined in California. This alarmed senators from primarily-agricultural states. Of course Leaird was ecstatic.

Wednesday evening, almost a week after the hearings had started, Barbara went to the bedroom to call Carol. The microphones in the living room wouldn't pick up her voice there.

Barbara couldn't stand the nagging of her conscience anymore. It was time to confess to Carol that she hadn't been honest.

But she had to wait to clear her conscience. Carol's first excited words over the phone were "Guess what? Larry's taking me on a picnic next weekend. His parents and daughter will be there, too. Sounds—"

"*Serious.*"

Barbara and Carol discussed what Carol would wear to the picnic, and what food she would bring. By then, Carol was calmed down enough to say, "I'm surprised to hear from you."

"Oh?"

"Every print-news organization in America is interviewing Matt these days, it seems like, and I keep seeing your living room on TV. So I figure that as soon as the Senate hearings end every day, you're stuck in maid mode."

"Maid, errand-girl, and hostess mode. It isn't only the American press—right now NHK is visiting."

"Professional curiosity: What's everyone asking?"

"The same question. `This Week' and `Meet the Press' cite polls that only 5 percent of America supports the treaty now, then they ask, `How does it feel, Senator, supporting a lost cause?' Everyone else asks, `Senator, why are you taking this crazy stand?'"

"Does that question have an answer?"

Barbara screwed up her courage. "It does. I—I don't know how to say this."

"Say what?"

"Remember after the Canadian ambassador's party, you were asking what was said?"

"So you *were* holding out."

"Yes, but—"

"You knew something about Matt and the treaty but didn't tell me, and you lied to me?"

"Yes. I'm sorry. I wanted to tell you that Matt wanted the treaty."

"If you *wanted to*, why *didn't* you?"

"Because then I wasn't sure."

"So you're sorry. Hell, it's not the withholding a story that bothers me most; you're a politician's wife."

"You think that means more to me than your friendship?"

"It seems so. You lied to me."

"I wasn't sure, dammit! After I told you about the party, you kept pushing. If I told you Matt was for the treaty, you might've printed it, and if it wasn't true—"

"You forgot I've been your friend forever. I'd *never* write a story about something you told me as your friend, without your permission first. But you didn't trust me."

"I wasn't sure. I'm sorry," Barbara repeated a second later.

Carol sighed over the phone. "It's done. What was it you didn't tell me?"

"Matt talked to Japan's ambassador at the party."

"What did they say?"

"I didn't hear, I had no need to listen in. Now I wish I'd listened."

"You wish, I wish, and every news organization in California wishes."

"Matt was staggering drunk by the end of the party. So I was driving home, and on the way he said, `I plan to swing the treaty. I talked with Ambassador Fujima, who started me thinking.'"

"What do *you* think all this means?"

"Carol, I think maybe he was offered a bribe. More likely, he asked for one."

"Would explain his endorsement. Face it, he's no saint."

"We can't let him go on. You should write something in the paper."

"Hold on, need to find a pad and a pen." A minute later, Carol said, "Okay, tell me again what was said."

Barbara repeated Matt's remarks. Carol wrote them down, then read them back. After Barbara had okayed their accuracy, she said, "So write this up, `An informed source said this,' and everyone relaxes."

"Um, it's not that easy. You said yourself last week, only two people at that party would talk to the San Diego newspaper."

Barbara smacked her forehead. "And could anybody think *Matt* leaked this? I couldn't hide."

"Exactly. So my choices are: I quote you by name, or we forget this."

"God, Carol, no! Matt must be stopped, but I can't have my name linked with this."

"Then these juicy quotes go into my desk drawer."

"You're serious."

"Very. No `Barbara alleges,' no story. But I'm saving my notes, trusting you to change your mind. Hm, today is April twentieth. The ambassador's party was, let's see. . .Saturday, the ninth?"

"Friday."

A scribbling sound, then Carol said, "Barbara, please—the public has a right to know."

"You see no other way? Facing Matt, my mother, the other Senate wives—you don't know what you ask."

"Look, what are we supposed to print? `We know someone alleging Senator Nakamura was bribed to champion the treaty. However, we won't tell you when he was bribed, or where, or by whom, because that would reveal our source.' Who'd believe us? Also, no reputable paper prints anonymous allegations without at least two sources. Know anyone else who'll tell me Matt was bribed at that party?"

"So no quote, no story. Quote me, only then the story runs."

"No other way's possible."

"No. I'm sorry."

"We have nothing more to say then."

Barbara turned off her digital phone. Next, she tried to convince herself she wasn't a coward—a wasted effort, that. Needing distraction, she remoted-on the TV and cable box to American Satellite News. Big mistake.

". . .talking to people in the street, finding out what they think about the California Treaty. Ma'am, what do you think about pawning California?"

The woman was young, with stringy blonde hair, and was holding a one-year-old baby. "I thought it was stupid, but if that California senator says it's okay, then it must really be good for the country, right? I guess I'm for it."

The next three people were against it, then the roving reporter asked a man in a light gray pinstripe. Pinstripe said, "Even before Nakamura spoke up, I thought selling California was a good idea. Now I'm even more sure. We really need the money, and maybe the money will start a ripple effect to create jobs."

Four more people questioned were against the California Treaty.

The final person asked was a college student. He said, "I don't know anything about it, sorry. However, won't that senator lose his job if California goes to Japan? He wouldn't do that if the treaty was no good. And he knows more about it than I do."

Barbara was stunned. She remoted-off the cable box and the television. Matt clearly had changed minds. *Should I reconsider?*

But deciding was hard. She felt pulled in so many different directions—

"I love you, Barbara. Never forget that. I love you, and I'm glad I married you."

"I'm sorry, Barbara honey, court ran late."

"Help him. If you cannot, be a silent flower."

"She's not a somebody, only a somebody's wife."

"It's decided, Barbara."

"I'm glad that our family isn't here to hear your shameful words. Our ancestors weep."

"It's betraying the people who elected you! It's treason against them."

"After Matt endorsed: 13 percent to 18 percent overnight."

"If that California senator says it's okay, then it must really be good for the country, right?. . ."

"I should leave him, but good wives stay with their husbands, but he's a real shit sometimes, but sometimes I still love him, but sometimes I feel like a whore."

"He wouldn't do that if the treaty was no good. And he knows more about it than I do."

Now she was even more confused. She felt the crush of giant responsibility, as the voices of memory came faster—

"I love you, Barbara. Never forget that."

"Be a silent flower."

"She's not a somebody. . ."

"It's decided, Barbara."

". . .your shameful words. Our ancestors weep."

"It's betraying the people who elected you!"

"If that California senator says it's okay, then. . ."

"I feel like a whore."

She was still undecided, still confused. The viewpoints in her head swirled around faster, like sharks closing—

"*I love you, Barbara.*"

". . .*silent flower. . .*"

". . .*not somebody. . .*"

". . .*shameful. . .*"

"*It's decided, Barbara.*"

". . .*betraying the people. . .*"

"I have no idea what to do," she moaned.

Then the clamor stopped inside, as a new memory spoke in Barbara's own voice: *"I have no duty to help Husband in dishonor."*

When Carol answered the phone, Barbara spoke in a firm voice: "Stop him, Carol. Print my name."

———————

About which, the Variety-Show Host joked—

A general testified that if California goes Japanese, the Army must put more posts in Nevada. Gee, the sacrifices our soldiers make for their country.

Derrick Russell said at the hearings, "When guns are outlawed, only outlaws will have guns." I have an idea: Outlaw baldness, then only outlaws will be bald. And outlaw cellulite, headaches, hail damage, refrigerator mold. . .

Part II
Twilight

t
a
s
o
g
a
r
e

CHAPTER 6
Thursday, April 21, 2005

Section Manager Masumi had called Hiroshi to his desk in mid-March. "Engineer, do you have a passport?"

Hiroshi had blinked in confusion. "Yes."

"An international robotics conference will be held in California in a month, and we want you to be one of the representatives for Matsumoto Robotics."

"I see. Section Manager, you honor me with your trust, though it isn't deserved. I have only been with the company two months."

"Which concerns us. But your spoken English is excellent, and you've a month to learn more about robotics. Nissan assured us you're disciplined and a fast learner."

When Hiroshi and Mister Masumi had talked then, the treaty hadn't yet been made public. So the fact that the conference was in California then had then of minor importance to Hiroshi.

Now Hiroshi, Ryuuji, and Section Manager Tsurumi were on a JAL jet, flying through darkness somewhere between Dutch Harbor, Alaska and Los Angeles, California. Hiroshi wondered how the three Japanese men would be treated in California.

Across North America in Alexandria, Virginia, the microwave clock showed 7:09 in the morning. Matt was thinking lewd thoughts—microwave ovens now always reminded him of Mela's ice-cube trick—when the Nakamuras' kitchen phone rang.

"Senator Nakamura? I'm Laura DuBois from American Satellite News. I'm glad I caught you."

Obviously another bedazzled reporter, about to write another puff piece about "Matt Nakamura, America's only unselfish politician." So Matt replied in Tone of Voice One (Friendly): "What would you like to know, Laura?"

Instead the reporter blasted him: "Senator, the *San Diego Union-Tribune* this morning is running a copyright story that quotes your wife. She believes you asked for a bribe, or accepted an offer of a bribe, from the Japanese ambassador at a party—"

"*What?*"

Matt glared over at Barbara, who was cooking the breakfast eggs. Barbara didn't notice that glare, or pretended not to.

"—to endorse the California Treaty, and push it through the Senate. My question is this: Did you ask for a bribe to support the treaty?"

"I don't know what you're talking about, Ms. DuBois. What does this article say? Who wrote it?"

"Some local reporter, uh. . .Carol Parks."

"Editor," Matt almost said. He made a face. *I'll bet Carol smiled as she typed every word.* Aloud he said, "But what's the damned paper *say*?"

DuBois read the article over the phone. Barbara hadn't overheard the conversation between Matt and the Japanese ambassador. But obviously to Matt, she'd figured out what had happened, from what Matt had said on the trip home. Fortunately, Barbara's theories wouldn't stand up in court.

DuBois was still talking: ". . .'Senator Nakamura could not be reached for comment.' So, Senator, what is your response to this *Union-Tribune* story?"

"I deny the allegation."

DuBois sighed. "Senator Nakamura, did you solicit a bribe from Ambassador Fujima of Japan to support the treaty?"

"I deny the allegation."

"Did the Japanese ambassador offer you a bribe to support the treaty?"

"I deny the allegation."

"How do you feel about Barbara making this accusation about you?"

"Thrilled to tears, of course. I have no other comments at this time."

After Matt slammed down the phone, he discovered the damned cup of water he'd microwaved had turned cold. Barbara was eating her egg at the table. His egg was on a plate on the counter.

He shoved the cup of water back into the microwave, stabbed buttons, then stormed to the kitchen table, grabbing the egg-plate on the way. "Barbara! *What the hell were you trying to pull?*"

"Barbara! *What the hell were you trying to pull?*"

Barbara told herself, *Don't let him cow you.* She put down her glass of juice and looked up at him. "I asked you to walk away from the treaty. You wouldn't, so I used the only way I could stop you."

"Where'd you dig up this bribery bullshit?"

She glared at him. "Cut the innocent act. You, a one-time crooked San Diego lawyer, then a crooked Washington politician—am I to believe that you'd *throw away* a Senate seat for the good of the USA? So I've thought about what you said that night, and only one theory works."

"You haven't a shred of proof. Coming from anyone else, I'd have open-and-shut grounds for a libel suit."

"But I *know* you. I dare you, look at me and tell me you don't expect to gain anything."

He paused an eyeblink. "I don't expect to get a dime out of this."

"I don't believe you, Matt."

"You *were* a sweet, dutiful Washington wife. What's happened to you?"

"What's happened is that I can't stomach sitting by while you sell out the people of California."

"Oh, you can't, huh? Then hear me well. You haven't stopped me, only *embarrassed* me; you haven't even slowed me down. I'm a senator and you're only an *amateur panhandler*, the Red Cross doesn't even respect you enough to pay you. You can't hurt me, so forget *right now* whatever other silly-ass media stunts you plan."

She played her only card. "Then you better expect to sleep on the couch."

"That's another thing: Forget any wifely retaliation. From now on, I'll be `working late' every night, and all day every weekend. I don't need your sanctimonious bullshit, in bed or otherwise, and I don't need your lines and wrinkles."

He came closer and wagged a finger in her face. "I haven't needed you for years; I keep you around only for the voters. But file for divorce and I'll see you penniless! I suggest you do as your *kaa-san*," mother, "taught you and remember your place."

The kitchen phone rang. Matt snatched it up. "This is Senator Nakamura's residence. . . .I deny the allegation. . . .I *said*, I deny the allegation!" A few seconds later, he shoved the receiver toward Barbara like it were a sword. "He wants to talk to you."

An hour and a half later, without leaving the house, Barbara had done two telephone interviews with television news shows. She was about to do a third telephone interview, with a fourth waiting.

"Remember," the "Today Show" news producer reminded her, "It's okay to watch the TV while he's on the phone with you, but you *must* keep the sound off."

"Thanks for telling me," Barbara said, though she already knew it.

The producer put Barbara on hold. At the moment, "Today" was finishing the news. Barbara's TV, obediently muted, showed Russian President Dimitrov and a man labeled as Syrian Prime Minister Al-Amin; the two leaders were shaking hands in Moscow for the TV cameras.

She kept the sound off. Syrian Prime Minister Al-Amin was not someone to concern herself about.

Then the TV showed the host talking. Behind him was a labeled picture of Barbara—at the edge of which, a man's waving arm was visible. Evidently the only picture of her that "Today" could find was a picture of Matt that she happened to be in.

The host put his phone to his ear, then the house phone clicked in Barbara's ear. "Good morning, Mrs. Nakamura. How are you?"

"I'm fine. How are you?"

"Great. Barbara, you believe that your husband asked Japan's ambassador for a bribe in order to support the treaty?"

"Yes."

"You allege the crucial conversation took place on the eighth, at a party at the Canadian ambassador's official residence."

"Exactly."

"But you didn't actually overhear your husband talk with the Japanese ambassador?"

"That's correct. Let me add that Matt never said anything to me before the party to hint that he would support the treaty."

"I see."

"At the party, I overheard him once telling someone that the treaty had no chance. He didn't mention supporting the treaty."

"But you've never overheard him say anything about *opposing* the treaty, have you?"

"Not so. We talked about the treaty on the seventh, the day the treaty was referred to the joint committee. Back two weeks ago, he made clear that he couldn't support the treaty."

"But obviously he changed his mind. Did you two discuss the treaty again, anytime before the party?"

"No reason to, no."

"A minute ago, you said that you only overheard him talking once about the treaty at the party. It sounds to me that you two spent the evening apart. Is that correct?"

"Yes, for the most part." *If this is fair reporting, I'm pregnant with elephants!* She resolved to put out her message despite the host's bias.

"About what percent of the time would you say that you were away from your husband? Twenty percent? Fifty percent? Ninety-nine percent?"

"About 80 or 90 percent, and that's his wish as much as mine."

"Why do you say—"

"But you're missing the bigger issue. Sacramento hasn't asked for this treaty, Californians—"

"Why were you and the senator apart so much at the party?"

"At social events he'll often schmooze, and I'm in his way. But as I was saying, Californians don't want the treaty, but Washington is treating California like the crazy aunt in the attic—"

"So you only know the content of his conversation with the Japanese ambassador by what he told you on the drive home? Quote: `Listen up: I plan to swing the treaty. I, Matt Nakamura. I talked with Ambassador Fujima, who started me thinking.'"

"Yes, I base my accusation on that statement."

"Such an ambiguous remark to draw such a charge from. Perhaps the Japanese ambassador is persuasive."

"I know my husband, sir. And I know that the treaty is a bad deal for everyone: California, the United—"

"Barbara, how would you characterize your marriage to the senator?"

How dare he, she thought. "It's, uh, okay. We have our differences, like any married couple. And his work keeps us apart a lot."

"But you're not particularly close."

"We've been married twenty-four years. This conversation is making me uncomfortable."

"Barbara, if you're going to make accusations against your husband the senator, the public has a right to know all possible reasons why."

A little after nine that morning, Barbara called the office of Senator Saunders. She wanted to ask Joe Bob to condemn the treaty publicly, as he had privately.

Joe Bob on the phone was eager to share his latest news: he and Marilyn were grandparents again. Marilyn

was still in Georgia, happily spending time with Joe
Tim and Lizzie Ella, and especially with brand-new
granddaughter Lizzie Sue.

But then Joe Bob was all business. "Barbara, if you
callin' me at work, Ah reckon you must be callin' about
the treaty."

"That treaty would be disastrous for the people of
California, Joe Bob. I'm sure Matt thinks he'll reap
something for supporting it."

"Yes, ma'am, Ah heard you say that on the news.
The deal supposed got made between those two with
me standin' right there."

"Kill the treaty, *please*. People will listen to you if
you badmouth the treaty."

"Barbara, Ah cain't make up my mind until Ah've
heard all the facts. We ain't heard yet from folks who
support the treaty."

"Well, yes, I know you want to be fair."

"Furthermore—and you ain't goin' to like this—Ah
think Matt deserves a chance to defend hisself against
the poison words you spoke about him."

"He'll lie to you."

"Yes, ma'am, he might well. But Ah still want to
hear lots more from folks before Ah decide anything."

----

*This morning is nuisance piled on irritant, and it isn't
even ten o'clock yet,* Matt thought.

Matt had given reporter Laura DuBois several
blanket denials. Then the house phone had rung again,
and again, and again. Half the callers had wanted to
talk to Barbara. In the Hart Senate Office Building he'd
been ambushed by reporters as he'd walked from the
elevator to his office.

Now he was in his private office, straightening his tie, while his hired help fought back for him. Through the door he heard Sherry tell a caller, "Senator Nakamura categorically denies that he has solicited or accepted a bribe from His Excellency Mister Fujima. A full explanation shall be given shortly. The senator is saddened and confused by this misunderstanding, but he cherishes and forgives his wife."

Matt took his seat in the Caucus Room promptly at ten. The number of press people had swollen yet again from yesterday. They reminded him of vultures perched on a fence.

"So how was the Canadian ambassador's party, Matt? Talk to any interesting people?" That was Leaird, who was leaning way back and covering his microphone with his hand.

Go sit on a nail, Leaird. You too, Barbara.

Matt's first priority this morning was putting out the fire Barbara had started. He had a plan, which he was sure would work. *But boy, am I taking a risk.*

Matt adjusted his microphone. "The hearings on the California Treaty with Japan now resume. All witnesses hostile to the California Treaty have been called. Beginning today, we will hear from those favoring the treaty's approval.

"Before we begin, a point of personal privilege. A news story came out this morning that quotes my wife as saying she thinks I was offered a bribe or solicited a bribe to push the treaty approved. These hearings and later committee meetings are meaningless, if my motives are in doubt. You deserve an explanation. I'll give you one."

"Ah hope so, Mister Nakamura," Joe Bob Saunders said, looking concerned. "The Senate can expel you, if a charge like that ever gets proved."

Matt read out the part of Carol's article that recounted Barbara's conversation with him during the drive home from the party. Matt told the room, "The quotes are accurate, and I was indeed drunk. Yet since my wife didn't overhear my one brief conversation with His Excellency Mister Fujima, she only can imagine what he and I said."

Joe Bob spoke, "Ah was with Mister Nakamura at the party. Only once Ah saw Mister Nakamura talk to the ambassador, when we all came out of the study after hearing the president talk. Their talk lasted only a few minutes."

Matt nodded.

Chris Ingram spoke up: "I guess I missed that. I was at the party, but I didn't see Mister Nakamura with the ambassador. What did they say, Mister Saunders?"

"Ah don't know. It was in Japanese."

Ingram asked, "Did anyone at that party see them talk any time other than right after the president gave his speech?"

The room hushed, as everyone waited to catch Matt in a lie.

Ten seconds later, Joe Bob sighed. "We all are still stuck. Ah cain't tell you what they said."

Phyllis Lamont added, "The Senate can't normally subpoena an ambassador. Yes, we're stuck."

Make it look unplanned. Matt turned to eye the other committee members. "I'm willing temporarily to step down, waive my senatorial privileges, and testify under oath about that conversation right now." If he could arrange a public hearing right then, and if he could convince Chris Ingram to chair it, he would be home free.

Ingram looked at Matt as if he were a lunatic. "Under oath? Why? This isn't the Ethics Committee, Mister Nakamura."

Joe Bob said, "We all know your wife, and Ah think she's a real fine lady. But that don't change the fact that she been the only one to accuse you, and she cain't back up what she said."

Ingram looked at Matt and nodded. "You know an unsubstantiated allegation can't be prosecuted."

Matt shrugged. "This isn't a legal problem for me, fellow senators, but a political problem. In the court of public opinion, politicians never are acquitted for lack of evidence, and *certainly* politicians never are innocent until proven guilty!"

Ingram looked uncomfortable. "Why not tell your story later, in a point of personal privilege before the whole Senate?"

"Because I want to resolve this right now, out in the open. This isn't some wild-eyed accusation from some yahoo whom nobody's heard of. My own wife says I committed a specific, wrongful act at a specific place and time. The specifics make the accusation seem believable. I'm here, you're here, we're on millions of TV sets. Why wait?"

"The Army-McCarthy hearings set the only precedent for this. Frankly, I don't like reinforcing that precedent, nor do I see the need. Consider a closed plenary executive session."

"And when I'm cleared in a closed session, people will scream `cover-up.' And open or closed, an executive session means a delay. Would *you* wait a few hours to defend your honor, Mister Ingram?"

"This is a public hearing, and you're chairing it." Ingram meant that nobody could stop Matt from talking, and whatever Matt said became public record. "When you're through talking, we'll ask you questions."

"Not good enough. I want everyone, both inside and outside the Senate, to know I'm serious. That's why I want to be sworn. Discerning colleagues, I insist on my testifying, here and now."

Since it would mean Matt's here-and-now vindication.

Sheppard said, "Then the next question is, who'll run this inquiry?"

Matt turned to face Chris again. "Actually, Mister Ingram, I'd like *you* to chair it."

"*Me?* Why? I'm a Republican!"

"And an attorney. Nobody will say that you made it too easy for me." *Even though you will—I have you figured out. When you acquit me publicly, nobody will listen to Barbara's bribe-talk ever again.*

Chris frowned. "If I decline the chair?"

"Then I must ask Mister Saunders, who's from my own party, which leaves open the future charge that he coddled me."

"Mister Nakamura, if you're open to a Republican chairing this, *I* could be persuaded," said Leaird. His smile was vampiric.

Matt gave Leaird a fake smile and said, "I appreciate your kind offer, but I prefer Mister Ingram."

Ingram's lips pursed in distaste. "I'll do it, but remember: You asked for this. The only break I'll give you is that I won't turn this into a Republican-versus-Democrat witch hunt."

"Thank you. Not every Republican would be so generous." Matt glanced at Leaird.

Step One, putting Chris in charge, was done. Matt's next goal: flimflamming Chris.

Matt leaned towards his microphone. "I turn over the gavel to Senator Ingram as chairman." Matt stood and carried the gavel to Ingram's chair. Ingram shrugged and took the gavel.

Thirty seconds later, Matt was standing in front of the witness chair, his right hand raised. Ingram was asking him, ". . .Do you solemnly swear that the testimony that you shall give before this committee shall be the truth, the whole truth, and nothing but the truth, so help you God?"

"I do." *Here's where I bet all my chips.*

"I do," Matt swore on television.

Sitting in her living room, Barbara had filled a large portion of her notebook with notes, and she would take notes for this part, too. The dij-VCR was humming away, for later playback; Barbara would make certain that she'd written down exactly what Matt testified.

On the screen, Ingram asked, "Mister Nakamura, please tell us what was said between you and His Excellency Mister Fujima."

"We exchanged pleasantries. He complimented me on my Japanese."

"Yes, yes. Please skip to the meat of the conversation."

"His Excellency complimented President Swensen's speech, noting that the president `was very informed about Japan's situation.' Remember, in the president's speech, he talked about diplomatic contacts between Japan and China. . . ."

A minute later, Matt was saying, ". . .His Excellency asked, `Senator Nakamura, may I please bother you to ask what is your opinion of the treaty's chances?' I used a Japanese expression meaning that the Senate would allow it to die. I explained, `Nobody in the Senate wants to champion the treaty. Even if somebody did befriend the treaty, pushing passage would be difficult.' His Excellency replied, `I wonder if the treaty has such a friend.'"

Matt swallowed; he seemed nervous. "I answered, `I know that if the Senate approved this treaty, that would be a huge gift to Japan.'"

Barbara sat up straight. "*What?*"

On television Matt said, "His Excellency replied, `Ah, would the prime minister and his cabinet agree?'"

Barbara said, "If they have, I'm going to be sick."

Matt was smiling. "I replied in essence, `Certainly they'd agree, in a thousand years.' That was a joke—I've noticed that when you gather together a committee of people, agreement about *anything* doesn't come quickly." Behind Matt in the gallery, people laughed.

"Or possibly," Barbara said with scorn, "you reminded the ambassador that Washington's clock still would be ticking while Tokyo was building consensus."

Matt said, "His Excellency said something; I said, `I'm sorry, I didn't hear you.' He told me then, `I agree, if the Senate approved this treaty, that would be a huge gift to Japan.'"

Pay dirt.

Barbara yelled at the screen, "Chris, that's *it!* Matt solicited a monster bribe, Japanese style, and he made the ambassador agree to it."

Matt said, "Then His Excellency asked me in English, `What do the people in California think of the treaty, Senator Nakamura?'"

Ingram said, "So after His Excellency agreed with you that it would be a real stroke of luck for Japan for the treaty to go through, that was the end of the Japanese talk."

"Chris," Barbara yelled, "smarten up, quit thinking like a lawyer. Merely because neither of them promised anything out loud, don't think they *made no deal!*"

On television Matt was smiling. "Yes, we spoke no more Japanese that evening, and only a few more words in English."

Ingram asked, "Have you received any gifts of cash or merchandise from His Excellency Mister Fujima since that conversation?"

Matt said, "I've received nothing from His Excellency except a brief handwritten note on his personal stationery, received at home the Tuesday after the party. He enjoyed talking to me at the party, he wrote, and he wished me well in my endeavors."

"I'm sure," Barbara said.

Ingram asked, "Since that night, have you exchanged any other correspondence with, or talked with, His Excellency?"

Matt said, "I've not spoken with, I've not sent surface mail to, and I've not sent e-mail to, His Excellency since that night. If His Excellency has sent e-mail or surface mail to me at the office, I'm not aware of it."

Barbara frowned with exasperation at Ingram's TV image. "Ask Matt if he talked with *go-betweens*."

Instead, Ingram asked, "So what was it that His Excellency said at the party that made you think?"

Matt said, "So what was it that made me think? Why, I told you: when His Excellency said, `The president saw how the treaty would benefit the United States.' Frankly, I'd wondered if the whole speech was only a face-saving for the president. But His Excellency talked as if the treaty was indeed mutually beneficial."

Barbara shook her head. "C'mon, guys, can't you see he's lying?"

Steve Leaird could: "His Excellency's statement shows me nothing to cause a political revelation."

"Go, Steve!" Barbara said.

Leaird said, "Now, I'm assuming that Mister Nakamura isn't deliberately leaving out anything important—because if we proved he did, his life would become very unhappy."

Matt sat up straight and proud. "I assure you, fellow senators, I've withheld nothing!"

"Of course not, because then you're open to a censure resolution. At least. Now, Mister Nakamura said at the party, `I know that if the Senate approved this treaty, that would be a huge gift to Japan.' This statement intrigues me."

Barbara made coaxing gestures. "Steve, you're close, you're close."

Leaird said, "Seems to me this means, `Japan, I know this means a lot to you.' But maybe *that* is a roundabout way of saying, `I know you'd pay me an awful lot if that were the only way to achieve this.' Look at it that way, and His Excellency repeating the sentence almost word-for-word means, `Yes, we crave this. We'll meet your price.'"

Barbara was trying to bounce with excitement, a difficult task in a papa-*san* chair. "*Bingo*, Steve!"

On television Ingram said, "With all due respect to the minority leader, his idea won't work. Politicians asking for a bribe don't make their requests vague, and they don't accept vague answers."

Ingram banged the gavel. "I'm satisfied that neither man discussed bribery. The witness is excused."

Barbara slapped chair-fabric. "Damn it, Chris, *no!*"

Ingram said, "I turn over the gavel to Senator Nakamura as chairman." He carried the gavel to subcommittee chairman Nakamura's empty chair.

On television seconds later, both Matt and Chris had retaken their seats. That's when the house phone rang in Barbara's living room. Startled, and still furious at Matt, she snatched up the receiver.

"Barbara Nakamura?" she heard. "I'm Laura DuBois with American Satellite News. Did you just see your husband on television?"

"I saw him."

"And now you think. . .?"

"He snowed Chris—snowed the joint committee big time. Under oath, too."

"Let me be sure I heard right. You're saying that your husband fooled the joint committee?"

"Yes." Barbara explained at length Matt's unholy bargain with Fujima, and how the American committee members could so misunderstand Matt's words.

DuBois asked, "You mentioned `Chris.' Were you starting to say something about Christopher Ingram?"

"Senator Ingram is the husband of my best friend in Washington. I know him to be intelligent, hardworking, and conscientious. I won't criticize him."

"Yet he cleared your husband. That must frustrate you."

"I don't wish to discuss my feelings about Senator Ingram."

"But you agree that your husband snowed Senator Ingram especially?"

Barbara said, "Matt took Chris for a ride, for sure. But more than everyone but Leaird on the committee? I don't know that."

"Barbara, we both know that you political wives are treated as part of the furniture, regardless of your talents. It's a shame, really, and you political wives deserve recognition."

"Long overdue."

"I want to appreciate, I really do, how you found something in your husband's testimony that smart Senator Ingram missed."

Amazing—an outsider who understands the problems of the Washington wife. Barbara said warmly, if modestly, "Laura, it's not like I'm so smart."

DuBois's voice was as warm as any politician's. "I know you're just saying that. So how did Senator Ingram go wrong? Let me understand."

"Look, I don't want to criticize Chris, but. . ."

Hiroshi's plane arrived in San Diego that afternoon. Hiroshi, Ryuuji, and Mister Tsurumi were met by the guide from California Japan Tours. She was a young Japanese-looking woman of college age, with hair and makeup in the California style, and dressed in a green blazer and a gray skirt. In one hand she held a green flag with the logo—a surfing samurai—of the tour agency. In the other hand, she held a handwritten tagboard sign saying in Japanese, "Welcome, Matsumoto Robotics."

In a few minutes, the men were in the company's car—a Toyota van with a Japanese on-board navigation system—and moving down the road.

Hiroshi gasped in horror, she was driving on the right! A head-on collision would occur any instant, all his blood would spurt from his body, he would die here in a foreign land so far from home, he would cause his mother great grief, and—wait, everyone else was driving on the right. *Americans are strange.*

Fifteen minutes later, the van stopped at the motel where Hiroshi, Ryuuji, and Mister Tsurumi were to be staying. At the motel, the three men went to deposit their luggage in their rooms.

Hiroshi and Ryuuji shared a room. After Hiroshi unlocked and opened the motel door, Ryuuji walked through, then stepped to the side and bent down to remove his shoes.

Hiroshi raised a hand. "This is America, Kinoshita-*kun*. Americans don't take their shoes off."

"What?" Ryuuji looked confused. He then looked down at his hands on his shoe as if they were zoo animals he were seeing for the first time. "The door is shut now; Americans can't see us." Ryuuji finished removing the shoe.

Hiroshi smiled. "Why don't we compromise, then? We only remove one shoe." Both men laughed.

Instead, they compromised a different way: Ryuuji took his shoes off, and Hiroshi kept his on. That settled, the two men next noticed—

"Beds! Real beds!" said Hiroshi.

Ryuuji dropped flat onto the nearer one. "I haven't seen beds since college."

"Me neither. Once or twice, I've missed my college bed."

"So have I, because of the memories I made there." Ryuuji feigned a sophisticate's smile. "Sex is *much* more comfortable in a bed than on a *futon*."

Hiroshi's smile was embarrassed. "It sounds like you had better luck than I did. Yonosuke"—Casanova—"I am not."

"Actually, I've pillowed only one girlfriend, but we were together for two years. You?"

"Same, only one girlfriend, plus an exchange student from Auckland."

Ryuuji looked impressed: "You sly badger. You talk about Miss Higashi Reiko and you pretend to be shy."

"The sex was only once. I asked Bronwyn the night before she returned to New Zealand forever." Hiroshi recalled how, after a night of "raging" (partying), Bronwyn had cried, then she and Hiroshi had kissed, then they'd made love.

Now Ryuuji's smile was wolfish. "Alas, I don't know about Kiwi girls. But I'm eager to learn if the stories about California girls are true."

Three time zones ahead in Alexandria, Tiffani's voice over the phone was accusing. "Barbara, how could you *hurt* me so with your lies about Chris? I thought you were my *friend!*"

Barbara wanted to keep Tiffani's friendship, but the problem was, Tiffani was pissed, and for good reason.

Barbara hung her head, though Tiffani couldn't see. "I *am* your friend, but sometimes even friends makes mistakes. The reporter—"

"*Mistake?* It's only a *mistake?* I caught you on ASN: `Matt took Chris for a ride, for sure,' you said. A minute later you said, `Senator Ingram was thinking like a lawyer. If it's unspoken, it means nothing. He forgot that in Japan the rules are different.'"

I'm-sorry-Tiffani had its limits. "It offends you, but I won't apologize for the truth."

"You as good as called Chris a fool."

"I admit I could've phrased my answers differently. Still, Chris refused to listen to what Steve Leaird was telling him."

"You could've kept everything vague: 'the committee this,' 'the committee that.' But *no*, you went nationwide and singled out *Chris*. Indiana heard you smear him!"

"It was *Matt* I was angry with. So I spoke without thinking beforehand—being newsworthy is new to me. But Chris goofed, he was conned."

"Would *I* tell ASN that Matt is a skirt-chasing lush? Let our politician husbands backstab each other—we wives are supposed to know better." Tiffani offed her cel phone before Barbara could say more.

Friday morning in San Diego, Mister Tsurumi, Ryuuji, and Hiroshi registered at the conference and received their nametags.

On Hiroshi's nametag, as with his English-language business cards, his family name was second: "Hiroshi Iwata." Hiroshi remembered when he was eight, Father had written Hiroshi's name in *rohmanji* (the Roman alphabet) in the backwards Western way, and little Hiroshi had laughed at how strange his name had looked. Yet here at the conference was his backwards name again, printed for real.

That morning, Hiroshi was busy: workshops on feedback design, cloth-tailoring algorithms, problems in stereo-optical processing in robots, and robots in a retail environment.

Upscale supermarkets in the United States, Japan, and Europe were just starting to get robots that would shop the aisles of the store. (A shopper chose items from a PC screen. The robot pulled those items off the shelves and put them in a cart, then returned to the checkout area.) Wal-Mart also was bringing shopper-robots into its stores. So the retail-robots workshop that Hiroshi attended covered all the hows and whats of setting up a robot-shopping system inside a store. But the workshop also premiered a breakthrough: a produce-selection algorithm.

"That's great!" said the woman next to Hiroshi. "I can sit down and talk to my friends while a robot does *all* my grocery shopping for me."

Hiroshi turned to the woman. She was a woman of thirty, ten kilograms overweight, with short blonde hair and a wedding ring. Her nametag identified her as "Margaret Snodgrass/Customer Service Engineer/ Deseret Robotics/Provo, Utah."

Hiroshi wondered if she expected him to reply. What was American-polite? Behavior by Japanese etiquette was clear: No mutual acquaintance had introduced them, so Hiroshi needn't talk to her. Yet Hiroshi knew that formal introductions were irrelevant to Americans.

Meanwhile, Mrs. Snodgrass had spoken to him. What to do?

Everyone liked jokes, he knew. He'd make a joke, to minimize the awkwardness if his saying something wasn't proper. He asked deadpan, "What if you want buy eggs? Do you ask robot check them? What if its software has a bug?" Still deadpan, he made egg-breaking noises as his hands crushed imaginary eggs. He clapped his hands once together and pantomimed being unable to pull them apart, then said in a robot's voice, "My hands are sticky. Error, error."

She howled with laughter. It amazed him. He knew, from television and movies, that an American woman laughed as unreservedly as a man. Still, it was unsettling when in person he experienced a woman's boisterous laugh.

She chuckled, "You're okay. . .Hiroshi. That was great."

When the retail-robotics workshop had ended and Hiroshi and Mrs. Snodgrass were walking to the door, she asked, "Where is Yokohama?"

"It's about thirty kilometers west-south of Tokyo. Where is Provo?"

"About eight hundred kilometers northeast of here. Is this your first time in America? If California is still *in* America." She laughed at her own joke.

Hiroshi then asked her, "Did you work on Fifi Fetcher?" He referred to the most coveted toy of 2004.

Margaret laughed. "I wish. Still, last Christmas I was the favorite relative of all my nieces and nephews. *And* their parents. That poodle was *impossible* to find in any store."

Hiroshi and Margaret sought out a soda machine and talked, and that's where he gave her his business card. Her nametag told Hiroshi everything he needed to know to figure her rank compared with his own. Yet exchanging *meishi* (business cards), as soon after meeting as possible, was ingrained in him.

Margaret showed surprise when he presented his card so soon. It took her half a minute, fumbling through her purse, for her to produce a business card of her own. Hiroshi put her card in the *meishi* box in his pocket.

Margaret looked at both sides of Hiroshi's business card. "How interesting. Does this Japanese writing on the back say the same as the English on the front?"

Hiroshi gave her a puzzled look—why was she insulting his country?—then realized she hadn't meant any offense. How could he correct her, without her losing face? Ah! "Yes," Hiroshi said, "Japanese writing on the *front* says same as English on the *back*."

Margaret blinked, then laughed. Hiroshi didn't laugh or smile, lest she interpret his laughter as laughing at her, instead of at his own clever remark. But her laughter meant he hadn't offended her; Hiroshi felt relieved.

She was asking a question about Japanese mechanical tea dolls when Hiroshi found himself thinking, *She keeps staring at me!* Margaret kept watching him while they talked, seldom and only briefly lowering her gaze. *She's not pushy like those American businessmen I worked with last month, but she looks at me too much, just like they did. Does everyone in America stare at strangers?*

Margaret told Hiroshi that she liked Provo and the people there, and she liked her job. She was married, yes, with a six-year-old daughter. Her husband was an electrical engineer at the company. She liked the company's owner, who was active in his local church and in politics.

Margaret's words gave Hiroshi another culture shock: *She's praising her chairman to a stranger?* Politeness in Japan dictated abasing oneself and one's entire group to outsiders. *But her loyalty to her company is clear. That's good.*

Margaret's next words unnerved Hiroshi: "Speaking of my boss, he testified before the Senate this morning.

He's for the treaty, he *wants* Japan to buy California. He thinks buying California will bankrupt Japan."

It was Friday night in Alexandria, and Matt was home—but not for long, if he could help it. "I need to make a call," he told Barbara as soon as he walked into the house. He dashed upstairs to the bedroom office.

Ten seconds later, he heard Mela's voice: "Jackson's."

"Hi, Mela, it's Matt. I'm—"

"Sorry, sir, I'm busy. Excuse me." The phone clicked.

Goddamn it, what am I supposed to do for sex? Matt grumped.

As Matt hung up the phone, he wondered if Mela was with Wendall Harland. Thinking about Harland reminded Matt of his three-way with Mela and Shirley the escort. That in turn reminded Matt of a remark of Shirley's: Before she became an escort, she'd been a stripper at a gentleman's club in Bethesda. If she was typical, the place was worth a look.

Matt decided *swank* was the word that fit Stares and Strips Forever ("A Refuge for Scoundrels"). Its parking lot boasted bright painted lines over new paving. The bouncer at the door wore a robot-tailored blazer—the club could afford it, and he was muscular enough to need it. The twenty-dollar cover was stiff, but Matt could afford it—and judging from the cars he'd seen in the parking lot, so could everyone else.

With the aid of a penlight, a hostess with eyes the color of fog escorted Matt to a table near the front stage. Nearby sat two congressmen; Matt and they exchanged nods. Behind Matt, he heard several voices in Japanese comparing TSE stocks. The hostess took Matt's drink order and told him what foods were available from the grill.

While he waited for his bourbon, he enjoyed the Seventies disco music and looked around. The largest dance stage, T-shaped with a runway, was at the front. Upon that stage two women danced apart and sometimes together. Smaller one-dancer stages were on the left and right sides of the room. Around the room were reproductions of election-campaign posters, and giant blowup pictures of politicians campaigning—oil paintings from the nineteenth century, black-and-white photos until the Sixties, and color photos after that.

The cocktail waitresses were wearing little, in either red, white, or blue solid. Their shoes were stilts. Every woman in the room—whether stripper, cocktail waitress, bartender, hostess, or disk jockey—was a goddess. Many of those gorgeous strippers were dancing on tables or laps around the room.

Matt felt lucky in this place. Good thing, because his plan was to relax, unwind, and go home with a hot stripper. Boffing a beauty with *all* her muscles toned was one of the best perks of being a national hero.

A cocktail waitress with a Eisenhower-Nixon button over one nipple and a Carter-Mondale button over the other, brought Matt's drink. He paid her, tipped her, and gave her two twenties, asking for change in ones. Of course when she brought the bills, they had lengthwise creases. He stuffed the bills—folded normally—in his breast pocket, underneath the open bomber jacket.

He watched the dancers for a minute or two before selecting a stripper. The sweetie on the front stage, left side, had waist-length black hair, a competition tan, bulletproof abs, nipples the color of chocolate, and long, slim legs. Matt took his place in line to tip her, behind three other admirers.

The DJ was playing "America the Beautiful" as a bump-and-grind instrumental when Matt stuffed his cash into Ms. Black Hair's cleavage. She ground her hips, shimmied her shoulders, and gave him a smile of aching, urgent, sexual craving—then she froze.

After a second, he noticed she was staring at something behind him. She gave him a horrified look, then looked behind him again. She actually took half a step back from him.

That's when he realized that, along with the blaring music, he heard yelling, whistling, and laughing. "Hoo boy, is *he* in for a surprise!" Matt heard a man say.

Matt turned around to see what the fuss was about—and found himself nose-to-nose with Barbara.

Barbara had the grin of a village idiot who'd just won the lottery. "Hi, honey," she shouted over the racket, "I heard you leave the house. I'm sure you didn't *mean* to ignore me. But I decided: if you won't spend the evening with me, I'll spend it with you. So, I followed you."

"Obviously."

Barbara was still disgustingly cheerful: "You should've heard me, trying to convince the hunk at the door that I wasn't here to make a scene." She took his arm. "Watching strippers together, won't this be fun?"

Matt glanced around the room. He, not the bimbos, was now the entertainment for the customers. Even the cocktail waitresses had stopped to watch the Nakamuras. "Go away, Barbara," he said through clenched teeth. "You don't belong here."

"But I do," she said with that same solar-powered cheerfulness. "All the marriage books advise doing something with my husband he enjoys."

"The books didn't mean this."

"No matter. Here I am, and wherever you go this evening, I'll follow you." She put her lips to his ear, and in her brightest, perkiest voice told him, "You shouldn't have threatened me yesterday, honey baby doll."

Matt was resigning himself to no frolic tonight when Barbara reached into his jacket and pulled out his wad of bills. "I need a dollar." She took a bill, then returned the rest.

He tried to snatch the bill back, but she was too fast. "What the hell you doing? What you need a dollar of *my* money for?"

Barbara's face showed innocent puzzlement. "The stripper, of course. She's working hard, she deserves a tip. Plus I'm sure the poor girl is freezing."

Matt groaned. "I'm trapped in a nightmare."

Barbara turned and held out the dollar to the stripper. Again ultra-cheerful, Barbara told the dancer, "Here you go, honey. Don't ever become any man's pyramid slave." It was hard to say who looked more uncomfortable: the stripper, or Matt.

"Lady, lady," a man yelled, "you don't *hand* money to a stripper. Wrong part of her body you're touching!"

"Money's folded wrong, too," someone else shouted. "Bomber, teach your wife how to tip a stripper."

Barbara turned to face the second man. "Oh, you fold it lengthwise? Sorry, first time here." She slipped her arm through Matt's. "But I'm sure my husband will explain everything to me."

The song had ended, and the black-haired dancer was fleeing the stage. Barbara nodded in her direction, then turned back to Matt. "Our business here is done. Shall we sit down?"

San Diego time was eleven in the morning, Saturday. Hiroshi's next workshop didn't start for another two hours, so he, Mister Tsurumi, and Margaret were sitting at a table inside the Mechanical Engineering building. At Mister Tsurumi's suggestion, Ryuuji had left with several other conferees to have a working lunch with a UCSD professor.

Margaret was saying, ". . .Hey, I'm starved. You men have any plans for lunch?"

Mister Tsurumi replied, "The student cafeteria sell ramen. That I planned to eat, then to here come and talk to other mechanical engineers."

"That's an option. Myself, I was told about a great Italian restaurant about fifteen minutes from here. I invite you to come."

Mister Tsurumi looked undecided. Hiroshi wanted to go, but Japanese etiquette required that the ranking person decide for everyone. In Japanese Hiroshi said, "If the ramen is made in Japan, I hope the import duty isn't too much. And if the ramen is made in America, I hope it tastes okay."

Mister Tsurumi looked surprised, then told Margaret, "I'll too go."

La Traviata Italian Ristorante turned out to be a hole-in-the-wall of only a dozen tables. As many traditional Japanese restaurants are small, Hiroshi felt, and Mister Tsurumi seemed to be, quite at home. The place was dark, making bright the candle on every plastic red-and-white checkered tablecloth. The room was pungent with garlic. From speakers overhead, an Italian opera was playing.

Hiroshi turned nervous when the waitress came by and put a silverware setting in front of each of them. Margaret said quickly, "Do you two like pizza? Our fingers will get greasy, but I hope you won't mind."

Neither Hiroshi nor Mister Tsurumi could hide his relief when each agreed to this.

———————

Hiroshi, Mister Tsurumi, and Margaret had begun eating their deep-dish pizza when the restaurant door opened and a man and woman came in. "Look at that!" the woman said. "First those sneaky Japs try to buy California, now. . ." (she spoke too fast for Hiroshi) ". . .can walk in and eat with us."

The man sneered. "That fat woman with them, she must be a Jap-lover."

The woman nodded. "She's got a wedding ring. . ." (Hiroshi lost more words) ". . .she's married to one of those Japs!"

Hiroshi had a problem. Did he try to resolve this, and perhaps violate some unknown American rule? Or did he sit and do nothing, and so lose face?

He stood and walked up to the man in the doorway.

Hiroshi was prepared for anything. He saw the man tense. The woman, Hiroshi noticed, wore a wedding ring with a huge diamond. Hiroshi also noticed that the entire restaurant had stilled.

Hiroshi looked into the man's eyes first, then the woman's. "Please, neither other Japanese nor I try buy California. We're not rich, like you. You are with our government angry, I understand, but you do not need be with us angry. Our American friend has not hurt you. You don't need be with her angry. Please, let's all eat in harmony."

The woman looked surprised. She opened her mouth, but the man spoke first. "Eat—with *you*? What would we eat, *fish eyes*?"

Hiroshi turned to the woman. "Our American friend is married to a man in Utah. She talks about her husband and children much. You have husband. Do you have children?"

The woman looked uncomfortable now. The man glanced at her, then glared at Hiroshi. "None of your business about our kids. So your friend has a husband back home. . ." (Hiroshi missed words) ". . .pick up two Jap men. . ." (more words missed) ". . .he would never know, right?"

"She is our friend, not the prostitute. She is the good wife. Like you have the good wife."

"Yeah, too good for eating in *this* cave. C'mon, Joanna."

At that point another customer, a man in his thirties with rippling muscles underneath a white shirt and tie, joined Hiroshi. "Yeah, if the presence of the Japanese and their friend offends you folks, I'm sure you'll enjoy a different restaurant more."

"Buddy, I don't know where you came from, but this isn't your problem, hear me?"

"Yes, it is. Your talk bothers my wife."

"Yeah? *My* wife and I are American and Californian, and we'll eat anywhere we want. I'll be *goddamned* if *we* leave here instead of some fish-stinking Japanese. Or are you a Jap-lover like the fatty, who'll lick their hand when they're running California?"

"*If* California gets bought, I'll live with it. But what I *won't* live with is jerks barging in and ruining lunch for my wife and everyone here!"

"I'm a jerk? C'mon, step outside, both of you!"

Hiroshi decided he could take the blowhard, if it came to a fight; but Hiroshi said instead, "I know you are brave. This is not the needed thing."

"Yeah? *I* need it!" The bigot's arms went up.

"Phil!" the woman yelled, as both her arms grabbed one of his. "Phil, stop."

"Dammit, let me go, Joanna! I can't let these two push us around." He struggled to pull his arm free.

Hiroshi sighed inside, then turned to his new ally. "Thank you for wanting help me. That is of you very kind and generous." Hiroshi turned to face both men. "You are here with your wives. I am with my friends here. They not want for us ruin the day in the fight. Please, let us together do the harmony."

Phil jutted out his chin. "Why? I'm no coward. Are you?"

Hiroshi kept a calm face. "Your wives and my friends think we are childlike if we fight. Please, let us together get back the peace."

Joanna whispered to Phil, "People are staring at us. Behave?" She let go of his arm.

"Fine! I prefer Mexican anyway, let's go." Phil and Joanna pushed through the door and were gone.

As Muscular Man shook his hand, Hiroshi again noticed the room's silence. Everyone watched Hiroshi as he took his seat.

Saturday night, the robotics conferees had enjoyed a show and catered dinner at Sea World San Diego. Sunday, Margaret had taken the Matsumoto Robotics men shopping in Tijuana for travel gifts; Hiroshi bought his mother a calf-leather purse. Monday at noon, the conference ended.

Soon after, Margaret and the Matsumoto Robotics men were making their goodbyes. Margaret sighed. "Well, it's time. Good luck to all of you." Everyone shook hands. "Thank you for the gifts, which were a nice surprise. I'm sorry I didn't get you guys anything in return."

A box with *sake* decanter and cups sat at her feet, a conference gift from Mister Tsurumi. Hiroshi's *kimochi no shirushi* to her had been a pen-and-pencil set, and Ryuuji had given her a beautifully wrapped box of Japanese candy.

Margaret looked around at the three Japanese. "Will you teach me how to bow the Japanese way?"

The men looked at each other, embarrassed. Margaret looked puzzled, then she realized: "It's like if Mrs. Tsurumi asked an American man how to curtsy."

Hiroshi nodded. "Yes, Japanese men and women bow differently, but now I show you."

After he demonstrated the proper bow for her, she bowed to the men like a Japanese woman, and they made deep bows back to her.

"Oh, this is wonderful! Goodbye, Mister Tsurumi, Mister Kinoshita, and Mister Iwata."

Mister Tsurumi gave her another bow; she didn't know to return it. "Goodbye, Mrs. Snodgrass. Thank you very much."

Margaret now turned to Hiroshi. "Thank you for defending my honor." She surprised him by stepping over the *sake* set and kissing him on the cheek. Ryuuji gave him a look of surprise, envy, and puzzlement.

A few hours later, Hiroshi was somewhere in the air between San Diego and Los Angeles. Hiroshi settled himself into his seat, turned on the in-flight music, and smiled to himself. After a few days in California, he'd become accustomed to cars on the right, and his English was faster.

And now he liked California.

Friday, four days later, Barbara's house phone rang a little before nine in the morning. Calling was Joe Bob Saunders. She hoped he had good news.

This Friday was a week and a day since Matt had testified in front of his own subcommittee. When Chris Ingram cleared him, instantly it was Barbara and not Matt who became the wicked Nakamura. The media trumpeted polls finding that Americans outside California booed her as a selfish, envious, lying shrew. "Saturday Night Live" caricatured her as a narc and a schoolyard tattletale. The mean words hurt.

This Friday also marked a week and a day of only treaty supporters testifying. As Senator Nakamura had boosted his respect and popularity, so also had the treaty improved its.

So when Joe Bob called on Friday morning, Barbara hoped he had good news—she needed it.

Joe Bob was saying, ". . .Marilyn and Ah are doin' just fine, ma'am. Barbara, this ain't a social call. Me and Matt talked yesterday in the Senate gym."

"The treaty."

"Yes, ma'am. After thinkin' it through, Ah'm backin' it. Thought Ah'd tell you before Ah told the press."

She was floored. "*Why*, Joe Bob? Remember at the Canadian ambassador's party, you told me you thought the treaty was silly?"

"Yes, ma'am, but Ah changed my mind. The treaty's good for Georgia—"

"Maybe."

"And for the whole country—"

"No way, Joe Bob."

"Barbara, a bunch of them folks who testified this past week was real convincin'. Then there's this: Ah don't think Matt got offered a bribe."

"But he *was* bribed." Barbara explained in detail Matt's "huge gift to Japan" dialog.

Joe Bob Saunders sighed when she'd explained. "Barbara, Ah'm truly sorry. You're a great lady. But no matter whether he was bribed or not, Matt has my vote now, and my help."

Three hours later in his private office, Matt couldn't wait for this day to end. *Only twenty-three minutes past noon—c'mon, clock, hustle.* That's when Jeff tapped on Matt's door.

"Mister Senator, I have news to make you dance when you hear."

"Right now I need all the good news I can get. I'm hungry and I need a nap. Tell me."

"This just came over ASN: Senator Saunders said that the facts show the value of the treaty, and he's endorsing it. Second, polls show support for the treaty outside California to be at 39 percent."

"That's still not a majority."

"Remember, slightly over a week ago it was only 5 percent. Wait, there's more."

"Yeah?"

"Your personal approval rating outside California is now 59 percent. It mushroomed after you testified last Thursday. Your wife's credibility rating is at 21 percent. American Satellite News called you `the first martyr to nullifying the debt.'"

Matt nodded. "The public thinks I'm a nice guy, and fewer persons than a week ago think I'm misguided. You're right, all this definitely is good news." Matt walked to the main door. "Jeff, when I return from lunch, I'll want to go over my notes with you on my talks with other senators."

Jeff nodded. "I'll have them over to the White House soon after. Oh, they told me to tell you: They're most grateful for current info on who's pro-treaty, who is anti-, and who's undecided."

"Of course. They can post messages to each senator's districts more effectively."

Jeff looked somber. "It looks as if the treaty's bad luck is gone. Speaking for everyone in this office, I hope you meant it about referrals and your help in finding other jobs."

About which, the Variety-Show Host joked—

My neighbor George tries to juggle beer bottles at parties. He has one thing in common with Senator Nakamura: His wife says he must be stopped at any cost.

Senator Nakamura has a 59 percent approval rating outside California. In California, his approval rating is 4 percent. It's the age-old problem—no matter how many friends you make, doing your job, the people you work for don't think you're earning your pay.

CHAPTER 7
Heisei 17-nen 5-gatsu tsuitachi, Nichiyohbi (Sunday, May 1, 2005)

Hiroshi and Ryuuji both had needed to work on Sunday, and so had planned to finish together that afternoon. Hiroshi completed his own work, then stood by the desk of Ryuuji, who was backing up files.

Hiroshi said, "Kinoshita-*san*, we could see that movie everyone's talking about, *Spring Bamboo*. Unless you have a cheaper idea."

"No, *Spring Bamboo* is fine. But why not see it with Miss Higashi?"

Hiroshi blinked. "A date? She's very pretty, but. . ."

Ryuuji smiled. "Pretend she's from Provo, and you'll be fearless."

"So you think. Still, I'm overcoming my shyness around her."

"Oh?"

"Yesterday I started a conversation with her in the lunch line. I even talked to her without stammering like a schoolboy."

"About work, or did talk turn. . .personal?"

"Work, mostly. But did you know she attended etiquette school?" Everyone in Japan knew etiquette-school grads were more desirable as brides.

Thirty minutes later, Hiroshi bought popcorn while Ryuuji bought a soda. After ten minutes' wait, the previous audience rushed out, Hiroshi and the rest of this audience rushed in, the lights immediately went down, and *Spring Bamboo* began.

Spring Bamboo begins in 1871, when former samurai KOBAYASHI Tadashi learns the government soon will eliminate the hereditary stipend of the *shizoku* (people of samurai descent). This disaster, ending the *shizoku*'s only source of income, comes four years after the samurai class itself was abolished (1867). Foreseeing a nasty trend, Tadashi swallows his humiliation and takes a job with the government, overseeing the construction of a railroad between Shinagawa and Yokohama.

Tadashi chooses wisely, for by 1876 the *shizoku* have lost every one of their samurai-class privileges, including the wearing of swords. With peasants drafted into the Imperial Army since 1873, *shizoku* are no longer needed as Japan's defenders. By 1880 Tadashi has watched helplessly as many good comrades and their families are ruined. Many of these men make their displeasure known, and Japan is rocked with assassinations and riots.

During all these years, mastering Western technology is both Tadashi's personal goal and Japan's number-one national priority. Japan is centuries behind, so the West scorns Japan as a technological and military weakling.

Worse, because of the lag, powerless Japan is forced to conclude humiliating "unequal treaties" with Western nations, beginning with the United States.

Under the "unequal treaties," Japan may charge only a puny 5 percent fixed tariff on what she sells foreigners, and foreigners in Japan who break laws are beyond the reach of Japanese courts.

Japan's treatment by the Western powers, and the reasons behind it, sting Tadashi's national pride. He travels for hours to attend public lectures on Western learning when he hears of them. He buys books about Western learning when the books are available, regardless of cost.

When the Shinagawa-Yokohama railroad is completed, Tadashi oversees the construction of a Kobe-Osaka railroad. In the 1880s, with government railroad construction scaled back, he takes a job building a railroad for a private company. By now he's learned quite a bit about the mechanics of a steam locomotive. He likewise by now has met many bankers, government bureaucrats, and foreign engineers.

In his forties, in 1885, Tadashi imports a safety bicycle from England at tremendous expense. He takes the bicycle apart and reassembles it, until he understands how it works. Then Tadashi, a carpenter, and an unemployed swordsmith build a wooden bicycle and finally a steel bicycle after much trial and error. Because he's *shizoku*, a guilt-ridden government loans him money to begin a side business: building bicycles for other Japanese.

Through hard work and wise use of his network of experts, within two years Tadashi's bicycle factory is a tremendous success. Now he has a decision to make: Japan's railroads, or his factory? Torn between conflicting senses of duty, Tadashi chooses to work for his bicycle factory.

Within five years, Tadashi is a wealthy man, yet even this success is not without pain. For becoming a merchant, which was three levels lower on the old social scale, he is deserted by some former friends.

Besides the railroad and bicycle, another idea that Japan had copied from the West was the daily newspaper. At the end of his life, Tadashi is congratulated on his achievements by a reporter for the *Jiji Shimpoh.* At the end of the interview, Tadashi leads the reporter to the alcove of his house.

On the wall of the alcove is a *daishoh* (two-sword set), the shorter sword above the longer. Tadashi takes the longer *katana* sword down from its place on the wall, and partially unsheathes it. "I couldn't meet my obligation to the emperor by the way I was born to serve, so I found another way. Rich I am because I wasn't allowed to unsheathe my swords."

When the movie ended, Hiroshi and Ryuuji rushed out of the theater as people for the next showing rushed in. Ryuuji said, "Everyone quotes those last two lines, applying them to Japan itself. Does Japan stay rich, or does Japan unsheathe its swords now?"

"Go on," Hiroshi said absently. He was imagining adventuring in the 1880s.

"Mishima II says—"

"Who? Oh, that ultranationalist with his own cable-TV show. Go on."

"Mishima II says Japan must rearm, Japan must reclaim its greatness. Now I wonder whether he's right."

Hiroshi grunted.

Ryuuji said, "You look thoughtful, too. Wondering about Japan's rearming?"

"Huh? I was thinking how exciting Kobayashi's times were, when Japan was changing so much. I want such excitement and change in my own life."

"How? Japan will never see another Meiji Era."

Hiroshi stopped walking, thunderstruck by an idea. "But Japan will, if we buy California. And when that time comes, I intend to be in the first wave of colonists."

Ryuuji shuddered. "Me, living in California, no thank you! But you, I hope your wish is granted."

Hiroshi turned to look at Ryuuji, his face serious. "It's more than a wish. I can't do much, but I will do everything I can to make California be bought. *Yooshi!* Here I go!"

Hiroshi knew the South Kantoh electoral region had twenty-three members in the Diet's House of Representatives. A twenty-fourth Representative served Hiroshi's election district within Yokohama. So that night, Hiroshi wrote twenty-four letters. Each read, "If America ratifies the treaty and sends it here, please approve it. Japan needs California."

When Barbara's digital phone chimed nine hours later, it was one o'clock on a Sunday afternoon in Alexandria. Barbara was dusting furniture while Matt was out who-knows-where, doing who-knows-what with who-knows-whom. In the meantime—

"Good afternoon, this is Barbara."

It was her father Ed calling. Father and daughter exchanged warm greetings, but then his voice turned serious. "Your mom and I saw you on television."

"I'm sure. So what do you think?"

"Barbara, this time you really kicked the skunks. What *I* think is that Matt did ask for a bribe, and you were right to step forward. Hell, he's probably been lining his pockets since he came to Washington. What *Tacky* says is—trust me on this, your mother has much to say."

"As I expected."

"Yeah, it's the most serious argument we've ever had. She's determined to talk to you now, and frankly, I'm doing all I can to delay that."

"I'm not eager for that, either."

Barbara heard her mother in the background. "Ed, I need talk to Barbara, please."

Ed's voice moved away from the mouthpiece. "In a few minutes. I promise."

Barbara waited for either parent to say more. After a second of three-way silence, Ed turned back to the phone: "So tell me what happened since Carol printed that story. I think you'll feel better if you talk it out."

"Dad, it's been unreal. After years as a senator's wife I thought I knew what the media attention would be like. Wrong! The house phone rings nonstop, and a few jokers even know my cel number."

"Yeah, I noticed you changed your standard greeting."

"I'm doing interviews for both print and electronic media, in both English and Japanese. The California press treats me as if I were a self-sacrificing saint for California. Everyone else tries to skin me alive."

"Yeah, I saw someone actually ask you, 'Why can't you ease up on your poor husband?' Sheesh."

Takeko in the background again: "Ed. I need talk to Barbara. *Now*, please!"

Ed's voice moved away from the phone again: "Tacky. I. Heard. You. Just a minute, please? I promise I'm going to give you the phone in *just a minute*."

"Dad, I'm glad I can talk to you, but let me get this over with."

"I'll handle your mother, honey. How has the Japanese press treated you? Them I can't watch."

"They ask me how could I shame my husband this way. How could I shame my mother? They quote the saying, `The souls of your ancestors weep behind grass leaves.' They ask me, Did I forget what my mother taught me, how to be a good wife?"

"So you're taking it from everybody."

Takeko spoke again, "Ed. Phone, please. Now, please."

Barbara sighed. "Yes, Dad—from everybody. You'd better give the phone to Mom."

"Yeah, it's time. Here's your Mom."

A second later, Barbara thought, *I will be strong. I've done nothing wrong.* Switching her language to Japanese was easy; sounding cheery was damned hard. "Good morning, Mother. How are you?"

Takeko was not deterred: "*Baaba-chan,* I am ashamed. You have shamed your husband, you have shamed your parents, and you have shamed your relatives in Japan."

Barbara dropped the "cheery" act as she replied, "It's unfortunate that my relatives feel ashamed. It's unfortunate that you feel ashamed, Mother. Father does not feel ashamed. Father says I'm fulfilling my *giri* to California."

"Your father is American."

"And so am I, Mother, always."

"Not always, Daughter. Japanese blood flows in you. You speak Japanese, you read Japanese, you write Japanese. You were born in Japan."

"But I am an American, Mother, raised in America or on American bases. Only in staying married to Husband am I Japanese."

"How is that?"

"If a man treated an *American* wife like Matt treated me, she would divorce that man."

"That is the only lesson on how to be a good wife that you've learned from me."

"No, from you I also learned a Japanese wife would keep silent about her husband's betrayal. Yet in this, too, I choose American."

"Americans do not say you are American in this. I saw the television shows about you."

"The Remaining States smell money now. They're already counting the sixty trillion dollars, besides all the jobs."

"Daughter, a reporter from the *Yomiuri Shimbun* called me Thursday a week ago. Monday morning, he called me again. TV Tokyo interviewed me Monday. Both of them asked, `Please, Mrs. Morris, why is your daughter acting like this?' I could not answer."

Score one for Mother. Barbara squared her shoulders to make herself feel strong. "It's unfortunate that you and they cling to old ways of thinking. Husband and Ambassador Fujima had *haragei*," intuitive communication where much could be left unspoken. "In not many more words than a haiku, it was agreed: When Husband delivers the treaty to the Diet, he earns a big reward.

"Mother, anyone who understands Japanese culture knows this. The American press says to me, `You're crazy, there was no bribe.' The Japanese press has never said this. Instead, they rebuke me that I revealed matters of my house to outsiders. Japan's media is wrong, and. . ." Barbara's voice trailed off.

"Am I wrong, too?"

"I am not ashamed, Mother."

"Daughter, now I'm twice ashamed. I spent so much time with you when you were a child, more than neglectful American mothers. I didn't abandon you to babysitters, unlike lazy American mothers. I taught you *ikebana*," flower arranging. "I taught you how to cook. I helped you with your studies in the American schools. I taught you how to speak Japanese and I taught you how to read and write it. I read you Japanese stories in the morning, and American stories at bedtime."

"Yes, I remember. Thank you, Mother. You taught me much."

"But not enough. You're individualistic, egotistical, and quarrelsome—a typical American."

That hurt. But Barbara rallied, invoking two famous Japanese traitors: "Should I silently sit on my heels, the submissive Japanese wife, while Husband becomes another AKECHI Mitsuhide? Another SAITOH Dohsan?"

"You should copy Princess Sahohime, who placed duty to her brother even above duty to her emperor."

"Copy her? Princess Sahohime shared a traitor's death."

"A good wife and daughter preserves harmony. You have fomented *disharmony* for all your family."

"You are unfair, Mother. *Ojii-san* opposed your marriage to Father. If a good Japanese daughter always preserves harmony and is never individualistic, how did you marry Father?"

"No good daughter of mine would speak like this. Now I'm three times ashamed."

Her mother's harsh words left Barbara feeling empty and lost when she turned off the phone.

Since Barbara had gone public, Matt was home only for as little time as possible. When Matt *was* home, now he was aloof and sarcastic. Yet the marriage wasn't much more sour than usual, so Barbara could bear Matt's anger.

Barbara was dismayed that Tiffani was upset with her. But even though Tiffani was her best friend in Washington, Barbara could bear up if that friendship were to end.

But her bond with her mother was to Barbara a precious treasure. Barbara's love for her mother, and Mother's love for her, was a source of soul sustenance even during Barbara's teenage years. So now Takeko's anger, disappointment, and refusal to understand stabbed Barbara's very soul.

But Carol was still Barbara's friend, and Carol knew Mother. Carol would understand. Barbara picked up her digital phone.

Click. Helloes. "Got time for sympathy?" Barbara asked.

"Matt being a jackass again?"

"No, my mother's why I'm calling."

"Your *mother?*"

"Uh-huh. My mother just ripped into me over the phone. For speaking out. For shaming Matt, and her, and all my relatives in Japan, she says. She's ashamed of me, she told me."

"That's awful. Poor Barbara, after all your treaty headaches, this you need like a shark in your bathtub."

"Yeah, isn't life wonderful. Mother's mad at me, and for all the flak I've caught about the treaty, I haven't hurt the damned thing one bit."

"All that would make me blue, too."

"Really. I want to call up Steve Leaird and we both get drunk."

"Say, what about teaming up with him somehow? Find a way to help him fight the treaty."

"Help him? What could I do?"

"Maybe nothing. Maybe pose with him in a grip-and-grin photograph. Stuff envelopes maybe, post messages online. Make speeches. Who knows?"

"Make speeches? Why didn't *I* think of that? Between campaign speeches and all my Red Cross fundraising, I can adjust a mike in my sleep. Yeah, anywhere Steve wants me, I'll give a speech. And I'll make the same offer to Hector DeGarcia. Matt's won't be the only Nakamura voice heard anymore."

Several suburbs away in Mela's apartment, Matt glanced at his watch. Mela asked him, "Want another bourbon before you go?"

"No, thanks. I need to be alert when I go to the office."

Mela gave Matt a sharp look. "On a Sunday? Maybe you're really spending the day with Barbara."

"After she humiliated me in that strip club?"

Those blue eyes were analyzing him now. "I can meet your needs much better if you're honest with me. Do you have a second girlfriend?"

Women—slip them your cock and they demand, "Talk to me." Aloud, Matt said, "It's absolutely none of your goddamned business, but I really am going to the office. The treaty is more important to me—"

"Than any ten other bills combined. So you've told me. Anyway, whatever it is you're working on, won't wait till Monday?"

With sarcastic patience, Matt spelled it out: "I'm going to the office, on a Sunday, to meet with that farmboy Saunders. We're going to plan strategy how we're going to gather enough votes in committee. Then we—or at least I—will make phone calls to the other committee members."

"You're not assuming the other Democrats on the joint committee will follow you two?"

"I can't afford to, although the voters in their states love the idea of sixty trillion."

"Go, then. I figured out yesterday what you're really doing with this treaty. It's so clever of you."

Shit. Tone of Voice Six (Casual): "And what am I really doing?"

"Your plan is *not* to swing the treaty, your plan is to *look as if* you're working to swing the treaty. It's part of your master plan to be president."

He relaxed. "Tell me more."

"You'll go through the motions for this treaty. You'll talk all about how you'll make this personal sacrifice for the good of the country. You'll protect the treaty against attacks in committee and on the floor. Then Fuller will force a floor vote. Of course, the treaty won't win two-thirds, but you'll look like you busted ass. Making all these efforts, you'll piss off the California voters, but people in the Remaining States will hail you as a saint."

"Saint Matthew Nakamura. Yeah, right."

"Then in 2006, rather than run a doomed re-election campaign for Senator from California, you'll announce you intend to spend time with your family."

"With Barbara? Who'd buy that?"

"I meant with your father and sister. Or announce you'll be performing community service. Anyway, you'll be out of office January of 2007, over a year before the New Hampshire primary. After you're out of office a few months, you'll say the people have begged you to run for president."

This is wonderful. Even if I don't collect the "huge gift," I still win big. Matt's smile was genuine. "Then why is Barbara saying I was bribed?"

"She's planning to divorce you and collect a fat settlement. If she divorces the `Martyr to Zilching the Debt,' media attention will force the family court judge to treat her as the selfish gold digger she really is. But if she divorces the scumbag who sold out California to get rich, the judge will be generous to her."

"Tsk, I'm shocked at her evil." Matt glanced again at his watch. "But I really must be going."

With his hand on the doorknob, he turned back to Mela. "What if I goof and the Senate actually approves the treaty?"

Tonight Mela's hair was up in a French twist, and tonight she'd done something unusual with her eye makeup. She was wearing elegant little gold earrings and a gold necklace. As she often did, she wore red polish on those dragon-lady nails, and red lipstick. Tonight she wore very high-heeled red shoes; and a deep-blue velvet, floor-length robe, loosely tied. The robe teased with glimpses of a white garter belt, white stockings, and American-flag panties.

Now Mela sashayed over to him, her toned muscles flexing and relaxing; the robe shimmered as she walked. She put her arms around his neck. Through his clothing and hers, he could feel her breasts squash against him, as her hips ground against his. He smelled perfume and clean skin and hair. Under his hands, the muscles of her back kept a dancer's firmness. She pulled his head down to hers to kiss him, licking his lips lightly with the tip of her tongue. The kiss was slow, measured, and intense.

She released him. Her eyes said she felt the titanium dowel in his briefs. She began throatily, "If the Senate approves the treaty? In that case—"

Her hands plummeted to her sides as she stepped back. Her eyes frosted. "—I'll drop you in a second."

───────────

It was eight o'clock Monday evening in Yokohama, and Hiroshi was on the phone to his parents. ". . .were watching the movie, and that's when I realized I want to live in Japanese California."

"And I thought Yokohama was far away," Mother said. "But with Mikio-*chan* here in Sendai, you're free to wander the world."

Hiroshi laughed. "Yes. But will Elder Brother envy me for going to California, or will he pity me?"

Father said, "Certainly if Japanese colonists were filling California, our national curriculum would demand even more spoken English."

"Finally they'd listen to you, Husband," Mother said.

Hiroshi said, "Father, this is another reason I'm working hard for the treaty. When pioneers report back how much they needed to know spoken English, I want Japan to see that you were right all along."

───────────

Monday morning in Alexandria, Barbara's clock said 8:15. It was time to call Hector DeGarcia, and offer him her help.

"Office of Senator DeGarcia of California, this is Tracie." Tracie sounded very young.

"This is Barbara Nakamura, Senator Nakamura's wi—"

"Yes, ma'am, we know who you are. You're a hero here."

She sighed. "If only I were." She had cowardly dawdled at speaking out against Matt.

"I presume you want to talk to Senator DeGarcia?" The senator was on another line; Barbara agreed to hold. "I'll make sure he knows it's *you* waiting. By the way, it takes lots of courage to step forward as you've done—people in this office are rooting for you."

Barbara was floored. "That. . .is very nice of you to say. Thank you."

"You're welcome. Mrs. Nakamura, you are *globally* mega-icy!"

Sometime later, Hector came on the phone: "Good morning, Mrs. Nakamura." Barbara heard no friendliness in Hector's voice.

"Hector, I'm Barbara, remember?"

"Very well, Barbara." Hector's words were slow, as if he was choosing every one. "What can I do for you?"

"I'm calling to let you know what *I* can do for *you*. I'm offering my help to defeat the treaty. I'll appear with you to speak against it."

"Hm. Mind telling me why you're doing this?"

"Huh? Isn't it obvious?"

"No. You're part Japanese, too, and you're Matt's wife."

"It's just *wrong*, Hector." Barbara went on to explain in more detail. She concluded, ". . .I'd talk the same way if it were some other state for sale. But also, this treaty would create real problems for Japan."

"Japan sure doesn't think so."

"Pride is a blinding emotion."

"One last question, Barbara. You know I had nothing nice to say about Matt before—now it's open war. If you join me, you'll be enlisting in that war. Is that a problem?"

"I'll help you with certain conditions."

His voice was cold: "I'm listening."

"I won't tell you anything about his treaty work that he tells me in confidence. As if *that* problem will ever come up. Nor shall I tell him anything that you tell me in confidence."

"There will be little of that at first. I don't trust you yet."

"I'm insulted; I think you know me well enough to trust me." She paused for him to assure her. He didn't. "I will not personally attack my husband in public, nor will I help you to do so. This might sound crazy, but I still love him."

"Which is why I don't trust you. Now, you went to the newspaper because Matt is betraying his state. Will it bother you that you're betraying your husband?"

"I'm not betraying my husband. He's making a mistake, and I'm trying to correct it." The problem was, nobody but her saw what she was doing in that way.

"Whatever." Ten seconds of silence, then Hector said, "Your conditions are reasonable."

She was committed now, even further. "So what do you want me to do?"

"You know where my office is. I'm going to be interviewed by someone with the Golden State Radio Network at three o'clock. Meet me at my office's waiting room at a quarter till, and I'll make it a joint interview. I'll tell them we're allies."

"I'll be there."

"If you're not there by 2:45, I'll assume you changed your mind."

"Impossible, Hector. I'll see you this afternoon."

After talking with Hector, she phoned Steve Leaird. The Senate Minority Leader welcomed her help.

The next step of Barbara's plan was calling Foreign Relations Committee and Armed Services Committee senators. The woman they had known only as wife and hostess was about to lobby them for a vote. She didn't know how they would react.

She couldn't let that bother her. She threw back her shoulders and touch-toned the first number.

"Senator Sheppard's office."

"Hello, this is Barbara, Senator Nakamura's wife. May I speak to the senator, please?"

"He's not in the office now. Are you calling about his committee vote regarding the treaty?"

"Yes, I am."

"He's made it clear to his staff that he fully supports the treaty. I'm sorry."

"How may I direct your call?" Barbara heard over the phone a minute later.

"Hello, this is Barbara Nakamura. May I speak to Senator Ingram, please?" Chris Ingram was wavering on the treaty. Barbara had to lock in his "Nay" vote.

"You're Tiffani's friend? Hold on, he's leav—Mister Senator? *Mister Senator!* Barbara Nakamura wants to speak with you."

Barbara heard Chris's voice: "Jesus. Yeah, I'll take it." Seconds later she heard, "Barbara, I have only a minute. What can I help you with?"

"This time it's business: to encourage you to hang tough on the treaty. I know you don't want a hole in America's nuclear fence."

Chris snapped, "Barbara, you're talking like nothing's wrong. Why should I listen to you?"

"Oh god, Chris, I apologize. The ASN reporter called seconds after Matt testified, and I lost my head."

"Apology accepted. But I'm late now, goodbye."

"Chris, I can't describe how sick with remorse I am because I hurt your feelings. Again, I'm sorry I offended you. Tell Tiffani again, I'm sorry I offended her."

"I will, but she still feels backstabbed. And nobody would blame me for ignoring everything you say."

"It Barbara!"

The time was 2:46 that afternoon, and Barbara was in DeGarcia's reception room. Through the open door behind the head receptionist was a small conference room. Several people in the conference room had been watching TV until a black woman in her thirties had spotted Barbara.

Within seconds, Barbara was surrounded by hand-shakers and well-wishers. "This treaty is garbage, you keep telling 'em!"

"He's really a slimeball. I can't believe you're still married to him."

Male voice: "Yeah, he's Benedict Arnold and Judas rolled into one, and he's from *our* state!"

Female voice: "But George Washington didn't have a Mrs. Arnold like our Barbara, and Jesus didn't have a Mrs. Iscariot like our Barbara."

Senator DeGarcia walked in. "Barbara, a pleasant surprise to see you. Come on back." In front of his staffers, Hector was Mister Cordiality. He gestured to the black woman who'd spotted Barbara. "Barbara, this is Sapphira Shaw, my chief of staff. Sapphira, what's the latest on C-SPAN?"

"Leaird done axed the committee to okay an amendment allowing American nuclear weapons in and through California. He keep trying to plant something Tokyo can't buy—that way, Japan kill the treaty and Delaware, they don't be blaming Leaird."

"Mm-hmm. How's the amendment stand up in committee?"

"It look like party line, Nakamura and the Democrats is against it. So when they be done debating, it probably be shot down."

Senator Gibson caught Matt slightly after four in the afternoon, pulling him aside in the Democratic Cloakroom. "This could be bad news," Ken said. "Your wife just announced that she's working with DeGarcia and Leaird."

"I don't see her as a problem."

"I do. Her public opposition to you makes voters wonder about the treaty."

"Then take care of her. You're from Nevada—I'm sure you know people who know other people."

Gibson gave Matt a hard look, then nodded.

When Barbara had returned to the house that evening, the answering machine held seven messages. Barbara had played back four when she heard—

"Barbara? Mrs. Nakamura? I'm Hazel Archer, and I'm president of the Santa Barbara Working Women's Association. And, uh, we'd like you to address our group tomorrow night. We, uh, I'm afraid we can't pay any speaker's fee, sorry. However, we can pay for the plane trip here and back, and a hotel for a night, and dinner. Well, maybe we can take up a collection for some kind of speaker fee. But we so admire your courage, and we're so glad for what you're doing, and we want to hear what you have to say."

Hazel gave her number and asked Barbara to call after six—"That would be, oh gosh, after nine o'clock in Washington. I hope that isn't inconvenient for you. I'm sorry it's such short notice. If you're too busy, that's okay, we understand."

"Too busy"? After seventeen years of being seen only as the candidate's wife, the congressman's wife, and the senator's wife, someone actually wanted to know what *Barbara* thought?

Barbara made the call, and agreed to give a fifteen-minute speech. A few hours away from Washington surely couldn't hurt.

Neither Monday night nor Tuesday morning did Matt remark about Barbara's partnership with Hector. Matt said nothing to her, and nothing to the news media. And when she told him Tuesday morning of her speech in Santa Barbara, that news likewise was answered with silence. She decided he considered her too little a threat to bother becoming emotional over.

A remark about her on Tuesday morning's news puzzled her. Secretary of State Wendall Harland was asked by a reporter what he thought the treaty's chances were of Senate approval. "The president and I are confident of approval," Harland insisted. The vote will be close—what if the treaty doesn't pass? Harland's reply was strange: "The president will be disappointed, and not only for the obvious reasons. If the treaty doesn't pass, that will make Senator Nakamura a more viable candidate for the Democratic nomination in 2008 than Vice President Collins. Unless, of course, Barbara Nakamura succeeds at sabotaging her husband's political career."

"This is ASN Newsbreak, 11:00 a.m. Eastern time, Tuesday, May 3.

"Senate Minority Leader Leaird, just defeated in one attempt to amend the California Treaty, has proposed another amendment. Leaird's previous amendment would have kept American nuclear weapons in Japanese California. After that amendment was voted down minutes ago, Senator Leaird proposed another committee amendment, to extend State of California gun laws from six months to nine years beyond California's turnover to Japan. The joint committee considering the California Treaty doesn't have authority to amend the treaty, but only to place into its report recommendations for amendments for the full Senate to adopt. . . ."

"In Moscow, Syrian Prime Minister Al-Amin is returning home after meeting with Russian President Dimitrov. Specifics of the talks are unavailable, beyond that the talks center on Syria's wish to buy weapons from Russia. The timing of Al-Amin's departure leads observers to believe that one side or the other broke off talks prematurely. Just before he boarded his plane homeward, Al-Amin described his meetings with Dimitrov as `frustrating and fruitless.' Dimitrov's office had no comment."

On the L.A.-bound airplane Tuesday afternoon, the man had frowned when he sat next to Barbara. As the occasional autograph seeker became a steady stream of fans, his frown deepened. Thirty minutes after the seat-belt lights were off, he stabbed the call button.

"Either move *her* or move *me*!"

The flight crew moved her, with apologies. They would've moved her into First Class at no extra charge, but she declined. They offered to fetch her royal-blue carry-on bag from under her old seat, and that offer she accepted. Of course they made sure that Barbara's new seatmate didn't mind her presence.

Barbara's new neighbor was from San Juan Capistrano, she was nine years older than Barbara, and she greeted Barbara with "Keep fighting, honey!"

Her name was Linda. "So is mine," Barbara said, smiling.

"Barbara Linda Nakamura or Linda Barbara?"

"The first one. It's a joke, actually. The rudest translation of *Barbara* is *female barbarian*."

"*Linda* means *pretty*. So you're a pretty barbarian?"

"Uh-huh. The joke is, which half of me—Japanese or American—is the barbarian half, and which is the pretty half?"

Linda smiled. "Your parents sound like a fun couple."

Barbara smiled back. "They are. New Year's Eve, they loved to play *Fuku Warai*. That's the Japanese version of Pin-the-Tail-on-the-Donkey, except you're trying to make a woman's face instead of a donkey. I think they often deliberately messed up the face to make everyone laugh. My parents like to joke around." Barbara's smile left. "Up till now."

"How's your mother taking all this?"

"Not well, not well." Barbara didn't want to dwell on that. "Linda, I've lived in San Diego for years, but I've never seen the swallows arrive at the Mission of San Juan Capistrano. What's that like?"

Hours later, Hazel Archer met Barbara at the Santa Barbara Municipal Airport. So did three television news crews from the Santa Barbara area, plus three crews from network news. Hazel hugged Barbara as if Barbara were a long-lost sister.

The two women headed to a steak restaurant a few blocks from the beach. Helen and Barbara found the meeting room packed with women of all ages and colors. Helen was openmouthed: "The attendance is the heaviest I've ever seen, Barbara. Heaviest in five years."

"All these women, on one day's notice?"

After dinner, Barbara gave her speech. The audience applauded long and loud, and gave Barbara a standing ovation at the end. She tried to put on the plastic, smiling politician's-wife face, but her eyes brimmed with too many tears. She and Hazel hugged again. It seemed the whole room came up to shake her hand and to hug her.

One woman told her, "If California goes Japanese, my company's moving out, and I can't afford to go with them. Keep fighting the good fight."

Another woman grabbed Barbara's hand. "When I was married, my husband kept stealing tools from the factory, and I never let on that I knew. I gave myself so many excuses. Still, I know I'm a coward and a thief. You did right."

A third woman said as she hugged Barbara, "I want my daughter to grow up to be like you."

Barbara found the flattery intoxicating.

Afterward Hazel put Barbara up in a Santa Barbara hotel right on the beach, so Barbara didn't arrive back into Ronald Reagan Airport until Wednesday afternoon. She found her car in Airport Parking, and paid the fee at the toll booth.

While she was paying, she saw a black Cadillac up ahead at the side of the road. The Caddy's hood was up, and a tow truck was behind it. As Barbara speeded away from the toll booth, she saw someone shut the hood and dash to the driver's side of the Caddy. Both the Caddy and the tow truck began to move. By the time Barbara had passed the tow truck, the Caddy was moving at freeway speed, right ahead of her.

The Caddy's rear window was tinted almost opaque black, so she had no warning when the driver slammed on his brakes.

"Damn!" Barbara said, half a second later.

Fortunately, she didn't hit him hard. She was thankful when the tow truck stopped behind the two stopped cars; with its flashing yellows, all three vehicles moved safely to the side of the road.

After finding her insurance card, she got out of her car. That's when the driver of the Caddy stepped out, as did a muscular man who was riding passenger in the tow truck.

She sighed as the tow-truck man walked up to her. "I didn't *think* I was following too close, but—"

He pulled his hand out of his pocket, and she stared in shock at what he held. *I've been set up.*

"Into the Cadillac. Back seat," he said.

She stood unmoving. He shoved her, then said, "They aren't here to kill you, just to talk to you."

She looked at the Caddy driver, who was himself watching her. *I hope you run*, his smile said. That smile chilled her.

Barbara realized that if they'd indeed wanted her dead, she'd be dying already by gunshot wound. Cheerful thought, that. She and the tow-truck man walked to the black Caddy.

The Caddy's side windows were also dark, so she didn't see the two other men until the driver opened the back-seat door for her. Ten seconds later, she was wedged between the two riders, her insurance card still clutched in her hand. *Be brave*, she told herself.

"Good afternoon, Mrs. Nakamura," the man on her left said. "Did you enjoy your trip to Santa Barbara?"

"Who are you?"

"I'm Mister A., from Las Vegas. Over there is Mister C., from Atlantic City. We're—you could say we're in the entertainment business."

"'Entertainment'? Is that the current term?"

"People need all kinds of entertainment. Joe back there"—his thumb meant the tow truck—"does odd jobs for me. The other guy you met is Bernoulli, he works for Mister C."

Mister C. nodded. "Bernoulli solves problems. He's good at solving problems."

Barbara turned to him. "So what is today's solution, breaking my kneecaps? Acid in my face?"

Mister C. said, "None of dat. You and us'll sit here and talk, three adults. Then you'll get into your car, go home, and leave da treaty alone."

"How's the plan change when I say no?"

Mister A. said, "Senators' wives don't get Secret Service protection—you don't want to say no."

Mister C. said, "Because then your brakes might go out sometime, all accidental-like."

Mister A. said, "Or some armed burglar breaks into your house, and shit happens."

Mister C. opened his door, and gestured for her to get out. "You're a smart lady. Act smart, and you won't get hurt."

She had to climb over Mister C. to get out of the Cadillac. By the time she was behind the wheel of her own car, both the Cadillac and the tow truck had left.

With a shaking hand she started her car. But her fear didn't change her mind: "Smart? Maybe. But I'm certainly stubborn—and stubborn ladies keep fighting till they win or they die."

When Barbara arrived back home in Alexandria, the answering machine held three messages. All three asked her to speak in California. They didn't want Matt, they wanted *her*.

To hell with Mister A. and Mister C. and their threats. She called everyone back and committed to all the speaking engagements.

Eight o'clock Thursday morning, Barbara was calling joint-committee senators again.

"Senator Holt's office."

"Hello, this is Barbara Nakamura. May I speak to the senator, please?. . .I'm sorry I missed him. I'll try again later." How odd that he was never in when Barbara called.

She touch-toned another number.

"Senator Lamont's office."

"Hello, this is Barbara Nakamura. May I speak to the senator, please?. . .Hello, Phyllis, how are you? How's Paul?"

"We're fine. Barbara, good to hear from you. You still working out?"

"Regularly—it keeps me sane. And you?"

"Once or twice a week—not nearly as much as I'd like. Honey, is this a personal call, or are you calling about the treaty?"

"The treaty. I'm calling to urge you to vote it out of committee unfavorably."

Barbara heard Phyllis sigh. "Can't do it—I owe Joe Bob a favor, and he's calling it in. Besides, Wyoming wants those trillions and jobs."

"Thanks for your time, then. I hope we can work out again sometime."

"Me, too, Barbara."

Barbara touch-toned another name on her list.

"Senator Powell's office."

"Hello, this is Barbara Nakamura. May I speak to the senator, please?. . .Hello, Kevin, this is Barbara Nakamura, how are you?. . .Thank you in advance for your vote against the treaty. Californians thank you."

166 Tom H. Richardson

"This is ASN Newsbreak, 10:00 a.m. Eastern time, Thursday, May 5.

"Senate Minority Leader Steve Leaird tries again to amend the California Treaty. Leaird just proposed an amendment that would raise Japan's annual payment from three trillion dollars to four trillion dollars. Leaird's new proposal came only minutes after the joint Foreign Relations-Armed Services Committee voted down Leaird's previous committee amendment. That amendment would have extended State of California gun laws from six months to nine years beyond the date of California's transfer to Japan."

In a committee room Monday morning, Steve Leaird said to the joint-committee chairman, "Joe Bob, I move that we recommend the treaty be amended as follows—"

The rules didn't let Matt interrupt. So he shook his head in exaggerated world-weariness.

"—below the text for Article 38, insert `Article 39. Japan shall have up to ninety days after the due date to make its annual payment to the United States. If full payment due annually is not received by the ninety-first day, or if the payment made is uncollectible, then California immediately shall become a state of the United States again, and all prior monies paid by Japan shall be forfeit.'"

Leaird adopted the voice of a kindly teacher, as he looked around the room: "Everyone, the president has proposed the most expensive land transfer in world history. If Japan can't make the payments, the treaty doesn't address how to resolve that problem. I've corrected this oversight."

Joe Bob glanced around. "There a second?"

Matt expected one of Leaird's Republican zombies to do it, but instead it was conservative Democrat Sheppard who raised his hand. Shit.

Sheppard looked around at his fellow Democrats. "Steve finally proposed an amendment I agree with. If Japan misses a payment, or if Japan's check bounces, we *repo* California!"

"This is ASN Newsbreak, 11:00 a.m. Eastern time, Tuesday, May 10.

"Japan might cancel the California Treaty, after what a joint Senate committee just voted to do. Within the hour the combined Foreign Relations-Armed Services Committee voted overwhelmingly to endorse the `Repossession Amendment' to the treaty. If the Senate amends the treaty as proposed, Japan might exercise its right to break the agreement. The `Repossession Amendment' requires Japan to make its required annual payments in full and on time, else California reverts to United States sovereignty. The only resistance to the amendment came from Senator Matthew Nakamura. . ."

Monday six days later, the time was slightly after noon, Washington time. Washington was the airplane's destination, nonstop from San Francisco. Barbara was returning from giving yet another speech to yet another adoring crowd.

168 Tom H. Richardson

Barbara was using the flying time to read that morning's *USA Today*. The headline read, "Rest of USA Wants Treaty." A joint *USA Today*/CNBC poll had found that 52 percent of Americans outside California favored the treaty.

Barbara was horrified. In not even six weeks, the percentage of those in favor had mushroomed from 2 percent to a majority.

With the new poll, the ninety-eight other senators all had an excuse to vote the treaty. Matt was about to succeed. Barbara felt scared for California.

The stewardess approached her. "Ms. Nakamura?"

"Is something wrong?"

"The captain just found out: the treaty, the committee voted for it."

"Reported out favorably. Damn. So now it all depends on a hundred senators."

"This treaty is important. I'm sure they'll do what's right for the country."

"But will they do what's right for California?"

About which, the Variety-Show Host joked—

> *Senate Majority Leader Fuller pledged this morning, "The Senate shall do what is right for California and the nation." Right, pal. Aren't the politicians the ones who brought California and the nation to this mess in the first place?*
>
> *Secretary of State Harland says that if the California Treaty doesn't go through, Senator Nakamura might be the next president. Of course, if the treaty <u>does</u> go through, Nakamura might be the next <u>emperor</u>.*

CHAPTER 8
Heisei 17-nen 5-gatsu
16-nichi, Getsuyohbi
(Monday, May 16, 2005)

On the Internet, Hiroshi found five message boards about the California Treaty. The first two were in Japanese, and held little value for him. Being at the moment unable to do more than watch Washington, those boards' contributors could only exchange rumors and daydreams.

As for the English-language message boards, Hiroshi didn't like spending time there—they had half the manners of a saloon brawl. Californian and non-Californian Americans insulted each other, when both weren't bashing Japan. Every time Hiroshi had posted a message defending his country, kilobytes of toxic e-mail had arrived within hours.

Still, the American message boards had information Hiroshi needed, so he kept coming back. Late Monday evening, Hiroshi learned the e-mail addresses of both Senator Nakamura and Mrs. Nakamura.

Hiroshi at once posted a message to Senator Nakamura's office. That note thanked Senator Nakamura for his courageous stand on the treaty, and wished him well.

Tuesday morning in Alexandria, Barbara was at home eating breakfast at the computer. Someone had revealed her e-mail address, so she had dozens of messages to wade through: Thanks for speaking out, You suck, Save California, How dare you, Thanks, You're a disgrace to wives everywhere, and so on.

Among such e-mail was a message, in English, from a Japanese man named Iwata:

> *Dear Mrs. Nakamura,*
>
> *You want help California people. You think the treaty will hurt California people. I understand these.*
>
> *I'm sorry, but I don't think the treaty will hurt the California people and I think the treaty will help us Japanese people. You know about Japan, so may I tell to you why I write these? Also I ask most respectfully, you stop your fight so the Senate passes the treaty and the Diet receives the treaty.*

Someone so polite and empathetic deserved a courteous reply. Barbara e-mailed back in Japanese:

> *Iwata-<u>sama</u>:*
>
> *I am not worth the trouble for you to honor me by explaining why you support the treaty.*
>
> *However, I commit a rudeness: I regretfully must decline your request to stop fighting the treaty. Like history's forty-seven masterless samurai, I have an obligation I must fulfill and which I cannot quit. While any means exist to fight the treaty, I must press on.*

Two hours later, Barbara stood beneath sun and clouds at the Washington Mall, making a speech at a rally of Californians. As Barbara stood behind the podium on the makeshift platform, she drew strength from the tens of thousands who surrounded the Washington Monument.

"Yes, the joint committee recommended the treaty," Barbara's amplified voice reverberated throughout the Mall, "but don't despair that the treaty's a done deal. Two-thirds of the Senate need to okay it, remember.

"Write every Republican in the Senate, then write every Democrat. Tell each senator you're counting on him or her to do what's right for the country. For the *entire* country!

"Above all, believe that this insanity *will* pass, and California *will* remain the best and brightest of the fifty united states!"

The crowd cheered loudly, then began to chant "Bar-b'ra! Bar-b'ra! Bar-b'ra!"

Hector DeGarcia took the podium when she left. Barbara sat down on the platform next to Steve Leaird and conversed with him—both of them shouting over the noise made by the crowd and by Hector.

Leaird smiled with self-satisfaction. "To do something good, that's why many in Washington went into politics."

Barbara gave him a skeptical look.

His look back was one of surprise. "What, you think this is an act?"

"The treaty is Charlie's baby. This is politics as usual."

He shook his head and sighed. "No, politics as usual is what it's *not*. The smell of those trillions is trashing discipline among Senate Republicans."

"Oh?"

"The hypocrites preach about slashing taxes. The honest defectors just talk about buying votes with bogus public-works projects."

"And Delaware?"

"Delaware voters keep flaming me for standing between them and part of sixty trillion."

"I apologize for doubting you. That's brave of you, planning to vote nay when Delaware wants yea."

He smiled. "Delaware and Gwen. Been a bit chilly around the house lately."

"You, too?"

"But I won't change my vote, not to stay in politics, and not even for Gwen."

"What if Gwen begged on her knees? That didn't work on Matt, but maybe you're different."

"In this only, I'm not. If I gave in to Gwen's appeals, I would be lax as a senator."

"Really? How?"

"No private promise or obligation may come before my public duty. That's in our Code of Ethics, and it's a good rule besides."

Barbara thought that over, nodded, then looked at Leaird again. "So you're telling Gwen no, and she's rationing you."

"And I'm suffering therefrom." He shrugged. "Even when she's pigheaded, a Senate wife's job doesn't include tolerating her husband's affairs." He gave her a searching look.

Barbara paused before speaking. "Assuming she knows about them."

"Now Hector DeGarcia over there, Joe Bob Saunders, Chris Ingram, and Jack Arbuckle, I believe that they are solid husbands, too." Leaird again looked at Barbara.

"Lay on, MacDuff," she said, then bit her lip.

"One of the Republican pages, yesterday he walked past Matt who was talking to a thirtyish blonde in front of the Dirksen. The boy didn't overhear what they were talking about, but he heard the woman say `panties.'"

"Thanks for sharing." Yet while she felt unhappy at adding a new suspicion to her collection, she also felt amazed at herself. People had dropped hints about Matt before, but this was the first time she'd been strong enough to ask them what they knew.

In Hector DeGarcia's office an hour later, Barbara frowned. "Actually, I blame myself."

Sapphira put a hand on Barbara's shoulder. "You stop that. How you to know the committee gonna vote it out favorable?"

"I should've been making fewer speeches on the road. I should've called more joint-committee members here in Washington."

"Now don't you be saying that. We been gotten lots of letters and e-mail since you started. Californians, they done felt forgot by Washington. But you comes home and you gives your speeches, and Californians they hoping."

"Because of me?"

"Sure enough. Senator DeGarcia, he also working hard against that treaty, but he ain't got time to do more, you knows that yourownself."

Sapphira's words banished the blackest part of Barbara's guilt, though much remained. "Sapphira, you're sweet. Still, I'm making no more speeches outside Washington until after the vote."

Barbara and Sapphira were talking in DeGarcia's large conference room, which had become the anti-treaty command post. Sapphira was directing DeGarcia's staff in the treaty fight; only a skeleton staff continued with regular business. Barbara was coordinating with Leaird and other anti-treaty senators.

As the two women watched, a young man erased the large whiteboard in the conference room, and began writing the names of senators. Next to each name, he wrote *For, Against,* or *?.* Barbara was stung to see—

"Chris Ingram? He's *for* the treaty?"

The man at the whiteboard nodded. "Yep, said so on American Satellite News this morning."

"I thought he was all bothered about Japanese California being nuclear-undefended."

"He said this morning, Swensen convinced him that Japan would have to join NORAD," the North American Air Defense Command. "So if a missile's coming, the United States would know and could work around Japan. The president also mentioned to Ingram that the California Treaty would bring more nickels for nukes."

"Gold-plated shark shit."

"I'm sorry?"

"It's what my best friend in San Diego would say."

———

Barbara eyed the whiteboard a few minutes later. "Twenty-one for, twelve against. The percentage scares me silly, but it's still short of two-thirds."

Sapphira shook her head. "But twelve for us ain't enough. We needs thirty-four or more."

"Less, if not everyone votes," Bill the whiteboard writer said.

Sapphira shook her head again. "Ain't no way *that* gonna happen."

Barbara, Sapphira, Bill, and others gathered to make plans. Bill sighed. "The problem is that no matter how much trouble this treaty creates for Californians, other senators can't suffer for it. We don't vote for those other guys, so we can't threaten them."

Barbara perked up. "Maybe we *can*. If this treaty goes through, lots of California people and businesses are going to move, right?"

Everyone nodded.

"Suppose Californians vow right now that if they don't move, they'll remember who their friends were when they plan out-of-state vacations. If Californians *must* move, they'll remember their pro-treaty senator when he comes up for re-election, and they'll canvass actively against him."

Bill chortled. "I love it. When one of those pro-treaty guys loses on Election Night, he'll realize ex-Californians haven't forgotten him."

Barbara snapped her fingers. "That's what we'll call our campaign: *We Won't Forget!* People, now we have a tactic to counter Matt's."

An hour later, Hector DeGarcia yelled, "Goddamn you, Nakamura! You lying, filthy, slimy crook, you disgusting traitor!"

So much for the Senate's no-name-calling rule.

Matt was caught alone in the senators' men's room with Hector. Up until now, Matt had managed to avoid this confrontation. Now forced into it, he was damned if he'd let Hector push him around.

Matt pasted on a haughty smile. "Your schoolyard words show your lack of class."

"Yeah? I have good reason for my `schoolyard words.' How many letters I've received start out, `I don't trust Nakamura one bit, so I'm writing to you.'"

"They write that? Great."

"You think so, huh?"

"Yeah, it means less work for my staff. Gives my people more time to work on projects of national importance—like the treaty."

"You slug. Not only do I have to worry about you costing me and all my staff our jobs, but you're gonna run us all ragged before you do."

"You know Ingram said I was clean."

"I also know Barbara says you bullshitted Ingram. You worthless collaborator."

"Ah, Barbara. You two have become so `close.'"

"Have a guilty conscience? Nothing is going on, you know goddamned well."

"And what if I tell the Ethics Committee otherwise? Better yet, what if I tell the press?"

Across the street in Hector's office, Barbara was hitting the phones again. But this time she had ninety-eight senators to sway, not just the joint committee's thirty-four.

She touch-toned the first number, and twenty seconds later she heard the voice of Rod Abernathy. "Hello, Barbara. You're calling about the treaty?"

"Yes, Rod. You voted against it in committee, and I encourage you to hang tough awhile longer."

"Relax. A few of us still care what's right, instead of what buys votes."

"Great. I know you're in a hurry, so bye, and thanks!" Barbara caught Sapphira's eye and gave her a thumb-up. Barbara made another call.

"Senator Porter's office."

"Hello, this is Barbara Nakamura. May I speak to the senator, please?" A minute later she was asking, "Hello, Roy, how are you this morning?"

"Big Roy" Porter sounded wary: "I'm fine, Barbara. Is this a social call?"

"No, I'm calling about the California Treaty. It's bad news all around, so I ask you to vote against it."

"Goddamn, I didn't realize you'd become a pesky lobbyist. Have you registered yourself with the secretary of the Senate?"

"No, because I'm working volunteer. No pay."

"Don't matter, to me you're a lobbyist, and I don't make time for them who don't support my position. I'm hanging up, Barbara. Don't call me about this again."

"But what about the treaty? Don't you even want to hear my reasons for opposing the treaty?" She thought, *You've eaten my food, you've drunk my liquor. I think I'm entitled to you hearing me out.*

"Barbara, I've already decided how I'll vote. Mississippi needs those trillions and jobs."

She sighed. "Okay, thanks for your time. Say hello to Holly for me."

"Don't call me again about this. Goodbye."

"This is ASN Newsbreak, 2:00 p.m. Eastern time, Tuesday, May 17.

"Japan might cancel buying California, after a recent Senate vote. The Senate just passed the `Repossession Amendment' to the California Treaty.

With the treaty amended, Japan now has the right to break the agreement. The `Repossession Amendment' requires Japan to pay in full and on time each year, else California reverts to United States sovereignty. Senate Majority Leader Fuller and Senator Nakamura of California unsuccessfully fought the measure."

At the health club that evening, Barbara thought, *There's Tiffani. Perfect.*

Barbara just had walked out of the women's locker room when she spotted Tiffani Ingram on a stair-climber. Barbara wanted to talk to Tiffani, but only partly because of friendship.

Tiffani, watching the mirror-reflection of a ceiling-mounted TV, didn't notice Barbara until Barbara had climbed onto an adjacent stair machine.

Barbara smiled. "Is this stair-climber taken?"

"Hi, come join me," Tiffani panted. She gulped from exertion. "Haven't seen you at the Red Cross lately."

"I'm spending lots of time at Hector's office, fighting the treaty. You know how it is."

"Uh-huh. Hey, the Red Cross is only volunteer work, who needs commitment, right?"

"You forget you were only a dim memory last year, when Chris was running for re-election."

"Hey, I'm joking, okay? Let's discuss something else. The president and Stephanie hosted a dinner for Republican senators and us spouses last night."

"How was it?"

"Steve Leaird was cracking jokes all night—even the president laughed. Then the president made a joke of his own." Tiffani's smile held mischief. "Maybe I shouldn't tell you. The president told us what a Democrat is."

"Okay, what's a Democrat?"

"Someone who believes that as long as the taxpayers still have money, the government can solve every problem."

"I did ask. What else happened at the dinner party?"

"Poor Chris had to talk Russian nukes again."

"Lament number one." This was Capitol Hill wives' code for their main complaint: Their husbands didn't dare completely relax at any public function.

"Yep. Chris discussed START III and the California Treaty, while *I* was free to savor the feeling of `*I'm* in the White House!' I love those rich gold curtains hanging tall in the East Room."

"I love the big portrait of George Washington. He stands there so tall and commanding, and obviously self-conscious about his wooden dentures. The painting makes him human."

"Don't you love the story how Dolley Madison saved the painting of Washington when the British set fire to the White House?"

"Sometimes Washington wives must be brave. Anyway, you enjoyed yourself last night."

"Lord, yes."

"You know, Chris said on the news that he and Charlie Swensen talked last night."

"Barbara, why'd you ask me about the dinner party if you already knew about it?"

"I didn't know it was a dinner party. All I knew was, Chris and Charlie talked last night."

"Chris also told the press that the president sold him on the California Treaty. Is that why you're talking to me?"

"Tiffani, Chris is making a big mistake, one that'll eat at him for years. Still, it's not too late to fix that mistake, I wish you'd tell him that."

"Is that why you're talking to me now? To con me into luring Chris back to voting your way?"

"I haven't visited with you in a long time. You're my friend, I—"

"You exercise with me, you ask me about the dinner party—it's all a ruse, isn't it? You were just following the manual: `Before asking for a donation, it's vital to find common ground and create a mood of camaraderie.'"

"Tiffani, again: You're my friend, and I miss you. That part's tr—"

"Is it?"

"Okay, I admit I thought about asking you to talk to Chris. *Satisfied?*"

"I can't believe this! Ever since Chris first got elected, everyone's tried to be *his* friend or *my* friend—"

"Same with me, Tiffani, so I never—"

"I made friends with you because you and I had so much in common, and because I thought you wouldn't ask for a `tiny favor.' Wrong! You're like everyone else."

"So what would *you* do if it were Indiana that Swensen was pawning, and Chris thought this was fine and dandy? I wish you'd be *my* friend and understand my problem!"

"You and I were so close. Why'd you need to wreck it? First you insult Chris, and now you want to *use me* to lobby him. I'm finished here; please excuse me."

Tiffani pushed herself off the stair-climber, grabbed her towel and her water bottle, and hurried away. The muscles of her back were stiff with tension.

Barbara felt wretched; she knew she'd lost her friend.

On television Wednesday afternoon, voting on one of DeGarcia's sabotage amendments had ended in Matt's favor. The presiding officer announced, "The yeas are forty-three and the nays are fifty-four. The amendment, which requires Japanese schools in California to be bilingual, is not agreed to."

In NBC News's Washington bureau that evening, anchor Sharon Hamilton gazed into the camera. "Back here again is Senator Matthew Nakamura of California."

She turned to face Matt. "Senator, right now the fight in the Senate is over poison amendments. For instance, today the Senate debated whether to keep military bases in California under American control for ten years. That amendment, if passed, would force the Diet to kill the treaty. My question: Do you think any of these poison amendments will pass?"

Matt turned on Tone of Voice Ten (Confident): "No way. Senators DeGarcia and Leaird are doing so only as a delaying tactic, to hold off the vote on the resolution of ratification."

"And how do you think this final vote will go?"

"I'm certain of passage."

"NBC News projects that if the vote were held this hour, only sixty-one senators would be in favor. You need sixty-seven, if everyone votes."

Matt steepled his fingers. "Perhaps I have more confidence in the wisdom of my fellow senators than does NBC News."

"Californians have started a petition drive to ask you to resign. How do you feel about that?"

"Sharon, I can understand their feelings. If I were still a corporate attorney in San Diego, I might sign that resign petition myself! But obviously it hurts, on a personal level."

"A lot?"

"Not much, I'm used to dislike. When I was a kid, I was pushed around and shunned all the time, because it was the early Sixties and I was Japanese."

Third grade, morning recess, sometime in November 1962: Dennis Goodman was taunting Matt, while Goodman's friends listened and snickered. Dennis said, "I'll bet your Dad helped bomb Pearl Harbor."

Matt was shorter than Dennis, but he glared and made a fist anyway. "You take that back!"

Dennis glanced at his friends and smirked. "Make me."

Matt tried to. That's when two boys grabbed his arms; Dennis and another boy punched him. After he got his wind back, Matt yelled, "My Dad's American, and he fought for America! In an artillery battalion in France and Italy. He's a real war hero, he showed me his medal."

Dennis still smirked. "They didn't send him to fight the Japs, everyone notice? Because they weren't sure which side he'd fight on."

Now Matt showed Sharon a forgiving smile. "Next to childhood taunts, what's a resign petition?"

Sharon, who was watching his face, nodded. "Wasn't `Bomber' originally a childhood insult?"

"That's right. A gang of kids teased me in third grade. Their ringleader was a kid named Dennis. He stuck me with the name."

Dennis Goodman yelled so that the whole playground could hear: "Hey, everyone, Nakamura wants to play with us. Go away, Bomber, we don't want you around. Your eyes look funny."

Matt now gave Sharon another forgiving smile. "But I didn't let bother me what those kids said. I moved past it."

She smiled—even this close, her smile looked sincere. "How wonderful. Please tell me about that."

"I decided that I couldn't stop them from disliking my name or my face, but I could make sure they didn't dislike anything else. I bought a copy of *How to Win Friends and Influence People*, the Dale Carnegie book."

Except Matt hadn't read it to become a wonderful human being, he'd read it to learn how to *fake* such.

Sharon nodded. "It's a wonderful book."

"Lots of people *read* it, but I *practiced* it. I listened to people, I remembered their names, I asked about events in their life—I followed all of Carnegie's rules. My junior and senior years in high school, I was elected class president."

"The start of your career in politics."

"When I was elected junior class president, I felt like I'd won the marathon. The outsider had become part of the inner circle."

"I'm sure that felt wonderful."

"Sharon, you don't know the half."

It was two days after Matt's election, in the high-school cafeteria. Rhonda Foster took Matt's arm as her eyes dismissed Goodman. "I told you we were through, Dennis. I'm with Matt now." Dennis looked like his dog had died.

Now Matt gazed at Sharon. "Much later, sometime in my first congressional campaign, I started wearing the bomber jacket. It was my way of saying, `Hey world, your insult can't hurt me. I've overcome it, I'm strong in my self-esteem.'"

"That's a very inspiring story, Senator." Sharon actually sounded like she meant it.

"Thank you, Sharon. It's very nice of you to say that." Matt wondered how Sharon was in bed. Was she a redhead all over?

Sharon leaned forward, her face sympathetic. "We all can brace ourselves when strangers say hurtful words. Yet it must have stung when your wife made those bribe allegations. . ."

Three minutes later, Sapphira phoned Barbara at home. "Barbara, is you watching `Our World in Depth' on NBC? You turn it on right now!"

"Sharon Hamilton's interviewing Matt. I'm skipping it."

"You got cable? You downloads this, you needs to see it!"

"Why bother? I know Matt's line by heart: `I can't think only of California, I must think of the whole United—'"

"No, Matt done called you a *slut*! You and Hector, Matt he blasted you two!"

"Why am I not surprised. Okay, I'll download it."

"Senator DeGarcia done axed me to record anything about the treaty fight. Man, he gonna blow a fuse."

Seconds later, Barbara was watching what she'd downloaded. Three minutes into Matt's interview, Sharon Hamilton asked, ". . .Yet it must have stung when your wife made those bribe allegations. Now she's campaigning against the treaty, teamed with Senators Leaird and DeGarcia. How much does this bother you?"

Matt was wearing his Forgiveness Face. "Sharon, I can understand Leaird's opposition. A Democrat president comes up with a program, it's Leaird's job as minority leader to oppose it. The treaty is a good plan. The treaty is what's best for our country. The treaty is of no net cost to the taxpayers. But Democrat Swensen made the treaty, so Republican Leaird is obligated to oppose it.

"Hector DeGarcia and my wife as a team? Understandable. Hector DeGarcia will lose his Senate seat if this treaty goes through. Of course, so will I, but again, DeGarcia's feelings are understandable. As for Barbara, she teamed up with DeGarcia mainly to achieve a great good, as she sees it."

Sharon frowned in puzzlement. "`Mainly?' Why else would they work together?"

Matt's shoulders hunched; his eyes darted. "Sharon, that was a slip—I mean, Barbara—it's personal—she—I don't know what to say."

Sharon's eyes widened, but she recovered: "I see. Let's change the subject. Senator Leaird—"

Matt took a shaky breath and wiped his hands on his pants. "Let me stress: I have no proof my wife and Hector are guilty of any wrong."

"That tomcatting hypocrite," Barbara breathed in horrified wonder.

On the screen, Sharon was leaning forward, one hand out, almost touching Matt. "Senator, you're hurting. We'd better change the subject."

Matt leaned forward, his eyes intent on Sharon's, seemingly unaware of the camera. "See, Barbara's a very attractive woman. Obviously I'm still in love with my wife after all these years. Barbara ditches me at parties soon as we're past the door, and this hurts, sure. She doesn't want to spend time with me, well okay. Meanwhile, Hector DeGarcia has that air of power that people talk about, and I can't be the only one who's noticed. I *hope* Barbara and Hector are only doing treaty work together—but I'd understand if they was involved in more."

By now the camera was close up on Matt's sadly smiling face. Even Diogenes would buy a used car from that face.

The next morning, Barbara and her homemade cookies arrived at Pam Case's house slightly after ten. Pam was this week's hostess for the Senate wives' Thursday-morning tea.

Barbara rang Pam's doorbell with mixed feelings. Up until Carol had printed Barbara's story a month ago, the Senate wives' tea had been the high point of Barbara's week. But since that day, Barbara's relations with some of the other women had become ever more strained. Still, she intended to forget about the treaty for two hours and to enjoy herself.

Pam opened her door and granted Barbara a polite smile. "Glad you could come, Barbara." The words held no warmth at all, though Pam always had acted friendly before—even last week.

From Pam's living room, Barbara could hear Betsy Lewis. "She actually *said* that, Tiffani? Who does she think she is?"

That living room went silent as Barbara carried her plate of oatmeal cookies to Pam's dining-room table.

Cookies put down, Barbara turned to the twenty or so women scattered about the room. The women ranged in age from thirty-two (Gail Tucker) to eighty-plus (Holly Porter). All were well-dressed, of course. Barbara knew she was likewise stylish, and her copper-and-silver chain bracelet rather bold, but only Marilyn Saunders made a compliment.

Barbara looked around the room at the women's expressions, and made herself smile. "Hello, Tiffani, how are you?"

Tiffani didn't smile. "Hello, Barbara."

Barbara paused, expecting Tiffani to continue, but Tiffani had nothing more to say. Barbara next greeted Marilyn Saunders, to cover her own discomfort. *Oh Tiffani, can't we still be friends?*

"Ah'm *so* glad you could come," Marilyn said. Marilyn's voice was unusually warm; her smile, bigger than usual.

Barbara helloed the other women, and only Gail Tucker and Marilyn Saunders acted friendly. Most women's replies were brief and superficial, their smiles were glued on. Barbara was getting a brush-off, and it hurt. "*Buenas dias,* Carmen," Barbara said.

Carmen DeGarcia's practiced smile was almost perfect, and the quick, furtive bite of her lip was almost unnoticeable. Carmen's eyes searched Barbara's face as the fingertips of Carmen's right hand kept brushing the spread napkin in her lap.

Barbara was aghast. *Carmen, you really believe I'm sleeping with Hector?*

It was Betsy Lewis who called court into session, with a smile and voice that were too sweet: "Tiffani tells us that you asked her to talk to Chris."

Barbara made her own face and voice reasonable, not defensive. "My need was urgent."

"Tiffani told us you said Chris was making a big mistake, one that would eat at him for years. How dramatic. You've held too many fundraisers in Hollywood, dear."

Cheryl Wade said, "Perhaps you need reminding: Washington puts pressure enough on us Senate wives, without politics intruding into our friendships." Barbara saw Tiffani nod.

"That's a rotten way to treat your best friend," Penny Wagner said.

Clearly Barbara would have to ditch forgetting the treaty and relaxing. What she had to do now was to convince her peers that it wasn't wrong to ask Tiffani to lobby her husband.

Barbara smiled and tried to charm them. "Everyone's getting excited over what is, remember, an *unwritten* rule."

Holly Porter waved that aside. "Will you be pushing *me* to talk to Big Roy? He endorses the treaty."

So much for charming them. Barbara dropped the smile. "Yes, Holly, I will. California's future is at stake."

Sandra Patterson frowned. "Will you badmouth Vernon for supporting the treaty? Like you did Chris?"

"No, Sandra. I blundered hugely with Chris."

Gail Tucker looked puzzled. "I don't understand why you said all that about Chris. Isn't Tiffani's your friend, and isn't Chris on Matt's committee?"

Barbara sighed. "A reporter called me when I was furious enough to strangle Matt, and I didn't think. You can't imagine how many times I've regretted my words." Barbara glanced at Tiffani, who looked away.

Gail nodded. "Sure. Last year I got waylaid in Minneapolis by a TV reporter."

Barbara smiled with relief, then turned back to Betsy. "This rule about us wives not lobbying each other, the rule didn't figure on my problem. Carmen's and my problem."

Holly sniffed. "Do you see *Carmen* working the room? Do you see *Carmen* pushing anyone?"

"So what, Holly?" Barbara looked into each hostile face. "Suppose Swensen were selling Mississippi? Would you say, `I'll play by all the rules. I mustn't lobby any senators' wives, I mustn't lobby any senators since I'm not a lobbyist.'"

Marilyn Saunders smiled at Barbara, then glanced around the room. "Ladies, if it was Georgia they wanted, Ah wouldn't hold back nothin'. When it was my turn to host, Ah'd serve tea and coffee in `Save Georgia' mugs that sat on `Save Georgia' paper napkins. Ah'd call y'all; Ah'd call your husbands. Ah'd make myself a downright pest—and Holly, don't tell me you wouldn't do the same."

Holly frowned. "Perhaps. But I wouldn't go on ASN and humiliate Barbara the way she's humiliated Tiffani. *I* was raised better than that. Also, *I* could defend Mississippi from Japan quite well, without *deceiving* Big Roy." Holly, sitting next to Carmen DeGarcia, squeezed Carmen's hand.

Wonderful. Not only did Barbara have to get the stupid no-lobbying-other-wives rule thrown out, but she also had to answer to Matt's slander. "Holly, Carmen, listen. Matt told Hector beforehand that he would smear Hector exactly that way."

"So Hector swore up and down to me," Carmen said. "He told me Matt made his threat in the Senate men's room. Of course no witnesses were around."

"To me it's obvious," Betsy Lewis said, "a man who would spread nasty lies about his own wife *certainly* wouldn't sacrifice his Senate seat. So I don't think Matt's telling nasty lies."

Barbara forced herself to remain at Pam's another forty minutes, but made no headway. Barbara tried to convince the other Senate wives to let her lobby them, but they kept throwing back to her the "affair" with Hector DeGarcia and her hot words about Chris.

Angela Hawkins said little to Barbara until Barbara was picking up her plate of cookies to leave. (Even Barbara's cookies had been shunned.) Angela eyed Barbara and said, "I adore Washington, but if the good of the country cost Adam his seat, *I'd* only shrug. I host next week, and I'll understand if you and Hector are so `busy' you can't attend."

Except for Marilyn and Gail, every woman nodded in agreement.

In the Senate chamber that afternoon, the presiding officer was saying, ". . .The amendment, which keeps military bases in California under American control for ten years instead of one year, is not agreed to."

At this announcement, Matt flashed Hector a smug smile. "*So* sorry your amendment didn't survive," that smile said.

Steve Leaird stood and faced the presiding officer. "Mister President."

"The senior senator from Delaware is recognized."

"Mister President: I believe that the United States will lose money on this deal, even at sixty trillion dollars. Thus I send to the desk this amendment that the annual payment be changed from three trillion dollars to four trillion dollars."

That amendment was voted down the next day, to Matt's relief. Then Steve Leaird yielded the floor to Norma Ehrcke, and she outsmarted the Senate.

"This is ASN Newsbreak, 4:00 p.m. Eastern time, Friday, May 20.

"The Senate again has amended the California Treaty, and again Japan is certain to be displeased. The Senate agreed to an amendment that requires Japan to sell boron to the United States at cost and without restriction for twenty years. Boron is mined in the United States only in California, and is essential for synthetic fertilizer and special steels. Though the amendment was proposed by Senator Ehrcke of Pennsylvania, Senate Minority Leader Leaird championed its passage. Senate Majority Leader Fuller and Senator Nakamura of California led the unsuccessful opposition to the measure. The Senate now has twice amended the California Treaty, and it is uncertain whether Japan's government would ratify the amended treaty if the United States ratified the treaty as amended."

It was shortly after five, Friday afternoon, when Barbara pushed her grocery cart out of the supermarket. A faded red pickup was parked next to her car. The truck's hood was up, and she heard two men talking. She turned to unlock her driver door.

Her arm was seized from behind, and something hard and cold was jammed into her side.

"Barbara, I have a gun," said a man's voice she now recognized. Joe, her tow-truck "greeter," said, "Unlock the back door."

"No. You won't shoot me in front of witnesses."

"You sure?" The gun poked her. "Unlock the back door."

Be calm. "You got it, Joe." Bernoulli appeared from behind the pickup and got into the back seat of her car.

Fifteen minutes later, the three people, plus an onion, were in Room 31 of a no-tell motel. Bernoulli put the onion down on a nearby table, and from there picked up a roll of silver duct tape.

Joe had his gun out and trained on Barbara. "Get on your knees, with your hands behind your back."

Bernoulli was watching her eyes as he reached into his pocket and pulled out a switchblade. Snick.

"No!" Still on her knees, she tried to back away—

Joe waved his gun. "Stop."

"Relax," Bernoulli said, "I ain't gonna stab you. Well, unless you make me."

Bernoulli taped her mouth shut, then taped her wrists together. Then he smiled. "It's a crying shame, what's in store for you."

He picked up the onion and cut it in half on the table. From each half he sliced off a disc as thick as his finger. He wiped the blade with his shirt tail, taking time to do a thorough job. With the knife retracted and put away, Bernoulli picked up the two onion discs and stuck them, an inch apart, to a two-foot-long piece of duct tape. Then he smiled at Barbara. "Women put *cucumber* slices on their eyes, right? Grab her head."

She started struggling as soon as Joe touched her. It did no good.

The agony was as if white-hot nails were being pounded into her eyeballs, a new nail each second. She turned her face sideways, trying to brush her face against a shoulder to rub the tape off, but she couldn't make contact. With other tape covering her mouth, she couldn't even scream properly. *I don't want to go blind!*

"Burn, don't they?" Bernoulli purred, as she was pulled to her feet. "Besides, they cover your eyes, which means you—"

She was punched hard in the stomach.

"—have no warning."

"Mmm!" she groaned. *I can't breathe!* She slumped to the floor.

"Your turn," Bernoulli said.

"She isn't breathing, dickhead," Joe said. "Help her stand, so she doesn't suffocate."

"Fuck that. She dies, how mad are our bosses gonna be?"

"When the whole FBI is hunting us? Our orders are to only work her over. Help her stand up."

Barbara was pulled to her feet again. "Now bring her to the corner of the bed," Joe said. She was walked several feet.

"You are pissing me off," Bernoulli said.

"Like I give a rat's ass."

She felt hands grab her shoulders, as a knee was put into her back. Her shoulders were pulled back and pushed forward, and then she could breathe. "You okay?" Joe's voice at her ear asked.

She managed to nod.

The hands let go, then Joe's voice was in front again. "Life is a real bitch sometimes."

Then she was knocked to the floor with a fist to the jaw.

Someone dropped to the floor and rolled her onto her stomach. Her right arm was seized, and pulled back and up. Bernoulli asked, "May I dislocate your shoulder, please?"

"Mmm!"

"I couldn't hear you, sorry. But I'll take that as `yes'." He forced her arm higher back.

"*Mmm!*"

"Or would you prefer I do the left one?" And suddenly it was her other shoulder in agony.

Her upper cheeks were now hot and wet with her own tears—tears caused first by the onions, and now by the tortures. But the duct tape acted as a waterproof seal, and those tears had no place to go.

"That's too much," Joe said. "Let her go."

"Fuck you, you pussy."

She heard the two clacks of an automatic's slide. "Let her go *now*."

"You think you can leap tall buildings because you got a gun? Put that down and we'll see how bad-ass you are."

"Enough to finish the job by myself. Cops won't do shit if I kill *you*."

"You bubble-balls," Bernoulli muttered. "Now I'm *really* pissed off." But Bernoulli let go of Barbara's arm—to slap her hard on the rump. "Hey lady, you ever had Greek?"

"Grow up," Joe said.

Barbara then was rolled over, and a strong arm lifted her to her feet again. "Fank oo, Choe," she mumbled through the tape.

Seconds passed before Joe spoke. "Don't thank me." Her face was slapped hard.

"You're *slapping* her?" Bernoulli said. "Yeah, you're so bad-ass."

"It hurts," Barbara tried to say.

"It does?" Bernoulli asked in sympathy. He giggled; "Then I guess I'll join in." Bernoulli's slap knocked her over. She was dizzy when she tried to stand, but nobody helped her up.

Punch. Slap. Punch. Slap. Meanwhile, Barbara's eyeballs boiled.

Then she heard metallic tinklings. "What's with her car keys?" Bernoulli asked.

From ten feet away Joe said, "I'm making sure nobody leaves while I'm in the bathroom. I've got the motel key, too."

"You worry too goddamn much."

"Why I'm alive. Which reminds me: If she dies in this room, so do you." Barbara heard the bathroom door shut.

"Boy oh boy," Bernoulli said, "I have you all to myself." Her left cheek was pinched hard. "Let's play."

"Mmm!"

"I know, let's play `School.'" A strong hand grabbed one of her wrists, turning it palm-up. The sleeve for that arm was shoved up past her elbow. "I'm in Penmanship class, and I'm practicing my letters. Hm, what do I use for a pen?"

Snick.

He dragged the blade-tip lightly across her forearm. "Hm, my pen's out of ink."

His grip on her wrist tightened. Just below the crook of her arm, the blade-tip stung her, then sliced across and around. He was carving a *B* into her forearm. The blood running down her skin was hot. She clenched her teeth and kept silent.

"Shit, this is so tame. Maybe I should just slice your wrist?" She felt the wet blade-tip there; she stiffened. "Or maybe slice your throat." She felt the flat of the blade on her neck, and she trembled. "Hell, I might just stab you." The knife-tip was at her ribs. She held her breath and braced herself. "Or maybe I won't hurt you at all." The knife-tip left, as she took a deep, shuddering breath.

She heard the toilet flush in the bathroom.

Bernoulli said, "But before I kill you or not, I *am* gonna kill Joe. I hate bossy people and besides, he's ruining the party."

From the bathroom Barbara heard water running in the sink.

"Show time," Bernoulli said. "Excuse me."

A second later, she heard the rattle of the doorknob. "Hey!" Joe said. She heard scuffling, then a man's sharp grunt of pain.

Oh god, Joe's dead! And now I'll be—

"You're killing my arm, motherfucker," said Bernoulli.

"Let go of the knife," Joe said, "or I break something." Something thumped the floor. "You'll get this back after we're done here."

Within minutes, Joe and Bernoulli had returned to punching and slapping Barbara. She heard Bernoulli's voice right by her ear: "You're feeling helpless, hm? Alone? Scared? Bet *that's* no fun."

Both her breasts were squeezed hard. "Hurt, don't they?" Bernoulli said.

"See what happens when you don't listen?" Joe said. "Quit the treaty, got me?" *Slap.*

After a time—minutes later? Days later?—Joe said, "That's enough."

"I think she needs more teaching."

"And what if there's an APB out for her car, huh?"

She heard the clicking of the deadbolt, then the outside door opened. A second later, Bernoulli's voice came from the doorway: "Nobody's outside."

Barbara was grabbed by the arm and dragged outside. Next to her, Joe's voice asked, "Car's back door still unlocked?"

"Hold on. . .yeah," Bernoulli said.

She heard a car door open, then she was shoved in. Her face collided with grocery sacks. She struggled to sit up. "Stay down," Joe told her. She stayed down.

"You forgot her purse, numbskull," Bernoulli said. "That's evidence."

Did they change their minds about not killing me?

She heard footsteps into the room, then out to the car. Something landed with a crash on top of her grocery sacks.

Three car-door slams, the car was started, and her captors drove her away. Barbara fought down car sickness because she couldn't see where they were going. Sometime later the car stopped and the engine was shut off. "No more treaty, understand?" Joe said.

"Because next time," Bernoulli giggled, "we won't play nice."

The driver's door opened. "Don't even think of leaving the car until you hear us drive off," Joe said. "I'll leave your car keys and digital phone where you can see them."

Joe and Bernoulli needn't have worried—by the time Barbara managed to sit up in the back seat, open the door, fall out onto the pavement, and get someone to free her, nearly ten minutes had passed.

The stranger was kind, but no genius. "Here, let me take this horrible blindfold off you." She was pulling the duct tape even as she spoke.

Barbara's hands were free by then, and she tried to push the voice away. "Please, not here, *indoors*—"

Barbara's eyes were exposed. Sunlight made her throw her arms over her eyes and scream.

––––––––––

Barbara was wearing sunglasses in the kitchen while she made breakfast the next morning. The sunglasses didn't set on her face right, because her cheeks were still puffy. Moving—heck, *breathing*—was still painful.

Matt walked into the kitchen from upstairs, his hair wet. "My god," he whispered when he saw her.

"The treaty," she said, as she studied his face. Did he know anything? Would Matt confess now, or would he console?

Matt paused a long time before saying, "The treaty. I see."

He brought the toast, marmalade, orange juice, sugar, and creamer to the table. After she cooked the eggs, he brought the plates to the table. When she sat down and began to eat, so did he. All this time, his eyes kept returning to her face and, when she shuffled about, her body.

When he was through eating, he rinsed his dishes in the sink. He walked into the hallway and got as far as the stair railing, then he turned back to walk over to her at the table. He touched her shoulder.

"Yes?" she said.

He looked into her sunglasses, as he ran a hand through his hair. "I'm sorry." He turned and left.

The place was Hector DeGarcia's office, in the large conference room; the time was two days later, soon after one in the afternoon. Hector's staffers and Barbara were watching CSPAN-2. Barbara no longer was wearing sunglasses.

On television, the presiding officer said, "The yeas are forty-seven and the nays are fifty-three. The amendment that allows American nuclear weapons in and through California, is not agreed to."

Barbara laughed through a twinge of pain. "You have to give Leaird credit for trying."

Sapphira smiled. "I know that's right. All the very same amendments that done got killed in committee, he keep sending them back out on the floor."

Bill sighed. "Where they're struck out again. The price raise to eighty trillion, extending gun laws to nine years afterward, and now this amendment with nuclear weapons in California: Three up, three out."

"Sorry, Bill, but that's four up, three out," Barbara said. "Ehrcke homered with that boron amendment."

On television, Matt rose, even as Fuller was speaking. "Mister President," Matt said.

The presiding officer frowned. "Mister Nakamura, the senior senator from Texas has the floor."

"Mister President, will the majority leader yield two minutes?"

Fuller leaned toward his desk microphone. "Mister President, I yield to the junior senator from California for two minutes."

"Very well. The junior senator from California is recognized for two minutes."

Matt said, "Mister President, I send to the desk an amendment, that essentially gives Japan the choice of buying half of California, for half price, if Japan can't afford the full sixty trillion dollars—"

"*What?*" said Barbara. "What's he up to?"

". . .amendment to the resolution of ratification as follows: Below the text for Article 40, insert ˋArticle 41. Japan may elect, prior to exchanging of ratifications to the treaty, to pay only 1.50 trillion dollars a year for twenty years, instead of three trillion dollars. If Japan chooses this option, then only the portion of California south of the thirty-seventh parallel shall be ceded to Japan, and California north of the thirty-seventh parallel shall remain a state of the United States.'"

Matt took his seat. Dave Fuller seconded Matt's motion, then took his own seat. Senators' voices clamored to be recognized.

Barbara and the rest looked at each other in amazement. Bill raised his eyebrows.

Barbara shook her head. "Sorry, Bill, I have absolutely no idea."

Sapphira nodded. "He gonna make Senator Gibson mad for sure. Whatever ˋBomber' trying, he stupid."

"This is ASN Newsbreak, 4:00 p.m. Eastern time, Monday, May 23.

"Senator Nakamura of California procedurally outsmarted treaty foes in the Senate. This happened minutes ago, when he withdrew his own `pay half, get half' amendment to the California Treaty. His move came just prior to a vote on his amendment, in the last half-hour allowing amendments to the treaty. Impatient senators then demanded that the Senate present early the resolution of ratification for the California Treaty, the final legislative step. The episode of Senator Nakamura's `pay half, get half' amendment is seen in retrospect as a brilliant ploy to prevent treaty opponents from further amending the treaty. The California Treaty now may be amended only by unanimous consent."

Mela's apartment was in a landscaped complex, with colored banners in front of the business office, and late-model cars in the parking lots. That evening, Matt was whistling as he locked his car, walked up to Mela's front door, and rang the doorbell.

When Mela opened the door, she blinked in surprise. "Champagne, Matthew?"

He beamed at her. "The world is beautiful tonight." He gave Mela a quick hug with his free right arm; he was too happy to care if her neighbors saw.

"Goodness," she said with a smile, as she shut the door behind him. "You've never hugged me before."

"Did you see me on CSPAN-2 this afternoon? Leaird and DeGarcia, I made them look like clowns."

"With `buy half, get half,' you mean?"

"Oh, I shut those assholes out, I was brilliant!"

"I'm confused. Your pushing the treaty is only an act."

"Um, yeah. But I need to make the act convincing, and Steve and Hector are worthless."

"May I?" She took the bottle from him and headed for the kitchen.

He sat down on her indigo-blue couch in front of the window, and looked around the living room of the apartment while he waited.

At his knees, the glass-topped coffee table was, as usual, carefully arranged—current issues of *Money*, *Cosmopolitan*, and *Time* magazines each were stacked neatly on their own corner. The coffee table's fourth corner held an ashtray, which was never used or else thoroughly cleaned.

The knickknack shelf had a new addition. Beside the little china cat figurines lay a paperback, *Power!— How to Get It, How to Use It*, with an emery board being used as a bookmark.

Still on a wall was that framed, greatly enlarged photograph. In it, Mela, about twenty years old and wearing a hot bikini, was posing with a lifeguard at the beach. The man must have been Mela's lover—their hands were on each other's butts, and their eyes, their smiles, and their bodies were turned toward each other. The lifeguard was handsome enough to be choosy: He had big muscles, a washboard stomach, a deep tan, and bedroom eyes. Matt always marveled how much smaller Mela's bust was in the picture.

Thinking now about that picture, it surprised Matt. The sex robot pouring his champagne didn't strike him as someone who could ever fall in love.

On a different wall of the apartment was her framed diploma (Master's degree in Business Administration from Kent State). Next to the diploma was that framed travel poster of Vail, Colorado in winter, with mountains in the background. Elsewhere on the wall were framed reproductions of watercolors and an art-gallery poster. Mela had taste.

A minute after she left, Mela returned with a filled champagne glass in each hand. "A toast: to enjoying your work."

"Yeah." They both sipped, and then he looked at her. "Do you enjoy *your* work?"

"Tax law, hours and hours each day? C'mon."

"No, I mean here and now. With me, or Wendall Harland, or whomever."

"Nice try about Harland," she said, smiling. "Do I enjoy servicing you? You have a handsome face, you have the shape of a god, and you always smell clean."

"You used flattery to avoid the question."

"Guilty."

"Then I'll ask another question, and no weaseling: What *don't* you like about being with me?"

"You don't confide in me. I want to know about the real you."

"Like what?"

"What you have nightmares about. What was your favorite Christmas toy. Why you entered politics. Why `Bomber' is an insult, yet you're famous for your bomber jacket."

"The `Bomber' stuff? That's no secret, just a lot of hellish childhood memories. Hey, I'm in a great mood, listen to this. . ."

Mela's blue eyes watched his expressions and gestures as she listened to him. The name of Dennis Goodman, his childhood tormentor, came up often. While Matt was telling his tale, Mela made sympathetic sounds as she stroked his hair. This caring side of her was new to him.

When he fell silent, she stroked his cheek. "How terrible for you. But now you've shown all of them up, the bastards."

Then she unzipped Matt, and knelt between his knees. "Thank you for confiding in me." For an hour after that, she said nothing more.

Sometime during that hour, Matt discovered that when Mela was acting this tender, he loved her.

In the Senate chamber Tuesday afternoon, the majority leader yielded the floor to Matt.

Matt said, "Mister President, I'm happy with the terms of the treaty as they are, so I don't ask for more amendments. However, I wish to send to the desk a *declaration* for the resolution of ratification, to help the deserving people of California.

"You know that I am supporting this treaty because it is what's best for America. Yet this same treaty will cause great suffering in California. I feel my people's pain, and I want to relieve that suffering."

Matt caught Leaird rolling his eyes.

Matt said, "What I propose will enable Californians who want to move away, to do so. Yet it doesn't change either country's rights or obligations.

"Mister President, below the text for Article 40, I move to insert `Declaration: at least ten billion dollars of Japan's first payment shall be used to assist individuals and businesses to relocate from California to states of the United States of America.'"

Matt intended the declaration as a Trojan Horse against Leaird and his ilk. Once Matt's seemingly harmless declaration was agreed to, senators could approve the treaty without feeling guilty. Senators could tell themselves, "If a Californian doesn't like Japan in charge, we'll pay him to move away. The treaty won't really hurt him."

Matt sent his declaration to the desk at one o'clock in the afternoon. By three, the Senate had appended it to the treaty.

At three eleven, the presiding officer recognized Hector DeGarcia.

Hector DeGarcia took a deep breath. "Mister President, I ask my fellow senators to defeat the resolution of ratification. . ."

At four o'clock, when the treaty's track time had ended, DeGarcia still had the floor. ". . .This in turn reminds me of something my high school Government teacher told the class. . ."

Matt was seething.

To kill a filibuster, Senate rules required a written cloture motion. Matt didn't wait for Majority Leader Fuller to start one. Matt needed only sixteen senators' signatures, but he presented many more than that to the clerk at one o'clock Wednesday afternoon. As Hector resumed talking. . .

"This is ASN Newsbreak, 11:00 a.m. Eastern time, Thursday, May 26.

"This just in: A teenage girl has been kidnapped in broad daylight in Washington, D.C. Kelly Eaton, daughter of computer mogul Anthony Eaton, was taken at a convenience store near the hotel where the Eatons were staying. According to witnesses, a thirteen-year-old girl matching Kelly's description was seized by two men in the parking lot of a Shop-N-Dash store, and was carried into a white van. The FBI is investigating. Anthony Eaton is the founder and majority stockholder of Cybersecrets. Kelly Eaton was last seen wearing. . .”

Friday, the Senate convened in chamber at 9:00 a.m. At ten o'clock, as per the rules, the presiding officer asked, "Is it the sense of the Senate that the debate over Senate Resolution 128 shall be brought to a close?"

Matt needed sixty votes to shut up DeGarcia. Sixty-three senators voted to end debate.

Around noon, Barbara was in Hector's large conference room, watching Bill update the whiteboard. She turned at the sound of footsteps, and found Hector next to her, also gazing at the whiteboard. "My filibuster couldn't stop the vote," he said. "But at least I delayed it."

Not quite two-thirds for the treaty, the tallies said, and that gave her an idea. She turned to Hector. "Speaking of delay, I have a plan. Right now the treaty is still on the one-to-four track, right? But soon someone will ask to drop that."

"Of course. Everyone wants to debate the treaty the whole day, so the Senate can run the cloture clock out that much faster."

"Uh-huh." Barbara gave Hector an evil smile. "When someone moves to drop the treaty track, here's what you do. . ."

In the Senate chamber that afternoon, Matt glanced at his watch: 3:56.

Phyllis Lamont was recognized. She said, "Mister President, by the rules, up to twenty-seven more hours of consideration can follow before we have a vote. If we would stay on the tracking system, we'd be here all next week. Of course, what I expect would happen is that we'd take our week off with the resolution of ratification unvoted—but this I don't want.

"I ask unanimous consent that we drop the tracks and remain in executive session until we've voted on the resolution of ratification."

Matt heard sighs, and everyone turned to look at Hector.

Hector stood. Instead of granting or refusing consent, he said, "Mister President, will the junior senator from Wyoming yield for a question?"

Lamont replied, "Mister President, I yield to the senior senator from California for a question."

The Chair said, "The senior senator from California is recognized to ask a question."

"Mister President," Hector asked, "would the junior senator from Wyoming explain whether she plans to 'remain in executive session until we've voted' without a recess? Is she intending an all-nighter?"

Matt fumed. Hector was wasting everyone's time deliberately, with malice aforethought.

Lamont said, "Mister President, I presumed that we would recess this evening, and recess in the afternoon or evening each day thereafter."

Hector wasted more time, by scrupulously and unhurriedly observing the parliamentary forms, to ask another question: "Mister President, would the junior senator from Wyoming explain whether, by `each day thereafter,' she meant tomorrow and Sunday, as well as the weekdays next week?"

Lamont patiently replied that yes, that was what she meant.

Hector again asked, after again sacrificing virgin seconds to the parliamentary gods: "Mister President, would the junior senator from Wyoming explain why she wishes to hasten the vote?"

Matt snorted. *Gee, Hector, she wants this so she can enjoy a week off in Wyoming, without suffering through hours of "helpful advice" how to vote when she returns!*

Lamont said, "Mister President, I read America's mood as impatient to get the California question resolved, and demanding we decide now about the treaty. I would be deeply grateful to my able and distinguished colleague if he again would display his generous nature to agree to dropping the tracks. In this request I speak only for myself, though I suspect others would agree."

Instead of answering Lamont, Hector sat. The presiding officer said, "If there are no objections. . ." His voice trailed off, as he looked at Hector and raised an eyebrow.

Hector sat inexpressive and rock-still.

Five seconds.

Ten seconds.

Almost fifteen seconds—then Hector nodded slightly.

The presiding officer said, "The Senate shall dispense with the 1:00 p.m.-to-4:00 p.m. track and shall remain in executive session, barring recess, until the conclusion of the vote on Senate Resolution 128."

The treaty was debated until six o'clock. The Senate then recessed until Saturday morning.

Matt drifted into the Democratic Cloakroom, where he found Ken Gibson saying goodbye to Dave Fuller. Ken looked sick. "Hey, Matt!"

"Yeah?"

Ken rushed over and whispered, "Hector tricked us."

"*How?*"

"Sylvia says the resolution of ratification's a few votes short. On the Republican side, McCoy says the same. But they also agree that if the vote had been delayed until after the Memorial Day recess, the treaty would pass."

"Money-hungry voters back home would've pushed the wafflers to vote yes."

"Right. So you saw Hector's big act, of reluctantly agreeing to Lamont's motion? What he really agreed to was to doom the treaty."

Less than an hour after the Senate recessed, Matt was sitting in a fire-escape stairwell in the Sheraton Washington. He was talking in Japanese to Asakawa, the lobbyist and go-between.

Asakawa asked, "How much time do we have left?"

"We have only twenty-five more hours of consideration to go, before we vote on the treaty."

"What about delays?"

"Timeouts aren't allowed, no extensions allowed. Anything done solely to delay is ruled out of order."

"Do you think the Senate will take the full allotted time? Maybe people will quit early. After all, isn't this cutting into your planned one-week recess?"

"Hard to say. Amendments are out of order now, so all anyone can do is to make procedural motions and give speeches. Senators' choices are limited."

"Go on."

"Still, I think everybody wants to be on record—they want to look good to the folks back home. I don't foresee many senators passing up their allotted time. So the debate won't end much early, if at all."

"I see."

"But yes, it's cutting into everyone's recess, and they're angry about that. Damn that *hinin-yaroh* DeGarcia anyway!"

Half a floor up, someone opened the fire-stairs door. Matt and Asakawa hushed. After a second, the door shut again.

Matt shoved a piece of paper at Asakawa. "I can't stay much longer. Here's the latest list of who stands where on the treaty."

Asakawa looked over the list. "Senator Young switched from undecided to opposed."

Matt frowned. "Yes, Wife's little trick worked. Young told me that he didn't want Californians coming to his state if it would cost him the next election."

Senator Arbuckle's receptionist was saying, ". . .Just a moment please."

Saturday morning, Barbara was making phone calls from DeGarcia's large conference room. Hector's staffers were hanging on her every word, and they were searching her face for any flicker of expression. She'd already called Senator Young, and her conversation with him had caused grins around the room.

Click. "This is Jack Arbuckle—hello, Barbara, I'm rushed, can't talk long! How you?" Jack was talking as fast as a tobacco auctioneer.

Barbara sped up her speech to match. "Fine, Jack. You?"

"I'm great! Treaty again?"

"Yes, Jack. Vote against that monster!"

"Still undecided, Barbara!"

"Vote's soon, Jack, decide soon!"

"Nah, flipped a coin before, maybe I will again! Gotta run, Barbara!"

"Bye, Jack!" Jack hung up, Barbara slowed her brain back to normal, then she touch-toned another phone number.

"This is Senator Frost's office."

"Hello, this is Barbara Nakamura, may I speak to the senator, please?. . .Good morning, Victoria, how are you?. . .The treaty, right, how'd you guess?. . .That `We Won't Forget' campaign back in California is *deadly* serious, Victoria. . . .You're right, Matt can throw away his seat if he wants, but there's no reason why *you* should. . . .You will? Thank you *very* much, and Californians thank you, too."

Barbara smiled as she broke the connection. She touch-toned another number.

"Senator Wagner's office, this is Lorinda. How may I direct your call?"

"Hello, this is Barbara Nakamura. Where's Colleen? She usually answers when I call."

"Her little girl has to go to the doctor. May I help you, Mrs. Nakamura?"

"Yes, may I speak to Senator Wagner, please?"

"Just a moment, please."

Twenty seconds on hold, then Lorinda came back on the line. "Hello, Mrs. Nakamura? Senator Wagner told me to tell you, `I intend to support my president and my party and vote for the treaty. Also, I don't appreciate receiving letters from Californians threatening to vote me out. Still, Penny and I will be glad to meet anytime with you and Matt, on a *strictly social* basis.'"

Barbara sighed. "Okay, Lorinda, thanks. Tell Colleen I hope her daughter gets well soon." Barbara hung up.

She glanced at the whiteboard, and that's when she realized: California was safe! She turned to Bill, who was waiting at the whiteboard with marker in hand. "Change Frost and Young both to `AGAINST.' That means"—shrieks around the room forced her to shout—"*thirty-five!*" She knew she was grinning like an idiot.

People around the room were clapping, were hugging, and were jumping up and down. Several men started singing "California Girls."

Sapphira was hugging everyone in the room, especially Barbara. "California stay a state, that what be important! We here gots jobs, and we from California gots homes to go to."

While Sapphira hugged, Bill erased and scribbled. Now the whiteboard read: sixty-three for, thirty-five against, and only Arbuckle and Hutton undecided.

Almost unheard in the Mardi Gras uproar, the phone rang. Bill answered it and turned to Barbara. "Elena asks if you could come see her. Head receptionist's desk."

Soon Barbara was there. "Yes, Elena. Do I have a call?"

"No—no, it's that I can't leave my desk." Elena's cheeks were wet. She took Barbara's hand and crushed it. "Everyone we know was so scared for such a long time—but now we don't need to be. We girls thank you, my family thanks you, and my friends thank you."

Elena made a gesture to include the telephone and the computer on her desk. "People back in California thank you. Do you know people are talking `Barbara for senator in 2006'?"

Barbara's mouth fell open. After a second, she said, "No. I didn't know that."

Tracie, the youngest receptionist, smiled. "I'm sure Californians would elect you."

Wanda, the third receptionist, smiled an evil smile. "Even if you were divorced."

Over in Matt's own office, Diane was telling him, "Mister Senator? It's the White House on the phone."

Matt took the call in his private office, and the White House operator promptly put him on hold. For half a minute, Matt wondered why Charlie had called him. Matt listed three possibilities—all were wrong.

"Goddamn, `Bomber,'" Swensen roared, "you have some explaining to do!"

Never before had Charlie called him "Bomber." Matt's voice didn't show his alarm: "What needs explaining, Charlie?"

"You know a guy named Asakawa?"

Matt gulped. It took effort to slip into Tone of Voice Six (Casual): "No, afraid the name doesn't ring a bell."

"Dammit, this is no time for games."

"Hold on, it just came back to me. He's a foreign lobbyist."

"For *Japan*. When's the last time you talked to him?"

"Asakawa? Gosh, I don't know. Three, four months ago."

"Listen, you can lie to the voters, you can lie to other senators, you can lie to your wife, your mother, and your little puppy dog—you're an adult. But now is *not* the time to lie to me, understand?"

"You've just insulted your best Senate ally."

"Matt, shut up for your own good. You listening?"

Matt's voice was as surly as a teenager's: "Yeah, I'm listening."

"I have on my desk a most interesting FBI report. Asakawa walks into the lobby of the Sheraton Washington Hotel at 6:35 yesterday evening. He immediately takes an elevator up to the fourth floor. You walk into the lobby at 6:39, and immediately take an elevator up to the second floor. At 6:51, Asakawa steps into the elevator from the second floor, goes down to the lobby, and immediately leaves the hotel. At 6:52, you ride the elevator down from the third floor and immediately leave the hotel. Report says the surveillance team was sure it was Asakawa—"

"Yeah? How?"

"Seems he carries his briefcase under his arm, instead of by the handle—makes him easy to I.D., even at a distance."

It wasn't *fair*, Matt had been so careful, so discreet! To regain control with Swensen, Matt went on the attack: "You sent the FBI *spying* on me?"

"You heard about the rescue of that kidnapped girl, I assume. The FBI filmed one of her kidnappers on dijvid, picking up his ransom. Your bad luck, it was in the same hotel, at the same time as your meeting—"

"Except that I haven't admitted to meeting with Mister Asakawa."

"Once a lawyer, always a lawyer. Anyway, the kidnapper's every step inside the hotel—including in the elevators—was caught with hidden FBI cameras. But replaying the dijvids, the agents noticed weird stuff with you and Asakawa. How is it you both arrived and left around the same times, and you each rode the elevator up to one floor yet rode the elevator down from a different floor?"

Admit nothing. "Your argument is speculative."

"But backed up with two facts. Asakawa wasn't registered at the hotel, at least under his real name. And you're famous enough now that the front-desk people would remember if *you'd* registered, and they say you didn't.

"Me, I have no idea what's going on with you and Asakawa. I *know* you're not queer. Whatever you two are up to, you're a fool after all the garbage that Barbara's been saying. So do you know what will really, *really* piss me off?"

Matt had no choice but to act meek. "What, Mister President?"

"If the press discovers you're sneaking around with the Japanese government. Understand what I'm saying? Stay away from Asakawa!"

———

"This is ASN Newsbreak, 12:00 noon Eastern time, Saturday, May 28.

"The Senate currently is in session to deliberate the California Treaty. Most senators expect the Senate to be convened on Sunday as well. If this happens, final voting on treaty approval would occur by Tuesday at the latest.

"The president this morning pledged to Democratic senators, `Vote for the treaty, and when you come up for re-election, I will work tirelessly to assist you in your campaign.'. . ."

"In international news, Syrian Prime Minister Ibrihim Al-Amin also wants to buy nuclear missiles from Russia. Prime Minister Al-Amin made public today his repeated offers to Russian President Dimitrov to buy Russian nuclear weapons at the same prices the United States would pay. According to Al-Amin, Dimitrov has repeatedly declined to sell such weapons to Syria. Al-Amin labeled Dimitrov's refusal as hypocritical, and accused Russia of violating the Non-Proliferation Treaty of 1968. The Non-Proliferation Treaty stops countries that have nuclear weapons from selling them or helping another country to develop its own nuclear weapons. The Non-Proliferation Treaty also stops countries that don't have nuclear weapons from buying or developing them."

"This is ASN Newsbreak, 1:00 p.m. Eastern time, Saturday, May 28.

"President Swensen joined Russia in defending that nation from Syria's accusation that Russia is violating the Non-Proliferation Treaty. White House spokesman Bob Garner stated only minutes ago, `START III is not a violation of the Non-Proliferation Treaty.' Russian President Dimitrov's office just issued a similar statement: `The START III treaty selling nuclear weapons to the United States will benefit the Russian people, the American people, and all peoples of the world. The proposed START III treaty fulfills the Non-Proliferation Treaty's intent: disarmament.'"

"This is ASN Newsbreak, 2:00 p.m. Eastern time, Saturday, May 28.

"Our lead story is from Syria: Syria now is threatening to build nuclear weapons if it can't buy them. In a nationwide address ten minutes ago, Syrian Prime Minister Al-Amin repeated his accusation that Russia is violating the Non-Proliferation Treaty. He said, `That treaty requires "each [nuclear nation] not to transfer to any recipient whatsoever nuclear weapons." That includes recipients who are themselves nuclear nations.' Al-Amin then declared, `Since our security needs are urgent, and since both Russia and the United States are parties to violation of the Non-Proliferation Treaty, we see no reason to honor the Treaty. Exercising our right under Article Ten of the Non-Proliferation Treaty, the Syrian Arab Republic shall withdraw from the Non-Proliferation Treaty three months from now. At that time we either will begin nuclear-weapon development, or will buy nuclear weapons from Pakistan.'"

"This is ASN Newsbreak, 4:00 a.m. Eastern time, Sunday, May 29.

"Russia has just told Syria in effect, `You can't buy our missiles now, but we'll let you buy them later.' In response to Syria's threat to become a rogue nuclear power, Russian President Dimitrov said that he shall give the United States exclusive rights to buy two thousand Russian nuclear warheads and their delivery systems for a two-year period after the START III treaty takes effect. After this two-year period, warheads not purchased by the United States may be bought by Syria at the same prices that the United States pays. However, Dimitrov's offer is made only if Syria shall otherwise remain in conformity with the Non-Proliferation Treaty."

"This is ASN Newsbreak, 9:00 a.m. Eastern time, Sunday, May 29.

"International tensions remain high as Syria stays mum on whether that nation will accept Russia's offer. Instead of accepting or refusing Russia's offer to sell missiles to Syria after a two-year delay, Syrian Prime Minister Ibrihim Al-Amin demanded today an explanation why Russia is giving the United States a two-year head start over Syria, Russia's longstanding ally. A Russian government spokesman explained, 'As Prime Minister Al-Amin was told privately, selling nuclear weapons to Syria at this time could seriously destabilize the entire Middle East region.' When questioned why nuclear weapons were being sold to the United States, a former enemy, the spokesman said, 'The Russian government trusts the United States to destroy the nuclear weapons.'

"In national news, the Senate is convening now for today's deliberations on the California Treaty. . ."

"This is ASN Newsbreak, 10:00 a.m. Eastern time, Sunday, May 29.

"This just in: Syria has accepted Russia's offer. Syrian Prime Minister Ibrihim Al-Amin just announced he would accept the offer made by Russian President Dimitrov to sell missiles to Syria after a two-year delay."

"This is ASN Newsbreak, 11:00 a.m. Eastern time, Sunday, May 29.

"International tensions resume: Now that Syria can buy Russian nuclear weapons, Israel wants to buy them, too. Israel has just announced that it intends to buy Russian nuclear weapons when Russia lets Syria buy them. . ."

"This is ASN Newsbreak, 2:00 p.m. Eastern time, Sunday, May 29.

"More Middle East nations have joined the Russian-warhead stampede. Following Israel's announcement that it intends to buy Russian nuclear weapons when Russia allows Syria to buy them, Egypt, Iraq, Libya, and the United Arab Emirates have announced that they also shall buy Russian nuclear weapons. . ."

"In national news, the Senate remains in session at this hour, deliberating the California Treaty. . ."

"This is ASN Newsbreak, 3:00 p.m. Eastern time, Sunday, May 29.

"Still more Middle East nations want to buy Russian nuclear weapons. In response to Israeli and Iraqi announcements today that they intend to buy

Russian nuclear weapons, both Iran and Saudi Arabia have just declared their intent to buy Russian nuclear weapons. Even Kuwait. . .”

Al-Amin, I could kiss you, Matt thought. *You brought me the senators whom sixty trillion couldn't tempt.*

Even when the Senate was in session, senators could be found elsewhere than in the Senate chamber. Matt found Doug Young and Victoria Frost in the Senate lobby; these two were sitting on a black leather couch, watching TV—

“This is ASN Newsbreak, 4:00 p.m. Eastern time, Sunday, May 29.

“Could the California Treaty solve the problem of the upcoming Middle East nuclear buyout? Every nation in the Middle East has expressed interest in buying Russian nuclear missiles in 2007. In response, President Swensen just issued a statement: ˋI urge the Senate to approve the California Treaty, to give us money to snap up Russian nukes. When Syria, Israel, and everyone show up in Moscow in 2007, all I want them to hear is “Sorry, sold out.”’

“In Kansas, a tornado ripped through. . .”

Matt gestured at the TV almost behind him. “Vicki, Doug, you heard Charlie. You still saying no?”

Victoria Frost frowned. “Mister Lincoln never had this problem. Yesterday morning the choice was easy: Preserve the Union. But now?”

Doug Young sighed. “Hell, I'm just worried about displaced Californians voting me out.”

Matt put on a sympathetic smile. “Folks, I understand. But please consider: Is it wise to enable OPEC to vaporize itself?”

"This is ASN Newsbreak, 5:00 p.m. Eastern time, Sunday, May 29.

"The Senate has just finished deliberations on the California Treaty, and begins the vote on treaty approval. This vote comes two days earlier than expected. Experts speculate that the recent crisis. . ."

Senator DeGarcia's staffers and Barbara were watching live coverage of the floor vote on NBC. The mood in DeGarcia's large conference room was relaxed, even festive—

With one exception. Barbara asked Sapphira, "Why the serious look?"

"Because I's nervous."

Bill looked confused. "Isn't it locked up? Thirty-five-plus votes against?"

Sapphira shook her head. "Syria and everybody buying nukes, that sure to done changed some minds here. How many, how few, can't nobody guess."

Sapphira's words put a pall on the happy mood. Noting this, Barbara replied, "I'm sure everything will be fine."

On television, the presiding officer said, "The clerk will read the title of the resolution of ratification."

The legislative clerk announced, "Senate Resolution 128, 'Resolution of Ratification to the Treaty between Japan and the United States of America, on the Sale of California.'"

The presiding officer said, "The yeas and nays have been ordered. The resolution requires two-thirds of those present and voting to carry. Fifteen minutes will be allotted for voting. The clerk will call the roll."

"Mister Abernathy," the legislative clerk said. Abernathy approached the platform. A moment later the clerk said, "Mister Abernathy, nay."

At the bottom of the television screen, the score read, "Yea: 0, Nay: 1, NV: 99, Time remaining: 14:54."

Barbara laughed. "That's a good start."

Soon the hundredth name had been called; Doug Young had voted nay. The score at the bottom of the screen read, "Yea: 48, Nay: 26, NV: 26, Time remaining: 10:43." Arbuckle, Frost, Vaughn, and Wagner, among others, had not yet voted. For Barbara and the others at the anti-treaty command post, the only disappointment had been when previously undecided Hutton had voted yea. Yet only Sapphira worried about the outcome.

———

Eleven minutes later, suspense made seconds drip. Then on television the legislative clerk said, "Mister Vaughn, nay."

Yea: 63. Nay: 34. Not voted: 3.

Thirty-four nay votes killed the treaty.

Pandemonium broke out in Hector's large conference room: hugging, clapping, cheering, singing, and jumping up and down. Sapphira, Bill, and Barbara improvised a high-kicking chorus line.

On television, Wagner approached the legislative clerk. A second later the clerk announced, "Mister Wagner, yea."

Yea: 64. Nay: 34.

Barbara smiled, unconcerned. "No sweat." Sapphira gave Barbara a hard look.

On television, Doug Young approached the clerk. This puzzled Barbara, for Doug already had voted. *Nah, it can't be.*

But it was. "Mister Young, yea."

"He changed his vote!" Bill said.

Barbara frowned. "The Russian nukes, that's what changed his mind." Sapphira nodded agreement.

Then Barbara smiled at worried faces. "We'll still make it okay."

Bill bit his lip. "I'm not sure anymore."

Yea: 65. Nay: 33.

On television, Victoria Frost approached the clerk. Barbara glanced at the whiteboard. "We need another nay, but she's gonna hand it to us."

On television, the clerk said, "Mrs. Frost, yea."

Sapphira sighed. "Man, I hates being right."

"Oh my God," Bill whispered. "Two-thirds."

Yea: 66. Nay: 33. NV: 1. Time remaining: 2:38.

Barbara's eyes ransacked the whiteboard. "C'mon, who hasn't voted? Arbuckle. Treaty passes unless Arbuckle votes nay."

On television, Arbuckle approached the clerk.

"*Will* he vote nay?" Bill asked.

Barbara sighed. "Don't know. He joked he'd flip a coin." She took Sapphira's hand, and Bill's hand, and squeezed them hard.

In the Senate chamber, Matt saw Jack Arbuckle take a breath. But Arbuckle wasn't allowed to speak.

"*Save California!*" someone yelled.

In one of the visitors' galleries, a young man and woman were yelling and each shaking a fist, while they held a California flag over the railing of their gallery.

Matt was offended by such misbehavior: yelling in the gallery, and hanging anything over the railing, both were against Senate rules.

"*Dollars and jobs!*" someone else in the galleries yelled back.

The presiding officer banged his handleless gavel on the desk. "Quiet! I order the galleries to be quiet! Remove that flag."

"*Vote yea, save Massachusetts!*" bellowed a third gallery voice.

Californians began stomping their feet, while clapping, while chanting. "Nay!"-stomp-clap. "Nay!"-stomp-clap.

The presiding officer banged his gavel again. "Quiet! *Quiet!* We shall have quiet, or the visitors' galleries shall be cleared!"

By then, the pro-treaty onlookers also were stomping while clapping and chanting. The Senate chamber shook from a self-made earthquake.

The presiding officer was gaveling steadily. "*Sergeant at Arms! Clear the galleries!*"

"Yea!"-stomp-clap. "Nay!"-stomp-clap.

And then the galleries were filled with Capitol Police. *About time those California hooligans were shut up*, Matt thought.

Clearing the galleries took a while. Time for voting almost had expired when someone screamed, "*Save California!*", a door slammed, and then the chamber regained silence.

"Mister Arbuckle?" the legislative clerk asked.

Sixty trillion dollars, Jack. As tens and twenties, sixty trillion would fill a trainload of boxcars. Now picture one of those boxcars unloaded in Oklahoma—how do you think Oklahomans would remember you on Election Day? Imagine all that, and your vote is easy.

On television the legislative clerk asked, "Mister Arbuckle?" Barbara was holding her breath.

Only the time had changed on the score: "Yea: 66, Nay: 33, NV: 1, Time remaining: 0:07." Arbuckle took a breath and stood straight. He spoke to the clerk.

The clerk announced, "Mister Arbuckle, yea."

Barbara sighed. "Damn you, Matt."

On television, the presiding officer was saying, ". . .sixty-seven, the nays are thirty-three, and the resolution of ratification is agreed to."

About which, the Variety-Show Host joked—

Since the vote, the Japanese are flocking into California. On the San Diego Freeway yesterday, there was a four tour-bus pileup. Meanwhile, the McDonald's down the street quit cooking their Filet-O-Fish Sandwich.

Some Californians already are acting Japanese. Rumor has it that the Lakers will require their opponents to remove their shoes on the basketball court.

CHAPTER 9
Heisei 17-nen 5-gatsu 30-nichi, Getsuyohbi (Monday, May 30, 2005)

It was very late Monday evening in Yokohama. On a side street in the entertainment district was a modest little bar, "Mister *Tora*." Outside the bar, its plain sign was unnoticeable in the thicket of its gaudy brethren. Inside the bar, one found no karaoke setup, no beautiful and flirty hostesses, and no expense-account big spenders. Instead inside were a bartender and six customers. Four were local men, silent and solitary drinkers all. The other two customers were singing.

> *Matsumoto Robotics!*
> *We make precision, we build excellence,*
> *We put spirit into motors and chips.*
> *We are gods of robotics.*

Ryuuji gave Hiroshi a pickled smile. "This drinking party was a smart idea, Iwata-*kun*."

Hiroshi shook his head. "Don't thank smarts, thank *ninjoh*," what I want. "I've wanted to celebrate since I watched the Senate vote this morning. Even Section Manager Masumi couldn't spoil my mood."

"I noticed your cheerfulness today. Certainly you were cheerful enough at lunch to walk over by where Programmer Higashi was eating. What did you tell her?"

"I told her she wore a very pretty hat to work this morning. It was dark red, my favorite color."

"And you still insist you're shy around her? You sly badger. Have you asked her on a date yet?"

"Soon." Hiroshi hurried to change the subject: "Hey, let's make a toast. To brave Senator Nakamura."

Ryuuji raised his glass. "I drink to the health of brave Senator Nakamura."

At that moment, brave Senator Nakamura was grinning in a First Class seat somewhere between Washington and Los Angeles. It was Monday morning in America, and it was morning in his mood.

Huge gift, I'll get a huge gift! I wonder what it'll be? Money? Real estate? Six months a year of expenses-paid vacation at the Imperial Palace?

And while I dream, Barbara has exiled herself in Coach with the rabble. I want to laugh and do cartwheels to the bathrooms and back, while she acts like she licked a toad.

In Yokohama, Ryuuji lifted his glass. "I drink to the health of brave Senator Nakamura." He drank. "My own toast now: to no more worries about his witch wife."

Hiroshi's expression went from silly to solemn. "I'll drink with you, but I fear you're mistaken."

"Oh?"

"Mrs. Nakamura doesn't believe herself a witch. Besides, she wants enough to kill the treaty to press on, and she knows enough about Japan to be resourceful. I'm sure she's building a new plan."

Meanwhile in Coach Section of the passenger jet, Barbara was racking her brain for new ideas how to kill the California Treaty.

"We Won't Forget" almost worked. She could try that again: threaten a boycott. That's it, she'd organize a boycott in California of Japanese products, to last until the Diet voted down the treaty. The boycott would turn Japanese business against the treaty, and the Diet would kill the treaty.

But what if the boycott wasn't painful enough? Worse, what if Americans in the Remaining States bought *more* Japanese goods, in order to sabotage California's boycott?

Damn—a boycott wouldn't work. She had to keep hunting for an idea that *would* work.

"And now, covering the news San Diego needs to know, this is News Eight at four."

Hours later Monday afternoon, Barbara was halfheartedly watching TV in the San Diego house. Meanwhile, she wholeheartedly was waiting for Carol to arrive. Barbara needed her friend's company.

Barbara was alone; Matt had raced off as soon as they'd arrived home. For once, though, Matt's absence was a relief: Barbara still didn't want to talk to him.

The TV anchor looked solemn. "Good afternoon. We begin with new developments concerning the California Treaty. First, Japan's Prime Minister Sasaki announced today he was approving the Senate's amendments, pending Diet approval of the entire amended treaty. Had the prime minister rejected the Senate amendments, the California Treaty would have been null and void. . ."

Barbara sighed. "Sorry, Steve. But thanks for trying."

". . .opposition leader Hideo Yamamura blasted the California Treaty today, calling it destructive to Japan." A clip showed a Japanese man in his fifties speaking. Barbara wanted to hear his words, but the voice-over translator was too loud: "The treaty will destroy Japan's economy, and we'll need crushing taxes to pay for it—"

The doorbell rang, and Barbara ran to the door. Carol Parks stood there with a sympathetic smile, and arms apart for a hug. Barbara said, "Carol, I feel so much better now."

The women hugged. Barbara asked, "How'd you convince the paper to let you out of your cage? Isn't the *Union-Tribune* hours from copy deadline?"

"Two words: `week's vacation'. Besides, they can't complain tomorrow when I fax in an in-depth exclusive. With hard-hitting questions like `Mrs. Nakamura, how do you feel now?'"

"Carol, I don't know strong enough words. I feel like I was raped by a man I thought was in prison."

"Doctor Carol prescribes a change of scenery. Grab your gear and let's go. Besides," Carol said, smiling, "we have all this Washington flab to tighten."

Barbara looked down her nose at Carol. "Is that so? And how many calories do *editors* burn off, just talking and typing all day? Hold on a sec." Barbara scooped up the remotes for the TV and cable.

". . .California sued today in the Supreme—"

———

". . .in the Supreme Court to have the treaty declared unconsti—" Click.

Carol began bouncing with excitement. "Congratulate me, Larry and I are getting married!"

"You *are*? Details!"

"Yesterday afternoon, I called Larry. Right after those idiot senators okayed the treaty, so at one point I said, `This makes me so unhappy.' `Well,' he said, `I know something that will cheer you up—or make you feel worse.' `What?' He said, `Did you hear my knee just pop? I want to marry you.'"

"I am so glad for you. Set a date?"

Carol's face turned serious. "Yes, Thursday at two in the afternoon, at a Justice of the Peace. We're afraid if we wait a month for a big church wedding, maybe can't get married." At Barbara's puzzled look, she explained, "Might be different laws in effect."

"C'mon, Carol, what laws?"

"I know it sounds silly. But if we're already married, we can't have any problems, right?"

"You're right, it makes no difference. Carol, if it's Thursday, then I can attend it! I've so much looked forward to meeting Larry."

Then Barbara sighed. "Even in your wedding plans, we come right back to discussing the treaty."

A few minutes later, Carol and Barbara drove by a moving-truck rental lot, where a line of people had grown far out the door. Barbara was reminded of fleeing refugees, each clutching his possessions.

The two women arrived at the health club. Fifteen minutes later, they had changed clothes and were pedaling adjacent stationary bikes. Barbara wasn't sweating yet, but her face and throat were flushed. "So tell me the news in San Diego."

"Usual stuff: weddings and funerals, conventions, infighting in the El Cajon mayor's office. No ground-breaking ceremonies, obviously."

"I'm sure." Barbara looked away.

Carol reached over to squeeze her hand. "Last few days have been rough on you."

"And rough on forty million other people."

Barbara and Carol were showered, dressed, and on the road an hour later. The two women made an emergency dash to a shoe store, so Carol could buy wedding footwear. At the cash register, the manager asked Barbara if Japan taxed shoes.

Back in the car again, Carol smiled and said, "Let me introduce you to Larry, okay?"

Larry had a nice house. He also had a nice bodybuilder shape; and full, thick, gray hair with memories of brunette. Barbara put on a good front, but Carol and Larry's clear affection for each other only made her want to go home.

Carol walked Barbara to her front door slightly before ten. The friends said goodbye in front of a dark house; Matt still wasn't home.

The next morning, Barbara sat in the kitchen of the San Diego house. She was sipping coffee, listening to the radio, and regretting her treaty-fighting performance. Matt was asleep, having come in drunk and belligerent at four in the morning.

I know people in Hollywood, Barbara thought. *How can I use those connections to spike the treaty?*

In the background the radio blared, "Did you know that the transmissions on some cars will break down if pulling a moving trailer? Absolutely free, at Tran and Nguyen Transmission, we'll tell you whether your car can manage a moving trailer, or if you'll need to rent a truck. . . ." Ten seconds later, the ad finished, "Don't risk an expensive transmission breakdown when you're driving alone through the desert. Tran and Nguyen Transmission—shops with convenient hours in La Mesa, El Cajon, and Pacific Beach."

Barbara thought, *Here's an idea. Hollywood stars who are popular in Japan hold a press conference in Tokyo, and explain why the treaty's a bad deal. I'm sure Derrick Russell would go.*

For Matt in the bedroom meanwhile, this was the "morning after" a truly worthless night. The main reason why: In the past eighteen hours, he hadn't been sucked or fucked once.

Since his marriage in his final year of law school, and certainly since he had announced his candidacy for Congress, Matt never had needed to work at finding a one-night stand. Always in the last seventeen years some stunner, her tits and ass and face still under warranty, had been willing to overlook that this Washington insider had a wife somewhere.

But not last night. Socially, he was in the ninth circle of Hell.

At his usual gold mine, bars near the universities, he had struck out. Before then, he'd been zero-for-three at three shopping malls.

Strip clubs had been no better luck. At the last one, he had chosen one particular runway dancer, a tall and athletic temptress with the mane of a lion and the prowl of a lioness. Yet she had looked through him as if he weren't there, and had glided past his five-dollar bill.

An instant later, his luck had turned worse. Matt had been jerked back at the shoulder by an overweight man wearing a Peterbilt cap. "You tha' traitor Nakamura?" Matt had run away then, to prevent being beat up. A thrown beer bottle had hit him in the back as he had been trying to unlock his car. The back of his shirt thereafter had smelled of beer, and he was sure he had a bruise.

All that had been last night. Now his head hurt, and the sunlight burned his eyes. His mouth felt as if it were filled with weevil-infested cotton, and tasted as if a sick dog had pissed in it. Meanwhile, Barbara's radio in the kitchen was blasting way too loud.

"This morning I can't solve my other problems, but I'll make *damned* sure Barbara shows the breadwinner some consideration." He lurched toward the kitchen.

In the kitchen, Barbara's radio asked with concern, "Are you *looking* for another job outside California? Are you *thinking* about looking for another job? Are you a professional? Then you'll need a professional résumé that highlights your skills. At Corner City Résumé, our résumés are computer-printed, and ready. . ."

Barbara was looking through the kitchen window into the back yard, while the radio played in the background. She was thinking that her plan didn't need only actors, California had many *musicians* popular in Japan. She could organize a series of free concerts in Japan, and between sets she'd slip the commercial in: "Hey Japan, the treaty is a bad idea."

Her thinking was disrupted by Matt's voice behind her. "I *really* am not feeling well this morning, so would it inconvenience you to crank down that *fucking* radio?"

Barbara turned. There stood Matt in the kitchen, needing a shave, his hair a mess, and his breath smelling like someone had poured whisky down a sewer. His bloodshot eyes glared at her.

She picked up the milk off the kitchen table, and strolled to the fridge. "I'll *think* about it, since you asked so *fucking* nicely."

Matt nodded at the radio. "I can hardly hear your yap over the foghorn. Not that your prattle's worth zip since you narcked to Carol."

"Radio's too loud? You have a problem then. The pyramid slaves went on strike a second ago."

"I don't know what you're talking about, nor do I care, so shut the hell up. Goddamn, I told you to turn that radio down!"

Without thinking, she started to reach for the radio at the refrigerator-end of the kitchen counter. Right in front of the volume knob, her hand stopped.

Maybe it was the stress she'd been under for almost two months. Maybe it was the emotional roller coaster she'd ridden because of the treaty vote, over the weekend. Maybe it was seeing Carol and Larry obviously in love last night. Maybe it was the disgust she felt at his appearance this morning.

No more.

She whirled on Matt. Her finger pointing at his face, five feet away, was aimed like her nightstand pistol. "No, I *refuse* to shut up. You sold out everyone to win the huge gift. Do you realize the cost now? How's it feel to be spit on, Matt? Did you figure on that?"

"I said *shut the hell up*, Barbara!" His voice shook.

She stepped closer. "So now no Californians want anything to do with you. Attorney Nakamura got the cuties, Candidate Nakamura got the cuties, and Representative Nakamura got the cuties. Senator Nakamura *used to* get the cuties. But now Senator Benedict Arnold has to sleep alone, and his feelings are hurt. You didn't figure on that."

"Barbara. . .," he growled too quietly.

"You threw away the only thing that makes you attractive. It's been years since your technique kept a woman coming back."

"Shut the *goddamned motherfucking* hell up!" His fists were clenched now.

Her anger was spent. Her voice became quiet, thoughtful: "When we were dating, I believed you were in law school to help people. Silly of me. Know why I fell in love? You were handsome, you were attentive, you were at ease with people, you were Japanese like me. Plus, you could make my blood boil with simply a glance or a touch."

His mouth twitched a small lustful smile.

Unconsciously she drifted back to the kitchen table. She picked up the jar of strawberry jam and screwed the lid back on. "That was another mistake I made. I thought it was passion and love for me that made you a skillful lover then. When I learned what a Don Juan you were, I thought it was a phase. I thought if I were a good wife, you'd grow out of it. You never have. First I loved you, Matt. Then for many years I switched—loving you one day, and the next day feeling nothing for you. Now I see you stripped of your masks and costumes, and you're only pathetic. I only feel pity for you."

In two lightning steps he was in front of her. His fist to the side of her face—

"*No!*"

—sent her sprawling across the kitchen table.

She dropped the jam jar. Dishes crashed to the floor, and hot coffee burned against her arm. Her jaw, her teeth, her lip—the pain! A salt shaker rolled off of the table.

"Uh. . ."

She found herself lying on her right side on the kitchen table. The left side of her face hurt. A spoon was pressing against her right boob. She pushed herself up to resume a normal standing position, and discovered she had a headache. Her hip felt bruised where she'd hit the edge of the table. She tasted blood in her mouth. One sleeve of her robe felt heavy, hot, and wet—it was coffee-soaked.

On the radio, a woman was singing, "Man, I gave you my number, so won't you please call?" Glass crunched beneath her house slipper. Strawberry jam was splattered about the kitchen floor.

Matt jutted his chin out. "I *told* you to shut up. That's also for humiliating me at the strip club." She saw anger there. Did she also see fear and uncertainty? She wasn't sure.

Matt spun to face the radio and, with a twist of the wrist, turned it off. "I also owed you big time for ratting to Carol," he said over his shoulder.

"*Damn you*, Matt." It was all she could trust herself to say.

In the bathroom, she wanted to shriek like a madwoman. She wanted to brain Matt with a hammer, see his red blood on the kitchen floor mix with the red strawberry jam. She wanted to scream curses as the police hauled him away in handcuffs and leg-irons. She wanted to bawl.

Instead, she rinsed her mouth with antiseptic mouthwash, then took two pills for her headache.

She cleaned up the mess in the kitchen while she ignored Matt. She watched Matt, who likewise did not speak to her, stomp out the front door. She showered and dressed. She threw the few dirty clothes, including her caffeinated bathrobe, into the washer. She dried the load, hung some clothes up, folded some clothes, and ironed some clothes. By then her thoughts were no longer awhirl.

She found her digital phone and speed-dialed Carol's digital. "Talk to me," Barbara heard.

"Hey, Carol. What, you're talking on the phone instead of romping Larry's brains out?"

"Barbara dear, after 965 times since midnight, we thought we needed a break. Anyway, sounds like *you're* in a happy mood."

"Actually, quite the opposite," Barbara said. "I'm filing for divorce."

"Matt stayed out late and got drunk," Ed said, walking as he talked. "He slugged you this morning during an argument. You called Carol, then you hired a divorce lawyer, and you're filing for divorce."

Barbara nodded during her own pacing. "Exactly."

Barbara was in her parents' living room that evening. Both she and her father were orbiting his green easy-chair.

Takeko sat in the other green chair, wrinkled hands folded in her lap, her face almost expressionless. Takeko's mouth held the hint of a frown, and the skin between her brows was wrinkled more—Barbara saw that her mother was angry. Takeko had not spoken a word since Barbara had reported the morning's events.

Barbara said, "I told Matt everything that had been bothering me. He'd never heard me talk so frankly."

Ed nodded. "Yeah, many times I wished you would tell Matt off, but you always kept quiet."

Barbara glanced at her mother and resumed her prowling. "The other reason I think he hit me is he finally realized: He is *so hated* here in California. I can tell he's upset."

Ed's smile was ironic. "You called Carol. Know what that means? Your divorce will be on the front page of tomorrow's *Union-Tribune*, then all over the U.S. and Japan within the hour."

Barbara shrugged. "I don't think telling Carol changed anything. It would've taken a few more days otherwise, that's all. Still, remind me not to talk to journalists when I'm emotional—I miss Tiffani."

Takeko broke her silence. "Why you say in a few days the news in the paper if you not tell Carol?"

"Some reporter always is assigned to go through the legal notices. He would've spotted my divorce petition and written a story. That is, if the courthouse clerk didn't call a TV station first."

Takeko stood on bowed legs and eyed Barbara. "Maybe nobody find out if you to Carol not talk. But now Matt shamed in San Diego, and California, and United States and Japan. Why not you asked Carol the secret to keep?"

Barbara couldn't believe it. *My own mother is siding against me?*

"Tacky," Ed said, "I don't see why this bothers you. Matt is a slimeball."

"Always he to me was respectful and polite."

Barbara frowned. She had to make her mother understand. "To *you*, he was respectful and polite. *Me*, he hit! Dad never hit you. And before Matt hit me, he lied I was having an affair with DeGarcia. You talk about shame—what about that?"

"I teached you to respect Japanese way. I know sometimes you act American, but this is *spitting on* Japanese way! If the wife of the samurai shamed her husband so much, he killed her." She glanced at Ed. "And maybe killed her father."

Ed made a gesture of frustration. "Once again: This isn't Japan."

Takeko ignored that, to continue whipping Barbara. "You now has nothing Japanese but name Nakamura, and you want to erase Nakamura name! Japanese don't talk outside and shame the family, but Americans go on the TV shows and say the about-family bad words. You are American."

Ed wouldn't be ignored. "Barbara had good reason."

"Ed, you let me finish, please! Japanese wives help their husbands work, but Barbara, you cut under what Matt works at. You are American."

Barbara stared. "*Help* Matt? What he did was *vile*."

"Now you are *kuse ga aruhito*," an argumentative or aggressive individualist, "and you forgetted the family and the good name. Of course Matt hit you—in last month, he hasn't the working-for-marriage wife!"

"Mommy, please don't be mad," Barbara wanted to cry. But she said instead, "I've done nothing wrong."

Barbara then stood straight to say, "As a wife, I've been *kata*," the model to copy. "But even if not, that still wouldn't justify his hitting me. Even that's nothing next to selling out California! Most women would've called it quits right then."

"Yes, the American women."

"Makes no difference. Is there one wife in Tokyo in 2005 who stays with the husband who hits her, cheats on her, and takes bribes at his job?"

"He hitted you because you said to him the lose-face words."

"Because I was upset. For good reason, too."

I'm not a bad daughter, Barbara thought. *I'm not.*

Ed turned to Takeko. "Don't dump on Barbara. She's not wrong—not by American standards and, I think, not by Japanese."

"Ed, I know you not understand. Japan buys California is the good action. You and Barbara not understand, but Matt understands."

"Mom, *Matt asked for a bribe.*"

"Maybe he asked, maybe he not asked, that not sure. But he not shamed you in the outside. If he pillows with the other woman, he not pillows where everyone sees. He not hitted you where everyone sees. But world sees that you want divorce."

"Mom, you're not being fair."

"Why you say not I am fair? The proper I tell you what is, nothing in that not is fair."

Barbara stepped to Takeko's chair and squatted down, now at eye level with her mother. "Mom, please trust my judgment now, the same way that *Ojii-san* finally trusted your judgment about Dad."

Ed nodded. "Yes, Tacky, please."

"Okay, Barbara. Since you born, much is different in United States and Japan. Maybe is okay, you divorce Matt. Ed, you ask, so I promise I keep the quiet—but only for some time."

Barbara had won, yet not won at all. "Mom, you don't promise because *I* asked?"

"Here's the story I wrote for tomorrow," Carol said to Barbara. "Thought you'd want to see it beforehand.

Lloyd promised me front page." Carol laid three double-spaced sheets on her kitchen table.

Barbara had gone straight from her parents' house to Carol's house. Barbara and Carol again were planning to hit the health club; Barbara needed the physical release of exercise.

But now in Carol's kitchen, Barbara tapped the working headline, "NAKAMURAS TO DIVORCE." Barbara said, "Next you'll by printing how I lost my virginity. Dad predicted front page, by the way."

"Sorry, but lots of people are eager for the latest on Barbara and Matt."

"Please don't take this wrong, Carol, you're a dear friend—"

"Hey, lots of people talk to a journalist, then regret it."

Barbara tapped the pages again. "I feel so naked."

Fifteen-year-old Bobby walked in. "Hi, Mrs. Nakamura." He opened the refrigerator and grabbed a can of cola, as he waved the digital phone in his other hand. "Doris says hi." Bobby popped the top on the soda. "She also asked me to tell you, she thinks it's globally icy that you're divorcing `Bomber.'"

"She does?"

"When he's on TV, acting all good and noble, he's so phone-sex it's tragic. We're glad you fought the treaty for us."

Barbara didn't feel like discussing her divorce, so she seized onto the side comment to respond to. "What don't you and Doris like about the treaty?"

"Our summer vacations will be only six weeks long—with *homework*! Classes will be forty kids. They'll make us bow to all our teachers, and bow to the seniors, and—this is awful—scrub the floors and clean the bathrooms."

"So awful, I agree," Carol said. "And sharks make the best opera singers."

"But all that is *women's*—"

Barbara's eyebrow went up.

Bobby coughed. "We'll have to learn Japanese. At least we won't have to worry about taking that tough test to get into high school."

"It's more than tough, it's *cruel*," Barbara said.

"Brr, high school turning Japanese, that's straight from a screamvid."

"Let me see what I can do about that." Barbara turned to Carol. "Since Monday, I've been brainstorming ideas how to kill the treaty. Let me bounce one off you."

"Please. California *needs* a good idea."

"Okay, California businesses place ads on Japanese commuter trains. They're don't-buy-California ads, ads that I write."

Carol and Bobby exchanged glances. "Um," Carol said after a pause, "it probably won't change anything." She plastered on a beauty-pageant smile before saying, "But keep thinking!"

Barbara and Carol shared a workout as promised, and afterward were changing clothes in the locker room. Carol asked, "If you're divorcing Matt, you keeping your house here in San Diego?"

"I told Matt he could use the house until he went back to Washington, and I'd rent a motel room. I didn't tell him I'd put all my stuff in storage so he couldn't make my things disappear."

"A motel? Why not your parents' place?"

"It's awkward now."

"Then why not stay with me? The family room has a day bed."

"You don't mind?"

Carol grabbed Barbara's arms and grinned. "It'll be just like college. Well, except for all our wrinkles."

In Carol's kitchen the next morning, Barbara saw that Bobby was beaming. "Globally icy, Mom. Look, 'NAKAMURAS TO DIVORCE.' You bagged front page."

Barbara shouldn't have been surprised that Carol subscribed to the *Union-Tribune*. A minute earlier, Bobby had dashed out to fetch the newspaper. Returning to the kitchen where Carol and Barbara were making breakfast, Bobby now displayed the front page like it was an award plaque. Which it was, for Carol.

The Nakamuras' upcoming divorce was reported at the bottom of the front page, next to a story about the television networks closing shop in California if Japan passed the treaty. All anyone had to do was unfold the newspaper, or turn the folded paper over, and he would learn that Barbara was a failure at marriage.

The next time I feel the urge to talk to a journalist, first I'll count to a hundred—in Gaelic. But Barbara saw no sense in ruining Carol's moment. Barbara smiled and kept her voice light: "Too bad Lloyd didn't give you the headline."

The banner headline read instead, "DIET ARGUES OVER TREATY."

A half-hour later, Bobby had left for school, Carol was out making wedding preparations, and Barbara was back at the San Diego house. Matt was gone, fortunately. An empty bourbon bottle and an empty six-pack in the kitchen trash can told her how Matt had spent his evening.

She carried from her car a thick stack of two-day-old *Union-Tribune*s. As most of Barbara's and Matt's goods were in Alexandria, she didn't need to pack all that much. She tried to work as quickly as she could, without making mistakes. She didn't know how much time she would have before Matt returned.

She packed kitchen items first, then books and knickknacks in the living room. When she walked into the master bedroom, she sighed, walked through the open door into the bathroom, and dug out cleaning supplies. As she knelt to clean the toilet, she realized she was wiping up Matt's puke for the last time.

Minutes later, Barbara was sorting through cleaning potions under the bathroom sink when she heard the front door open and close. Her survival instinct told her that being on her knees in the bathroom, with only one way in and out, was dangerous. She leaped up and hurdled the open packing box that now blocked the bathroom doorway.

Footsteps approached, then Matt stood in the bedroom doorway holding papers. Divorce papers, unless she was mistaken. He said, "So you weren't lying yesterday." His face and voice were tight.

He's blocking the door, and I won't be able to call 911 before he's on top of me. Carefully she said, "Why would I lie? It's over."

"Want to know what the process server said? `Are you Matthew Lucas Nakamura? You are hereby served.

And you deserve it, scumbag.'" Matt looked at her, waiting for her to speak.

He didn't seem violent, but she did not relax. "We have nothing left, why continue this? Whatever your huge gift turns out to be, I want no part of it. For me, this is what's best."

"Not so long ago I threatened to leave you penniless if we divorced. Do you remember that?" His face and his voice were still tight, but now his eyes were searching hers.

She was too tired of his mind games to be manipulated anymore. "I'll fight you. Even if you win, I'd rather be broke than in this marriage any longer."

He shrugged. "Perhaps indeed `this is what's best.'" He gestured to the toilet bowl. "But it means I'll have to clean up my own messes."

"Yes." This whole conversation felt strange; she didn't know what else to say. She was dumfounded he was being so agreeable. Why couldn't he have acted like this more often?

He walked out of the room. Seconds later, she heard the front door open, and his steps through the house. She dashed out of the bedroom. *I'd better find out real fast what he's up to.*

It turned out that he was loading her sealed packing boxes into her moving trailer. All her concerns were groundless.

Once he'd loaded her boxes, he walked back into the house, his car keys in his hand. She stood in the entranceway, looking at him. She couldn't read what he was feeling.

Nor could she pin down her own feelings. Love, regret, pity for him, amazement, anger, self-doubt, hope—each heartbeat brought another emotion.

After a moment, she said, "Thanks. The boxes, I mean. The books were heavy, it would've really been hard for me."

He smiled like everyone's best friend: "Sure, no problem." The smile vanished. "I. . ." He jammed his keys into a pocket. "So this is the end." He raised his hands in the beginnings of an embrace. "It's been years since I've held you—I mean, only held you, with no trying for sex."

"Yes." When he hugged her, she neither stepped into the embrace nor flinched away. She wanted his comforting, yet she also wanted him gone.

His hug was as nervous as a seventh-grader's. After a moment, his arms dropped. "We had good years, Barbara." His voice turned thick. "I remember the weekend you first made love to me. It was only your fourth time, you said. Since then, you've become a skilled lover. I remember the first time you baked a cake. It fell. Since then, you've become a wonderful cook. You helped me a lot—in law school, during my practice, and in Washington. I know you put everything you had into the marriage. You've sacrificed a lot for me. Thanks for all you've done."

"Those are lovely words." She shook her head. "Said too late, but lovely."

The next morning, Barbara was driving from Carol's house back to hers to check her mail. The sky was partly cloudy; the clouds were undecided whether to be white fluffs or gray rain clouds.

Barbara emptied the mailbox and unlocked the front door. She heard the living-room TV, tuned to an Eighties sitcom. When she walked into the living room, she found Matt passed out in his recliner. She turned the TV off, stepped over the beer cans, and headed to the computer in this house's home office.

She pulled up the database of big contributors and found Gene Hill. Gene had attended a thousand-dollar-a-plate fundraising dinner for Matt's re-election campaign in 2000. Gene also was a Malibu record producer and concert promoter.

Phone in hand a minute later, Barbara was explaining to Gene her idea about California musicians staging free concerts in Japan. Gene got excited at once, and he and Barbara spent ten minutes discussing what artists might be interested, what Japanese cities they could tour, and when for Barbara to take the stage to make her anti-treaty pitch.

Barbara was excited, and Gene was excited—until just before the call ended. "Barbara baby, *love* your idea, look forward to working with ya, you're really a sweetheart. But I have one tiny question. Don't take me wrong, but—will this work? Will these free concerts save California?"

After talking to Gene Hill, she called Governor Dodson's office in Sacramento. Jim Dodson's voice was friendly and loud: "Hey, Barbara, great you called! How are you?"

Pretty glum, actually. In the shower this morning she'd recalled how many times when she'd been an imperfect wife. It was no fun admitting she shared fault for the end of her marriage.

But now Barbara said, "Um, okay. How are you? How's Lydia and the girls?"

"We're all fine. My only real problem right now is this damned treaty. Meanwhile, Lydia is wrapping a shoot in Marin County. The girls can't wait for school to finish, especially since Lydia will be home by then."

"I'm sure you're all looking forward to that. Speaking of 'this damned treaty,' how's California's fight in the Supreme Court progressing?"

"We're pinning our hopes on one sentence of the Constitution: `. . .Nothing in this Constitution shall be so construed as to prejudice any claims of the United States, or of any particular State.'"

"An excellent argument, Jim."

"Not really. Don't tell your editor friend I said this, but the argument's shaky. Our attorneys made several more arguments, which they swear will win our case."

"But you don't believe them?"

"C'mon, they're *lawyers*. Anyway, if California loses the case, then we figure we have at least nine weeks before we're handed over."

"*Nine weeks?*"

"That's if the Japanese act quickly to run it through the Diet favorably and then can throw the money together quickly. It's a worst-case scenario."

"So it could take longer."

"It could take much longer. If the Diet shoots it down that's great, but we can't afford to count on that. Anyway, is this why you called?"

"No, I have an idea how to redeem myself and save California, and Lydia is essential."

"Barbara, you don't need to redeem yourself to me. But what's this with Lydia?"

"I want to organize a troupe of Hollywood stars that will go around Japan and speak against the treaty."

"Lydia being one."

"Right. They'd speak in English, I'd speak in Japanese. Lydia herself is popular in Japan, and I'm sure we three can persuade many other big names to fly there."

"Granted, Hollywood stars will draw huge crowds, and put on a helluva show wherever they go in Japan. But will they do any good?"

"I can't talk to the lawmakers in Tokyo, Jim. This indirect approach is the best I can do."

⁂

Minutes later, Barbara was locking the front door of the San Diego house when she heard air brakes and the rumble of a diesel somewhere close. That was odd, for the house was near no truck routes, and the nearest bus route was several blocks away.

She was walking down the driveway when the bus turned onto her street, coming from the left. It was green and white, with "California Japan Tours" on all four sides. On the left and right sides were pictures of a surfing samurai.

As the bus approached, Barbara could see the tour guide beside the driver. The tour guide was talking into a microphone, and pointing to Barbara. The bus stopped in front of the house. Dozens of Japanese tourists were pressed against the windows, snapping photos of Barbara and the house. She felt amazed.

After a second, the bus door *chish*'d open, and the tour guide came out. College-aged, her name tag identified her, in alphabetic and *katakana* writing, as Kathy Shimizu. Kathy put out her hand and smiled. "Good morning, Mrs. Nakamura, how are you today?"

Barbara absently shook hands. "I'm fine, but what's all this? Am I a tourist attraction now?"

Kathy looked embarrassed. "You've been for several months. Actually, it's the house: Japanese want to see where Senator and Mrs. Nakamura live."

"Oh."

"It's a real treat for them to see you in person."

Barbara's smile was dry. "It's maybe not a treat for them, but it's clearly a rare event." Just inside the windows of the bus was a solid wall of humans, each working a camera. A young woman's hands flew as she jammed film into her camera. Barbara turned back to Kathy. "I've never seen San Diego as a tourist. Where do you go—the zoo, Sea World, the beaches, Tijuana?"

"Well, it's, ahem, not a vacation tour anymore. Since Monday, we've been offering our `Familiarization Tour.' It's for Japanese who've never lived in California, but who think they might be living here soon."

"Oh."

"Besides the places you mentioned, we drive through residential areas, visit Japanese grocery stores and American supermarkets, drive by hospitals and schools, and so on."

"Oh."

"I see two cars here. Is Senator Nakamura at home?"

"Yes, but he's still asleep." *Mother, you should be pleased: I can't admit he's passed out drunk.*

Kathy touched Barbara's hand. "Could we ask a favor? Could you please pose for pictures and give autographs? The people on the bus would like that."

They'd much have preferred Matt to her, Barbara knew, but Kathy was kind not to mention that.

A car was coming down the street. As it moved closer, Barbara recognized Mrs. Harper, the elderly neighbor who grew spring tulips in her front yard. Mrs.

Harper stopped with a screech and stared wide-eyed at the bus. Barbara caught her eye, waved, and shrugged.

Barbara turned back to Kathy. "Pictures and autographs, sure, *if* anyone wants them. But tell your tourists it's only for fifteen minutes. Your bus is an inconvenience to my neighbors."

Seconds later, the bus spurted tourists. Each departing tourist bowed to Barbara, who bowed back. Mrs. Harper's eyes widened more, then she reversed her car to find a different way home.

The first tourist to talk to Barbara was a young man who asked in slow English, "Please, your car which is?"

Barbara, smiling, said in Japanese, "Mine's over there, the yellow one."

He blinked, then replied in kind. "Thank you very much for answering in Japanese, Mrs. Nakamura. I wasn't sure in which language it was proper to speak with you. Please pardon me for my rudeness if it is too great an inconvenience, but may I please take a picture of you standing next to your car?"

She shrugged, and walked to the back of her car. He sucked air through his teeth. "I am rude, but may I please ask if you could trouble yourself to move to either the right or the left by half a meter? I want to also include the license plate of your car in the picture."

Her mouth flew open as she realized what he meant. "You think American California license plates will be history soon."

Unless I find a way to prevent that.

———

The time was half past noon, which was an hour and a half before Carol's wedding. The bride was rushing around her bedroom as she dressed, while Barbara sketched the morning's events.

Carol shook her head. "Amazing, your house a Japanese tourist attraction. Oh, those pumps I bought yesterday, where—"

"Top of the closet."

"Could you find them and toss the box on the bed, please? So what was giving the autographs like?"

"Very strange. I've posed for pictures and given autographs for about a month now. But it's the first time I've written autographs in Japanese, and it's the first time I've posed for pictures in my own front yard."

"You're one-up on me. We editors manage to avoid celebrity quite nicely."

"They took their souvenir group photo right on my front lawn."

"That's a big deal, right?"

"Uh-huh. But while I was playing celebrity, I was thinking about what the tour guide said. Now the question in everyone's minds about California's transfer isn't *If?* anymore. The question is *How soon?*"

"Can you zip me up?" Carol had just donned a white dress with celadon-green trim at the hem, wrists, and throat.

"Sure."

Carol picked up the belt that was on the bed. "Nine weeks, god. What will you do after the changeover? That is, *if.*"

Barbara said jokingly, "I'll party my life away, in a houseboat smack in the middle of Lake Tahoe." Then Barbara's expression sobered. "Japanese won't want me in California; Americans won't want me in the Remaining States."

Carol walked into the bathroom with her makeup. "There's always Canada. I hear they have great lobster."

Carol was prettying her face as Barbara asked, "So what are your own plans afterward? *If*."

"All three of us talked it over. Larry leans toward staying. He's lived here since the Marines, and thinks he'll keep his job at the bank. Bobby's girlfriend is staying. As a newspaper editor, I can work anywhere. I'd prefer to leave, but won't push it."

A few minutes later, after curling her hair, Carol was sifting through her earring collection. "Barbara, this is exactly like in college—one of us is dressing up to go out, and we're talking."

"Except now you're not going on a date, you're going to get married."

"On the contrary, it's a years-long date. And I've decided, tonight I'll let him go all the way."

After the wedding and reception, then after helping Carol's mother and Bobby clean up Carol's house, Barbara got on the phone. Five minutes later, she had the phone number of treaty opponent (and two-time Academy-award nominee) Derrick Russell.

"Hello, is this Derrick Russell? This is Barbara Nakamura. . . .Thanks, but I already *have* a divorce lawyer, so I won't need yours. . . .Oh, your third ex-wife's? Why him?. . .That's what I need, a smooth-talker with the conscience of a heartworm when we go to court. Why didn't I talk to you a few days ago?. . .Derrick, I was kidding. But seriously, your movies do great box office in Japan, right?. . .I'm trying to round up California movie and TV stars who have many fans in Japan, to organize a junket to Japan to speak out against the treaty. Think of it as a cross between a `Voice of America' propaganda broadcast, and a USO tour. . . .Great! Know anybody else who'd want to sign on?"

Friday night, Carol and Larry were still on their honeymoon. Barbara had picked up Bobby after work at his grocery store and now they were in his living room, watching "The X Files: New Cases." The cordless rang, and Bobby answered it. After a moment Bobby, amazed, handed the phone to Barbara. "It's Japan."

Barbara took the cordless into the kitchen. "*Moshi-moshi*, this is Barbara Nakamura."

"*Moshi-moshi*. Mrs. Nakamura, let me introduce myself. I am YAMAMURA Hideo." He added that he was a member of the House of Representatives in the Diet.

Barbara nodded. "*Hajimemashite*. I remember now, you're the senior party president among the parties in the Progressive Coalition."

"Yes, the City-Dwellers Party ignores my many glaring faults to keep me on. Mrs. Nakamura, please let me say why I've called."

"Please."

"Within a few days I presume your Supreme Court will rule for the treaty, and the president will ratify it."

She sighed. "True."

"Once it moves to the Diet, the frank truth is that the Conservative Coalition has enough votes. We Progressives cannot stop the treaty's passing."

"Yes, I've read that. Go on."

"I'm asking for your advice how to kill the treaty."

"You have a whole army of experts you can ask, right there in Tokyo."

"*Soh desu.* Yet you are a Californian who also knows our language and our culture."

And then she saw her answer: Yamamura could bring her face-to-face with Diet members. Yamamura was her best way to fight the treaty.

So Barbara said, "Yes, I'm all those things, so why stop at a phone call? I can help you fight the treaty much more effectively than by over the phone."

"Fight it how?"

"Senior Party President Yamamura, please, invite me to Tokyo. Let me talk to the Representatives `belly to belly.'"

"Ah, I had forgotten how *direct* Americans are." He wasn't paying a compliment.

Barbara bowed, though Yamamura couldn't see. "That I have offended you, *moshiwake arimasen*," she said, using an apology for serious offenses. Barbara followed with a humble request for forgiveness: "For my rude directness *o-yurushi kudasai*—but please consider my request."

"Mrs. Nakamura, you know a politician can't afford to take offense—"

Which wasn't the same as saying he wasn't offended, she noted.

"—but I foresee problems. You're a woman. . ." In the Japanese manner Yamamura let his voice trail off, rather than voice an unpleasantness.

"Women are elected to the Diet, *ne*? Women lobby the Diet, women contribute to election campaigns, and women vote for Diet members, I understand." Her uncertainty was by form only.

"But as a woman, your status. . ."

"My status is that I am an international celebrity because I oppose the treaty. Japanese tourists have asked for my autograph, and have taken their souvenir group photo on the front lawn of my house. Please, bring me to Nagata-*cho*." Please bring me to the Diet.

"It perhaps is said by some that you have *chased after* such fame." His tentativeness likewise only polite form; he was making a finger-pointing accusation.

"Those who say that are mistaken. I didn't ask for this."

"Your notoriety perhaps might hurt our cause. I have seen Japanese news media interview you. The television people don't actually *say* that you ignore your obligations as a wife and daughter. . ."

"As a politician yourself, you know that Husband could not have progressed as far as he has without my *active* help. Mother and I always had enjoyed a good relationship, right up to the time I spoke out against the treaty. Always and everywhere, mean or ignorant people spread lies. Please invite me to come."

"It's not true you curse the land of your mother's birth? It's not true your relatives in Japan are ashamed of you?"

"Japan is also the land of *my* birth, though I was born on-base. I do not know how all my Japanese relatives feel about me."

"Mrs. Nakamura, *wa uchi no mono ja arimasen zo; aka no tanin desu zo.*" You're not a 'regular Joe,' but as much an outsider as anyone can get.

"Senior Party President, you said yourself: I *know*—I don't need to guess—how Americans and Californians think. I have a bigger perspective than anyone who has lived only in Japan. When you've introduced me to a Representative and I tell him buying California will bring disaster, he'll know he can't dismiss what I say."

"In Washington you already knew the legislators socially, and only a *third* of them you needed to sway. Yet you failed. But in the Diet, every Representative will be a stranger to you, and *half* of them you must bring to no."

"I've learned from my Washington experience. Also, in Washington, I was asking the senators to vote against receiving trillions of dollars."

"Go on."

"In Tokyo I'll be asking Representatives to vote against killer tax increases. I actually think my job in Tokyo will be easier."

She frowned. She was stuck, not advancing. She'd have to try something risky.

With more confidence in her voice than she felt, Barbara said, "Please forgive my rudeness, but are you resisting the idea of my meeting with Diet members because the idea is new, or for some other reason?"

"Mrs. Nakamura, you have pushed me hard. You've cultivated no spirit of harmony, and you've made no attempt to build consensus. You've shown no trace of *enryo*," you've behaved with selfish bad manners. "Perhaps it could be said that, even among big, arrogant, bullyish Americans, you excel at rudeness."

He paused. "Yet in Tokyo you could help us much."

They made plans. Yamamura would speak to individuals and groups who opposed the treaty, and he was confident he could arrange sponsorship for Barbara. He insisted on booking her flight, reserving a hotel of suitable status, and providing her with enough money for eating.

Monday, she would be back in Alexandria, where she would be vaccinated for smallpox. She already had a valid passport. A visa shouldn't be a problem—she could enter Japan without a visa for up to 90 days, and Yamamura could arrange for an extension to 180 days, if needed.

Barbara's final words to Yamamura were heartfelt: "Senior Party President, I cannot thank you enough." *I have a second chance to stop the treaty!*

"Mrs. Nakamura, please give *me* a reason soon to thank *you.*"

———

Seconds later, Barbara turned off the cordless. As she replayed the conversation in memory, her joy died. Everything Senior Party President Yamamura had told her was true:

She was going to Tokyo, where she was not only a foreigner and a woman in a male-dominated culture, but where her reputation was worse than in the United States. In Washington she had known the face and first name of every senator; in Tokyo she wouldn't know a Dietman from an *oshiya* (train packer) without their clothes to clue her. Despite their being strangers, she had to persuade half of the Diet lower house lawmakers to vote her way, not merely a third as in the Senate. To sway so many Dietmen, she needed the help of Senior Party President Yamamura—whom she'd just offended.

"What have I gotten myself into?" she asked the ceiling. The ceiling made no reply and gave no advice.

Right then, Bobby strolled into the kitchen. "Who was that, a relative? I've never heard you speak Japanese before. What did he want?"

"He wants me to help him fight the treaty in Japan's Congress. He's—"

"You're going to Tokyo to talk to their politicians? California's still in the game?"

"Yes, still in the game, but—"

"*Globally* mega-icy! Boy, if Mom were here, she'd go leptic for sure. We need to phone her, right now!"

Barbara smiled. "Bobby, adults don't want work-related calls on their honeym—"

"Okay, okay, she promised to phone every day. We'll wait for tonight's call."

Carol over the phone didn't sound happy. "Barbara, want you to know: If you weren't my *very* best friend, I wouldn't be sacrificing my time this way."

After talking to Senior Party President Yamamura, Barbara had phoned Lydia Dodson, and had left messages for Derrick Russell and Gene Hill. Barbara had explained that she was changing her plans. The Hollywood stars' press conferences in Japan, and the California musicians' free concerts, would need to go on without her. She'd apologized for any inconvenience. No sooner had Barbara put her digital phone back in her purse but Carol's cordless had rung again.

Now on the phone to Carol, Barbara smiled. "Nonsense. Nobody's *forcing* you to interview me; nobody's forcing you to do *anything*. Unless you and Larry share interests you haven't told me about?"

"Pervert. I'll—Larry, you devil, stop that! I need to work."

Barbara heard Larry's throaty laugh over the phone. "*Honey*, remember the time Daphne called me? I'm paying you back."

"Larry, I'm interviewing Barbara, I need to think clearly now. And what you're doing, *oh god* I'm not thinking clearly!" Ten seconds later, Carol could talk again. "*As* was saying. I'll do you this one-time favor— interview you, fax it in—but I ask you to stay off the news afterward, until I return. *Okay*?"

Barbara laid on her sweetest politician's-wife voice: "Of course, Carol my good friend. But if you're *too busy*,

I could call up Sharon Hamilton, and tell *her.* Even sneaky ASN bitch Laura DuBois might be worth a call."

"Don't you dare."

"Let me know when you're ready. . .to write."

Carol was back on the line half a minute later. "Go. Who's this guy, uh, Yamamoto?"

"Hideo Yamamura." Barbara spelled it. "He's a Representative in the lower house, and head of the Progressives who are fighting the Liberal-Demo—hm. Let me start at the beginning.

"Japanese politics has two Coalitions, the smaller Progressive Coalition and the bigger Conservative Coalition. The Conservative Coalition contains the Democratic Party of Japan. But the far bigger party in the Conservative Coalition. . ."

Barbara explained at length, because it became clear that Carol was in Japan-politics kindergarten.

"Whew," Carol said when Barbara had finished. "You know a lot about this."

"Remember, I took a class in Chinese and Japanese Government at UCSD?"

"No, not really—yes. You read a book on *sword-fighting* for extra credit."

"Right, Miyamoto's *Book of Five Elements*, which the professor felt was Japan's business bible. Anyway, besides that course years ago, Matt's had a subscription to the *Japan English Weekly* for years, and I've talked to Ambassador Fujima at parties."

"While eating Canadian lobster, I'm sure. Now, since I'm going to call in a world exclusive, okay if I check my facts?"

"Check away."

"This guy Yamamura's in their lower house, which, like our lower house, is called the House of Representatives. Except that the Diet's lower house has the final say on the treaty in Japan, so it's not like our House of Representatives, but like our Senate."

"Right," Barbara said.

"In Japan's parliamentary system, the legislature elects a lower-house representative to be prime minister. Thus the prime minister always comes from the majority party or majority coalition. So the majority coalition gets two branches of government for the price of one."

"Uh-huh."

"But you're allied with Yamamura. Yamamura is head of the Progressive Coalition that opposes the Conservative Coalition, so he's like Fuller. But the Conservatives outnumber the Progressives there, so he heads the minority coalition, so he's like Leaird."

"Right again."

"Making up the Progressive Coalition are four little parties. But some of those parties are conservative, even though they're part of the Progressive Coalition fighting the Conservative Coalition."

"Right a fourth time."

"While the big party in the enemy Conservative Coalition, the party the prime minister belongs to, is called the Liberal-Democratic Party."

"Strange name for a conservative party, I admit."

"Whew, I thought our presidential election system was confusing. Finally, today you talked Yamamura into bringing you to their House of Representatives, so you can talk against the treaty."

"Yes."

"Barbara, must ask this. Did you remind him you tried that trick once before, and it didn't work?"

Barbara sighed. "*He* reminded *me*."

"Mother," Barbara said into her digital phone, "a Dietman invited me to Tokyo to help him fight the treaty. I accepted."

"*Dame yo,*" Takeko said. "You miss sleep to plan new ways to shame me, don't you? Why did he ask you to come?"

"Because I know California and Californians; I know Japan and Japanese."

"You think so? Did you tell the Dietman about when I told you `Stop'?" Takeko used the English word.

Barbara's voice was stiff. "No, I didn't tell him about that." She thought, *That was mean of you, Mother, reminding me of that.*

"So what's the problem with *Stop*?" Bobby asked. "Mom tells me it all the time, and it doesn't bother me."

"When my mother said that, she saved me from showing my grandfather that I was an ignorant fifteen-year-old lout."

"You were once my age?" Bobby looked amazed. "Listen, if I promise not to tell kids at school, or my mom, can I hear the story?"

"Why? It's embarrassing!"

"Because it's good to know how a genuine American hero was once a lepty like me."

"No Doris either. Tell nobody."

"Swear on a Bible warehouse," Bobby said. He looked at Barbara expectantly.

She sighed. "Okay, this happened the second time my father was stationed in Japan. One Saturday he had to work, so Mother and I decided we'd visit my grandparents. *Ojii-san* had lost his entire left leg in the war, so he always needed to use a crutch."

"Poor dude. That sucks."

"Anyway, Mom and I walked into the room while he was trying to go from standing on one leg and a crutch to sitting on a cushion. Neither *Obaa-san* nor Mom tried to help him, so I stepped forward."

"Well of course, that's acting polite."

"In *America*, yes. In Japan, no. As soon as I started to move, my mother said, `Stop, he not wants your help.' She said it in English."

"I don't get it."

"Mom talks to me in English only when my dad, or your mom, or other Americans are around."

"I don't understand—no Americans were there."

"Mom saved me from a major social blunder. By giving help unasked, I'd be implying that my grandfather couldn't sit down by himself, so he would've lost face. Worse, by helping him sit, I'd oblige him to return the favor in the future."

"And he never could pay you back that way."

"Uh-huh, and I'd be placing someone with higher status than me in debt to me."

"Different rules. So why use English?"

"Had she told me to stop in Japanese, so that my grandparents were sure to understand her, then both my grandfather and I would've lost face."

"Him for being weak, and you for being a dummy?"

"Yes. My grandfather understands some English, but can anyone prove he understood Mom? The way she handled it, everyone could pretend that nothing happened, and nobody lost face."

"So why are you so embarrassed about it? It's a mistake I or Mom or anybody I know would've made."

"We were playing by Japanese rules, and Mother's been teaching me Japanese stuff since I was small enough to be tied to her back. But watching *Ojii-san* trying to sit down, I thought American instead of thinking Japanese."

Bobby considered that, then looked into Barbara's eyes. "Then I hope you've learned by now, when to think Japanese. California needs you to figure out how to charm Japan's Diet into trashing the treaty."

Matt almost missed it.

In the living room of the San Diego house later that night, Matt was watching ASN Newsbreak and draining a twelve-pack. For the first time in years he was relaxing at home like a working stiff, instead of spending all his recess sucking up to potential contributors to his next campaign. But the reason why he was idle, made Matt frown. *I might as well relax at home, because I'm sure as hell unwelcome everywhere else in California.*

A minor story on ASN Newsbreak covered a dinner party that the president and the first lady threw for Swensen's Cabinet. Most of the secretaries and undersecretaries of the various Cabinet departments attended it.

Panning the room, ASN's camera found FBI Director Frederick Hahn with a woman. ASN Newsbreak didn't name her, but Matt recognized her.

"Mela!"

The Nakamuras returned to Washington Sunday afternoon—Matt to return to work, and Barbara to pack and move, and say goodbye to friends.

Sunday night, Matt and Barbara divided up the furniture and personal possessions in their Alexandria house. Monday morning, Barbara found a clinic to vaccinate her for smallpox, then she resumed packing up cardboard boxes.

Monday morning, the Supreme Court in a 7-2 decision upheld the treaty.

The instrument of ratification had been ready for a week, awaiting the Court's favor and the president's signature. At four in the afternoon Monday, in the Rose Garden beneath a cloudless sky, Charles Swensen ratified the treaty.

Barbara was in the Alexandria house late Monday night, packing kitchen appliances. Matt stepped into the kitchen to announce that Marilyn Saunders was at the front door with home-made sandwiches. The two women hugged several times, and Barbara thanked Marilyn for offering to help with the move.

The next morning in Washington, Barbara had finished packing and had priced movers. She visited friends and said goodbye.

She and Sapphira cried in each other's arms. Joe Bob Saunders kissed her on the cheek, and Barbara envied Marilyn.

Barbara cleaned out her office at the Red Cross, and thanked both her state fundraising managers and their volunteers for their hard work. Tiffani and the other state manager gave Barbara a goodbye gift, a teddy bear. The soft, tan teddy bear was as big as a toddler and was covered by a large Red Cross T-shirt. The T-shirt in turn was covered with autographs that were written in black laundry pen.

Barbara cried, the Virginia-D.C. fundraising manager cried, and the volunteers cried. Tiffani was dry-eyed and looked uncomfortable. Everyone hugged Barbara goodbye, but Tiffani's hug was brief. Barbara did not show her hurt, but instead congratulated Tiffani on her promotion.

Yamamura called Barbara slightly after noon. He told her he had arranged a round-trip flight to Tokyo from San Diego, leaving the next day. After turning off her digital, Barbara drove to her bank, closed her savings account, and converted the money into traveler's checks.

Back at the Alexandria house that afternoon, Barbara answered the house phone. "Senator Nakamura's residence, this is Barbara."

"Barbara, dis is Mister C. Remember me?"

"The mobster from Atlantic City. What do you want?"

"You don't listen good, so I'll tell you one last time: Leave da treaty alone. You got me? You go to Japan, you die."

The phone clicked.

Later that afternoon in Washington, Secretary of State Harland delivered the instrument of acceptance to His Excellency Mister Fujima, in front of the Embassy of Japan. Every television-news organization in the United States and Japan that could dash a dish to Washington, covered the exchange live. California TV showed nothing else.

The United States of America had officially agreed to the treaty. The time had come for Japan to decide.

Barbara wanted the Diet to say no.

Hiroshi wanted a yes.

Matt didn't care one whit how the Diet voted. What Matt wanted was to collect his huge gift—and he would squash anyone who interfered.

About which, the Variety-Show Host joked—

Secretary of State Harland took the treaty to Japan's embassy. I don't see why Japan's ambassador couldn't have come to the State Department instead. If Japan can afford sixty trillion smackers, Japan can afford round-trip cab fare for its ambassador.

They demand three trillion bucks a year for twenty years, and not one penny less. But enough about what the moving companies are quoting to move my furniture from L.A. to Seattle.

Part III
Does the Sun Rise in the West?

A N A
s i r
a s u
h h
i i k
  a
g n
a i

CHAPTER 10
Heisei 17-nen 6-gatsu
7-ka, Kayohbi
(Tuesday, June 7, 2005)

It was after America's Supreme Court had okayed the treaty, and before America's Secretary of State would hand the instrument of ratification to Japan. As soon as Hiroshi arrived at work Tuesday morning, he asked his boss if he might discuss something important. Section Manager Masumi grunted assent.

Amid much honorific language, Hiroshi said this: "Section Manager, Matsumoto Robotics is an excellent company to work for. The people here are great folks to work with. Yokohama is a wonderful city. But *if* Japan buys California, and *if* Matsumoto Robotics puts a branch operation in California, then I most respectfully request a transfer."

Mister Masumi grunted a promise to inform the Personnel Department and his own boss, Sales Department Manager Wagatsuma.

That night, Hiroshi took another step to become a pioneer to Japanese California: He wrote a second batch of letters to his twenty-four Diet lower-house Representatives. Each letter was brief: "Now you have the treaty. Please approve it."

While mailing the letters, he wondered, *What do I do next?* Whatever he could devise to help the treaty, he'd do. He needed to know he was doing everything he could to make the treaty proclaimed—even though his help might not be needed. After all, Japan's news media were predicting the treaty was sure to win approval in the Diet.

But Mrs. Nakamura was headed for Japan, and Hiroshi felt sure the Japanese press was wrong to dismiss her. What if her work succeeded enough to endanger the treaty?

Somehow, he decided, he'd Nakamura-proof the Diet. Carrying out such a decision sounded impossible, for so many reasons. But he was an engineer, and engineers solved problems.

Walking back to his apartment from the mailbox, Hiroshi spoke his resolve aloud: "If Mrs. Nakamura threatens the treaty, I'll stop her threat."

―――――――――

"Goodbye, Barbara," Mrs. Nakamura heard Matt say.

It was Tuesday afternoon in Washington, and Barbara was in Matt's private office. She stood on the other side of his desk, and she felt choked up, looking at him. He kept running one hand through his hair, which meant he also was emotional, but she couldn't read his face.

"Goodbye, Matt. I. . ." She had no idea what to say next.

Matt clasped his hands together on the desk and squared his shoulders. "What about your stuff, how are you going to move it? Your junk was still in the house this morning."

If he could switch gears from the emotional to the practical, so could she. "I asked Marilyn Saunders if she'd supervise moving my things out."

"Marilyn has enough to do already, without you imposing."

He's actually lecturing me about "imposing." Matt, who only twice in sixteen years has gone to the dry cleaners himself. "I don't have another choice, do I?"

"Excuse me, how many other Senate wives do you know?"

"I don't know Gail Tucker that well, and the other Senate wives think I'm dirt."

"Still, you *do* have an alternative—two, actually."

"Enlighten me."

"The better one is for you to stay here till the movers leave."

"Yamamura needs me in Tokyo as quick as I can fly there." *Besides, as rude as I was to him over the phone, no way can I call him back and tell him, "I'll come when I'm ready."*

"The other alternative is that *I* ship your stuff."

She gave him a skeptical look. "Really, you? You'll only ship to San Diego what fits in a matchbox, then keep the rest. While you spout nonsense about possession being nine-tenths of the law."

"You don't trust me."

"Give the man a gold star."

"Sorry, *I* think I'm a decent guy."

This from the man who'd punched her? Her nostrils flared. "Decent guy? Exhibit One: At Taylor, Finch, and Holmes, you came home late once and told me court ran late. It hadn't. Exhibit Two—"

"I'm sure I gave you a good explanation."

"Yes, a real doozy," she said with smile withering. "Exhibit Two: That biker-chick campaign volunteer back in 1988—"

"This is time-wasting bullshit. You still need to move your stuff out, but your silly idea is a royal pain for both Marilyn and me."

"Live with it. I don't trust you."

"Then I refuse to cooperate with Marilyn. *Now* what do you do?"

"You always need to stomp me, don't you? You always need to play power games with me, always need to win. This is a trivial housekeeping detail—sheesh, take a break."

"*Think*, Barbara, how busy I am. But if Marilyn's at the house, I'll need to be there so she won't ship my stuff by mistake."

"I'll give her a list of what's mine. Credit me with *some* smarts."

"Yeah? Your way, I'll have to coordinate my schedule with Marilyn's, and she with Farmboy Saunders. Anyone has a change of plans, I'm back to square one. Bottom line: Your idea's ridiculous, and I'm being sensible."

Actually, he was playing another mind-game at her expense. But she had no alternative.

Barbara zipped open her purse and jerked a piece of paper out to thrust at him. "Moving estimates, I'll pay you back when I return." She grabbed her purse, went to the door, and jerked it open.

Then she remembered something, and turned back to him. "By law, *you're* now responsible for informing the movers they're transporting a firearm. My nightstand pistol is in the box marked `kitchen and bedroom misc.'"

A little after eight p.m., Matt was unlocking his car to go home. He had not taken Barbara to the airport.

When he'd walked Barbara to the elevator five hours earlier, he had realized: *I trusted her. A long time ago, she trusted me. Soon I can marry a woman younger and prettier, but I'll never again know such trust in a marriage.* But he'd refused to let that awareness, how much he was losing, bother him then.

He refused to let the loss bother him now. Still, Matt was hungry but for some reason didn't feel like playing senator at some fancy restaurant. He didn't feel like grabbing a burger with Mela. "I don't feel like talking to a goddamn soul," he yelled into the silent parking lot.

What he felt like doing was stopping at the supermarket to pick up a frozen pizza and a twelve-pack, then watching hours of TV.

Twenty minutes later he set the beer and pizza on the kitchen table. He noticed the wall calendar with fresh eyes. Every day of the month of June had an entry—his appointments were in blue, Barbara's in red. For June twenty-first, there were no words, only overlaid red and blue hearts and a bold, black *25.* Matt took a pen and X'd through all that.

While the pizza was cooking in the oven, he looked for the pizza cutter. That was Barbara's now, so it was in one of the packed mover's boxes. But she couldn't object if he washed the cutter afterward and put it back, right?

The pizza cutter was in the last box he tried, "kitchen and bedroom misc." In the box, along with the cutter, was an electric fryer, Barbara's nightstand light, some other kitchen and bedroom knickknacks, and an oddly shaped object that was wrapped in cloth inside a plastic bag.

Curious, Matt pulled out the strange bag and opened it. He smelled rustproofing gun oil, which told him that the cloth-wrapped object was—

"Just as Barbara said, her nightstand pistol."

Matt resealed the bag and put it back in the mover's box.

A few hours later in San Diego, Carol and Larry met Barbara's plane at the airport. Barbara saw Carol brimming with love for her new husband.

The next morning Carol and Larry took Barbara to the airport to catch her flight to Tokyo. Well-wishers and press people were both in force at San Diego International. Barbara's smiles were real.

Once the plane to Tokyo had taken off, Barbara discovered that sitting behind her was a young Japanese couple returning from their honeymoon. They, like Carol and Larry, were affectionate and excited about their future. Barbara stared at clouds, and she thought about newlyweds.

It was April of 1981, late in the evening in San Diego. Barbara and Matt had been married almost a year, and Matt was only an entry-level attorney at Taylor, Finch, and Holmes.

She stood beside Matt's chair in his half of a tiny office. "Hello, Perry Mason, it's dinnertime." She bent down and kissed him on the cheek.

Matt's smile was that of a gigolo, not an attorney. "Is *that* all I get? Kiss, Take Two." He stood, wrapped his arms around Barbara, and gave her a long, slow, French kiss.

"Sir, if you don't stop kissing me like that, I will retain an attorney." Her husky voice gave *retain* a double meaning.

"'Your Honor, I plead temporary insanity. I saw Mrs. Nakamura's shapely legs, and I lost all control.' Looks like the Colonel's chicken again."

"Which means the conference room again."

During their walk to the conference room, she asked, "So what are you working on?"

"I have two women as clients, nurse and a retired teacher. They teach nutrition and childcare to teen mothers. These two need a nonprofit but can't afford to set one up, so we're doing it *pro bono.*"

"Honey, that's so sweet of you."

"And you know what's great? Gloria—the retired teacher—knows people in the county Democratic Party. When this is finished, I'll ask her to introduce me."

"Does the Democratic Party *need* an attorney? Sure, I've heard the rumors—"

He smiled at her joke. "No, no, as a volunteer. I want to lick envelopes, make phone calls, whatever. Politics in high school was a rush, and I miss it."

They laid pages from a castoff *Wall Street Journal* on the conference table to absorb the grease, then took their seats. Once seated, Barbara kicked off her pumps. As she was laying out the food, she gave Matt a sidelong look. "You got me *very* turned on with that kiss, tiger."

"Oh, you mean *this* kiss?" The second long kiss was as arousing as the first, and this time Matt added kneading a breast. "I love you, Barbara."

"Cool it, tiger, someone might walk in," she said, sounding practical and modest. She felt anything but.

"Nobody's on this floor but Alan." He kissed Barbara again, as he ran his hand slowly down her back. Her nipples tingled.

"Oh, *really*, nobody but Alan? So nobody will see if I do *this*?" She started rubbing his hard-on through his pants. He clutched the chair's armrests in a death grip.

Then he pulled her head to his and kissed her with all he had. At the same time, his other hand slipped under her dress. He lightly caressed her leg from knee to panties, moving with tantalizing slowness. By the time he had worked his hand up her leg and under her pantyhose, and slipped a finger inside the crotch of her panties, those panties were wet. She gasped and thrust her hips against his hand when he touched her clit.

"I want you," he growled.

"Really?" She grabbed his front and felt a flagpole. "Mmm, I want you, too."

His hand on her back found the zipper of her dress. She twisted her body to stop him. "Alan—"

"Might be having sex with *his* wife, right this instant." He unzipped her dress to the waist, then began one-handed work to pull her bra straps off her shoulders. "I want to lick your tits, Barbara. I want to suck your nipples."

What the hell. She reached behind and unfastened her bra. Shortly thereafter, he'd bared her to the waist. He sucked on one tit, while he caressed the other tit, while she pulled on his black hair. She felt jolt after jolt of sexual shock that went straight from breasts to brain, and from brain to crotch.

"Fair is fair, tiger. If I get half-naked, so do you." She pushed Matt back into his own chair and began unfastening his belt. Then she unzipped him and pulled down his pants and briefs. His cock was straight out and twitching. "Mm, steel sausage. Bet it tastes good." He remembered his manners and moaned all the time her head was bobbing.

His voice was a series of gasps: "If I don't fuck you right now, I'll go out of my mind."

"Same here, tiger. The hell with Alan."

She pulled off his shoes, pants, and underwear. He helped her shuck pantyhose and panties. The young couple spread more newspaper sheets at the far end of the table, and then Matt laid her on top of the pages. She was just deciding that the table was too hard for comfortable sex when Matt knelt and went down on her. After that, she didn't notice the table much, especially once Matt slid his cock into her.

"Oh Matt, tiger, I love you, oh God."

She spent the next twenty minutes in a orgasmic haze. Only two things could she clearly remember afterward: clenching her teeth to keep Alan from hearing her screams, and Matt telling her at one point, "My shoulder, leggo, you're squeezing too hard."

A minute after Matt had grunted and collapsed, he helped her sit up. As soon as she stood on the floor again, he kissed her chastely on the lips. "I love you, Barbara. Never forget that. I love you, and I'm glad I married you."

Never before had she felt so close to a man, so in love with a man, and so womanly.

In Terminal Two of Tokyo's Narita International Airport, it was now early Thursday morning. For once, going through an airport was a breeze for Barbara. She zoomed through Immigration; she zipped through Customs. Only a minute after opening her bags in Customs, Barbara was piling her suitcases and her still-wrapped presentation gift back onto her luggage cart. A minute after that, Barbara had pulled her suitcases to the arrival lobby nearby. It was good to have friends in high places.

Her sponsor Yamamura was a naturally thin man in his sixties, of average Japanese height. Barbara recognized him on sight, from recent TV news. Likewise, he walked up to her without pause.

She stepped forward and bowed to him as he bowed to her. Though Barbara was a woman, his was the much deeper bow, for she was his guest. Television and still cameras and extension microphones recorded the scene. Round-eye press people were still in force, but now they were outnumbered by Japanese media people.

"Nakamura-*fujin*, thank you very much for honoring my poor effort with your help." Yamamura spoke the ritual words gravely.

"You honor me by asking me to add my puny strength to your worthy cause," she said.

"Please forgive my rudeness. Let me give you this, as a sincere expression of my gratitude for your help. It is of no value, but please accept it anyway." He handed her an envelope, around which were tied red-and-white *mizuhiki* cords.

"Yamamura-*sensei*, this is clearly a very valuable gift, which I cannot possibly accept." That said, Barbara accepted the envelope but did not open it. Since she had no entourage to hand it to, she dropped the envelope into her purse.

Barbara then said, "In return, I ask you to accept my poor gifts." She stepped back to her luggage cart and fetched her travel gift that lay against her carry-on bag, then she walked back to Yamamura.

Barbara bowed again. "They are only trifles, but they come from California." She handed Yamamura a big boxy shape, wrapped in maroon paper with neither ribbon nor bow. Inside was a skillfully woodworked chest made of California incense cedar. The chest in turn was filled with a basket of dried California fruit, foil-wrapped California cheese, and California-packed cans of shrimp.

Yamamura bowed to her, made polite noises, and handed Barbara's gift to the man behind him.

"Nakamura-*san!*" a man from the press yelled, addressing her with bare-minimum politeness. "Why are you here?"

"You know I want to save California. I also want to save Japan."

A second hostile man asked, "What makes you think that you'll affect, even slightly, treaty deliberations in the Diet?"

Barbara pasted on a smile. "Because I'm familiar both with Japan and with California. The people in the Diet thus must consider what I say."

She got more of the same for another ten minutes, until she called a halt. It wasn't a press conference, it was a kangaroo court.

A few hours later, in Washington it was after eight in the evening Wednesday. Once the Senate had approved the treaty, Matt's work had become routine again. He was trying to finish such work when the phone rang in his private office. "This is the White House," Matt heard. "Please hold for the president."

Twenty seconds later, Charlie was saying, ". . .Matt, I need some information that only you can give me. That is, if you can lay aside your feelings about Barbara for five minutes."

"We'll see. Ask."

"I need to instruct our ambassador how much a threat Barbara will be. The Japanese press thinks she's wasting her time. Are they missing something?"

"Only that she's a bore in the sack."

After a pause, the president said, "So not to worry. Good."

Barbara still owes me for tattling to Carol. Hitting her was amateur; now I have the perfect way to even the score. Matt said to Charlie, "I see one way to make sure you have no worries: Remove her."

Charlie spoke slowly: "What are you saying?"

"I'm sure you have CIA men at our embassy who have diplomatic passports and time on their hands. If not the CIA, I'm sure we have Special Forces men sitting idle at one of our bases in Japan. The prime minister won't complain, because Barbara is a problem for him as well as for you."

"You monster. I will not murder your wife for you."

Matt changed course: "Of course I'm not suggesting you kill her. Put her in protective custody—tell her you've saving her from Mafia goons again beating her up. Once you have her, slip her back to the States. Maybe she gets two black eyes due to `turbulence.' Anyway, you set her free after the Diet votes."

"This is sick. You're mad at your wife, and you want me to get your vengeance for you."

What would Dale Carnegie advise? Show Charlie that doing what I want gets him what he wants. "Charlie, do you want future schoolchildren learning that the Elementary School Curriculum and Standards Act was your only success? Two years from now, do you want every sunburned Son of Abraham to control his own pet Russian missile? Removing Barbara saves your legacy, and preserves world peace."

"Matt, you don't give a goddamn fig about world peace."

The line went silent, while Matt waited. Then the president said, "I'm ashamed to say that you've tempted me—but the answer is still no."

Matt talked to the president for another minute, worked another half hour, then rushed to his car. Matt had an appointment to keep—and an overdue huge gift to collect.

Promptly at nine, Matt zipped his car into an empty space on the third level of a certain parking garage, shut off the engine, and waited.

A minute later, Minoru Asakawa opened the passenger-side door and climbed in. "Good evening, Senator Nakamura," Asakawa said in Japanese.

Matt frowned. "It's a terrible evening for me, Lobbyist. Wife just arrived in Tokyo, still trying to kill the treaty. She misses sleep to devise new ways to embarrass me."

"We are confident that her efforts will accomplish little."

Matt made a gesture of dismissal. "You and I haven't much time, so let's move to what's important. I want to know, Asakawa-*kun*, when I can expect—"

A car came up the ramp to their level and parked. *Damn! Couldn't he have waited five minutes?* The driver climbed out of his car, locked it, and began to walk toward the elevator. His path brought him right in front of Matt's car.

"Down!" Matt told Asakawa, who obeyed. Matt felt foolish at his own nervousness.

The new arrival was a trim young man in his mid-twenties. Whistling as he walked, he played a game with himself in which he threw his keys over his head, then tried to catch them behind his back. He wasn't practiced: Several times he dropped his keys. Near Matt's car was one such time: the keys hit the hand behind the man's back and fell to the ground. The young man squatted down and retrieved the keys, stood, and continued his whistling walk to the elevator. He never once glanced in Matt's direction.

When the elevator doors closed on the keys-tosser, Matt spoke again. "I want to know when your government will thank me, Asakawa-*kun*. It was my understanding with Ambassador Fujima that Japan would show its gratitude as soon as the Senate approved the treaty. That was almost two weeks ago."

Asakawa sat up. "Some think a gift to you now might be unwise."

"Why unwise?"

"If it were noticed. . ."

Matt understood. "A scandal in both countries."

"And the treaty's opponents in the Diet would use this scandal to advantage."

"*I* would, were I in their position."

"We feel the treaty's future is not enough assured for needless risks. Our only other choice would be to give you a gift so small that it can't be noticed."

"Okay, I'll wait. But your explanation better not be a story. I threw away my Senate seat for this treaty—I'm counting on that not being for nothing."

Mister Asakawa slid out of the car. "Don't worry, the government of Japan most generously shall meet its social-debt to you."

"It had better. I don't like people who don't meet their obligations."

Mister Asakawa shut the door and walked away, not looking back. Matt started the car and headed for the exit.

"This is ASN Newsbreak, 9:00 p.m. Eastern time, Wednesday, June 8.

"Japan's prime minister has explained why he wants California. Appearing before a Diet committee, Prime Minister Sasaki gave three reasons for wanting California. Buying California would provide many crucial natural resources that Japan lacks. These natural resources are iron and boron, food, fuel, and timber. Buying California also would provide a frontier for Japan's young people, to relieve the social stress caused by Japan's rapidly graying population. Finally, Japan buying California would enable the U.S. to buy many missiles from Russia under the Nickels-for-Nukes Treaty. Effecting world nuclear disarmament is a major goal of Japanese diplomacy. The prime minister appeared before the Foreign Affairs committee of the Diet lower house. He was required under Japan's Constitution to answer Diet members' questions. This questioning, called interpellation, has no counterpart in U.S. law."

"This is ASN Newsbreak, 10:00 p.m. Eastern time, Wednesday, June 8.

"Japan's Prime Minister Sasaki has answered more questions about why Japan is buying California. The prime minister confirmed President Swensen's statement that the U.S. was Japan's second choice for a seller. Under questioning, the prime minister stated that among possible states, California was Japan's first choice, followed by Washington, then Oregon. The prime minister said Alaska is too cold, and Hawaii was deemed vulnerable to attack."

It was just after noon Thursday in the Matsumoto Robotics company cafeteria. Ryuuji smiled and said, "Well, Iwata-*kun*, you did right."

Hiroshi gave him a puzzled look. "Doing what?"

"I heard it on the radio before lunch. The prime minister said that Japan needed a new frontier for young people, so that's why we're buying California."

"Thanks for telling me. Since you heard the radio, wasn't Mrs. Nakamura to arrive this morning?"

"Yes, she gave a short press conference. She said she hoped to talk to House of Representatives members, but I don't think she will."

"Go on."

"Even if she does talk to any, who'd listen to her?"

Hiroshi's expression turned sober. "Anyone who wants to hear a worldly expert on California, who also understands us Japanese. Those who underestimate her are careless."

"That almost sounds like admiration for Mrs. Nakamura."

"She ignores her debt to her mother, and that bothers me. But yes, I admire her."

"Please remember, she fights the treaty."

"And she betrayed her husband's trust when she spoke out. Yet she faces the Diet's Conservatives like TOMOE Gozen and her halberd braved the Taira army."

"You're amazing. You of all people are praising Mrs. Nakamura."

"Lord UESUGI Kenshin ordered his own vassals to mourn the death of Lord TAKETA Shingen. Surely then may I speak good words of *my* enemy?"

"You're amazing."

"Such a woman. Alas, if only Nakamura-*fujin* didn't ignore her mother's pain. Mrs. Nakamura forgets *tsukiai*," social debt.

The owners of the restaurant were both wearing kimono. The elderly couple bowed low as the man said, "Welcome again, Yamamura-*sensei*. Welcome to you, Mrs. Nakamura."

Hours later in Tokyo, it was almost eight p.m. Jetlagged Barbara at noon had left the lower-house chamber to get some sleep at her hotel. Yamamura had been too much enjoying grilling the prime minister to be offended. Now after six hours' sleep, Barbara wasn't rested, but she was again human.

Where Yamamura had put her up had turned out to be a *ryokan* (traditional Japanese inn). She suspected it was one of those ¥100,000-a-day inns she'd read about. Her inn was first-rank.

Just as now the *ryohtei* (exclusive restaurant with private rooms) where she was about to eat, was first-rank. The restaurant boasted a live trio: two women playing the *koto* and a man on the *samisen*.

Barbara and Yamamura were shown to a small eating room that was only six *tatami* mats in area. She and Yamamura removed their slippers right outside the room, and then she exchanged bows and business cards with the three men already waiting there. These men were, like Yamamura, members of the Diet's House of Representatives, as well as the heads of their respective political parties.

Now began the task of meshing with these four men to form a strong anti-treaty team.

Since she was the guest of honor, they were waiting for her to eat. She was given the place at the table farthest from the door and facing the door. She sat on the straw-stuffed *tatami* mat, her knees together and her rear resting on her heels. She placed her hands on the mat in front of her and bowed to Yamamura opposite her, who bowed back. Then she bowed again to the three other men, who returned her bow.

"*Itadakimasu,*" she said. *Bon appétit.*

"*Itadakimasu,*" the men repeated.

She unwrapped the cool, damp *oshibori* towel, and wiped her hands with it. She uncovered her rice bowl and her soup bowl, and placed her rice bowl on the waitress's serving tray. When her rice bowl was filled, Barbara thanked the waitress and took the bowl, touched the bowl briefly to the table, then brought it beneath her face. She took a bite of rice with her chopsticks, and put the rice in her mouth. Now everyone could eat.

After dinner, the men poured each other much *sake*, while Barbara nursed the tiny cup that Yamamura had poured her at the beginning. After she finally finished that, she drank only soft drinks, apologizing that she was still feeling jetlag.

"So is it true, Mrs. Nakamura, that most Californians shop at malls, sunbathe, and drive around in convertibles?" asked middle-aged Mister Teramura. His business card said that he represented a district within Hyohgo Prefecture, and that he was president of the Social Democratic Party.

Barbara smiled to soften her correcting him: "Many do, but not most, Representative Teramura. Exactly as Texans don't ride horses to work, and women of Japan don't wear kimono every day."

"Texans don't ride horses?" asked smiling, black-pinstriped Saitoh. Still smiling, he asked, "But Texans still carry guns everywhere and have shootouts in the streets, right?"

Saitoh's full, thick hair was the distinguished shade called "romance gray" in Japan. Barbara approved.

She smiled back at him. "You mustn't believe everything you see in movies. Texas in 2005 doesn't have shootouts in the streets with guns blazing." A second later, she added deadpan, "Only gangsters in Chicago do that."

Yamamura's smile was indulgent. "Mrs. Nakamura, you must understand that Saitoh hasn't enjoyed the benefit of growing up in Tokyo. He's from backwater Kagawa prefec—"

"I'm from *Kohchi* Prefecture," Saitoh said, "home of fierce fighting dogs and of beautiful coral jewelry. The senior party president pretends to forget."

Yamamura waved that away. "Kagawa, Kohchi, they're the same."

"They're the same? Kohchi, home of Matsuo Shrine's banyan trees, and Kagawa—"

Yamamura ignored that. "In any case, Mrs. Nakamura, Saitoh doesn't represent any district in Thingamabob Prefecture. Instead, he won the Twenty-first Century Party's only seat for Shikoku Region. As he represents all of Shikoku Island, it doesn't matter where in Shikoku he's from."

Saitoh's smile looked neither natural nor friendly. "He only says that, Mrs. Nakamura, because I graduated higher in my class at Tokyo U. than he did in his. It still rankles him."

"You have a college degree, Mrs. Nakamura?" asked the youngest man there, Kada. Kada was from Aichi Prefecture, and headed the Full Prosperity Party.

Barbara nodded. "Yes, in History."

"What junior-college is your degree from?"

Correcting him could turn awkward. "From the University of California at San Diego."

"Indeed, I recall now that you have no brothers." Kada changed the subject: "Which of these foods can you cook?"

She felt Kada's `no brothers' remark was in poor taste, but she let it pass. She said, "I've offered *shabu-shabu* twice at dinner parties. I try to make *nigiri-sushi* in San Diego, where I can buy the fish fresh, but this was better than what I make. Exactly as Charles Swensen likes to bake bread at home, but the president knows the bread tastes better if he lets others bake it."

Barbara saw Saitoh was grinning (secretly laughing?) at Kada. "What she's saying, Kada-*kun*, is that simply because someone can cook, doesn't mean that they can't talk politics."

"It's true." Barbara gazed into every eye. "Politics is why I'm here. Treaty Article 32 is key to swaying proportional-representation Conservatives—"

Yamamura waved his *sake* cup to interrupt her. "Ah, it's good to eat and drink and relax with friends this evening."

"Yes," Barbara said. Yamamura was reminding her that in Japan one first built rapport, and only then did one talk business.

She smiled. Still sitting, she bowed to Yamamura. "I thank you for that artful reminder."

Teramura turned to her. "I presume that you've eaten raw fish, but have you ever eaten *fugu*?"

"No, never. I never tried blowfish when I was a teenager here in Japan. Few California restaurants ask to be licensed for it."

Kada snorted. "Their timidity is no surprise. Americans are so fond of lawsuits."

Yamamura's voice was calm and quiet, like a garden in which ninja were hiding. "Kada-*kun*, please remember where my guest is from."

Kada glanced at Barbara, then bowed to Yamamura. "If my words are offensive, this is regrettable." He didn't sound regretful, though.

"Mm," Yamamura said.

Saitoh smiled at Barbara again. "Would you like to try blowfish while you're here?"

"Please forgive me for not being brave. Thank you for the kind offer, but. . ."

Yamamura said, "I'm with you, Mrs. Nakamura. I don't like how blowfish numbs my mouth."

"It's *meant to* numb your mouth," Saitoh told him. Saitoh turned back to Barbara and teased, "Our senior party president doesn't like eating blowfish because it's different and risky. Also why he opposes the treaty."

Teramura turned to her and pointed to Yamamura, then Saitoh, with his chopsticks. "These two are competitive."

No kidding, Barbara thought.

Thirteen hours' difference meant that what was late evening Thursday in Tokyo was early morning Thursday in Alexandria. Matt had been about to step into the shower when the phone had rung. Could Matt meet with the president this morning? Matt had figured the president wanted to beg a favor of the "Martyr to Zilching the Debt."

Now an hour later, Matt strolled past Mrs. Cooper and into the Oval Office.

"This will be mine soon," Matt murmured with a smile. He surveyed the room from the viewpoint of a future owner, and a future bachelor who'd have to do his own decorating.

The place in truth wasn't so big—not twice the area of a typical American living room. And like a typical living room, it had two couches, four chairs, tables, and lamps. The furniture was practical, so it could stay. What else would he keep? He liked the mahogany grandfather clock; the marble mantel, with twin antique Chinese vases setting on it; the bronze bust of Benjamin Franklin; and the cast-bronze Frederic Remington statue, "Bronco Buster."

What would he change? Those ceiling-to-floor burgundy drapes behind the desk, paired with cool-white walls and blue carpet—that trite red-white-and-blue scheme would quickly be changed to all-blue. Some of the oil paintings on the walls weren't to his taste, so they, too, would be banished to the basement.

And the first painting to leave, Matt decided, would be that portrait of George Washington over the mantel. Right now, sit in the president's chair and you couldn't help but see old George staring back at you from across the room. Nuh-uh, not for Matt. When President Nakamura met with bigwigs and foreign dignitaries in the Oval Office, or when he addressed the American people from the Oval Office, the last thing he would want is the President Who Could Not Tell a Lie always watching and listening.

So much for decorating the place. After all, Matt knew, no visitor to the Oval Office ever noticed the decor. Instead the visitor noticed the two flags behind the desk. He noticed the presidential seal, both woven into the blue carpet and set into the ceiling. He noticed the presidential coat of arms that was carved into the desk. He noticed the phones on the desk, and remembered whom those phones could call. He felt the power of this room, and of the man who worked here.

Charlie Swensen, the man who currently worked here, was sitting behind his desk. On that desk stood a picture of himself and Stephanie, who were sitting on the four-poster bed in the Queens' Bedroom. The photograph-Swensen was grinning, but the real Swensen was frowning. *Odd*, Matt thought.

Matt stuck his hand out as he donned his most photogenic smile. "Good to see you again, Charlie. What can I do for you this morning?"

The president didn't rise, and ignored the proffered hand. "I hear if the treaty folds, you'll be running against Collins for the nomination in '08." Swensen's face and voice showed disgust. "You better drop that whole goddamn idea."

The handshaking hand dropped. Matt's smile disappeared. "W-what?"

"Barbara was right. You betrayed California, and now here's proof."

Fear seared Matt's body like lightning.

The president picked up a several-page report that had been lying face down on the blotter. Swensen's voice dripped loathing. "Shall I tell you what I know?

"You were on the third level of a parking garage last night, sitting in a car with Minoru Asakawa. Says here, Asakawa is more than a simple lobbyist, he's one of Ambassador Fujima's unofficial errand boys. Lucky for you that Asakawa isn't a true spy, only a gopher, or I couldn't be so kind to you."

"This is kind?"

"Hush. Your car's plate was a California-tag senatorial license plate—talk about blending in. Then the report turns interesting.

"Let's see, 9:02 p.m., `Nakamura and Asakawa in car. Conversation already in progress. All conversation was in Japanese.

"`Nakamura: I want to know when your government will thank me, Mister Asakawa. It was my understanding with Ambassador Fujima that Japan would show its gratitude as soon as the Senate approved the treaty. That was almost two weeks ago.'"

Swensen flipped through the report. "You two continue to discuss why you, Nakamura, will have to wait for your payoff. At 9:05, Asakawa exits your car and you drive away."

The keys-tosser, he was an FBI spy! Damn, what do I do? I need to move off the defensive, stop the damage. "Charlie, you had no right to spy on me! I'm no threat to national security, you infringed on my rights—"

"Stop with the lawyer tricks. But you're lucky today, damned lucky."

"Yeah? How is that?"

"Because I plan to do nothing but sit on this report."

"Let me guess why. You're sweet and generous."

"I'm keeping this quiet because you elected me in 2000, and our success with the ESCSA put me on the map politically in 2001. I've owed you big, but this squares us."

"Not to mention, you don't want the public realizing you knew about this the whole time."

"You're deluded, or full of shit."

"Stow it. The day we received the treaty, you had to bribe me not to strangle the treaty in its crib. *Remember?* Then a few days later, I'm saying on TV that this same treaty is wonderful, and you never asked why? You knew."

"You're wrong."

"If you're not lying, you're stupid. Either way, you're a hypocrite."

"You stinking weasel, you *dare*—"

"What do *you* call that deal we cut over the phone?"

"Politics and good preparation."

"Spare me. Anyway, *if* I solicited a bribe, so what? Kids on hot TV shows earn much more than I do, and they only learn lines and do sit-ups." Matt gestured at the FBI report. "If I solicited a bribe, I saw a way to get what's owed me."

"Believe me, I'd love to see you get what you deserve, but I'm burying this. I'm not even going to tell my Cabinet."

You won't tell anyone? Charlie, you chump, you just threw away your bargaining chip. "Is that why you called me in here, to tell me about this report?"

"I called you in because I didn't dare risk discussing this over the phone. I told you at the start why you're here: Forget any presidential campaign in 2008."

"Just because you're president, don't for one second—"

"I also called you in to say that you're a turd-licking rat. Last night I saw your wife welcomed at Tokyo Airport by a big Diet opposition leader. I watched her on CNN and I said to the kids, `Matt should've been the one to go to Tokyo.' But not only didn't you go, now you plot to jail Barbara on a pretext because she spoiled your party."

"So my motives are selfish. But you *do* need to remove her, for national security."

"National security? This I've got to hear."

"Iran or Iraq with Russian missiles doesn't threaten us? How about missiles in Mexico? Or Cuba? Put a handkerchief soaked with chloroform over Barbara's nose, and you'll never get hit with a second Cuban missile crisis."

The president paused too long before replying. "No, forget it, the end. And forget the 2008 campaign. Run in any way at all—even as running mate to a write-in candidate—and I'll make sure this report is leaked. Then how far will you make it?"

"You're bluffing, Charlie. Said yourself, if this report goes public, it will hurt you as well as me." Running for president was Mela's idea. Still, if the chance was offered, why should Matt walk away from it? No way would he let Charlie bully him.

Swensen's eyes on Matt's were lasers. "I'm not bluffing. Run for president, and I'll leak this report *myself*, got me?" A pause. "No matter what happens to me afterward."

Matt didn't say, "Quit wasting my time, loser." But he stood there and let Charlie spew, and all the while he thought, *You know my secret, but won't reveal it. Whereas I'm tempting you to hunt Barbara. Who's really on top here?*

Four hours later was very late in the evening in Tokyo. Barbara and Kada were sober; Yamamura, Saitoh, and Teramura were smashed.

"Waitress!" yelled Saitoh. "Our American friend needs more tea, hurry please."

The kimono-clad waitress rushed in on socked feet and bowed deeply. She placed a full teapot of green tea in front of Barbara, and took the empty one. "Does anybody need anything? More *sake*? Beer? Pickles?"

Teramura belched. "I've had too much *sake* as it is. Please bring me some *ochazube*," green tea poured over rice, "to calm my stomach."

After the waitress had left, Saitoh smiled at Teramura. "*Ochazube*—is that food for a real man?"

Teramura burped. "I see nothing manly about puking all over myself. Besides, if I get too drunk, who'll help me walk?"

"Just me," Kada said. "Mrs. Nakamura has only a woman's strength, and all of you are as wobbly as Teramura-*kun*."

Saitoh looked at Barbara, smiled, then turned back to Kada. "Mrs. Nakamura could walk him, she's strong. Have you noticed her muscles? She's sleek."

So cute Saitoh thought she was attractive, too? "Thank you very much for those compliments, Representative. Still, I am certainly not as strong as you men." She saw no harm in giving Saitoh a flirtatious smile. She noticed Kada noticing that smile.

Saitoh leaned toward her. "If Kada tries to carry Teramura, he'll hurt himself. Teramura never was a sumo wrestler, it was years of sitting behind a desk in an Education and Science Ministry job that made him look like this. That, and too much beer and *sake* over the years." Saitoh laughed.

Yamamura looked at Saitoh talking to Barbara and twitched a frown. "Saitoh shows poor memory. He neglects to mention his own years with the Ministry of Agriculture, Forestry, and Fisheries, and those years' effect on his own girth."

298 Tom H. Richardson

"Girth? I'm within fifteen kilograms of what I weighed in college."

"But I'm within ten kilograms. As I've said before, over in Kagawa Prefecture—"

"Kohchi Prefecture," Saitoh said. "Home of two rice harvests a year and hectares of hothouses growing food, all to keep smug *Tokyo* residents from starving."

"Anyway, over in Kohchi, agriculture, forestry, and fishing, that's all they know."

Saitoh's smile was amused, probably at Yama-mura's attempt to bait him. "True, it wasn't a prestigious Ministry, but enough Shikoku people knew me for my party to elect me to the lower house upon my retirement. I'm not complaining."

Kada, who had been watching Barbara, now spoke. "So what kind of political experience have you had? Have you ever been elected to anything?"

"No, not at all. My political experience has consisted of campaigning for my husband, traveling with him or sometimes alone across California for his three Congressional and two Senate campaigns."

"Go on," Saitoh said.

"Wait, I also wrote some of his position papers for his first Congressional campaign."

Kada frowned. "So you haven't attended a great American university, but you're a great cook. You've never held political office, in California or anywhere."

Teramura gave her a tipsy smile. "Ah, yes, California. That's why you're here in Japan, talking to us drunken politicians."

Before she could answer, Kada replied instead. "I don't understand how this woman can help our goal. To me, her presence seems an expensive waste."

Seven hours later was early evening in Falls Church, Virginia. "C'mon, Mela." Matt again knocked hard on her apartment door. "Let me in, please."

"Why are you here, Matthew?" asked Mela's voice through the door. "Have you forgotten what I said?"

"I hoped you might have changed your mind." If not, he'd come to persuade her to take him back.

"Not tonight, not tomorrow, not ever. Go home."

He couldn't bear losing Mela, too. "Only for a moment, okay? I need to talk to you. Please, Mela. Only for a minute, I swear."

A pause, then she unlocked and opened the door. "A minute, tops."

She was wearing a plain pink cotton bathrobe with cartoon teddy bears dancing over the pockets. He'd never seen it before, but it looked well worn. Her hair was wrapped in a wet towel and she was barefoot. The blue easy chair had a bowl of popcorn setting on it, and a can of diet cola beside it. A bookmarked user's guide to a database software lay atop one armrest. A bottle of red nail polish sat on one corner of the coffee table. Matt sensed no sign of another male visitor.

She eyed him, arms crossed. "What part of `it's over' do you not understand?"

"We can't end this—"

"Why not?"

"I'm in love with you."

She inhaled to speak; he added, "Not because of the ice-cube trick."

She was silent, waiting.

He added, "See, it's because you're strong, you're my match."

She looked hard at him.

She wasn't buying; his shoulders slumped. "Okay, forget that. Can't we just be friends?"

She looked at him, with a Nevada blackjack dealer's expressionless eyes. She said then, "Friends. Us. Why?"

"I need you."

"You need me. Sure."

"And if the treaty doesn't work out, the presidential race—"

"What about *my* needs? Your political career is in the coffin. You have left—two years? Two months? Two weeks? It's time for me to cut my losses, invest my time more profitably—"

"But the presidential campaign coming up—"

"No lies, Matthew. You can't run, ever."

The fear kicked him again. "What's *that* mean?"

"I know facts. Facts that would become public if you did run, facts to end your political career. Maybe even end *you*."

"There's only one way you could know that!"

"How I know isn't important. What's important is that I *do* know. That's why I'm dropping you."

I need to regain the initiative. Put her on the defensive. "You learned that from Hahn, didn't you? The FBI Director? You set up a threesome for him, then he probably let you read what my first-grade teacher said about me."

She smiled, amused. "Exactly." The smile vanished. "Righteous anger from you isn't believable, Senator. I want you gone now."

He knew the perfect way to put her on the defensive. "You're nothing but a goddamned whore!"

She drew up straight. "And a damned fine one."

"You're *proud* of it?"

"If I charged for it, I could earn a thousand dollars a night here. I actually did that, one winter in Vail. I'm a whore for sure, but *not a slut*, Matthew—I haven't done it for free in years. But my coin now isn't money, it's power. Give me power, political power, or at least introduce me to powerful men. I'm patient, I can wait for my own power. But right now, you can do nothing for me, so it's *au revoir, Monsieur* Nakamura."

"You're foolish enough to think you can sleep your way to the top."

"Watch me. The only reason that it hasn't been done before is the women's own limitations."

He snorted. "It's Eva Braun's fault she didn't win Hitler's job."

"A woman wanting power can fuck and suck and moan, but it's not enough. Can she manage? Can she negotiate? Make alliances? Deliver on promises? Can she *consolidate her power*? Until now, no. So when her lover lost power, or else when her lover tired of her, she was powerless."

"Yet you think *you'll* be the exception—you, a tax specialist with tits."

"Give me power, I'll be able to keep it." For a second she pulled apart the lapels of her robe, to plunge the neckline. "Men think my chest means I'm stupid, but it's they who become the drooling idiots. My money was well spent."

"Your money was wasted. If a fine chest and a hot cunt were all that anyone needed to grab power, Capitol Hill would look like a porno-actress convention."

"You overlook that I have a brain, too. Senator, your minute is long past."

"You can't throw me out like this! Without me, you'd never have met Harland. And maybe Harland introduced you to Hahn, so I get credit for him, too."

"What I've owed you, I've paid you for—or have you forgotten you and me and Shirley in bed together? Now I've asked several times for you to leave, *Senator.* Do I call the police?"

Screw trying to win her back. "Why, you goddamned little tramp. You think because you're gangbanging the FBI that you can *threaten* me? You need reminding of your place."

He grabbed the towel around her hair, and dragged her into the bedroom. She'd made him, a senator with power to make laws, beg at the door for entry.

About twenty minutes later, he pulled up his pants and left. She hadn't screamed, but she had scratched him, often and deeply. She also had bruised him, almost as much as he'd bruised her.

Before and after Friday's legislative session of the Diet, Barbara walked around the House of Representatives with Yamamura, who introduced her to other lower-house members. Again and again the pattern repeated: Yamamura made introductions, Barbara and the visited Dietman exchanged business cards, the visited Representative offered green tea and rice crackers or other snack, the two Representatives and she made light conversation for a few minutes, and in less than five minutes after they'd arrived, Barbara and Yamamura were bowing their goodbyes. At the end of the day she'd discussed flower arranging, current movies, swimming at various Japanese beaches, *go*-game strategy, and soccer. What was *not* mentioned, by anyone that day, was either the treaty or California.

Barbara met Yamamura's staffers, and everyone (including Barbara) was amazed when she met Miiko-*san*. Barbara stared at the young woman—*She looks just like me!* Miiko-*san* was only in her twenties, with black hair, in the uniform of an OL (clerical helper), but she had Barbara's height, and even a similar face.

Everyone exclaimed how the two women looked like mother and daughter.

Laying on Miiko-*san*'s desk was a novel, *Geigi to Supai* (Geisha and Spy).

Only seconds after opening his eyes, Matt said, "Shit, what was I thinking? That was a damned stupid and risky thing to do."

A few hours later was Friday morning in Alexandria. Matt woke from a night's sleep and realized: What he'd done to Mela the night before was thirty ways foolish.

He feared the unexpected ring of the phone or the doorbell. He feared walking naked out of his bathroom, there to be jumped by FBI special-unit commandoes. He feared starting his car and it exploding.

By Sunday morning for Tokyo, Barbara was now over the worst of the jetlag. Diet members were spending the day with their families. So after giving two TV interviews and a newspaper interview, she took the commuter train to spend the day with her relatives.

Grandfather lived in the city of Shinjuku, west of Tokyo, along with Mother's next younger sister, Makiko. Aunt Makiko had moved in with her father after her own husband had died. Grandmother already had passed on.

After the train trip, Barbara took a taxi. Now she stood face to face with Aunt at the apartment door. Aunt's face had aged much in thirty-odd years, and her hair was completely white.

Aunt bowed low, as etiquette demanded, and Barbara bowed back. Aunt said with formal modesty, "You honor humble-us with your visit, Niece. Our home is small and filthy, but please enter it."

The apartment was completely traditional, not partially or completely Westernized as were most Tokyo apartments. Barbara exchanged outdoor shoes for indoor slippers at the entryway, then stepped up to the short hallway. A few seconds later she removed the slippers at the hallway's end, as Aunt opened the *fusuma* sliding door into the *ochanoma* (traditional-style living room).

She found Grandfather sitting calmly by a small, low-legged table. Grandfather sat as usual: half-on, half-off the edge of a low *seiza* meditation bench that he used for sitting without falling over. His crutches—aluminum, unlike those of thirty years ago—lay within reach behind him. Just as thirty years earlier, Grandfather wore a *hara-maki* (stomach-warmer band).

Barbara bowed low to Grandfather, who sketched a bow in return. She presented her visitation gift, a big can of California almonds.

"You honor this house with your visit," Grandfather said. His voice was reedy. "Please sit there." He indicated the *kamiza*, the place of honor at the table where her back would be to the alcove.

Aunt entered and served green tea and *monaka* (cakes filled with bean paste) to everyone, as Barbara took her place.

"The One-Eyed Dragon is gone," Barbara said. She was referring to a vacuum-tube television that Grandfather had built, and which had still worked when Barbara was a teenager.

Grandfather nodded. "When it needed a picture tube, parts for that model were no longer carried."

Aunt smiled. "It never ate me, despite Older Sister's prediction."

"And how *is* Takeko-*san*?" asked Grandfather.

Grandfather and Aunt looked at Barbara, who felt her face redden. It took self-control not to squirm. "Mother is in good health."

"*Soh desu*," so things are, Grandfather said without expression. "What does she think about your being here?" Grandfather gave no clue whether he himself approved or disapproved.

Calm, be calm. "Grandfather, she feels that I fail in my duty by opposing the treaty, I fail in my duty by contradicting Husband in public, and I fail in my duty by divorcing Husband."

"Go on."

"She thinks that I am too American in my nature. Perhaps she is ashamed of me."

"Mm. Do you feel ashamed, Barbara-*san*?"

His deliberate erasing of expression was making her nervous, but she would answer honestly. "No."

He frowned. "I joined the Imperial Navy because the United States insulted my country. The United States said it knew better than Japan about governing Manchuria. Now you say the United States knows better than Japan about governing California?"

"Yes. I'm sorry," she told the floor.

"Please tell me why you have taken these actions."

Barbara explained, then said, "Grandfather, Mother feels that I have shamed my relatives in Japan. Please, if I may dare to ask: Do you feel ashamed of me?"

"I'm not sure, Barbara-*san*."

The next day, Monday, Yamamura again took Barbara around to meet more lower-house members. Again, everything but the treaty was discussed. She was growing anxious, but she didn't think it showed.

A few hours later, which was Monday morning in Washington, Matt decided he could relax. Mela never had called the police; Matt decided she knew better than to fight a senator.

In Tokyo, Barbara spent Tuesday walking around the National Diet Building with Yamamura, talking with the House of Representatives members she'd met Friday and Monday. At last, the treaty was discussed. As in the Senate, Dietmen's reactions to her ranged from seemingly sincere support and interest, all the way to haughty disdain. Yet overall she considered the day a net gain.

She looked forward to the next day, when she could attack the treaty at its most politically vulnerable point: Article 32.

Of the five hundred members of the Diet lower house, three hundred came from three hundred single-member districts, and two hundred members were elected on a party-proportional basis in Japan's eleven electoral regions. Treaty Article 32 decreed that sixteen of those two hundred party-proportional Representatives would lose their seats—but nobody knew who those sixteen would be. So all two hundred proportional Representatives felt endangered. The majority of the two hundred were Conservatives, and all two hundred wanted to keep their seats.

In the Diet it was traditional to vote on treaties unamended, but observing the tradition created a dilemma. America would cancel the deal if the Diet gutted Article 32, which guaranteed fair Diet representation for Japanese California. Yet with Article 32 unharmed, the Diet's proportional-representation Conservatives were in danger.

The proportional-representation Conservatives were searching for excuses to vote against the treaty. Barbara's strategy was to wield her California expertise to teach the proportional-representation Conservatives plenty of great excuses.

Her plan couldn't miss, she knew.

By the next day, however, Barbara learned she had more obstacles to overcome. The treaty needed only a simple majority in the Diet's lower house to pass, and a casual survey showed about 55 percent support. Prime Minister Sasaki and Foreign Minister Utsumi—and even a former prime minister named Matsuzaka—were making friendly calls and visits in the treaty's behalf.

She sought out Representative Hidaka, who was not only a proportional-representation Conservative, but a faction leader within the Liberal-Democratic Party. If she could've subverted him, he would've brought at least forty votes with him. But his "Sorry, I'm voting yes" was firm. *Damn.*

"Barbara! Ms. Nakamura!" the American woman yelled.

Five days later, Barbara just had left her Japanese inn when a young woman hurried over. "Thanks for agreeing to the interview," the woman said, panting. "Here's the map I promised."

The stranger was a blonde in her late twenties, her eyes hidden behind sunglasses. She was holding an envelope out to Barbara. The printed return-address had been destroyed by ballpoint pen and black marker.

"Sorry, I don't remember—"

The young woman jabbed Barbara in the stomach with the envelope. "I put in an explanation—I mean, a reminder. Everything you need is here."

Something was going on, but Barbara couldn't guess what. "Are you print, or electronic?"

The woman lowered her voice and leaned closer. "Truth is, I'm from the embassy, but—"

"*Embassy*? Then you've wasted your trip. Tell Swensen and the Secretary of State I won't stop."

The woman's head turned slightly, as presumably she checked for eavesdroppers. "I was never here. With this, you can help my parents in Davis."

Barbara shook her head in confusion, unable to guess the woman's game. Meanwhile, no way did Barbara intend to touch that envelope.

The blonde bit her lip. "I'm in Consular Section. I broke laws just by reading this myself. *Please*."

With a nervousness she hid, Barbara took the envelope. The blonde spun on the ball of her foot and hurried away.

Inside the envelope was a photocopy of a message from the U.S. ambassador to Foreign Minister Utsumi:

"Secretary of State Harland holds proof that Senator Matthew Nakamura awaits a conspicuous bribe payment from Japan. The Secretary instructs me to respectfully inform you: The United States would be greatly embarrassed if that bribe were to be paid."

About which, the Variety-Show Host joked—

Prime Minister Sasaki explained that Japan didn't want Alaska because it's colder than Japan's coldest island. Hey Diet, did you know Sacramento is hotter than every place in Japan? Then there's Death Valley. . .

Politician Yamamura says that all of Japan's cash and gold isn't enough for even one three-trillion-dollar payment. God forbid I help Japan, but Californians have this problem beat. Japan, put California on your credit card.

CHAPTER 11
Heisei 17-nen 6-gatsu 20-nichi, Getsuyohbi (Monday, June 20, 2005)

Barbara jammed the message about Matt in her purse, dashed back into her Japanese inn, and asked excitedly how she could place an international long-distance call. Two minutes later, she was connected to Carol at the *San Diego Union-Tribune*.

"Carol, at last: proof Matt sold out California!"

"Who told you?"

"A woman who works in the U.S. Embassy."

"How'd she learn about the FBI reports?"

Huh? "*What* FBI reports?"

Carol explained that she, too, had received a delivery not ten minutes earlier. Yet the Sunday-night delivery to the newsroom was not what was most remarkable about Carol's envelope.

Sent anonymously to Carol from Washington were copies of two FBI reports. The reports detailed Matt's secret meetings with somebody named Asakawa, and Matt's own words damned him. The entire newsroom was in an uproar, as everyone pushed to confirm those reports with the FBI.

Barbara told Carol her own news. Both Barbara and Carol were puzzled how Secretary of State Harland had obtained his proof. Likewise mysterious was the identity and motive of Carol's anonymous source. How the two events were connected was a third mystery. But what was no mystery were the results, once Carol's story were printed.

"All this time." Barbara shook her head in wonder. "All this time, I couldn't make anyone listen to me. Now here's Matt, demanding his huge gift, and make it snappy. And you have it all in black and white."

"Yes," Carol said. "Now you're cleared."

Two hours later, Barbara was still at her Japanese inn. She was trying to call Matt through the phone in her room.

The operator had a trained speaking voice and a fully polite manner. "Firefly-River Inn switchboard, how may humble-I direct your call?"

"This is Nakamura again. I wish to place another international call to the United States, please."

The operator took the number for Matt's office private line. She then said, "Thank you. It will take humble-me about forty-five seconds to place the call, so please stay on the line." As during Barbara's call to Carol, the line seemed to go dead.

While waiting, Barbara mused aloud. "I need to know, Matt, what went wrong with you? Did I so misread your true self when I was young? Did I somehow drive you to this, later on? When we were dating we told each other everything. So drop the lying and let's be frank one last time."

The operator came back after a minute of silence. "*O-machidoh-sama*, but that line doesn't answer."

"*Arigatoh gozaimashita.*" Barbara tried again, giving the operator the number for the Alexandria house.

The operator was back after another minute. "Nakamura-*sama*, humble-I am sorry, but I have reached an answering machine."

". . .name, phone number, time you called, and a message if you wish," beep.

Barbara couldn't afford another international call, which meant she wouldn't have that final heart-to-heart with Matt. Damn.

But in the meantime, Matt's machine had beeped at her. She'd always thought that people who hung up without leaving a message were rude, so Barbara said, "I'm still in Tokyo, but I know all about those FBI reports. *Really*, now—`I threw away my Senate seat for this treaty; I'm counting on that not being for nothing`? `I don't like people who don't meet their obligations`? Who *are* you now? Why'd you do it? What happened to the man of honor I married?"

Monday afternoon in Washington, Asakawa's message had been urgent: *Please meet me.* Soon after, he gave Matt the bad news—

Foreign Minister Utsumi had sent a message to Ambassador Fujima early that morning. "Somehow Secretary Harland knows, so the arrangement with Senator Nakamura is ended."

This disaster has Mela's fingerprints all over it. But I don't dare retaliate, or she might hit me with something worse. What a pisser.

Matt's response to the message, after saying sullen goodbyes to Asakawa, was to head to Stares and Strips Forever and become a belligerent drunk. First Barbara's taunts on the answering machine last night, now Fujima's bombshell tonight, and Mela was clearly the cause of both. Why, Matt asked himself, did everyone pick on him?

When he drove his car into his own garage, sometime after eleven, he was in a foul mood. His fender pushed against one of Barbara's moving cartons that he'd carried into the garage, making a small tear in the cardboard. "If you'd shipped out your shit yourself before you left, I wouldn't be bumping into it," he told the absent Barbara.

From the garage, he staggered to the kitchen refrigerator and its beer. From the fridge, he stumbled to the answering machine in the bedroom.

The answering machine held thirty-six messages. He swayed back and forth as he listened to them—then he smashed the answering machine on the floor.

It seemed those damned FBI reports had wound up on the front page of a special-edition *San Diego Union-Tribune*. Under Carol Parks's byline. It didn't take Einstein to figure who'd leaked Carol the story.

Barbara would pay.

About which, the Variety-Show Host joked—

The FBI caught Senator Nakamura whining that Japan hadn't paid his bribe after he delivered the treaty. Now he knows what ordinary folks suffer: He busted his tail to meet all the government requirements, then the government delays paying.

I think spying on Capitol Hill should be a regular job of the FBI. It keeps the politicians honest. Of course, the FBI might have trouble getting this part of its budget approved. . . .

CHAPTER 12
Heisei 17-nen 6-gatsu 21-nichi, Kayohbi (Tuesday, June 21, 2005)

At eight in the morning, Japan's television and radio exposed the scandal linking the Foreign Ministry and America's Senator Nakamura. Hiroshi was canvassing outside the Yokohama train station, so he didn't hear the news until later.

Hiroshi was at Matsumoto Robotics an hour later, standing by Ryuuji's desk. Hiroshi stifled a yawn. "Please excuse me, Kinoshita-*san*."

"You're tired and it's only nine in the morning. Were you up late with a lady? Another Auckland girl?"

Hiroshi smiled. "No, the entire Takarazuka All-Girl Revue."

"Well, when you decide to cut down to only one woman, remember Miss Higashi likes you."

"She does?"

"Please notice, blind one, how much she smiles when you speak to her at lunch."

"Huh! Around her, I'm too busy worrying about sounding like a fool. But to answer you: No, I haven't been staying up late, I've been waking up early."

"Doing what? Exercise? Study? Writing a novel?"

"No, everyone knows you need a Literature degree to write a novel. I've been standing outside the west entrance to Yokohama's train station, asking people to sign my petition."

Ryuuji blinked. "What petition?"

"It reads, `Dietmen, we want you to buy California.'"

"How many names do you have now?"

"Just over five hundred."

"That's not too many, in a country much over a hundred million."

Hiroshi felt hurt. "I apologize for seeming argumentative, but five hundred names is a lot for only one person."

"You don't feel, uh, outside the mosquito net?" *You don't feel like a foolish weirdo?*

"Yes, so I must constantly push myself. I'm shy, remember?"

"You weren't in San Diego."

"True, but watch me around Higashi-*san* sometime."

"You insist you can't talk to her, but alone you petition strangers at the train station. You're amazing."

"I'm only an ordinary man, nothing special," Hiroshi said, embarrassed. "As for the petitions, humble-I have a request." Hiroshi's mouth went dry as he said, "I know this is an imposition, but it would mean much if you please would join me."

"I don't feel strongly about the treaty like you do."

Sounds like a "no" coming, but I'll keep trying. "I understand."

"Besides, by myself approaching strangers who would give me scornful looks? Aggh!"

"Yes, it's hard, but I'm doing this for Japan."

"Still, I can't let people here think you're a weirdo loner. But even beside you, I'm not sure I can endure the rejection for long."

Hiroshi was surprised and deeply moved that his friend would do this scary thing for him. The very polite words "Kinoshita-*san*, *dohmo arigatoh gozaimashita*" weren't nearly enough to express Hiroshi's gratitude.

"Mister Senator, sorry to disturb you, but—"

Twenty hours later, Washington time was just after 4:00 in the afternoon Tuesday, and Matt was furious. A long day after a sleepless night was one cause of his rage, all day enduring a cold formality from his fellow senators was another.

But head receptionist Melissa, who'd burst into his private office without knocking, was the top irritant of the moment.

"Melissa, what's the idea of—"

She was close to hyperventilating. "A bomb, it's here! Just now, we caught his VEMM," video e-mail message. "He sent a letter bomb! The man had a fake voice, and a paper bag over his head. Said the bomb's in today's mail. I already called the Capitol Police. Somehow he knows we already picked up the mail. It's addressed to you, he says. My mother lives in Eugene, Oregon, in case—"

"Melissa." Matt's voice was slo-o-ow now, it was soothing, it was hypnotic: "I've been a senator for ten years. I've received death threats before. I'm still here—"

"But Janice and Cecilia and I have taken four death threats this morning!"

Damn you, Mela. "Melissa, the newspaper story has only been out since yesterday afternoon. There's no way a bomb really could've been mailed from California to here by now."

"Maybe he flew to Washington yesterday and mailed it here in town."

"They X-ray luggage."

She took a deep breath and tried to stretch the tension out of her muscles. Matt decided her moves would've looked very sexy if she weren't so scared.

Melissa found some sense: She tried to agree with the boss. "Okay, it's maybe a fake. Still. . ." Her voice trailed off.

Melissa refused to leave Matt's office, convinced that the wood of his door might shield her. He was still trying to calm her when Sherry walked in with a stranger. At the door's opening, Melissa flinched.

The new arrival had a straight back, a crew cut, a digital camera that wound around his neck and under his left arm, a satchel with strange bulges inside, and constantly sweeping eyes. The "Hazardous Devices Team" patch on his sleeve confirmed Matt's deduction. He was a very thin, ruddy-skinned blond man.

"I'm Lieutenant Riggins, U.S. Capitol Police."

"How do you do, Lieutenant, I'm Sena—"

"I know you. I hear you got a lotta people ticked off at you. Who's the lady who caught the video message, that you?"

Melissa glanced at Matt; at his nod, she nodded to Riggins.

"You didn't erase it, I hope."

"I wanted to, but no sir, oh no, it's evidence."

"Then I'd like to see it. Senator, I ask you to look, too. You might know the guy or spot something I miss."

Matt and Melissa walked to Melissa's computer in the front reception area. Riggins kept going, striding past them to the main door and opening it. A Capitol Police Canine Unit officer and a small white curly-tailed dog entered. Riggins rejoined Matt and Melissa at her computer, while the dog handler and dog remained just inside the door.

By now the entire staff crowded the floor near Melissa's screen. "Get back to work!" Matt yelled. People shuffled their feet but nobody spoke, or left.

Melissa pulled up the bomb-threat VEMM. She'd been right, the message sender had been wearing a paper bag over his head. He had drawn a monster face on the bag with marker pen. Paper Bag wore a USC sweatshirt. The hand holding the microphone belonged to a white male, age indeterminate.

Paper Bag spoke in front of a white wall. His voice sounded synthetic. "Mornin', Senator. Now that ya just got your morning mail, I wanna tell ya what ya got. I sent ya a letter bomb. Y'see, I know lots of guys here in California, and I keep hearin', something should be done about Nakamura. Well, I'm the guy doin' something. Ya shoulda stayed close to home when ya put your hand out, Senator, know why? Those Japanese take over, then some of us guys in California, we're gonna find it *real hard* to make a livin'. *Capisce?* Rule is, ya mess with us, we make ya *hurt real bad.* Yer nickname is `Bomber,' so I sent ya a bomb."

Five minutes later, Riggins was on his knees in the office mailroom. By then he'd donned surgical gloves, and had unfolded his camera.

He and the white dog had already cleared one mail tray. Now Riggins pulled the second tray in close. Immediately he picked up a large tan clasp-envelope, thicker than a woman's wrist. To Matt, the only other thing unusual about the envelope was that the sender had gone overboard with the postage. Also, the paper was covered with oily blotches—one such was a huge blotch right above where the sender had written "Personal and Confidential." The envelope was postmarked Takoma Park, last night; it had been mailed locally.

Riggins touched the blotches, sniffed his fingertips, then brought the envelope close and smelled the biggest blotch. Evidently he wasn't smart enough to see the obvious explanation: A postal worker had used the envelope as a tray for his onion rings.

Riggins eyed the dog-handler. "Harv, we won't need Snow-Wolf. I'm calling a Code Red Alarm."

"Oh, jeez."

"He's using a book to disguise the bomb. Bet it's an old almanac."

The dog-handler whistled. "Shit, if he hollowed out that whole book, and we had an Event. . ."

Riggins shrugged. "Beats a slow death by cancer. Anyway, tell the team, the building superintendent, and the Watch Commander's office. We need an orderly evacuation." The dog-handler and dog left. Riggins grabbed his camera.

Who does this moron flatfoot think he is? Matt glared at the back of Riggins's head. "Excuse me for pooping your party, but this *is* my office. Do I understand that you're going to evacuate my office without even your goddamn dog sniffing this goddamn envelope?"

Riggins looked up from shooting close-ups of the envelope to lock eyes with Matt. "You nailed it. Except I'm not gonna evacuate only your office, but the entire Dirksen-Hart Building. I'm gonna piss off lots of motorists by shutting down Constitution between First and Maryland. And if this little honey were sent by some fruitcake terrorist instead of a mobster with a grudge against you, I'd be evacuating everyone within an entire *block*."

"But your dog didn't sniff it. If he had, he would've proven it safe."

Riggins ignored Matt, and stood to address the throng. "I want you to leave the building. Don't run, *walk*. Leave purses and briefcases behind. And don't touch *nothing*. We've got everything under control."

Matt's staffers glanced at their boss; nobody moved.

Matt grabbed Riggins's arm. "I *said*, your dog didn't sniff the envelope. I see no reason to leave."

Riggins pulled his arm free, to put his fists on his hips. "Senator, do I order the Capitol Police to evacuate this office *forcibly*?"

Matt glared at Riggins. Riggins glared back.

"Oh, what the hell," Matt said, and stomped out the door.

As he was walking out the building's front door, a bomb technician walked in. The man was carrying a thick metal case.

As Riggins had commanded, both the Hart Building and the adjoined Dirksen Building were evacuated. Many people left those two buildings by the underground electric-car subways that led to the Senate Wing. Yet many people left Dirksen-Hart at street level, in order to watch the show. Add them to the usual horde of tourists, and the result was crowds of people outside.

Those of Matt's people who came outside stood near him in a loose group. That is, until Sherry wandered away and began talking to Senator Dag Anderssen of Minnesota. As soon as Sherry left, the rest of Matt's staffers also drifted away, to haunt the barricades and watch the bomb squad. *Good riddance.*

A black bomb-disposal truck with a red trailer sat in the middle of blocked-off Constitution Avenue. Next to the truck and trailer, a bomb technician and a District of Columbia policewoman were talking—too quietly for Matt to overhear. Matt recognized a *Newsweek* reporter named Alice; she and a CBS television crew were pressed against a barricade, straining to record the words of the bomb technician and the policewoman.

Twenty yards behind Matt, Senator Gibson stood with his staffers gathered around. Gibson caught Matt's eye and glared.

Matt spotted Mela in Gibson's crowd, and took only enough time to catch her shark's grin before he turned around. He had better things to do than look at some tax staffer with delusions of grandeur.

Mela walked past him a few seconds later, supposedly headed to the barricades. As she came beside him, she murmured, "Such a pretty day for a bomb threat."

Matt acted unworried: "Such evil genius, be proud. You brought me two disasters for the price of one."

"Yeah?"

"You sent those FBI reports to Barbara, *knowing* she'd pass them to Carol."

Mela shot him a look of surprise—did she really think he wouldn't figure everything out? Then she smirked. "I sent them where they'd erase the boredom." She strolled down to the barricades.

That's when he discovered that the CBS team had left their barricade to ambush him. "Senator," a balding reporter asked, "will this bomb be the first of many?"

Matt put on his confident face. "I'm convinced there is no bomb. All this is a joke by an isolated loser."

"Level with me, Senator. With millions of Californians given even more reason to be enraged, you really don't fear for your life?"

"Assassination is rare in American history. Men thought much worse than me have lived to old age."

"If you don't fear death, then do you fear expulsion? Majority Leader Fuller has said that if the treaty dies—"

"I'll face the Senate Ethics Committee. Yes, he told me yesterday afternoon."

"We hear that if the Ethics Committee summons you, your prospects look grim. Comments?"

"Of course my future looks bleak. I deserve to be cleared, but Fuller will tell every Democrat the president wants me gone. With Charlie Swensen and heartless Steve Leaird teamed against me, what hope do I have? And the White House will ensure Fuller and Leaird don't stop with my censure."

"Are you actually saying, Senator, that you'll be expelled not because you're guilty of abuse of office, but because of a White House plot?"

"Folks, Hank Collins masterminded these fake FBI reports. I understand why: Politics as usual, the V.P. is looking to the next presidential race. But what really dismays me is that my friend Charlie agreed to `plant the bloody glove.'"

"And why would the president do that?"

"Swensen had to choose whom to back in 2008: his V.P. or me. I'm a cinch for the nomination, but it seems our president still begrudges my not campaigning much for him last November."

"If the reports are fake, why release them now? The 2008 campaign doesn't start for another two years."

"Wouldn't it look suspicious if they were discovered a week before the New Hampshire primary?"

The dog-handler stepped out of the front entrance of the Dirksen-Hart Building and waved. The bomb technician by the trailer waved back. The dog-handler disappeared into the building again.

The bomb technician by the trailer walked over to a contraption that Matt hadn't paid attention to before. The technician picked up a set of controls attached by springy wire to the machine. He pressed buttons, and the machine unfolded itself to become a waist-high robot spider. The Deseret Robotics spider lumbered toward the steps of Dirksen-Hart, with its puppeteer following at a distance. Alice the *Newsweek* reporter photographed this.

Matt turned back to the balding reporter. "But the vice president's scheme has backfired. I hear not only loose talk of expelling me, but also of impeaching Swensen as well."

The dog-handler and dog hurried down the front steps of the Dirksen Building. The bomb tech with the metal suitcase hurried down the steps of the Hart Building a few seconds later.

Matt continued, "I admit it looks bad. Yet I trust that when all the facts come out, the American people will continue to believe in me as they have up till now."

"Senator, if a bomb does kill you, doesn't it bother you that you'll be remembered not as the `Martyr to Zilching the Debt,' but as the `Traitor to California'?"

"As I said before, I maintain my innocence. I trust in the judgment of history."

The reporter made the throat-cut sign to the cameraman, and the television crew wandered off. No sooner had they left than Alice from *Newsweek* pounced on him. Matt endured more minutes of reporter grilling.

While Matt had been jousting with Alice, the robot spider had come out the front door. Now the spider, carrying the thick envelope, was almost down the steps.

Alice dumped Matt for the spider. Matt wanted the planet to leave him alone then; the planet didn't oblige. About twenty yards away was a gaggle of teenagers, all wearing "Lubbock High School" T-shirts. Several kids pointed at him. One boy left the group to talk to him.

The mama's-boy was crying. "Why'd you have to take the bribe?"

Matt gave the kid a smart-aleck grin. "Because it seemed a good idea at the time."

"We believed in you. We thought you were a miracle."

Matt was still flippant: "Didn't they tell you your trip to Washington would be educational?"

"I hope they throw you in prison, or do whatever to you. What you did was rotten."

"Enjoyed the talk, kid. Your teacher's waiting for you." The boy glared and left.

The spider was down the stairs, and was headed toward the bomb-disposal trailer. The puppeteer bomb-tech and Riggins followed at maximum distance. Riggins had binoculars trained on the spider, and spoke words to the puppeteer every few seconds. Just so everyone knew Riggins was Somebody Important, he was carrying a bullhorn in his other hand.

A hand fell on Matt's shoulder. "That boy gave you a rough time," Joe Bob Saunders said.

Matt's voice was bitter: "Be careful, Joe Bob. Ken over there"—Matt jerked his thumb at Gibson—"will report you to Dave Fuller. Showing kindness to the bad boy of the Senate isn't allowed."

Saunders shrugged. "Two thousand years ago lived another Matthew who also was called a traitor to his people. Jesus chose him to be an apostle, so Ah think Ah can be seen talkin' to you."

"At least you're not screaming. Hector did that. Did you know he cornered me in my private office yesterday? Just charged straight in, Sherry and Lisa and Melissa couldn't stop him."

"Yes sir, Ah heard that."

"I thought he was going to cut me open right in front of all three women." The memory of the fear was still strong.

"Can you blame him?"

Matt sighed. "No, I guess not. Christ, look at everyone stare at me. I'll be glad to leave this circus, I don't care when or how."

The robot was at the bomb-disposal trailer. Set atop the trailer was a red thick steel cylindrical tub, three feet tall and three feet in diameter. A second thick tub, of matching height and slightly smaller diameter, was set inside the first tub. A two-inch air gap separated the two tubs' walls. A circular railing, at the top of the outer tub and coming radially outward from it, suspended a net. The net hung atop and into the tubs.

The arm that held the envelope, the spider moved it up the side of the tubs, over the railing, then down. Obviously the puppetmaster's intent was to drop the envelope into the net.

The spider brought the envelope down too soon. The bottom tip of the envelope found a hole in the net, and jammed itself between the inner and outer tubs.

"God, the bomb's stuck!" Matt heard Melissa scream.

"It's not a bomb, Melissa," Matt tiredly called out.

Riggins lifted the bullhorn. "Ladies and gentlemen, we are evacuating the area. Please cooperate with the police for your own safety. . ." Riggins was loving this, Matt was sure.

Five minutes later, the area was deserted but for the statue-still robot spider, the bomb techs, and the District of Columbia police. And one stubborn senator.

Riggins was in Matt's face. "When I said `evacuate,' that means you."

"I see no reason to leave."

"We have a suspected bomb caught in our—"

"You have my mail stuck in your washtub. When you're done with your street theater, I'm taking my envelope back."

"I'd love to let you fetch it. Lucky for you, I'm responsible for your safety."

"I'll stand where you're standing. Get on with it, I have work waiting in my office."

Riggins made an angry gesture to the puppeteer. For the next few seconds, the robot's motors were the only sound in the utter silence of the onlookers. The spider slowly rocked the envelope's free end to the left and right, forward and back.

The envelope slipped free from the spider's grippers and tumbled into the net, the envelope ripping free from its jammed tip.

Nobody was hurt by the explosion, and neither the trailer nor the bomb-disposal truck was damaged. Yet within a hundred yard radius, every window cracked. The robot spider, of course, was a total loss.

Fifteen minutes later, almost everyone was back in Matt's office. With the slam of the door, Sherry returned, several brown paper sacks under one arm.

Sherry strode to her desk, popped open the first sack, and began bagging her personal effects.

"That's it, I quit!" she yelled.

Matt noted that Diane and Lisa were staring dumfounded at Sherry's activities. Sherry's dramatics irritated him. "I demand two weeks' notice."

Fury gave the mouse a lion's spine. "I'm not *asking* you, Mister Senator, I'm *telling* you. It's been bad enough, handling your dirty money and lying to your wife. Then this disgusting treaty came along. I worked for the treaty, though I felt like *shit*, because I needed the job. But now Senator Anderssen needs a new chief of staff, and I refuse to die for a stinking traitor."

As soon as Sherry could pack up her belongings, she was gone. Everyone but Matt hugged her goodbye and wished her well.

By the time Sherry left, Melissa and Diane had given their own notices. Matt was relieved that they, at least, would stay two weeks.

Fuck! Matt thought. His life had turned into fermented garbage, all because of Barbara. Alone in his private office, Matt fumed, then he decided, then he schemed, then he gloated.

"You crossed the line twice, Barbara. Now you pay. When Dennis Goodman wronged me, did I forget? No, I repaid him eight years later by stealing his girl. I hope I made him cry—but his pain is a dime-store hell next to what awaits you.

"You will die soon, dear wife, alone and in disgrace."

Fifteen minutes later and a mile away, Matt walked into FBI headquarters. The FBI had hurt him; The time had come for it to help him.

Back in April, two Japanese businessmen had been killed in San Francisco, and the FBI believed the men's killer or killers had ties to the yakuza. The FBI hadn't made any arrests yet, but surely it had a list of suspects. Since Matt's plot against Barbara needed a connection to the yakuza, he needed to learn who those suspects were.

Matt spelled things out for the FBI legislative liaison: "You show me the case file on those two Japanese businessmen killed in April. I'm alone with the file for just five minutes. I won't remove anything, I won't change anything. In return, I won't screw with your funding. I ask so little, really." Thus did Matt wrest from the FBI the address of the prime suspect, Kazuo Ebara.

Ebara lived in San Francisco. From the Hoover Building, Matt headed to the airport. He caught the flight that would be first to arrive in San Francisco.

Two hours after Matt's flight departed Washington was nine o'clock Wednesday morning in Tokyo. Yamamura, along with Saitoh, the other party leaders, and Barbara, sat atop *tatami* mats in a private room in an expense-account restaurant in Shinjuku. Saitoh was a regular at the restaurant, and so was playing host.

Saitoh swallowed a spoonful of sugared corn flakes, then took a sip of coffee. "Mrs. Nakamura, how do you feel, now that you've been proven right?"

"Relieved, so relieved. Can you imagine the horror, my knowing that I was not a terrible person, yet millions throughout America insisting that I was?"

"How do you feel," Kada asked, "seeing everyone involved with the bribe exposed and censured?"

"Representative, that's awkward. I don't want to look as if I'm criticizing Senior Party President Yamamura, who has been very helpful to me—"

Kada made an impatient gesture. "But?"

"Yes, Mrs. Nakamura, please finish," Yamamura said.

Be careful, she thought. "But I've never blamed Ambassador Fujima, or anyone above him, for agreeing to pay Husband a bribe."

Teramura blinked. "Never?"

"Husband in effect said to Ambassador Fujima, `I'll fix your impossible problem, and you make it worth my while afterward.' So what options did Ambassador Fujima have?"

"No others that I see," Saitoh said.

Kada glanced at Saitoh, then eyed Barbara. "To refuse to bribe your husband, and to hope for approval anyway. This saves the ambassador's honor."

She chose the tactful answer: "Honor was another option."

Kada's gaze was piercing. "Do you understand honor?"

She ignored Kada, and turned to Saitoh. "I don't blame anyone of Japan for making that evil deal, I blame only Husband."

He nodded. "Your words would `rub their ears gently,' considering how much has happened to them in the last twenty-four hours. Do you know that both Ambassador Fujima and Foreign Minister Utsumi made atonement resignations? And the Progressive Coalition demands that Prime Minister Sasaki resign as well."

Barbara sighed. "Much has happened to those men. And much has happened to Husband."

Saitoh looked sympathetic. "I regret that you saw that bomb unpleasantness on the news this morning."

"Thank you."

Kada eyed her and Saitoh in turn. "So devoted to your husband you are."

Yamamura said, "Yet the release of those FBI reports, a misfortune for your husband, is fortunate for us who oppose this treaty."

"Please forgive me for being a silly woman, Senior Party President, but I feel sorry for Husband."

"Go on."

"The deal is off for Husband's bribe. He committed these shameful acts, and now he has nothing. He has no bribe, no marriage, no friends, and no honor."

Saitoh looked at her. "Many people have told me they couldn't bear the weight of your husband's shame as well as you have. If you now feel sorry for him, you are both stronger and more civilized than I."

"Ah, Saitoh-*kun*," Yamamura said, "how you flatter *my* honored guest."

Barbara surprised everyone when she bowed to Saitoh, eight fingertips in a row touching the *tatami* mat in front of her knees, while she still sat on her heels. Her head went low, nearly touching the mat. "*Sumimasen wa ne*," she said, my guilt never ends. Her voice broke: "I really do not deserve your kind words."

Not when I was sitting in front of the TV during the Senate subcommittee hearings, howling, "Stop Matt! Stop Matt!" Not when I filed for divorce against him. Perhaps my mother is right: Maybe I am a bad wife.

As Saitoh was making a reply-bow to Barbara, she saw Yamamura's mouth twitch.

Yamamura abruptly turned to the men. "We have much to do. The prime minister refuses to resign, so we must force a no-confidence resolution."

Saitoh frowned. "I commit a rudeness, but to me it seems you don't need for him to resign, and you don't need a no-confidence resolution."

There they go, Barbara thought, *butting heads again.*

Barbara listened and worried as a stormy strategy session followed.

The Dietmen agreed that they had two foolproof treaty-killers. The first way was to remind nervous proportional-representation Conservatives that Treaty Article 32 was lurking nearby, slavering at the chance to unseat some of them.

("Article 32 only helps us as long as the press doesn't notice whom we're talking to," Kada said.)

The second sure strategy was for Progressive Coalition members on the Foreign Affairs committee to keep the treaty bottled up in committee.

The plan was for the committee to hold the treaty until August 24, the last day of the ordinary session. This would prevent the lower house from passing it, and any bill passed by neither house by the end of a session automatically died. The upper house wasn't receiving the treaty until the lower house was through with it, and the full lower house couldn't see the treaty until the committee freed it.

The treaty could actually be locked up in committee for the entire session? Oh yes, the four Dietmen assured Barbara, the Progressives could imprison the treaty in committee "forever."

These plans the Dietmen agreed on. But they were split over Yamamura's idea of pressing for a no-confidence resolution to dump Sasaki and his Cabinet.

Teramura said, "The Conservative Coalition might fracture on a no-confidence resolution. I think Senior Party President Yamamura's course is wisest."

"Yet I agree with Saitoh-*kun*," Kada said. "*Maybe* the resolution passes. *Maybe* we gain seats in the resulting election. But no matter what, we won't hurt the treaty. Even if we choose a new prime minister, he might pledge only to not bribe foreign officials."

Teramura waved no. "We make renouncing the California Treaty a condition of his selection. I believe that we can pass a no-confidence resolution, and that it will bring us what we want. I'm with Senior Party President Yamamura."

"It's good that one man here has sense," Yamamura said.

After half an hour more bucking Yamamura, Saitoh "reluctantly" agreed to push for a no-confidence resolution. Kada surrendered then, but he was blunt as usual: "I'll work for it, but it's a waste of time."

To silent Barbara the conclusion was obvious: Saitoh had taken too long to agree. She had watched Yamamura grow angry by how fiercely, and by how long, Saitoh had questioned Yamamura's plan. Clearly to Barbara, Yamamura would neither forgive nor forget Saitoh's gall.

Whether a no-confidence resolution would fracture the enemy Conservative Coalition remained to be seen. But Barbara worried the California Treaty might well fracture her four allies in the Progressive Coalition.

Two hours later in San Francisco, it was after eight Tuesday evening when Matt rented a car from a sullen car-rental clerk. Matt drove the white Dodge Intrepid to the address of Kazuo Ebara, suspected murderer and yakuza soldier.

To avenge himself on Barbara, Matt's plan required enlisting the yakuza's help. So now Matt was in San Francisco to recruit Ebara.

But first, Matt had to get Ebara where law-enforcement types couldn't listen to their conversation. But Ebara hadn't made it so far by trustingly climbing into cars with strangers.

When Matt rang Ebara's doorbell, a lawn sprinkler was going, but nobody answered the door. Rather than leave, Matt rang the doorbell again. And again. . . .

After five minutes, the door was opened a handbreadth by a man in his thirties. "Hello," he said, in a Japanese accent. His shirt collar was open, and Matt saw a chest tattoo that went up to his throat. On Ebara's left cheek was a white scar shaped like a numeral four. Both the tattoo and the scar were confirmations: Ebara was *gokudoh* (a yakuza gangster).

Matt switched to Japanese. "Good evening, please pardon my rudeness. Are you Mister EBARA Kazuo?"

The man paused, then said, "Yes. You're Naka—"

"No names. Yes, it is so. The yakuza, I understand it would gain by California being sold."

"Sir, humble-I am a simple exporter."

Matt switched to acting tough: "Nice tattoo you have. I know how the yakuza and I together can eliminate the obstacle to California being sold. The *gokudoh* who helps me, helps himself. Are you man enough for the challenge?"

Ebara stiffened, but said, "You want to help the yakuza?"

"Ebara-*san*, if you take a ride in my car, I'll be honored to explain how you can gain yourself status within your organization."

"What do *you* get from this?"

"Blood vengeance on the person who dishonored and shamed me."

Ebara nodded. "Wait while I lock my door. California has many criminals."

A minute later, both Matt and Ebara were in the rental car. Matt drove several blocks away from Ebara's house, as he checked his mirrors for tails.

Neither man spoke.

Once Matt satisfied himself he and Ebara weren't being followed, he studied his passenger. Ebara's face showed no emotion, but he sat with his back stiff, and with his hands on his thighs, his fingers pointed inward. To Matt's surprise, Ebara had all the parts of all his fingers. Matt realized that Ebara's hair wasn't permed either. Apparently Ebara Kazuo was an undercover gangster.

Ebara broke the silence with blunt Japanese: "You planning to drive, or to talk?"

Matt frowned, then began: "Being arrested is much more disgraceful in Japan than in the United States, right? It's not unusual for an arrested Japanese to be shunned by family and former friends, right? And what's a crime that's sure to bring an arrest in Japan?"

Ebara studied Matt. "Smuggling in methamphetamine, I've heard."

"Or assassination of the prime minister."

"How does this involve your wife?"

"We use Wife's gun, which is in my garage. We smuggle it into Japan."

"How stupid. Yeah, you get revenge on your wife, but our man will be hanged."

"No, make him put on gloves, a wig, and tearaway clothing. I don't want him caught, but he's to throw the gun away."

"I see. We go to much trouble and expense to bring it in, then our man lays the piece on the sidewalk before running off. Or would you prefer he run into a *kohban* and lay the piece on a policeman's desk?"

Matt was annoyed by being on the receiving end of sarcasm. "I *want* the gun found. Sooner or later the National Police will discover that the pistol is registered to Wife."

"If they tap into an American police database."

"The gun is American-made. When the National Police try America, that's when the *pachinko* rings."

"How so?"

"Wife is in Japan, the pistol that is registered to Wife is in Japan, so the public prosecutor concludes that Wife brought the pistol into Japan."

At last Ebara sounded respectful: "Sure."

"The frame works in Japan because she's American, it doesn't matter that she has a clean record."

"Sure, Japanese think Americans are gun-crazy cowboys. But why this trickery? Why not just have us kill her?"

"You kill her, she dies with honor, and she gains public sympathy in Japan. Who knows how many Diet votes that would change? My way, she loses all honor and public sympathy, and dies `a dog's death' by rope."

"Mm."

"When Wife is arrested and disgraced, those she's allied with are themselves disgraced and want nothing to do with her. Treaty opposition is routed, the Diet approves the treaty, California goes to Japan, and the yakuza expands."

"Yeah, I see it. But how does this help me?"

What did Dale Carnegie say? Everyone wants to feel important. "When we carry out the plan, only you can be the go-between. Then when the plan succeeds, your seniors in the Sawayama-kai know you're the man who gave them California."

"Hey, for a politician you make a good plan."

"Actually, I have *two* good plans. To ensure Wife's arrest, I have another illegal idea. . ."

It was Friday morning in Yokohama. The Hat Woman herself, Higashi Reiko, stood at Hiroshi's desk. "What are you working on, Engineer Iwata?"

She's talking to me? Don't say anything foolish. "This design is for the bid for Mitsumi Paper Recycling."

"How's it coming?"

"I have most of it figured out, except at the start."

"What's left?"

"I haven't decided yet whether the truck should be unloaded by an overhead or ground robot, nor whether the robot should be fixed or on-track."

"Overhead-track seems the most logical, but this isn't my specialty."

"I agree. But overhead-track is also the most expensive."

"True."

She smells good. "If I must submit an expensive design, I better have looked at all the options first."

"I'm sure you'll do a good job. What Section Manager Tsurumi told me when he introduced us, was how highly Nissan had praised you."

"Perhaps Nissan had not yet noticed my many faults, but thank you for the compliment."

Her gaze at him was warm. The corners of her mouth turned up to smile.

I think she likes me! "Um, then I decide not only the truck-unloading robot's platform, but I also look at whether a Model 6000 or a Model 7000 would give a better value."

"Software Section recently upgraded the support software for the Model 7000s. I'd be glad to e-mail you the new specifications, or I can bring them by your desk if you wish."

Is she finding an excuse to talk to me again? Hiroshi took a breath, and made his muscles relax as he tested her: "Please, if you see me away from work, I am Iwata, though to my mother I am Hiroshi."

"I see."

No clue in her face or voice to her reaction. Had he blundered and embarrassed them both?

He kept worry and disappointment out of his own voice in his formal reply: "The new specifications would be great. Thank you very much, Programmer Higashi."

"Please don't mention it. Please, Iwata-*san*, if you see me away from work, I am Higashi. For those whom I'm close to, I am Reiko."

He felt overjoyed, but his "Very well, Higashi-*san*" was calm. They both were silent for a beat; that's when Hiroshi decided Reiko had beautiful skin.

She dropped her gaze. "Do you have any of your petitions here, Iwata-*san*?"

Huh? "How'd you learn about my petitions?"

Reiko said, "Engineer Kinoshita," Ryuuji, "he told Section Manager Tsurumi. The Section Manager told R&D Department during Tuesday's tea break."

Hiroshi made a rictus smile of embarrassment. "*Sa.*" Well, then.

"Speaking to so many strangers, by myself, how frightening! But you stood up to that angry Californian, so Yokohama Station must be easy for you."

He was still embarrassed, but also wondering, *She doesn't think I'm a fanatic? She thinks I'm brave?* "Well, then," he said again.

"Please, I want to sign your petition. I live in Yokosuka."

"Um, here are my petitions right here." He extracted them from under his umbrella. She wrote her name and address, and her writing was beautiful.

"*Sumimasen yo.*" Hiroshi's bow was crisp as he could make it. "Please pardon me for the trouble I've caused you," he recited.

"It was no trouble. I'm glad that I could do my small part to help."

He seized on any excuse to continue the conversation. "You said you live in Yokosuka."

"The train ride isn't all that bad. Well, I'd better be returning to my desk."

I don't care if she already has a boyfriend, I need to know. "Of course. Say, Sunday is the one day I'm not working the train station."

She smiled slightly. "Go on."

"I know an excellent *sushi* restaurant and a great gourmet coffee shop, both in Kurihama. I would like very much to show them to you. That is, if you're not busy then."

While she was saying yes, Hiroshi decided that Reiko had a beautiful smile.

Over in Tokyo, Barbara thought, *This is like the anti-American demonstrations in Dad's stories.* Tachikawa Air Base, where her father had been stationed as an Air Policeman in the mid-Fifties, had been the site of many bitter protests then.

Barbara was looking at another bitter protest now—twin protests, in fact.

In front of the National Diet Building was a fence and a gate. A four-lane street ran north-south alongside that fence and gate, and a ten-lane street approached the gate from the east. But Barbara saw no cars, no trucks, no busses move on either street. The only four-wheeled movement was by police vehicles that turtled their way through two angry throngs.

In front of the gate, riot police buffered opposing lines of raised fists, raised voices, helmets painted with slogans, undulating placards, and windblown, handheld, red-painted banners. Barbara was too far away to read many of the banners, but she heard the chants clearly.

To the north, behind roadblocks, many demonstrators shouted anti-treaty chants: "Sasaki resign!", "Shame, shame, shame!", "Keep Japan pure!" and "Stop the treaty!"

To the south, behind a second line of roadblocks twenty yards from the first, other demonstrators countershouted. "Japanese knowledge, Japanese wisdom, worldwide!" "Japanese mind, Japanese soul, worldwide!" "Don't think small!" "Progress, for our ancestors, for our children!"

Safe on the Diet grounds, up the stairs and amid the tall pillars of the Diet building's Central Porch, Barbara and a fifty-year-old man listened to the tumult.

The man, SHOHJI Shuujiroh, was a mild-mannered proportional-representation Conservative. Barbara was meeting with Representative Shohji to convince him to vote against the treaty.

Shohji gestured at the demonstrations. "Prime Minister Sasaki is responsible for this upheaval, whether he knew of the bribe or not. Perhaps his time is over."

Barbara felt Shohji watching her. Since she was unsure what to say, she played it safe: "I have no thoughts on a no-confidence resolution. No thoughts I'm qualified to share."

"But didn't Yamamura-*sama* send you? Aren't you here to rile up us Democratic Party of Japan members against our LDP allies?"

She sighed. She couldn't second-guess Shohji, so she spoke honestly: "You highlight my dilemma. Yamamura-*san* wants this no-confidence resolution, and I owe him much. Yet how could I push a resolution I obviously take no interest in?"

"You're a foreigner. I wouldn't believe you care who our prime minister should be, were you to ask me to vote nonconfidence. Still, Yamamura-*san* expects you to ask me. You need his support, and it would be rude not to do him this small favor." Shohji returned to watching her.

She was silent for five seconds while she decided. "Shohji-*sensei*, please vote yes on the resolution of no confidence in Prime Minister Sasaki and his Cabinet."

"Mrs. Nakamura, I regret I must refuse."

She sighed. "Politics feels so different when I'm the player rather than the spectator."

"I so agree." Shohji sneaked a glance at his watch as smoothly as Barbara had ever seen it done. "Today we've discussed the Red Cross, baseball, and James

Bond movies; the no-confidence resolution; and the woes of political life. Anything else on your mind?"

"Representative, if the California Treaty leaves the Foreign Affairs committee, I urge you to vote against it."

"Please, why should I enrage the prime minister and the Conservative Coalition to do that? Plus, many `special-interest tribes' in South Kantoh Region want me to vote yes."

"Yes, but other special-interest tribes are asking you to vote no. They say this because the treaty's a bad deal for Japan."

"Go on."

"Even without Article 32 endangering your seat, the California Treaty deserves your vote no." She was proud of herself, how artfully she'd reminded him of fearsome Article 32.

Shohji gave her a look—of anger? Confusion? Surprise? She couldn't tell. "Why are you mentioning Article 32?"

She blinked in surprise. "Because. . .because the sixteen seats that Article 32 will vanquish will come from among you two hundred proportional Represen-tatives. This treaty could get you fired."

"Once in Japan, obligation meant losing one's life if required. Next to death, what is a Diet seat?"

"But Miyamoto wrote that the true Way of the Warrior is not dying, but winning. There is no honor in squandering one's life, he wrote; Can a corpse still win for his lord? You're no coward if you don't squander your seat."

Shohji had startled at her citing of Miyamoto— apparently Shohji hadn't expected an American woman to have read a book on sword-fighting and war-making. But now Shohji said, "South Kantoh Region has twenty-three representatives. Let Article 32 reduce that to twenty-two, even twenty-one—so what? Next election, my party will be sure to highly list a man with Diet experience."

"You."

"Yes. You may explain how mixing Japan and California would smash Japan's society like a typhoon. I want your views about the headaches that the treaty would give the National Police Agency. But please don't refer to Article 32 again."

In Representative Masukawa's Diet office that afternoon, Barbara and Saitoh were being given the bum's rush.

Masukawa's office manager said, "Masukawa anticipates hearing your well-considered reasons for a no-confidence vote, Saitoh-*sensei*. Mrs. Nakamura, Masukawa greatly admires your fervor and dedication to keeping California American. Yet once again the Representative is unable to meet with either of you."

"I see," Barbara said, not believing a word.

"For this he sends his most sincere regrets."

"I understand. Thank Representative Masukawa on my behalf for those generous words, which I do not deserve from such an esteemed person. I hope that we will be fortunate soon to enjoy the honor of meeting with him."

"Thank you for honoring us with your visit, Saitoh-*sensei*, and you, Mrs. Nakamura," the office manager recited as he bowed them out.

Since Wednesday, Barbara had been escorted around the Diet offices with Yamamura, with Saitoh, or with Teramura—Kada had been "too busy" to escort her. Yet no matter whom she was with, Conservatives didn't want to talk with them. Barbara was starting to take it personally.

A few minutes after being gracefully thrown out of Masukawa's office, Barbara and Saitoh stood alone in Saitoh's office. That office was decorated in *wabi* (calming simplicity).

She made an ironic face. "It certainly is curious how suddenly no Conservatives are in their offices."

"It's not you they're avoiding, it's me. You they find very charming."

"Perhaps." Then she smiled. "Thank you for sensing my feelings."

Saitoh smiled back.

The flash of awareness was like hot *sake* in her belly: Saitoh was handsome, intelligent, witty, and considerate. His only major flaw was his silly schoolboy rivalry with Yamamura. Saitoh was the man Matt could have been.

The thought came to Barbara unbidden: *I wonder how good at sex he is.*

She felt her cheeks warm. *Stop that, I'm still married.*

—Only technically.

Can I inflict on his wife the pain I've suffered?

—But I want him.

She took a breath. *Does he sense how I feel? Back to business!* "I—I was worried that nobody was meeting with us because my perfume was too strong, or something else about me."

"Your perfume smells sweet. It's not so heavy as to distract, either—unless a man wants it to." As he spoke, he moved too close, breaking a rigid Japanese rule. "Anyway, it's not you they're avoiding, it's the man you're with."

Her heart beat faster. *Calm down!* She smiled at him and said, "Twice you've reassured me of that." She liked the smell of Saitoh's aftershave.

His smiling eyes, less than arm's-length distant from her own, matched the smile of his lips. "Mrs. Nakamura, you want to talk about the treaty, but the Conservatives know that we Progressives want to talk about the no-confidence resolution." The words were those of a teacher; the voice was that of a lover. "If Masukawa doesn't meet with me before the no-confidence vote, he's spared awkwardness if he plans to vote no."

"Ma—Representative Masukawa isn't forced to tell you no, to lie, or to hedge." She wanted to touch SAITOH Taijiroh's bare skin.

Saitoh moved yet closer. "Also, if Masukawa hasn't talked to me before the vote, then afterward he can flatter me, 'I'm sure if I had heard your arguments, I would've been persuaded.'"

"Undoubtedly true. I'm sure you're very persuasive." *His voice is so husky.*

Her left hand he lightly touched with his right hand, breaking an even more rigid rule. "Yesterday and today, whenever I tried to see him by myself, I also was turned away. I suspect Masukawa is hiding under his desk."

She made herself break the touch of their hands. "Representative Saitoh. . ." Her voice cracked once.

He looked down at her hand that he had been touching. Though he continued to stand too close, he kept his gaze politely averted. Quietly he said, "I don't know whether you still have *giri* to your husband, Nakamura-*fujin*. But I have a duty to my wife not to shame her. Duty owns me, though it be crushing." He was saving both their faces, by pretending the idea of stopping was his.

She nodded. "Duty owns me, too—"

He leaned forward, his eyes again on hers, and his lips brushed her cheek. In America, such a mild kiss might have meant little. But she was in Japan, and the kiss electrified.

"—Though it be crushing," she breathed.

Yamamura had been quiet for most of dinner.

It was evening dinner, Monday three days later, in a favorite restaurant of Teramura's. Three days had passed since Saitoh had tempted Barbara, and five days had passed since the Progressives had decided to push for a no-confidence resolution.

Scarcely two hours had passed since the no-confidence resolution had been voted down.

"It seems that you both were right," Barbara said, to cheer Yamamura up. "The no-confidence resolution failed. Yet some Conservatives did vote for it, and the prime minister didn't dissolve the lower house."

Teramura looked glum. "Still, a disappointment. Does anyone besides me feel like downing a big, cold bottle of *sake*?" No one answered.

Saitoh looked around at everyone. "We still have the treaty imprisoned in committee. Be glad of that."

Yamamura spoke up. "True. Progressives on the committee assure me the treaty will remain stuck there until the ordinary session ends and the bill dies."

"How?" Barbara asked.

"Our people forced the Conservative majority on the committee to agree to only considering the treaty on Tuesdays and Wednesdays."

Kada said, "So? The Conservatives can drag the treaty out of committee, in plenary session."

Yamamura waved that away. "They know the chaos we'll create in vengeance."

Kada eyed Yamamura but said nothing.

Saitoh said, "At least, we can count on Article 32 to split the Conservatives. The treaty terrifies farmers, fishermen, and wood-industry workers, right? And they are both Conservative parties' core supporters, right? So even some prefectural Conservatives will be forced to switch to `no.'"

"That's good," said Barbara, smiling.

"Finally," Saitoh said, "there's our whispering campaign: `If the treaty's so wonderful, why did our Cabinet choose to cheat?'"

Yamamura stared Saitoh down. "That last remark isn't much of an argument, so that strategy isn't much of a defense."

Saitoh stared back. "If you have a better idea, I await high-you's wisdom."

"It's taxes, keep talking taxes! Remind everyone: eye-popping taxes for the next twenty years."

"That is one option," Saitoh said. His voice still had anger, but he also gave Yamamura a stiff head-bow.

Yamamura grunted, and turned back to Barbara. "Right now the treaty to the committee *obuareru*," is bound like infant to mother. "We are not defeated."

"I'm relieved to hear that."

"Now we must look inward, past current disappointment, and seek calm."

Kada eyed Yamamura. "Calm with good strategy is what wins battles. Right now, we need a strategy how to overcome the tempting prizes that Prime Minister Sasaki and former Prime Minister Matsuzaka can offer our colleagues."

"True," Yamamura said.

"Before we proceed further, perhaps we should review our methods of today. Perhaps we've been making mistakes."

Yamamura's voice was quiet, like a sword slowly drawn from a sheath. "Oh?"

"Mrs. Nakamura cannot contribute votes, influence, or yen to any of our fellow Representatives. Perhaps it was a mistake to rely on her so much. Perhaps it would be best to minimize using her in the future."

———

Ten hours later was Monday afternoon in Washington. At first Matt was relieved when the wire service reported a man arrested for sending the letter bomb. The bomber told police that he was hired on the day that news broke about the bribe. After making the bomb, he confessed, he drove down from Pennsylvania and mailed the bomb from just north of D.C.

Matt was frightened to read that the bomber couldn't, or wouldn't, identify who in California had hired him to make the hit.

———

Barbara stared in shock. "But you told me, Senior Party President, you *assured* me that the treaty would stay in committee forever. What happened?"

Tuesday afternoon in Tokyo, Barbara and the Progressive Coalition party presidents were meeting in Yamamura's Diet office. The Progressives had just been zapped by the Conservatives.

Yamamura frowned. "It was at today's plenary session. The Conservative Coalition rammed a measure through that demanded an interim report."

"The problem," Saitoh told Barbara, "is that when a committee reports on a bill, no matter why or how, then the bill is out of committee."

Barbara looked for a face with happy news. She found none. "So now the whole House of Representatives can consider the treaty?"

Teramura sighed. "Yes."

"You men assured me this could *not* happen. Yet you knew it might."

Yamamura sighed. "Whenever the majority tried it before, opposition members gridlocked the House. It seems that the Conservatives today decided they'd pay that price."

Kada eyed her. "Mrs. Nakamura, you wail like a woman, as you ask why didn't we tell you this might happen. Some might wonder why didn't *you* think to ask more informed questions?"

"Kada-*kun*," Saitoh said, "please remember that Mrs. Nakamura is a high guest here."

Yamamura frowned. "In turn, Saitoh-*kun*, please remember that Mrs. Nakamura is *my* guest, and so it's *my* place to rebuke Kada-*kun*. Kada-*kun*, Saitoh-*kun*, you both forget your place."

Barbara looked from face to face, and only Teramura's face lacked anger. "Please, may I say something?" She had to stop the others from fighting over her. "Yanking a bill out of committee is a rare practice in either house in Washington. Yet this does not excuse my ignorance here. Yes, I should've asked more questions. Then I whined like a child, and for this I am ashamed. Though such admission is difficult, I admit that Kada-*sensei* was right and I was wrong."

Kada gave a satisfied grunt. Everyone else looked embarrassed for her.

"Mrs. Nakamura," Saitoh said, "you needn't lose face to save Kada's."

"Saitoh-*kun*," Yamamura said, glaring, "perhaps you need to take an ice bath. Both you and Nakamura-*san* are married to other people."

Kada said, "But Mrs. Nakamura is married unhappily, and her husband is thousands of kilometers away. Your poor guest must feel lonely." Kada glanced at Barbara and then Saitoh, smirking all the while.

She saw Yamamura's jaw muscle tense, and she wasn't feeling too serene herself. She lasered Kada with an unblinking stare. "Representative Kada, your remarks that belittle me because I'm a woman, I find them unacceptable. Please tutor me if you have good reason for such words?" She was letting Kada save face, while still making her message clear.

But it was Yamamura who replied to her: "Mrs. Nakamura, whatever intimacies you shared with Senator DeGarcia are your own concern. But if the Tokyo press were to link you with Saitoh, the scandal would destroy all hope of defeating the treaty."

She realized she'd lost Yamamura.

About which, the Variety-Show Host joked—

The Postal Service is undecided about arresting the guy who mailed the letter bomb to Senator Nakamura. True, the bomber endangered employees and property. But the Postal Service doesn't want to discourage someone who uses too much postage.

Japan's ambassador to the U.S. made a big mistake. He resigned because of it, but so did his boss, the foreign minister. In Japan, if you the <u>*employee*</u> *really goof up, your* <u>*boss*</u> *might lose his job. At last, the secret to happiness.*

CHAPTER 13
Thursday, June 30, 2005

"This is ASN Newsbreak, 12:00 midnight Eastern time, Thursday, June 30. . . ."

"Moving now to Japan: In the Diet House of Representatives, opposition members won a parliamentary battle against the California Treaty. Members of the opposition Progressive Coalition within the Managing Committee succeeded at pushing the California Treaty to the bottom of the legislative agenda. As the Managing Committee is multipartisan and is traditionally unanimous in its decisions, members of the majority Conservative Coalition were forced to agree. The Progressives' hope is to keep the treaty's bill of ratification from coming to a vote before August 24, the end of the ordinary session. Any bill that is voted on by neither house of the Diet before the end of a session dies automatically."

Four days later, an OL (office lady) told Hiroshi, "I'm sorry, Shohji is meeting with someone. But he'll be honored to talk to you soon."

In Representative Shohji's waiting room, Hiroshi was waiting with a bundle of photocopies of signed petitions. He was in Tokyo, stopping by the Diet offices of his twenty-four Representatives. Hiroshi was visiting Representatives to present the petitions his team had gathered thus far—and maybe to commit each Representative to a "yes" vote on the treaty. Hiroshi hoped this, despite knowing better.

It was the night of Monday, July 4—ten days since Hiroshi had dared to ask Reiko for a date. Eight days since they'd gone on that date. Six days since the Diet courageously had overpowered the Foreign Affairs committee's Progressives to rescue the treaty held hostage, and four days since the wily Progressives had endangered the treaty again. It was one day since Reiko and he had gone on their second date.

Now the OL said, "That's a thick stack of petitions you have."

Hiroshi's smile was modest. "Yes, my friends Kinoshita and Higashi, and coworkers Shinohara and Fukuda, are generous in helping me gather names."

After that first date with Reiko, she'd volunteered to join Hiroshi and Ryuuji at train-station canvassing. Hiroshi would've been overjoyed to have her regardless, but she'd turned out to be a treasure. Even the most hurried, workaholic commuter found it easy to stop once he'd looked into Reiko's bright eyes and he'd caught that warm smile.

Reiko wasn't the only addition to the petition team. Only hours after Reiko's first time at the train station, Hiroshi at lunch had recruited clean-room assemblers Shinohara and Fukuda.

Now Hiroshi told the OL, "It's very kind of Shohji-*sensei* to see me so late in the evening."

"Rather, it's you who is kind to come here after work to express your views."

Two hours earlier, when the workday for Matsumoto Robotics had ended, Hiroshi had offered the petition team the evening off while he headed north to meet Dietmen. The team had refused, and instead had escorted him and the box full of petition-copies to the Yokohama train station. Ryuuji, Reiko, Shinohara, and Fukuda had been gathering still more names, even as

Hiroshi had bought his Tokyo-bound ticket. Hiroshi was grateful to have such friends as them—

Now the door to the waiting room opened, and a man and woman walked out. The man was wearing a maroon chrysanthemum lapel pin, the mark of a lower-house member. As for the woman, Hiroshi was alarmed to recognize Mrs. Nakamura.

She was saying, ". . .Not much time is left, Representative. You must decide soon, please remember."

Representative Shohji raised a hand. "I have time enough to study my choices. I'm deciding Japan's future—I won't be rushed."

Hiroshi was surprised that Representative Shohji's reply was a firm refusal rather than the usual pretty evasion. Then Hiroshi realized the words meant that neither would the Representative buy from Hiroshi.

Hiroshi wouldn't walk out with the promise of a yes-vote. Still, he'd pitch his best presentation. He'd better, with Mrs. Nakamura standing only two meters away.

⸺

A minute later, after the OL made introductions, Hiroshi greeted Representative Shohji. Then Hiroshi turned and bowed again. "Mrs. Nakamura, I'm pleased finally to meet you."

"Mister Iwata, I'm pleased to meet you, too," she recited.

"Perhaps you don't remember me, but we swapped e-mail in May. I asked you to stop fighting the treaty, but you likened your obligation to that of the forty-seven masterless samurai."

Her smile was indulgent. "I remember. I found your innocence charming."

Representative Shohji said, "Mister Iwata, she not only didn't stop fighting, this is the second time she's lobbied me to vote against the treaty. She's used every argument she can think of, too." Representative Shohji shot Mrs. Nakamura a look that Hiroshi couldn't read. "Yet you're here to present for the treaty. Please."

Mrs. Nakamura had talked to Representative Shohji twice before? Hiroshi took a breath. *I must stay calm and watchful.* "Shohji-*sensei*, I've brought you copies of petition names that my friends and I have gathered. . ."

Hiroshi read the text of the petition, and mentioned that the petition had gained 2,742 names. Then he sketched Nissan's Oppama Plant, his reaction to the movie *Spring Bamboo*, and his friends at Matsumoto Robotics joining him at the Yokohama train station. ". . .Now while I talk to you, they endure rain and summer heat as they take still more names."

Representative Shohji smiled. "Soon you'll be back with more, you're warning me?"

Hiroshi smiled back. "Yes."

"You recruit people to help you gather twenty-seven hundred names. Mister Iwata, regardless of their politics, Japan needs more young persons like you."

"*Sensei*, I'm not worthy of such kind words. . ." As Hiroshi reciting the disclaimer, he noticed the expression change on Mrs. Nakamura's face. The condescending smile vanished, as alarmed eyes flicked between Representative Shohji's face and Hiroshi's.

After a pause, she said, "Ah, youth. When I was in my twenties, the world seemed simple. Finding answers to the big problems seemed easy."

Hiroshi, generous in victory, wouldn't match her veiled insult. "Yes, young people view the world simply. That perhaps is why, while their elders are talking, young people are doing. Young people and you."

"*Dohmo arigatoh gozaimasu.* Of course, it's not enough to do, one must do effectively. For all your work, you can't reach more than a sliver of eligible voters," she replied.

Unworried Hiroshi replied with only a smile, then he turned from her to Representative Shohji. "I forget why I'm here. *Sensei*, I ask most respectfully for you to vote for the treaty."

"Mister Iwata, I want to hear all the facts before I decide."

Mrs. Nakamura said, "Fortunately I've been able to widen your perspective with an American and a Californian viewpoint."

Hiroshi looked into the other man's eyes. "The treaty now is solely Japan's problem; doesn't listening to what Americans think only confuse you? `Ignorance is Buddha.'"

"`Blind men do not fear snakes,'" she replied.

Representative Shohji nodded. "Mrs. Nakamura is correct. I don't dare pass up any information."

"I'm pleased to hear that," she said, showing relief. "I've made transcripts of my interviews on Japanese TV, in which I explain why Japan must say no to the treaty. May I e-mail them to you, please?"

Hiroshi waved the petition-packet. "Here are hundreds of voter names."

Representative Shohji nodded to Hiroshi, then turned to Mrs. Nakamura. "Thank you very much, I accept your offer. But I promise nothing after I read your information."

Hiroshi took a risk: "You want information. If you'll permit me, I'll tell you more about why the treaty is good for Japan—"

"Representative," Mrs. Nakamura said, "you mentioned a speech you're to give tonight?"

"Mm. Mrs. Nakamura, thank you for interesting conversation. Mister Iwata, thank you for bringing me these petitions." Giving first Mrs. Nakamura and then Hiroshi a preemptive bow, Representative Shohji said, "Thank you for coming."

The contest had ended up a tie. Hiroshi didn't make Representative Shohji forget Mrs. Nakamura's international stature and expertise, but she couldn't wash away Hiroshi's voter signatures. And neither Hiroshi nor Mrs. Nakamura moved Representative Shohji to decide about the treaty.

"Again, Nakamura-*sama*, it's a pleasure to meet you," young Iwata told Barbara a minute later. The two of them were in the hallway outside Shohji's office. They bowed to each other, then he picked up his big cardboard box. Barbara watched him head down the hall, eyeing nameplates as he walked, until he entered another office.

That young man is sharp. He had Shohji in his pocket for a minute there. The memory made her feel disappointed in herself: She'd sunk to artfully mudslinging her opponent Iwata, in order to win the argument. And then her trick hadn't worked. She'd looked not only mean, she'd looked foolish.

But regrets were useless. As she headed off to talk to another proportional-representation Conservative, she discarded thoughts of Iwata Hiroshi.

Hiroshi meanwhile was meeting with Representative Yuuki. Representative Yuuki was the one prefectural

Dietman on Hiroshi's visitation list, mixed in with South Kantoh Region's twenty-three proportional Representatives. After Hiroshi bowed hello, he remarked, "I'm surprised that Mrs. Nakamura didn't follow me to your office."

Representative Yuuki looked confused. "Mrs. Nakamura? Oh yes, the American. Surely she knows better than to pitch me, because I belong to the prime minister's faction."

Hiroshi was surprised. "She's never come here, to your office."

"*Hai*." That's correct. Yuuki's expression asked, *Why would she be so foolish?*

Hiroshi was puzzled. *Mrs. Nakamura has met twice with Shohji, but not even once with Yuuki? Strange. Representative Shohji isn't a famous politician, so why is she interested in him?*

Hiroshi frowned. Mrs. Nakamura was following a plan, but what was it?

Barbara's last Dietman prospect that night was Representative Ishii. By then it was late, so she walked him to his car. While they were talking, a camera flashed. Barbara thought nothing of it.

The next morning, Hiroshi and his petition team again were working the Yokohama train station. Lying on the ground was a castoff newspaper, folded so that a photo of Mrs. Nakamura and an older man was displayed. The man was walking somewhere in the dark, as his head was turned to listen to Mrs.

Nakamura beside him. She was striding beside him as she talked, her gestures and face emphatic.

The picture was titled, "DOESN'T QUIT." The caption read, "Mrs. Nakamura presses on, trying to sway the lower house against the California Treaty. Here she talks with Representative ISHII Isau (LDP-Kinki Region)."

Representative Ishii? Hiroshi had never heard of him. Again the mysterious Mrs. Nakamura had met with an obscure politician.

Hiroshi tore out the photo and caption, and put the clipping in his pocket. Ryuuji gave him a puzzled look. Hiroshi said, "I don't yet know Mrs. Nakamura's plan, but this is another clue."

Hiroshi and the petition team worked Yokohama Station for another hour that morning, then rode the bus to work. After work and evening canvassing, Hiroshi returned to his apartment. By then he had an idea how to solve Mrs. Nakamura's puzzle.

A minute and a half after he'd walked through the door, he was at his computer, looking at the *San Diego Union-Tribune*'s home page. He double-clicked on "Barbara Watch."

According to "Barbara Watch," yesterday Mrs. Nakamura had given an interview to Television Tokyo Channel 12, and met with a list of lower-house members. Shohji and Ishii were two members on that list. Yuuki, sure enough, wasn't on the list.

"Barbara Watch," intended for a Californian audience, listed nothing about the Dietmen. Hiroshi would need to make the connection.

From "Barbara Watch" Hiroshi made a detailed printout of Mrs. Nakamura's activities in Japan. Hiroshi next pulled up the lower house's home page, and printed out its much more detailed list of the five hundred lower-house members.

Comparing the two printouts, Hiroshi quickly spotted that Mrs. Nakamura was spending *all* of her time talking to Conservatives. Why waste her time on something so futile? He was missing something.

He looked for a geographic connection. He couldn't find it. Mrs. Nakamura had sought out Conservatives throughout Japan, from northernmost Hokkaido Region to southernmost Kyushu Region. She'd spoken to lower-house Conservatives both from rural Chuugoku Region and from urban Tokyo Region—

It hit him: He'd cross-checked twenty-one names so far, and he hadn't found one *prefectural* representative.

Further work only confirmed the pattern, from which Mrs. Nakamura had never veered after her sixth day in Japan.

"She's talking only to region-elected Conservatives. Why?" Hiroshi leaned back and stared at the computer, wishing the screen would show him the answer.

Wait—didn't the treaty mention something about region-elected lower-house members? Hiroshi pulled up the text of the treaty and text-searched for "region."

Article 1? Nope. Article 6? Still no. . . .Article 32?

"Aha. She's talking to the Dietmen scared of being laid off."

So why was she talking to region-elected Conservatives? It couldn't be to persuade them; they already wanted to vote down the treaty. But they couldn't vote no, because otherwise they'd have no excuse for their disloyalty—

"Excuses, she's teaching them excuses. She's teaching `facts' about California to repeat back home."

How to stop her plan? Hers was a political strategy, so political rules applied: Appearance was what mattered. So—

"If I expose her plan, I ruin her plan."

He felt proud of himself for solving the puzzle. But how to publicize his discovery and stop her? He shut down his computer and tried to think.

His digital phone played can-can music. "Is everything okay?" Reiko asked.

"Uh, sure. Why?"

"You seemed distracted tonight, then you hardly said anything to me when we said goodbye."

"I'm sorry. Don't worry, it isn't you."

"A problem at work?"

"No, I was trying to solve a puzzle about Mrs. Nakamura. But I beat it! Listen to the great scheme she's using. . . ."

He told Reiko the story, finishing with ". . .at this moment she's probably bewitching still more region-elected Conservatives."

"No, right now she's on the radio."

"The radio?"

"She's a guest on `What Thinks Tokyo?' Hang on please, I'll let you hear—"

". . .listeners should know that everything bad you've heard about me are all Husband's lies—"

Reiko again: "Everyone's asked her, `Why'd you say such-and-such in Washington?' `Why'd you do such-and-such in Washington?' Nobody's asked her what she's doing in Tokyo."

"Until now. Do you have the show's phone number?" Hiroshi's smile was bared fangs.

Two minutes later, Barbara was still in the radio studio. Headphones covered her ears, and a bulbous, foam-rubber-covered microphone floated in front of her mouth. The host, facing her from three feet away, was equipped the same, plus he had a keyboard and screen in front of him.

"Our next caller," the host said, "is Hiroshi from Yokohama. My screen says you talked to Mrs. Nakamura yesterday?"

And then Barbara was stunned to hear young Iwata again: "Yes, we spoke in Representative Shohji's office about the treaty. Mrs. Nakamura, I know your plan."

"My plan?"

"Her plan to do what?" the host asked.

Iwata said, "Her secret plan to lure enough Conservatives into voting against the treaty. Proportional-representation Conservatives who want to keep their seats."

Oh god, he's on to me. Aloud she said, "I don't know what you're talking about."

"Why are proportional-representation Conservatives so important?" asked the host.

Iwata's explanation missed nothing, he knew all about Article 32 and region-elected Conservatives. Iwata finished with ". . .Mrs. Nakamura has spoken to nobody else since her sixth day in Japan."

"So what is she saying to them?" the host asked.

"She's teaching them how to excuse themselves after they vote no."

Barbara had to divert everyone's attention. "Mister Iwata, yesterday I told you nothing like that. Where'd you get your information?"

"From the San Diego newspaper's home page today."

The host looked over his mike at Barbara. "Is this correct, Mrs. Nakamura? Have you been meeting only with these proportional-representation Conservatives?"

"No, I've met with Progressive members, and prefectural members."

Iwata said, "Any of those after your first five days in Japan?"

"Sorry, I didn't bring the members' business cards with me tonight."

"Please, just one name outside the pattern."

"I can't recall," she lied, and knew she sounded the liar. So she borrowed a trick from Matt: She attacked. "Hiroshi-*san*, isn't it okay for me to lobby the Diet members? To say to them, `Please vote against the treaty'? That's why I came to Tokyo."

"Then please, talk to all five hundred members; any fewer is foolish. But you're not foolish. You know exactly which Dietmen to talk to, and exactly what message they're desperate to hear."

The host looked at Barbara. "Your reply?"

She tried to evade: "At Nagata-*cho* I try to spend my time wisely."

"Mm," the host said. Bad sign.

Then the host turned his eyes to the computer screen. "Hiroshi-*san*, thanks for calling. Any last words to the guest?"

"No, but I'd like to say something to any listening Conservatives threatened by Article 32."

"Please."

"Dietmen, you know Japan needs California. Please don't let Mrs. Nakamura sweet-talk you into becoming an Article 32 coward."

Half a day later was Tuesday evening in Washington. Matt drove from Washington to Bethesda with a pocketful of change. He chose a gas station whose pay phone was on the far corner of the property, by the coin-operated air compressor. He hid his car behind the Dumpster where the senatorial license plates wouldn't show. He walked to the air compressor and fed it four quarters, to make a racket to clog any listening FBI directional microphone. At the phone he touch-toned Ebara's San Francisco number, then inserted the requested change. Matt's calling card stayed in his wallet.

Ebara answered in gruff Japanese. "Yes."

"You know who this is?"

A pause, then Ebara said, "Yes. You're calling because the *pachinko* hasn't rung."

Matt shifted to Tone of Voice Two (Angry): "I demand to know when I'll have satisfaction. It's been two weeks."

"And it'll take weeks more, but you'll get what you want. Anything else?"

"No, but—"

The phone clicked in Matt's ear.

About which, the Variety-Show Host joked—

A politician named Ishii was photographed talking to Barbara Nakamura, who can promise him neither money nor a vote. But here, the mayor's office won't even return my calls about a pothole in front of my house.

The Diet lower house Managing Committee is usually is unanimous in its decisions. Could those people come here and teach their secret? Democrats and Republicans in Washington fight like they're in the WWE—except wrestlers show more sportsmanship.

CHAPTER 14
Heisei 17-nen 7-gatsu
12-nichi, Kayohbi
(Tuesday, July 12, 2005)

Each day thousands of people came to Yokohama to work, and most of them came through the Yokohama train station. That's the main reason why, at any instant, JR Yokohama Station had so many people in it. The other reason was that, one level up from the train tracks, the train station also was filled with an underground shopping mall.

Thus if someone wanted to talk to strangers, plenty of strangers could be found entering or leaving the two entrances of the Yokohama train station.

A week had passed since Hiroshi had revealed Mrs. Nakamura's scheme. Japanese news media had grabbed Hiroshi's "Article 32 coward" sound bite, and one editorial writer had used Hiroshi's phrase to effect. But also during this week, Hiroshi's team continued collecting petition signatures.

Now morning found the petition team again at the west entrance of JR Yokohama Station. Reiko, in an expensive hat, was thanking a petitioner for affixing his *inkan* (signature stamp) to the petition.

She walked over to Hiroshi and dropped her voice: "Uncle likes how serious you are." Hiroshi and Reiko had gone to Reiko's uncle's house Sunday evening, supposedly so her relatives could meet the man who'd twice dueled Mrs. Nakamura.

Now Hiroshi gazed long at Reiko. "Around most people I'm serious. Around one person I want only to write poetry by the hour."

Reiko's return gaze was warm. "Yes, Aunt told me later how you acted around me `stuck to her eyes.'" Reiko stepped in closer and murmured, "Aunt thinks we're lovers."

"Soon. I've noticed how you enjoy stroking the front of my shirt when we kiss."

"Mm, while I'm smelling you, while I'm tasting you. I'm savoring you."

That afternoon in his office in Tokyo, Representative Tsunoda was smooth. "Mrs. Nakamura, thank you for your thorough presentation."

Not another one. Barbara refused to quit. "Representative, please remember that when you vote yes, you might be voting yourself out of office."

"Temporarily. But if I'm labeled an Article 32 coward, my political career is ended. Permanently."

Barbara was dismayed but not surprised. Since Iwata Hiroshi blindsided her last week, proportional-representation Conservatives had been bleating much too often that they didn't dare vote no.

She'd talked to Shohji that morning. She took a grain of comfort that he hadn't joined the chorus of weak-willed naysayers. However, Shohji hadn't said yes, either.

In the meantime, she'd better undo Iwata's mischief, and fast.

That night Barbara figured out what to do about Iwata. But the calendar conspired against her.

Japan's Bon Festival was an important three-day Buddhist holiday to honor one's ancestors. It always fell on July thirteenth through fifteenth. In 2005, those days fell on Wednesday through Friday.

Many Japanese observed the holiday, regardless of what days it fell. Every year they traveled to their ancestral homes and cleaned their ancestors' graves. (Indeed, Barbara, Grandfather, and Aunt Makiko made pilgrimage to Tokorozawa, Saitama-*ken*.) But not everyone observed the holiday, instead claiming they "needed to work."

But everyone in Japan with three days' vacation time noticed that this year, the festival ended just as the weekend started. And even in allegedly workaholic Japan, when a man had a choice between everyone believing he dishonored his ancestors, and getting a five-day weekend, which would he choose?

Politicians, of course, had no choice at all. It would not do to have voters thinking that a politician's family was unimportant to him. Besides, weeding a grave made a great photo op.

In short: Starting Tuesday night, Tokyo was politicianless. It was an eternal six days later, Monday morning breakfast, before Barbara could explain to Yamamura and the men how to counter Iwata's "Article 32 coward" plea.

Kada's response? "Her idea won't work."

"Or so it seems to me," he then said for form's sake. "Remember Mrs. Nakamura's last idea, to talk up Article 32? That at least *seemed* like it might work."

Saitoh looked at Kada. "May I remind you, even you were in agreement about Article 32. None of us foresaw our plan being exposed by some amateur. That isn't Mrs. Nakamura's fault."

Yamamura glanced at Barbara, then at Saitoh who sat next to her, and frowned.

She wanted to say, "Yamamura-*sama*, please don't rush to conclusions. Saitoh-*san* and I *aren't* sleeping together." But she kept silent.

She had a proven idea how to fight Iwata Hiroshi's inflammatory "Article 32 coward" tag line. She'd just finished explaining her idea to the group, and she needed to convince them. Kada, as usual, was sabotaging her, and Yamamura was harboring suspicions about her sex life.

Kada was the more immediate threat. She began polite: "Kada-*sensei*, if you know of a good reason why my infomercial idea won't work, please tutor me. If you *know* of a good reason why."

She had a plan for an infomercial that would sell the idea the treaty was bad for Japan. And while the political infomercial had been proven effective in the United States, it had never been tried in Japan. This meant the public would be curious to watch it, and the Conservatives would be defenseless against it.

Teramura turned to Kada. "Infomercials for vacuum cleaners, golf drivers, etc., wouldn't be on Japanese TV unless they work."

"Oh, her kind of infomercial works in the United States. But it won't work *here*."

Saitoh said, "We don't know that."

As Yamamura's eyes were noting that Saitoh spoke up when Barbara was criticized, Kada criticized again. "I don't think you realize how much this costs."

Saitoh started to speak, but she stopped him with a gesture. "Can I rattle off a yen-figure? Nobody here can. Still, the cost of production, plus buying thirty minutes' prime-time airtime for three consecutive nights—I know it's expensive."

Kada looked at her as if she were a moron. "Then why do it?"

"It swayed public opinion in the United States in 1992. Move Japan's public to send `vote no' messages, and the Representatives must vote down the treaty."

Kada the optimist again: "You're planning to interview ordinary people? Viewers won't care what people like themselves think. My advice: Show Japanese who are rich or famous or successful."

Teramura said, "Sorry, but they're also who'll be soaked the worst when the treaty makes taxes skyrocket. Voters won't trust their words."

"True," Barbara said.

Teramura looked around. "Men, Mrs. Nakamura's commercial will be seen by millions of people. It will sour public opinion on the treaty, enough to make our colleagues kill the treaty."

"I also agree with Mrs. Nakamura," Saitoh said, touching Barbara's forearm in reassurance.

Saitoh, stop! Too late.

Yamamura eyed Barbara's arm. "Of course you agree with her, Saitoh-*kun*." Yamamura turned to Teramura. "You think this is a good plan?"

"Yes," Teramura said.

"No," Kada said. "But I'm willing to let you proceed and prove me right."

Yamamura looked at Teramura and at Kada. He didn't look once at Barbara or at Saitoh. The room became quiet.

"We'll do it." Yamamura looked only at Teramura and Kada.

Barbara had her infomercial, but now Yamamura was convinced she was sleeping with his rival.

———————

That afternoon, Barbara and Okano, who was Yamamura's chief of staff, both bowed to Salesman Maeda. "Thank you."

The three were in a meeting room for Nippon Television. Barbara had asked to buy thirty minutes of airtime, starting at 7:00 p.m. next Friday. Stunned Maeda then had excused himself to consult with higher-ups. Within minutes a steady stream of suits had come to the meeting room to meet Barbara, and to hear her say, "Yes, the entire thirty minutes, prime time, that's what we want." After two hours' wait, Maeda just had rushed back with a yes.

Now Salesman Maeda—he was still breathless from his dash—responded to Barbara's and Okano's bow with a much steeper bow of his own, and effusive thanks. Maeda then panted, "So what else may I help you with?"

Videotape editing, Barbara told him.

Salesman Maeda made a phone call, and two minutes later the trio walked into the control room for Nippon Television's six o'clock news show. Maeda explained to the dijvid (digital video) editors about the infomercial, and stressed that corporate management *fervently* wished Mister Okano and Mrs. Nakamura shown every courtesy.

The place reminded Barbara of Mission Control in Houston. There were five rows of six technicians in the room, each technician wearing headphones and looking at a computer screen. The technicians faced an enormous wall tiled in TV screens.

Along the top and bottom were two rows each of small screens, some of whom displayed still-pictures that were being cropped, captioned, and otherwise adorned. Other of the small screens showed glitzy graphics, including maps of Japan, of parts of Japan, and of foreign countries.

Between the small screens, medium-sized screens showed silent dijvid. Among the clips: Charlie Swensen mouthing words in the Oval Office, an update on construction of Space Cruise Ship *Amaterasu*, and an anti-treaty demonstration in front of the Diet building.

In the center were two large screens. The right screen was labeled "Broadcast," and now it was showing an ad. A father, mother, and two cute children were playing in a playground. This was no tiny city park typical of Japan, a fact obvious both because the playground was enormous, and because California-type palm trees were everywhere. Then the fun-loving family was replaced by a spinning globe and the caption, "Mitsui World Moving Lines." The ad's message was clear: *Parents, move to California and your children finally will have room to play outside.*

Barbara's gaze returned to the Swensen-screen. The senior dijvid editor must have noticed, saying, "President Swensen concluded the treaty with Russia about buying their nuclear weapons. He's just sent the treaty to the Senate."

Barbara sighed. "That treaty with Russia will be expensive. Yet the president must believe he'll have money to pay for it."

"So it seems."

"He doesn't believe I'll stop the California Treaty."

Three nights later, Barbara was watching a taping for the infomercial.

The taping of interviews for the infomercial was in a meeting room of a Tokyo executive hotel. The room had rush-mat *tatami* floors and unpainted walls. The large room was divided into smaller spaces by sliding doors; each door was covered with a picture of fog-shrouded mountains. The meeting room's alcove had a *nageire* flower arrangement and an ink-painting hanging scroll of swimming carp. The interviewer and guest each sat on a cushion on either side of a low table, in front of an antique folding screen that depicted the Battle of Sekigahara. The place was traditionally Japanese from floor to ceiling, which was why it had been chosen.

At the moment, MORI Kumiko, Mother's lifelong friend, was the person being interviewed. Age had not lessened the old woman's fervor. She told Mister Matsuura, the interviewer, "If we buy California, Japanese people will die from senseless shootings."

"Go on."

"Japanese know how to settle conflicts peacefully. We talk, we build consensus, we compromise, we go to mediation if we must."

"Right."

"We strive never to offend or to make the other person lose face. Americans only know how to solve disputes by shooting each other."

"What about the treaty article that six months afterward, Californians must meet Japanese gun laws?"

"It makes no difference. California has many criminals, and the criminals will smuggle in guns."

"I see."

"Japanese in California will be shot to death by drug-crazed California criminals, or by California cowboys overconcerned about private property."

"Mrs. Mori, what would you say to those who would argue that not all Californians are that way?"

"Of course, not all are gun-mad, but enough are— and I only need to meet one, to die."

Right after Mori Kumiko finished taping her anti-treaty interview, Barbara walked up to her and bowed deeply. "Mrs. Mori, thank you for speaking up against the treaty."

Mrs. Mori bowed back, halfheartedly it seemed to Barbara. "You're welcome. Goodbye now."

Huh? "I'm sorry, I thought we had time to chat."

"No, sorry, I need to leave now."

"Is something wrong?"

"It would be rude to speak of it."

"Have I offended you?"

"It would be rude to speak of it."

"Please, tell me. You'll feel better if you do."

"That is the way of California, not the way of Japan."

"Then I am deeply sorry, but I don't know. I'm not fully Japanese, so we're missing *haragei*." We haven't achieved full unspoken communication.

"Exactly," Mrs. Mori snapped.

"I don't understand."

"You're not fully Japanese. Look at you, you're American."

"And you detest Americans."

"Americans are arrogant. Fifty years ago, Americans claimed to know better than Japanese, what was best for Japan's defense." In the mid-Fifties, the U.S. Air Force wanted to extend the runways at Tachikawa Air Base into the nearby farmland, and Kumiko had been one of many young Japanese protesting against that.

Now Barbara said, "I know *one* thing that I don't know better than Japanese about."

"What's that?"

"How to heal my relationship with my mother."

Mrs. Mori's face showed no kindness. "Ask your grandfather. Ask your aunt."

"I have. You are, and you were, Mother's friend. You know her in ways we relatives don't."

"Takeko-*san* and I are friends because I no longer speak of her great mistake. We don't discuss the treaty in our letters, so I don't remind her that if she'd behaved properly years ago, she wouldn't need a treaty to live in Japan."

Be calm, take a breath. "'Properly,' you say. Mother told me of the two times Grandfather hired a matchmaker for her." The two men introduced to Mother had been poor, and she'd turned them down. "If Mother had behaved 'properly,' she would've spent married life poor and probably miserable. Did you want that of your friend?"

"There's no shame in enduring in silence. Goodbye now." Mrs. Mori turned to leave.

Barbara bit back the first seventeen things she wanted to say next. She told Mrs. Mori's back, "In Japanese, Father asked Mother for their first date. She was cooking hamburgers and he read from a paper, 'Please go with me to the movie on Saturday.' She giggled at his accent before she caught herself. An arrogant American would've stayed with English, instead of working so hard to embarrass himself."

Mrs. Mori turned to face Barbara again. "If your father was so open-minded, why did he take her to see an American film instead of a Japanese film?"

"For the same reason that he took her to a theater in Tokyo that had subtitles, instead of to the theater on-base."

"Did she tell you what people in the theater whispered about her?"

"She was a young, beautiful woman, together with a serviceman. I can guess what Japanese people called her." *Pampan*—streetwalker for GIs.

"She cried when she told me the next morning. But a week later, she went on a second date with him."

"And you don't remember why? She often told me that during their courtship he was funny, he was handsome, and he always treated her like Lady Murasaki, never like a poor cripple's daughter. And certainly never like a *pampan*."

"I'm leaving now, goodbye. But since you ask for advice about your mother, I'll give it. Do two things. First, become more Japanese. Japan is the most civilized country in the world."

"I see," Barbara said without expression.

"Second, do not speak of what troubles your mother. Avoid disharmony."

"But then nothing is resolved."

Mrs. Mori called over her shoulder as she shuffled away, "Your answer is so American."

———

Eight days later, a Friday night, the first infomercial ran on Nippon TV. Had the Progressives' commercial swayed enough voters? Barbara couldn't answer, and the suspense was almost painful.

Saturday morning, Barbara needed distraction from that suspense, and she wanted to deepen ties with her Japanese family, so she took Aunt Makiko shopping.

Saturday afternoon, Barbara and Aunt were back in Grandfather's apartment, where Barbara was modeling the *hohmongi* (matron's kimono) and *obi* (sash) that she'd bought with Aunt's help.

The kimono made Grandfather smile. "It pleases me that you did something so Japanese, Barbara-*san.*"

"Thank you, Grandfather."

Aunt said, "You certainly pleased *me* when you asked me to come with you. Father, when I saw her trying on the matron-kimono, I told her I didn't think of her only as American anymore."

Grandfather said, "Yes, I understand your feelings." He watched Barbara model the clothes. "Granddaughter, I am surprised."

Barbara looked at her grandfather and aunt. "I did this for Mother."

"Go on," Grandfather said.

"Mrs. Mori reminded me of all that Mother lost when Mother chose Father. Mother lost friends, reputation, the country that was her home, and the goodwill of her family."

"Yes." Grandfather left volumes unsaid.

"And I'm here to fight the treaty that Mother wants so much. I must continue my fight, but I know I add to Mother's hurt. This matron-kimono is my way to say, `Mother, I respect who you are, what you feel, and what you've lost. Mother, please let's stay close.'"

"That is good, Granddaughter." He paused, then looked at her. "When Takeko-*san* married, I was ashamed of her. Then, I saw only that she was Eldest Daughter, but had disobeyed me."

"Go on."

"I behaved properly as the sages wrote, and that cut the rope of love binding me and her. Years and years lost, so regrettable."

"Yes," Barbara said, voice faint.

"One day Takeko-*san* will regain harmony when she accepts that she cannot ever truly know you. As I cannot, and as your American relatives and friends cannot. But until then, hurry to heal this rift between you and Takeko-*san*. Do not let her grow even older, estranged from you."

After visiting with Grandfather and Aunt, Barbara rode a train back to her station, then caught a taxi to return her to her Japanese inn. The first 99-plus percent of the trip was unexciting.

Joe, the enforcer from Las Vegas, was standing across the street from the inn. He was looking at every car, but gave her blue taxi only a glance.

He's watching for me to arrive in Yamamura's limo!

The taxi driver was in the far left lane and slowing, his signal flashing. "No!" Barbara said. "Don't stop, don't turn. Go, go!"

"Huh? You don't want to go here?"

"Turn right at the corner and drop me there! Hurry, *go!*"

As the taxi speeded up again, she turned to look at Joe. Had he spotted her? Was he now watching her taxi? No—she sighed with relief.

Two minutes later, she had paid the taxi fare and had walked back around the corner. Joe didn't notice her. She ducked into a drugstore, to stand where she could watch Joe watch for her.

She needed to think. She knew Joe was here, but he didn't know that she knew. How could she use her momentary advantage?

Probably Bernoulli was here, too, but she had no clue where. She also didn't know whether Joe and Bernoulli could talk to each other. She could call the Tokyo police and get Joe picked up, because the Alexandria police had a report of her assault by these two men. But with Joe arrested, Bernoulli might just hide for a while.

Desperation boosted Barbara's brain. Now she recalled a trick she'd seen in *Sanjuro,* besides in several Westerns: "Hey bad guys, the good guys aren't here, they're over there! Hurry, leave now and you'll catch them!" She'd trick Joe, and with luck, she'd snare Bernoulli as well.

She pulled out the digital phone Yamamura had given her, and called his driver. She explained her problem, but don't worry, she had a plan. Did he know the phone number for a second Japanese inn, one that would do a favor? She was in luck: She was given a phone number. Next Barbara asked, "Remember Miiko-*san*, who looks so like my daughter? Does anyone know how to get hold of her?" No problem, Barbara was told, Miiko-*san* was at the office, though it was late Saturday afternoon. Barbara's luck was still holding.

Barbara called the phone number for the other Japanese inn. Her fortune continued: The staff there was willing to help.

Next Barbara called Miiko-*san*. "Hello, I need your help for a dangerous mission," Barbara began.

Barbara explained the plan, finishing with "...When you're out of the limousine, this is important, you must never look at the American man across the street. When you arrive at the second inn, have the staff there put your coat and scarf wherever they keep my suitcases. Then call a cab. Joe won't realize that the office lady he sees leaving in a taxi is the same woman he just saw arriving in Mrs. Nakamura's limousine."

"This is *exciting!*"

"Yes, but these men are *dangerous.* You'll be in less danger than I'd be, but still, if you want to keep clear, I can do this mysel—"

"No way. Do I wear a trench coat and sunglasses?"

Barbara laughed. "Sorry, you'll need to wear an expensive dress coat, one long enough to cover your office uniform. No fedora either; I need you to cover your hair with a scarf."

After talking with Miiko-*san*, Barbara called her Japanese inn. She confused the staff at first. If Barbara wasn't checking out, why did she want them to load all her luggage into the limo when it came? No, no, she explained, not her luggage, just her suitcases, please load the empty suitcases into the limo. "*Empty,* you say?" But a minute later they'd understood and agreed.

She called back Yamamura's driver. Begin Operation Fake Move, she told him. *That's one problem gone soon,* she thought. *I hope.*

A half-hour later the limo pulled up to the front of Barbara's inn. Joe was watching, Barbara noticed. The limo driver got out and then opened the door for his passenger, whose hair was covered with a scarf, and whose tall body, a dress coat.

Driver and passenger bowed to each other, then the driver moved to get back into the limo. "Wait," Miiko-san yelled. Joe startled at this, and looked ready to run. The bellman came out of the inn with Barbara's suitcases loaded on a cart, and Joe looked confused.

The bellman made a show of straining to load the suitcases into the trunk. By then the inn's whole staff had come outside. With much bowing all around, the staff said goodbye to the fake Mrs. Nakamura.

Miiko-*san* was helped back into the limousine, then the driver got back behind the wheel. Barbara looked away to Joe. Gone. But when the limo drove past the drugstore, Joe soon followed, in a green taxi.

But Bernoulli wasn't with Joe. She eyed every car that drove past, but she didn't spot Bernoulli.

She'd overlooked him, she told herself.

Thirty minutes later, Barbara received a call on her digital phone. A man said, "Hello, this is the Plum Blossom Inn. The muscular American is outside, watching our entrance. The young woman has left."

"Thank you for what you've done. What about the other American? Has anyone seen him?"

"I'm sorry, no. Do you wish us to call the police now?"

"That's kind, but no. I'll give the other man a few more minutes to arrive, then I'll make the call to arrest them both."

"Thank you." The relief in the manager's voice was obvious.

Seconds later, digital phone back in her purse, Barbara walked into her inn. She intended to warn the inn's staff to beware of two dangerous Americans.

Before Barbara could speak, Mrs. Bekki the hostess did. "Ah, Mrs. Nakamura, you have an honored guest. An American man has been waiting for you."

Barbara turned and saw Bernoulli—wearing a black-hair wig. Now Bernoulli was too close, and getting closer. *No!*

His smile was cruel. "Honey, I'm home. Did you miss me?" She felt a knifepoint in her side. "Start walking now, real slow, real quiet. You got me? Slow and quiet."

She planted her heels. "Am I an idiot?"

The tip of his knife pricked her. "I said *walk*."

"Or what, you'll kill me?"

"I'll carve you to the bone, here and now, if you don't move."

"Plan C: *KEISATSU O YONDE KUDASAI! KOROSOH!*"

Guests fled to their rooms; front-desk staff grabbed phones. "Shit!" Bernoulli said.

His other arm snaked around Barbara's throat. "*Back off!*" he yelled, waving the knife around.

Mrs. Bekki, the kimonoed hostess, took a tentative step closer. Instantly Bernoulli laid the knife blade against Barbara's carotid artery. "Come close, she dies."

Mrs. Bekki halted, looking scared and confused. She turned to the front desk for instructions. No instructions came.

Barbara took a slow breath to calm herself. She recalled what Miyamoto wrote: "When your body is quiet, your mind shouldn't be quiet; when your body is moving fast, your mind shouldn't at all be moving fast." *Think hard!*

Bernoulli's hands were both busy; neither of Barbara's were. While she bit his arm, her right hand reached back and squeezed his balls hard as she twisted them, while the heel of her right shoe slammed down on his instep.

While he was shrieking, she broke and ran.

"Bitch, you'll *beg* before I'm done," he yelled.

She dashed out, planning to find a *kohban* (neighborhood police station). But throngs of pedestrians made walking slow. And she had no idea whether she was headed in the right direction.

She heard a startled and outraged scream behind her. Then another and another. She looked back. Bernoulli was shoving people out of his way, and gaining on her.

Get away from him, I must get away.

She heard police sirens converging on her Japanese inn. A police car even raced past her, not noticing Bernoulli either.

Stop! Come back, come here!

Two blocks further, she was trapped in a crowd at a corner when she heard Bernoulli's voice behind her: "Face me, you whore." She spun around.

He had the knife out. Someone screamed. Everyone was backing away from the two Americans.

The onlookers then fell silent, except for three talking into digital phones. She presumed they had dialed 110, but she couldn't spare attention to them.

She was calm now. "You'll hang in a Japanese prison," she said.

He smiled. "The boss has money, and money buys lawyers. Also judges." He lunged; she stepped sideways almost in time. *Oh, the pain!* Hot, wet blood flowed down her left arm.

Bernoulli smiled again. "Sliced your arm, honey pie. You should've stayed in Washington, serving coffee and smiling pretty. They're gonna write on your tombstone, `She was outclassed.'"

She stared openmouthed at him. Part of her was horrified how he'd crafted a taunt so on-target. Another part of her feared he was right.

And while Barbara stood paralyzed with anguish, Bernoulli slapped the knife into his left hand and lunged with that. She twisted sideways—again, almost in time. The crowd gasped; Barbara screamed.

She put her left hand on her abdomen—the movement was agony for the sliced triceps. Her hand came away sticky red. "Nothing internal," she told the crowd in a shaky voice. "Cut only my obliques."

Bernoulli hadn't understood her Japanese. "You dying?"

She locked her eyes on his. "No."

He swaggered up to her, his wrist relaxed as he waved the knife back and forth. "Then I'll need to change thi—"

Barbara, while still keeping her eyes on his, using only her peripheral vision, seized Bernoulli's forearm with her right hand.

Her left hand followed; she ignored the agony the movement caused.

Only then did her gaze shift away from his surprised face. Her hands pushed down while her knee shot up, slamming into his wrist.

Her right hand slid back, grabbing the knife away from his loosened grip. Only two seconds had passed since he'd spoken.

He froze when he saw his own knife pointed at him, as the police sirens were approaching now. He slowly raised his hands to shoulder level in surrender. "Game over."

His gaze darted to her neck.

His hands shot forward for her throat, even as her right hand lunged forward and up.

His hands brushed her throat without strength for a second, then he slumped to the pavement. His eyes were wide. His black wig fell onto the cement and laid there like a dead animal.

Wobbly on rubber legs, through the flashing green haze of her own pain, Barbara looked down at the corpse. "Miyamoto wrote to strike swiftly when the enemy is slow and lax. He also wrote to observe without rolling your eyes around. But you haven't read *The Book of Five Elements*, have you?"

Barbara's ambulance arrived five minutes later; by then the police had searched Bernoulli's pockets. Other police were on their way to pick up Joe. A policeman showed Barbara an employee I.D. card for Isadoro G. Bernoulli, issued by Cappello's Boardwalk Casino of Atlantic City.

"Could this Cappello be the `Mister C.' who kidnapped and threatened me?" Barbara asked.

Bernoulli's carvings on Barbara hadn't cut any nerves or major blood vessels, nor had he hurt her gastrointestinal tract. Thus she was not seriously injured—but the main reason the hospital released her the next morning was that she was so insistent.

A nurse wheeled her out into early-morning sunshine to where Yamamura's car and driver waited. Merely standing up and walking was hard and painful for Barbara, but neither the nurse nor Yamamura's driver moved to help her.

But a stranger did. A brunette woman in a salmon-colored suit stepped in front, grabbed Barbara's right arm near the armpit, and pulled her up. "Mercy, is nobody else going to help you?" the woman asked in American English.

"It's okay. Ask me sometime about my grandfather and you'll understand."

The brunette released Barbara and gestured to Barbara's right. Over there stood an American man shouldering a professional's dijvid camera; beside the man stood a blonde focusing a digital still-camera. The brunette raised a cordless microphone in her right hand to her mouth. "Barbara, I'm Audrey Garza, from NBC4, Los Angeles. L.A.—correction, all of California— is relieved that you survived the attack yesterday. You were so brave. I count eight stitches in your arm."

"Plus ten at the beltline. Audrey, relish life while you have it."

"So true." Audrey smiled at Barbara as the still-photographer handed Audrey a sheet of newsprint. Though folded many times, the sheet was still too big to fit in a briefcase. What Barbara could see of the paper was covered with handwriting.

Audrey asked, "Could you help me unfold this, Barbara? I'm glad it's not windy."

Audrey laid down the mike and helped Barbara unfold the paper on the ground. Since Barbara was forbidden to bend at the waist, and her left arm had a dogleg splint, she functioned mainly as paper-kicker and paperweight. Hospital visitors, both those leaving and those arriving, meanwhile had gathered around into a silent audience.

Audrey reclaimed her mike. "Barbara, this is a joint gift from NBC4, the *Los Angeles Times,* and the people of Los Angeles. As the banner says, we in L.A. are with you 100 percent."

Unfolded, the paper was not quite five feet tall by eight yards wide. Typeset in letters a foot and a half tall was "L.A. believes in Barbara!"

Filling the rest of the space were handwritten messages, hundreds of messages covering both sides of the paper:

"Barbara, please save California. Roger Light."

"I know you can do it! Don't give up. Isabella Hernandez."

"I dont want to groe up in Japan. Jerry Scalpelli. P.S. I'm nine."

Barbara thought, *I can't let all these people down.*

The next morning, Barbara had breakfast with Yamamura and the coalition leaders. Three of the four men were sympathetic and supportive about her attack; Kada, no surprise, said only a lukewarm "It's good you're all right."

Over breakfast, Yamamura read aloud an editorial: "'This week the Progressive Coalition is full of surprises. A *Yomiuri Shimbun*/Nippon TV poll taken Sunday night found that only 32 percent favored the California Treaty, while 58 percent opposed. This highly significant drop in public support can be directly credited to the three thirty-minute infomercials broadcast this weekend.'"

Teramura made a silly face. "And Kada said it wouldn't work."

Kada made a dismissive gesture. "The polls only matter if they persuade enough Conservatives to switch their vote. If Conservatives keep together, the treaty passes. It's simple arithmetic."

An hour later, still Monday morning, Barbara visited Miiko-*san* at Yamamura's office. Barbara thanked Miiko-*san* formally and at length, returned her coat and scarf, and repaid her for the taxi fare.

Barbara's splint, stitches, and painful movements sobered Miiko-*san*.

"This is ASN Newsbreak, 9:00 p.m. Eastern time, Sunday, July 31.

"Barbara Nakamura is no murderer, say Japanese police, and she won't be charged with any crime. Nakamura `clearly acted in necessary self-defense to prevent her own homicide,' according to Japan's National Police Agency. Such self-defense clears her under Japanese criminal law. Two days ago, Nakamura took a switchblade knife away from Isadoro. . ."

Hiroshi and his big box were back in Representative Shohji's Diet office Friday evening. An office lady was asking, ". . .here before, right? Shohji is out and I don't know when he'll return."

"I don't need to stay, but thank you. Could you please give these to him?"

"Thank you. What are they?"

"Copies of more signed petitions, respectfully requesting the Diet vote yes for the treaty. Mrs. Nakamura's show makes interesting television, but these people know Japan needs California."

Monday morning, eight days after Barbara had received L.A.'s banner, it was the mayor of San Francisco making the presentation. "Barbara, we're sorry we're late. Thanks for staying behind to meet with us, at such a charming hotel." The presentation was being shot in the garden of Barbara's Japanese inn.

Barbara's smile was as big as the mayor's. "My pleasure." Actually, by now, the fourth banner presentation, she was slightly bored.

"On the news yesterday, your own beloved San Diego gave you their autographed banner."

"Yes, with over a thousand signatures."

"And of course, Los Angeles gave you one. Yet we in—"

"Sacramento, too."

"Really? I wasn't—"

"Less than two hours ago. Sorry, since you came straight from the airport, you probably haven't seen the news yet."

The mayor presented San Francisco's banner. It was fifty-five inches by ten yards, "longer than La-La-Land's," the mayor said—

"But wait, Barbara, we also have a second present for you. The students at San Francisco's School of the Arts drew this mural for you. This photograph shows what it looks like, unrolled and unfolded."

The mural showed California's scenic wonders: the Golden Gate Bridge; the San Diego Zoo; San Francisco trolley cars; a redwood forest; Death Valley; a snarling saber-toothed tiger, its feet trapped in tar; surfers; bountiful vineyards; gold prospectors; and the "Hollywood" sign. A red-white-and-blue border framed each picture.

These other pictures surrounded the large central picture: a heroically rendered grizzly bear, facing left atop a hill.

Barbara smiled for the cameras. "Quite an effort. San Francisco is very generous, Mister Mayor."

"Barbara, we're only thanking you in advance. We know you'll save California."

"This is ASN Newsbreak, 10:00 p.m. Eastern time, Sunday, August 7.

"Twenty minutes ago someone shot at Prime Minister Sasaki of Japan. An unknown gunman fired twice at the prime minister, missing him both times. Japanese police don't have the gunman, but they do have the gun, which the gunman discarded in a trash can. Japanese police identify the recovered weapon as a 9-mm semiautomatic pistol. Prime Minister Sasaki was about to meet with senior bankers from Japan's largest banks to discuss raising money to pay for California, should the Diet approve the California Treaty."

"You *baka-yaroh*," Matt yelled into the pay phone, "I wanted you to *kill* the prime minister."

"Shut up, it's not *your* neck on the block," Ebara yelled back from his own pay phone. "We got no gripe with Sasaki."

"But—"

"Listen, a miss is the same as a murder under Japanese law. Your wife is still headed to Tochigi Women's Prison for years and years."

"I don't want her in prison, I want her dead."

"Still the plan. You ever heard of GOHDA Sadako, the `Pantyhose Strangler'? Right now Miss Gohda is serving time, and feeling broke."

About which, the Variety-Show Host joked—

Did Barbara Nakamura <u>really</u> need to run three thirty-minute commercials to turn Japanese against the California Treaty? Listen, <u>I</u> only need five seconds. People of Japan, do you really want a Hollywood agent maybe becoming your next-door neighbor?

Barbara Nakamura is okay, the hit man she killed didn't seriously wound her. But Barbara, next time <u>pay</u> the library fine.

CHAPTER 15
Heisei 17-nen 8-gatsu
9-ka, Kayohbi
(Tuesday, August 9, 2005)

"We're sorry for the intrusion," Detective Araki said, "but we'd like to ask a few questions."

It was early in the morning. Right after Barbara had returned from the hot tub, the hotel maid had come to tell her that the police wished to speak with her. Barbara had felt curiosity, but no alarm. When Barbara had finished dressing, the maid had brought two policemen to Barbara's room.

Araki's partner, Detective Kawakami, had the unchanging fierce expression of a temple stone lion, and a persistent cough. Now Kawakami watched her. "Mrs. Nakamura"—he coughed—"do you know that someone shot at the prime minister yesterday, then threw the weapon away?"

"Yes, it's terrible. Have you caught the man?"

His body was stiff. "We're investigating leads at this time." Kawakami watched her. "Let's talk about your Smith and Wesson Model 5906 9-mm semiautomatic pistol. You bought it in Alexandria, Virginia, in January 1989. Do you still own it?"

She gave him a puzzled look. "Yes."

Detective Araki needed only tusks and a mustache to look like a walrus: He was tall and broad, with an enormous belly. "Do you know the same model was used in the attempt on the prime minister?"

Before she could answer, Detective Kawakami asked, "Where is your own pistol?"

She gave them another puzzled look. "Yes, I read about the crime weapon in the newspaper. I was surprised by the coincidence, but I didn't think it remarkable—"

"Why not?" Kawakami asked.

"I'm sure there are thousands of guns in America of that model. As for my own handgun, it's in a moving box in Alexandria, or in San Diego, or somewhere on the road between."

"So"—he coughed—"you didn't bring the pistol to Japan?"

"Of course not. That's highly illegal." Why were they asking her such odd questions?

Araki asked, "Mrs. Nakamura, may I please ask where you were at 10:40 a.m. yesterday, and for three hours before?"

"Where *I* was? Am I somehow a suspect?"

"Please, Mrs. Nakamura, we need you to answer the question."

She wasn't worried, for the whole situation was too bizarre. "Let's see, I was. . ." She gave a detailed explanation, mentioning breakfast, the hot tub, a ten-minute meeting with the Sacramento delegation promptly at eight, and the San Francisco delegation ". . .who asked me to meet them here at nine o'clock, but they didn't arrive until 9:45. I talked with them for fifteen minutes. . ."

"Who can confirm that?" Araki asked when she'd finished.

She cited names of several hotel employees, the names of several hotel guests, and the name and mobile-phone number of Yamamura's driver.

Kawakami was watching her again. "So between 8:10 and 9:45 a.m., you can't confirm your whereabouts." He coughed.

They're acting as if I'm involved in the crime! "May I ask how you think I'm connected to the attempt on the prime minister, and how my pistol fits?"

Araki repeated Kawakami's question: "So between 8:10 and 9:45, you can't confirm your whereabouts? Please answer."

"No, I can't. Please, will *you* answer *my* question? How do you think I'm connected to the shooting?"

Kawakami gave her a cop-look. "The description and serial number of the recovered weapon exactly match the pistol you admit you own. How do you explain this?"

In her shock, Barbara mixed languages: "Oh, God. Oh, God. *O-benkai dekimasen.*" I can't explain it.

Detective Kawakami had progressed from watching her to staring her down. "Mrs. Nakamura, what do you know about the attempt on the prime minister?"

What they were saying was impossible, ridiculous. But how could she convince these two? She said, "Only what I read in the newspapers. I'm not involved, please believe me!"

Araki this time: "Then you deny involvement?"

"*Hai wa.*" Emphatically yes.

"How did the man who shot at the prime minister get your pistol?" Kawakami asked.

"Please understand, *I don't know!*"

Kawakami looked at Araki and nodded. Araki pulled a folded paper from his inside coat pocket. "Barbara Nakamura, this is a warrant to search your hotel room.

Please step out into the hallway, but remain where we can see you."

She left, with relief. She knew they wouldn't find anything.

After five minutes, she heard Kawakami say, "Please look, Araki-*kun*." He coughed. "A false bottom."

"Mm. With a padded cutout for a pistol. Clever. But wouldn't the metal case show up on X-ray?"

Araki stood in the doorway a minute later. "Mrs. Nakamura, we found this in your bedding-closet. It has a hollow bottom."

Kawakami was holding a carry-on bag. It was the same size as the carry-on she'd brought to Japan, and had zippers in the same places. Kawakami's bag was identical with her own suitcase in many ways.

But the carry-on bag Kawakami held was black. The bag she'd brought to Japan had been royal blue. Her carry-on bag had been supported on the bottom by a reinforced black plastic skirt near the wheels. The black imposter carry-on featured a flat-black metal pan down near its wheels. With the black suitcase open, and with its false bottom in Araki's hand, she saw that inside the metal pan was foam rubber, with a pistol-shaped cutout.

Matt had framed her.

She was thoroughly in shock, only half listening, when Kawakami pulled a different folded paper from his own pocket.

"Barbara Nakamura, this is an arrest warrant. You are charged as an accessory to the attempted homicide of Prime Minister Sasaki. You are also charged with violation of the Firearms and Swords Control Law, specifically illegal importation of a Smith and Wesson Model 5906 9-mm semiautomatic handgun, with serial number of. . ."

". . .and violation of the Customs Tariff Law, specifically importation of a prohibited object: a Smith and Wesson Model 5906 9-mm semiautomatic handgun, same serial number.

"The law lets you decline to answer incriminating questions. Whatever answers you give can be used against you in court. The law lets you hire a defense attorney to be present during questioning. As a foreigner, the law lets you request an interpreter during questioning, at public expense. If your case comes to trial and you do not have a defense attorney, the court shall appoint one if you wish, at public expense. Your embassy shall be informed of your arrest once you request this in writing. Please come with us."

About which, the Variety-Show Host joked—

Barbara Nakamura was arrested for helping an assassination attempt. Listen, Japan, I'll prove she doesn't shoot politicians: "Bomber" Nakamura is alive.

The news reports are wrong, assassination and gun-smuggling aren't why Barbara was arrested. She refused to sing in a karaoke bar.

CHAPTER 16
Heisei 17-nen 8-gatsu
9-ka, Kayohbi
(Tuesday, August 9, 2005)

Fifteen days until the end of the session:

It was a quite civilized bust. Kawakami and Araki didn't frisk Barbara in her hotel room, but Araki took her purse and passport. With both policemen watching, she was allowed to pack one of the two unseized suitcases with toiletries, makeup, and clothing to take to jail. They didn't handcuff her, but they walked on either side of her, and Kawakami gripped her arm when the three of them passed through the inn's lobby.

Why did you frame me, Matt? Why did you betray me? Barbara kept asking herself.

Barbara was further distressed by all the averted gazes in the lobby.

I wish I'd wake up and all this were a bad dream.

After she was fingerprinted and photographed at Tokyo Detention House, she asked when she could make her one phone call. She wanted to phone Yamamura and explain. No phone calls were allowed, she was told. Likewise denied: visitors, except for her attorney or someone from the U.S. Embassy, and mail from anyone except her attorney or the embassy.

She asked how much a defense attorney would cost. She was told at least a half-million yen, about eighty-three hundred dollars, to handle her case. She didn't have that kind of money.

A minute later, Detective Kawakami and Detective Araki walked Barbara to a small interrogation room.

Said room was standard issue: It had no window, and one wall was a mirror. The only furniture was a table, with one chair on one side that faced the mirror and three chairs on the other side. The only door was next to the mirror. A microphone hung from a hole in the ceiling. Lighting was from three ceiling-track spotlights, all aimed at the single chair. On the wall behind the single chair was a no-smoking sign.

They marched her to the hot seat, then took the two outer chairs on the other side. She tried to sound casual: "My dad was a cop. I've done homework in rooms like this." Yet in truth she was intimidated. No wonder, the place was *designed* to be intimidating.

Kawakami had carried a battle-scarred metal ashtray into the interrogation room, and had tossed it on the table. Now, from a pocket he produced a pack of cigarettes and lit up.

Kawakami blew smoke at the microphone. "Mrs. Nakamura"—he coughed—"tell us who shot at the prime minister."

Barbara crossed her arms. "I don't know who the shooter is. I'm not involved in any crime."

Araki asked, "How'd you sneak the pistol past airport security in Washington and San Diego? The suitcase's metal part is obvious on X-ray."

"I didn't bring the pistol to Japan, I left it in Alexandria. That's not the suitcase I brought to Japan."

Kawakami leaned forward and eyed her. "This suitcase walked into your room all by itself, while yours was walking out."

"Talk to the staff at the Firefly-River Inn and the Plum Blossom Inn. They handled my carry-on bag when I was trying to escape two Mafia men. The bellmen will tell you my bag was blue then."

Araki pulled a notebook out of his jacket, opened it, and scribbled something. "We'll check that."

"But that doesn't explain the pistol," Kawakami said. He blew smoke past her ear. "How'd it come to Tokyo if you didn't bring it?"

"Ask Husband."

"How do you explain our finding a suitcase with a hollow bottom in your hotel room?" He coughed.

"Husband somehow switched my carry-on bag."

"He sent the gun to Japan, and he switched your suitcase here in Tokyo, without leaving Washington? How did he manage that?"

The cigarette smoke in the small room was starting to sting her eyes, but she wasn't about to give Kawakami any satisfaction. "How? He's a senator."

Araki asked, "Mrs. Nakamura, what did you want to achieve by shooting the prime minister?"

"I'm not involved in shooting the prime minister."

Kawakami asked, "How did you get the pistol past Customs at Narita Airport?"

"I didn't have the pistol at Narita. I didn't have a trick bag at Narita. Husband framed me."

Araki asked, "What were you doing between 8:10 and 9:45, the morning of the shooting?"

"I was in my room, waiting for the San Francisco delegation to arrive. I was reading ENCHI Fumiko's *Onnazaka* while I was waiting. You moved the book when you searched my room."

The questioning went on for hours. The detectives repeated their questions and Barbara repeated her answers. Her eyes and nose burned from cigarette smoke, and she recalled Bernoulli's onion mask. In the still air of the interrogation room, the cigarette smoke had formed its own cloud layers.

And as the air became toxic, so did Barbara's attitude toward Kawakami. After sixteen years in Washington of putdowns and humiliation from Matt, ditto most recently from Kada, Barbara was in no mood to take more. Had it really been only four months earlier that she'd actually apologized to Matt for fixing her flower arrangement? That sweet doormat was gone forever. Besides, she'd beaten Bernoulli in a fight to the death—did Kawakami think mind games could cow her now? Kawakami, watch out.

". . .Mrs. Nakamura," Kawakami was saying, "I know you brought the gun to Japan. Now tell me why."

"Has the goo in your lungs clogged your ears, Detective? I say again: I didn't bring the handgun to Japan. I brought a *blue* carry-on bag to Japan, and when you talk to the bellmen, they'll agree. *Wakaru da*?" Understand, buddy? "Husband framed me."

"Mrs. Nakamura," Araki said, "please tell us again what you were doing between 8:10 and 9:45."

She sighed. "At 8:10 I shook hands with the Sacramento delegation, in front of my *ryokan*. I went inside, to my room. I resumed reading *Onnazaka*, while waiting for the San Francisco delegation. At 9:45 the hostess came and said I had visitors. Sheesh, I've lost track of how many times I've said this."

"Thirty or twenty times, at least," Araki said, smiling at her. "I admire you for that. You've stuck to your story and you've kept calm, which under this stress is commendable."

"Thank you."

Kawakami snorted. "Yes, quite commendable, for the accomplice of a bungling assassin."

Kawakami stubbed out the last of a pack's worth of cigarettes as he eyed her. "Nakamura, you want to play a game with us? That's okay." He coughed. "While I'm here listening to Husband-framed-me stories, I don't have to fight Tokyo traffic, and I'm not out in the rain— I'm happy, you understand?"

"Perfectly. It was your ever-present grin that tipped me." She laughed at his angry expression.

"When I slam your jail door shut, we'll see who laughs."

Araki looked at Barbara and Kawakami. "My partner was starting to say, He's not who'll suffer here if you're not open with us."

"So I don't care," Kawakami said. "You confess now, so the judges give you three years' forced labor but no fine? Or you decide to be a hard case, so the judges hand you life at forced labor, and a five million yen fine? Either way suits me."

Araki nodded. "Here in Japan, a `document of reflection'—"

"A what?"

"A written apology to the court shows the judges you're contrite. This reduces your sentence. Refusing to confess lengthens your sentence. Life with forced labor plus an eye-popping fine, do you want these?"

Barbara leaned forward and looked hard at both men. "Has either of you heard the word *acquittal?*"

Kawakami grunted. "Only when talking about lenient American courts. In Japan, public prosecutors have a conviction rate over 99 percent. And prosecutors in Japan don't reduce the charge in exchange for a guilty"—he coughed—"plea. But cheer up, maybe you can request transfer to a prison in California. Who knows, we might reopen Alcatraz."

This scared her, and Kawakami looked smug as though he knew that. But her posture was straight, her voice steady, as she said: "I might surprise you. I might take the stand and convince those judges."

"Not with your story. This isn't America, don't think you can fast-talk yourself to an acquittal."

"I'm willing to risk it."

"*Soh da?* Then you don't understand how Japan's judges think." He coughed.

She turned to completely face Araki, snubbing Kawakami. "What does he mean?"

Araki said, "A defendant can't be forced to testify. But if he does testify, he's automatically considered incompetent and so he isn't sworn. Whatever he says, the defendant never commits perjury."

"What stops the defendant from lying?"

"Nothing. Knowing this, the judges are free to ignore everything she says."

This was *not* good news.

Araki tried a new approach: "Mrs. Nakamura, the judges will be easier on you if you confess. The judges will be still easier if you also write a letter of apology to the prime minister."

"I've done nothing to confess, and I don't need to apologize to anyone."

"Then please think of your mother. Please think of your debt to her, to your family in Japan, and to Representative Yamamura who sponsored you. You have an obligation to ease their embarrassment. Please, for them, confess and apologize."

"How do you know I won't confess, only to recant later? What if I claim that my confession was forced?"

Kawakami blew smoke in her face. "Feel free to try. In Japan a confession can't be retracted once made."

Kawakami didn't even rate a glance. To Araki she said, "Then I regret to say, I cannot confess."

Araki's sympathy looked sincere: "Then I likewise regret to remind you that soon you'll be known in Japan as 'one who doesn't know indebtedness.'"

This, being called ungrateful to a benefactor, was the most vile insult in Japanese.

Araki added, "Even were you to gain release from custody, California would be no better off. You'd be unwelcome everywhere in Japan, and you could only hurt California."

Thirteen days until the end of the session:

Barbara peered closely, then sat back. "I know you."

Barbara had requested that the police contact the U.S. Embassy; two days later she was visited in jail by consul Amber Connor. Barbara immediately recognized Amber as the mystery blonde with the envelope.

As consul, Amber's list of Cannots was longer than her list of Cans. The embassy couldn't represent Barbara in court. The embassy couldn't attend any of her hearings, nor attend her trial. The embassy couldn't give her legal advice. The embassy couldn't accept custody of her, nor guarantee her appearance in court. The embassy couldn't post bail for her, should a judge decide to set bail.

Barbara was on her own.

She had written a note for Yamamura. She begged Amber to rush her note to him any way possible. Amber looked doubtful, but agreed. Clearly Amber had second thoughts about her hero.

This was beside the immediate problem that the guards at the jail wouldn't let Barbara pass to Amber the note she'd written to Yamamura. But Amber had a small datebook and pen in her briefcase, and eight years of school Japanese in her brain. Barbara sat on one side of the divider glass, Amber the other, and Amber wrote as Barbara read aloud:

> *Yamamura-<u>dono</u>,*
>
> *By now you know I've been arrested. I apologize for the embarrassment my arrest creates for you.*
>
> *The police think I smuggled in the gun that someone used to shoot at the prime minister. But I didn't smuggle anything! That is my pistol, yes, but I left it in Washington. I came to Japan with an ordinary carry-on bag, not the one the police found. Somehow Husband arranged for my gun to be smuggled in and for my suitcase to be switched. Somehow Husband framed me. . .*

As Barbara read that last sentence, Amber gave her a skeptical look. "I was framed" is the universal jailhouse whopper.

An hour later, Detective Goodcop and Detective Badcop were collecting Barbara, so they could haul her to the public prosecutor's office. The procedure was that the public prosecutor either would release Barbara, or else would request from a judge a Warrant of Detention to hold her during further investigation.

Yet Barbara wasn't worried—once the prosecutor heard testimony that Barbara's carry-on bag was recently blue, she'd walk.

But as Barbara was being marched to the police car, Kawakami said, "We talked to the staff at both Firefly-River Inn and the Plum Blossom Inn. Nobody remembers what color your suitcases were. Nobody remembers if they were all the same color. Want to change your story?"

Barbara sighed. "The bellmen don't want to get involved."

"Yeah, that's one explanation."

Once Barbara was facing the prosecutor, he read the charges to her, then asked her to tell her side of the story. She did, but it was clear he didn't buy a word.

The police presented their evidence. Kawakami's report highlighted that between 8:10 and 9:45 a.m. on the day of the shooting, Barbara's whereabouts couldn't be verified. She was unsurprised to see her pistol, with an evidence tag on it; a fax sheet of her gun registration from Virginia; and the black imposter carry-on bag.

But Barbara was stunned and dismayed to see the Narita Airport Customs dijvid. On television, only her gift-wrapped cedar chest was X-rayed.

"What's in here?" the Customs inspector asked, when he saw the black shapes on the monitor.

"You're seeing foil-wrapped cheese and cans of shrimp," Barbara said.

He nodded and set the gift aside, unchecked.

This was bad for her case. Her carry-on bag wasn't X-rayed, and it received only a few pats. This was worse for her case. Worst of all, nobody could tell what color her carry-on bag was at Narita—for the Customs dijvid was in black-and-white.

How lucky for Matt, how disastrous for her.

She claimed her carry-on bag at the airport had been a different color from the bag the police had seized. But she couldn't prove her claim to a judge.

"This is ASN Newsbreak, 4:00 a.m. Eastern time, Thursday, August 11.

"Did Barbara Nakamura smuggle her pistol into Japan? Her baggage inspector can't say she didn't. You're seeing the actual Japan Customs videotape of her bag-check two months ago at Narita Airport. Shinsuke Kubo is the official seen rushing through the inspection of her bags. Kubo has told ASN that his bosses encouraged him to give Mrs. Nakamura preferential treatment. . . ."

Twelve days until the end of the session:
The day after Barbara was brought to the public prosecutor's office, she went before the judge in a closed detention hearing. Again Barbara told her story. The judge heard her out, then ordered her held for ten more days' investigation. He also denied bail. The entire hearing didn't take ten minutes.

In ten days, the public prosecutor would release her, or else ask the court to charge her. The smart money wasn't on release.

She needed either to contact Yamamura or for him to contact her. She wished she knew if he'd received her note, and what he thought of it.

"This is ASN Newsbreak, 1:00 a.m. Eastern time, Friday, August 12.

"This just in: Barbara Nakamura's sponsor to Japan has turned on her, calling her the `ingrate cowgirl criminal.' Nakamura's sponsor, Hideo Yamamura, also just resigned his seat in the Diet as an act of atonement for bringing her to Japan. In his resignation speech, Yamamura apologized for breaking the law by using his influence to hurry her luggage inspection at Narita Airport. . . ."

In Alexandria, Matt had cable TV on as he was brushing his teeth.

"This is ASN Newsbreak, 8:00 a.m. Eastern time, Friday, August 12.

"Barbara Nakamura now has a powerful character witness in Japan's Diet. Taijiroh Saitoh told reporters, `I've worked closely with Mrs. Nakamura for two months now. She's neither cowgirl nor criminal, nor does she forget others' help.' Saitoh is the new senior party president among the parties in the opposition Progressive Coalition. Saitoh's comments carry considerable political risk to himself, both because he hasn't yet firmed his power base within the Diet's lower house, and because sentiment in Saitoh's home region is overwhelmingly hostile to Barbara Nakamura."

Snarling, Matt muted the TV. "The plan was *supposed* to be that all her allies desert her. No matter, the main part of my plan still works. Barbara is headed for prison, where the Pantyhose Strangler awaits."

Three days until the end of the session:

Sunday night, Hiroshi was leaving Reiko's apartment in Yokosuka. Reiko said, "I heard a rumor today, and I think it's true."

"What rumor?"

"That Matsumoto Robotics is interested in a big robotics factory somewhere in California. If the treaty goes through, our company plans to buy it."

Hiroshi beamed. "A transfer—I can receive a transfer to Japanese California!"

In jail in Tokyo, Barbara gave a searching look to her visitor. "Tell me about the treaty."

Amber stared at her. "You still can't prove you're innocent, and it's now the night before your arraignment hearing. *Hello?*"

"I'm not crazy, I know my future: years in prison. Maybe life."

"So then why—"

"I need to be sure the treaty's dead."

"'Sure'? Today the treaty's the *least* sure thing on the planet."

Amber explained that by recess Friday evening the treaty had moved to the head of the lower-house agenda. The Progressives filibustered, and proposed poisonous treaty amendments and spurious procedural motions, all to prevent a vote on the treaty in the time remaining. None carried, but the House had recessed for the weekend without a vote on the treaty. The Speaker was growing impatient.

Barbara now asked, "And the voting, if the Progressives can't stop it?"

The Japanese public, thanks to Barbara's infomercials, now hated the treaty and the taxes it would bring. Thanks to public hatred, and Article 32 cowards using public hatred as an excuse, the vote now was a mystery.

"*How much* a mystery?"

"The embassy reads it as 249 yes, 250 no, 1 undecided, and the Speaker voting yes if a tie."

"Who's undecided?"

Amber shrugged. "A Conservative from South Kantoh Region."

That didn't tell Barbara much—South Kantoh Region had thirteen Conservative Representatives.

I wonder if it's Representative Shohji?

A second later, Barbara leaned back and sighed. "Is there anything else I should know?"

"Yes." Amber made a face. "Last night Consular Section received a message from Senator Nakamura to give to you—"

"Matt wrote me?"

"Who else would say this? `Karma strikes back for you passing those FBI reports on to Carol. See you at the hearing.'"

"Huh. At last I know his reason."

"Reason for what?"

"For framing me. I wasn't who sent Carol those reports—but it seems like Matt thinks so. Isn't life beautiful sometimes?"

"I'm sorry for what I've thought about you since—"

Barbara smiled sadly. "Matt's fooled you only once. Be glad."

"God, I hate him. Bad enough to be a traitor to California, but does he have to be so *mean,* too?"

"To the wife he thinks snatched away his huge gift? Yes."

"You deserve better. How I wish for your sake you could've killed the treaty."

Barbara cocked her head. "For my sake?"

"People will always link you with him. I wish you could've killed the treaty, then you wouldn't be known as `Bomber' Nakamura's wife anymore. You'd be called instead `Barbara, treaty slayer.'"

Barbara stared at Amber, stunned. "What you said," she breathed.

Now it was Amber puzzled. "What did I say?"

"During sixteen years in Washington, how often did a reporter ask me for a solo interview? Once a year, maybe. And then it was clear that the reporter was only interested in whether I was playing my role. Was I putting on weight? Did I smile winningly, and mouth sweet words of support? Could I out-fawn Nancy Reagan? Nobody wanted to hear what *Barbara* Nakamura thought."

"Only what the *Honorable* Matt Nakamura thought." Amber packed sarcasm into one word.

"I want—I *need*—to be recognized again as myself. Not as Matt's wife, not Matt's ex, but as Barbara! And you say the way out of Matt's shadow is to stop the treaty?" Barbara shook her fist. "I resolve *again*, Amber: I must get out of jail and kill the treaty!"

***

The next morning, two days until the end of the session:

A man walked up to Matt outside the courthouse where Barbara was to have her arraignment hearing. Though Matt's visitor wore a Japanese press badge, his clothes were too loud to be a reporter's. He wore a hat in August—to cover a perm? His hand, missing a pinky, shoved a piece of paper at Matt.

Matt glared at him. "Fool, I can't read Japanese. What's it say?"

The thug's eyes narrowed, then he remembered who Matt was. In a low voice he said, "The deal is set. A hundred thousand yen goes to the Pantyhose Strangler when she kills your wife."

"That's *if* Wife has been tried and sent to prison. Right now, she hasn't even been arraigned yet."

"All that will happen; we made sure of it. Your wife will die."

In the courtroom twenty minutes later, the judge said, "I order Barbara Nakamura held for trial."

This meant Barbara's time to kill the treaty was gone.

The previous night with Amber in the jail, Barbara had felt excitement along with her renewed determination. But now Barbara was looking at dull gray reality.

The reality? She hadn't found proof of her innocence, so no time was left to kill the treaty.

In the Diet, meanwhile, it was unlikely the Progressives would be allowed to continue blocking a vote on the treaty. Meaning, the treaty was at the mercy of one undecided Dietman.

Even so, call Barbara a fool but she refused to quit. She still pushed her brain to find a way to bust out of detention prison somehow, race to the Diet Building, and kill the treaty.

But now she didn't even have her hands free. She was wearing a robot-tailored tan suit, and handcuffs, when Detectives Kawakami and Araki escorted her out of the courtroom.

Meanwhile, time was up.

Amber had warned Barbara that the detention prison would be harsher than the jail Barbara had left. Kawakami knew this, too.

"Mrs. Nakamura, I'm so sorry," he now said, smiling. "Yes, the judge just provided you with a defense attorney." He coughed. "Yet your new life does have unpleasant parts. The prison has rules about everything, even how you sit in your cell. You'll be required to submit a written request merely to write a letter or to buy snacks. You'll be locked in your own cell and the prison makes it tough to talk to anyone else."

"So? The only person I want to talk to is my defense attorney."

Kawakami snickered. Araki told her, "Your attorney will spend very little time on your case. And most of that time will be spent reviewing the prosecutor's evidence, not talking to you."

"How much time *will* I have with him?"

"You'd be wise not to expect more than one or two visits from your attorney, two or three weeks before your trial."

Barbara realized she wouldn't talk to her attorney before the Diet voted. Even if the attorney could spring her, it would be too late to hurt the treaty.

This meant she had no more time.

Now she and the detectives were almost to the outside doors. Kawakami was smiling at her again: "I see your press club, they're interviewing your husband. Do you wish us to remove your jacket and drape it over your head?"

She gave Kawakami a look of defiance. She strode outside between her keepers, her bare head held high. Sure enough, TV cameramen, TV sound technicians with their furry microphones, TV and newspaper reporters, and still-photographers, both Japanese and American, all were outside with Matt. She recognized the Japanese press as the same antagonistic pack that had tracked her since Narita Airport. Now at the sight of her, the press people frenzied.

Suddenly the reporters were shouting and moving. Matt looked over to see Barbara, who was being escorted from the courthouse.

Inside, Matt smiled. *Barbara, you'll live only long enough to see the Diet pass the very treaty that you fought so hard.*

The Japanese press in its eagerness reminded Barbara of hungry wolves. To Araki she said, "They definitely didn't show me such interest when I arrived at Narita."

When I arrived at Narita? her mind repeated. That's when she remembered.

She was at Narita Airport, standing by her luggage cart in the arrival lobby. At Yamamura's approach, she took a step forward and bowed to him as he bowed to her. To her right, digital still-cameras flashed. Among the photographers, TV cameras stared unblinking at her and Yamamura. Seconds later, Yamamura stepped forward and handed her a gift envelope. TV cameras recorded this, too, as more still-cameras flashed.

Then it was time for her to present her own gift. She stepped back to her luggage cart with its three suitcases: two monster suitcases on the bottom, and the carry-on bag atop them both. Her travel gift sat atop the second suitcase and rested against the carry-on bag. She picked up the gift-wrapped wooden chest and stepped forward to rejoin Yamamura. No still cameras flashed during the moment she'd stood by her carry-on bag—the shot was uninteresting—and only one or two TV cameras still tracked her. But one or two was enough.

Now she wondered, *Is there real dijvid proof I'm innocent? Then why didn't any press people notice before now, my carry-on bag changed colors between the airport and my arrest?*

But as soon as she asked, she knew the answer: The few who had the proof, hadn't bothered to look for it. After all, the police also had her gun in evidence.

She wanted to whoop, she wanted to dance. "Somebody has proof I'm innocent!" she said in English.

Only two seconds had passed since she'd spoken to Araki. Barbara now said, voice trembling, "Detective Araki, I need to talk to the TV people, please."

Kawakami spoke instead: "That's fantasy, Nakamura. The only people you're talking to are the guards at the detention prison."

She touched Araki's arm. "Detective, please."

Araki looked across her. "Please be generous, Kawakami-*san*. What harm can it do?"

"If she wants it so bad, she must be planning something. Next she'll ask me to remove the cuffs so she can play volleyball."

I won't let him stop me now. Barbara's foot shot forward and around, kicking Kawakami hard in the shin. He stumbled. She spun a quarter-turn as she squatted, and so twisted free of both men's grasp. She dashed forward, straight toward the press throng. She needed only a moment.

The reporters, fear showing on their faces, were backing away as Barbara the seeming madwoman rushed them. But the photographers, cameramen, and soundmen stood their ground. Excellent.

She stopped two yards from Matt and the press people, as she heard feet pounding behind her. Her heart was racing, and not only because of the sprint. She shouted, "Listen, please! Please review the dijvid of me at Narita Airport—"

Ten fingers bit painfully into her right arm, and ten strong fingers seized her left arm. The detectives dragged her away.

Kawakami couldn't cover her mouth. She yelled, "Please replay me fetching my gift for Yamamura-*san*— my carry-on bag was *blue*! The bag that the police seized is black!"

I still have time! I still have time!

She eyed Matt as she was dragged off—she saw he was no longer smug, but shocked.

———————

About which, the Variety-Show Host joked—

Japanese and Californians now are united: Neither want the California Treaty. But this hasn't changed the big difference between them—Japanese value artificial conversation, and natural breasts.

Japan doesn't let arrested suspects make a phone call. Japanese police used to, until they arrested a man for obscene phone calls. . . .

CHAPTER 17
Heisei 17-nen 8-gatsu 22-nichi, Getsuyohbi (Monday, August 22, 2005)

Less than forty-eight hours until the end of the session:

It was late Monday evening in Yokohama. In front of the copy center, Hiroshi and Reiko said their goodbyes to the tired but hopeful petition team. Fifteen minutes later, Hiroshi, Reiko, and a box full of petitions were in Hiroshi's apartment.

Outside, a loudspeaker truck was cruising residential streets. Hiroshi and Reiko could hear it clearly, right through the wall: "You don't want a 70 percent income tax, right? A 15 percent consumption tax is bad, right? You don't want your children to spend their lives in a ruined Japan, do you? Please demand your representatives vote down the treaty."

But Hiroshi and Reiko were ignoring the misinformed sound truck. They were sitting on the living-room floor of Hiroshi's apartment and, between kisses, were watching a downloaded news program.

The news devoted ten minutes to Mrs. Nakamura. At the courthouse that morning, Mrs. Nakamura dramatically had improvised a "press conference" about the trick suitcase. The TV ran several more news stories about Mrs. Nakamura, but Hiroshi was too busy kissing Reiko to heed them. When Hiroshi noticed the TV again, the public prosecutor's office still intended to try Mrs. Nakamura.

Reiko nodded at the TV. "I have a question, Iwata-*san*, but it's not about Mrs. Nakamura."

"Oh?"

"What do you want to do with your life? Besides pioneering Japanese California."

Hiroshi shut off the TV and cable. "Why do you want to know?"

Her smile held mystery. "Because, because. Please, what do you want to do with your life?"

He should've been nervous, afraid she'd think him a fool. But he surprised himself, he felt confident. Either she'd understand—or she wouldn't, too bad. He gazed into her eyes, then began:

"For months, I've felt truly alive. Also frightened, afraid I'll fail and people will point at me—but *alive*. What I want to do is to keep this liveliness. I don't want to be a tiny leaf, helplessly floating down the stream; I want to be a frog who swims in the stream how I choose. I can't push myself like this often, I know. In years to come I'll have duties to my wife"—he glanced at her—"and to my children, and to Matsumoto Robotics. But at least once more, I want to plunge into another worthy but new and dangerous project."

"That's beautiful. Why'd you say I wouldn't like it?"

"Don't women crave security? Don't they want men whose lives are as predictable as *asahi*?" As predictable as the sunrise?

"Yes, but we also want to admire our men, and we want others to admire our men. TOKUGAWA Ieyasu, TOYODA Sakichi, SEN no Rikyuu, SUGIHARA Chiune, SOGO Shinji—all the men of history whom people admire were suns rising in the west. You're the same as they, Hiroshi-*san*."

He blinked in surprise. "You admire *me*?"

"The whole petition team does, as do Section Manager Tsurumi and many others. You're the bravest man we know, our twenty-first century Peach Boy."

Reiko was likening Hiroshi to the hero of Japan's favorite children's story? Hiroshi waved "no," then said, "I'm not brave. Whatever Section Manager Tsurumi told you, I think the American in the restaurant never intended to hit me."

Reiko only smiled in reply.

He changed the subject. "Please tell me why you asked me that."

"To learn if you would confide something so personal to me. It's important to me that I'm important to you."

He rose to a kneeling position as he faced her, pulled her up by the shoulders so that she was kneeling and facing him, then he took her in his arms. "You're to me the most important person in the world."

She lowered her gaze. "I hope you mean that."

For answer, he gave her a gentle kiss that slowly turned hot. Nothing new there. She matched him in kissing, reserve for reserve and heat for heat. Nothing new there. But this time—as he felt her shape and her muscles moving and her body heat, as he smelled her, as her hands on his shirt hardened him—this time he chose to not let shyness with Reiko limit him anymore.

He ran his hand in a languorous caress from the nape of her neck, down her back, across her thigh, and up her stomach to her left breast.

She lightly bit his lip in response.

His left hand on her back found the zipper of her dress. When her dress was unzipped, she shrugged it off, then stood to kick it away. She was wearing expensive American underwear. He stood, running his hands up her body as he rose. Her shoulders were soft and smooth and warm to his touch.

She was still standing. She took his face into her hands and looked into his eyes. His gaze showed the love and desire for her that he felt. Her eyes and hands dropped to his shirt, which she unbuttoned. When his chest was naked, she bent forward and planted a single modest kiss on his breastbone.

They finished undressing each other. She had a wart on her left arm. Her waist was slim. He felt embarrassed for his slight paunch—mornings and evenings no longer spent playing racquetball were starting to show.

Hand in hand, they proceeded to the bedless bedroom. From the *oshiire* (bedding closet) they pulled out and unfolded the *futon* mattress and coverlet.

He was sucking on her breasts when he proved himself overexcited. Hiroshi was sick with embarrassment, but Reiko stroked his earlobe and kissed him. "Such an honest way to say I'm pretty. As for the problem, it corrects itself." She stood up, walked across the soft, fresh-smelling *tatami* mats to a box of tissues, wiped off her leg, and returned to the *futon*.

A few minutes later, her hand squeezed his *kohgan* (balls) too hard, and it was his turn to reassure her. Her lack of experience relieved him.

She put her mouth on him, which amazed him. He remembered what Bronwyn the New Zealander had taught him, how to touch a woman in her moonlight places. His caresses made Reiko's *chitsu* pungent and slurpy. Reiko bit his lip again, hard this time.

She'd been correct. Now Hiroshi was able to maintain control of his *inkei* long enough to make both of them climax. He believed Reiko had come twice, and for that he felt proud of himself.

When it was over, he caressed the nape of her neck. "Reiko-*san*, your turn. What do you want to do with *your* life?"

Her voice was amused: "Hiroshi-*san*, I wonder if you'll like my answer."

"Please, try me."

With one finger a writing-brush, she started writing a *kanji* character on his chest. "My goal since I was fifteen always has been to find that special man—a man who attracts me sexually, who's also a man I can talk about anything with, who's also a man destined for grand success. If I have him, everything else comes."

The character she'd written was *kekkon* (marriage).

Less than fifteen hours until the end of the session:

The guard opened Barbara's cell. "You're being released."

Tuesday evening, less than a day and a half after Barbara had been taken to detention prison, she was free. Amber, who was already at the prison and waiting, with bright eyes filled Barbara in:

Ten minutes after Barbara's courthouse "press conference" Monday, Nippon TV aired split-screen the police evidence dijvid and the Narita gift-exchange dijvid, to highlight the carry-on bag's color change. TV Asahi broadcast its own dijvid a minute later.

Seventeen hours later, CNN revealed that Senator Nakamura, on the day he'd received the letter bomb, had pumped the FBI for information about yakuza in California, had immediately flown to San Francisco, then had left San Francisco a few hours later. Whatever Senator Nakamura had done in San Francisco, CNN couldn't find one constituent, contributor, or local politician he'd met with.

Six hours later, an American Satellite News reporter in San Francisco interviewed a neighbor of Kazuo Ebara, who the SFPD and FBI suspected was a yakuza soldier. The neighbor told ASN that a man who "looked just like" Senator Nakamura had driven up to Ebara's house in a white Intrepid during the hours Senator Nakamura was in San Francisco.

Five hours after that, San Francisco TV station KRON found a car-rental clerk who clearly remembered renting "the traitor" a white Dodge Intrepid for a few hours that day. The clerk held up Senator Nakamura's rental-car agreement for KRON's camera.

Three hours later, the DEA and the FBI jointly busted Ebara for drug manufacturing. In a search of Ebara's house, the FBI found a Rolex watch inscribed with the name of a murdered Japanese businessmen. When shown the inscription, Ebara promptly offered to talk about Senator Nakamura.

One hour later and only ten minutes ago, the Tokyo Public Prosecutor's Office announced it was dropping all charges against Barbara.

Now Barbara asked Amber, "So what has Matt to say about my release?"

Amber shrugged. "Senator Nakamura fled for Washington four hours ago—about the time Tokyo reporters' questions turned nasty."

"Yakuza gangs also hate questions from Tokyo reporters. I've made Matt's new friends very unhappy with him."

Two minutes later, Barbara was speaking to reporters in front of detention prison. ". . .As for Nippon TV, TV Asahi, CNN, ASN, and KRON, thank you so much. To Yamamura-*sensei*, who invited me to Japan, and to my mother's family, for embarrassing you there is no excuse, please forgive me. To the musicians and movie stars who came to Japan giving `Save California' concerts and speeches, who all pledged your unwavering support for me when I was in jail, your trust moves me to tears."

This was when her press club became distracted by the arrival of the helicopter.

Senior Party President Saitoh jumped out as soon as the chopper touched ground. "Mrs. Nakamura, please!" he yelled. He gestured with his whole arm as he shouted over the engine noise, "I need to rush you to the Diet, hurry please!"

Barbara was still adjusting to the idea of release from prison, but she would deal with that later. She pressed through the reporters to reach Saitoh. Calls of "Barbara!" and "*Dohzo denaide kudasai!*" followed her.

The engine was revving up even as she climbed into the helicopter. Once airborne, the chopper raced for the Diet Building.

She had to shout it: "What's the crisis?"

Saitoh shouted back, "The treaty vote is set for tomorrow morning, and we can't stop it."

Tomorrow, August 24, was the last day of the ordinary session. This afternoon, with the treaty still unvoted, the House Speaker had used his prerogatives and had scheduled the unamended treaty for a vote first thing tomorrow morning. The Speaker hadn't first consulted with the Committee on Rules and Administration, the normal custom. Meaning, the Speaker hadn't given the committee's Progressives a chance to thwart him. The Progressives in the lower house thus were furious with the Speaker.

Now Saitoh yelled, "But all that isn't why I grabbed the helicopter. The vote is tied except for Shohji of South Kantoh Region. He still hasn't decided."

"So that's why we're rushing? So we can hurry to his office and talk to him?"

"No, we're rushing so *you* can hurry to his office. Shohji doesn't listen to me about the treaty now."

"Why not?"

Saitoh's smile was amused. "He tells me that perhaps South Kantoh Region has different needs from Shikoku Region. Yamamura-*san* is gone, but his snobbery towards Shikoku lingers."

"Hm, maybe Representative Shohji suspects you plot to use the treaty's defeat to foment a Progressive takeover." She shouted it in mock seriousness.

Saitoh leaned back and smiled dreamily. "Well, as soon as Shohji decides how such a scheme works, I hope he'll tell me. I'd enjoy being prime minister."

She smiled. "You'd make an excellent one." He smiled back as their eyes met, and she felt those longings again.

Their talk turned to her experiences as a crime suspect. Saitoh was a sympathetic listener. Thus it seemed sudden when they spotted the Diet Building.

Saitoh turned to face her. "I'll take you past Security, but beyond the metal-detector, you're alone."

Her reply began in full honorific language: "Thank you very much. Before we land, let me thank high-you for your help and support these last two months. Humble-I humbly-am not worthy of your risking your new promotion to defend me publicly—sheesh, this sounds too stilted. You're no stranger."

She reached over, caressed his cheek, and kissed him on the mouth as the pilot pretended not to notice. The kiss lasted but a heartbeat, because she didn't trust herself for any longer.

But then she permitted herself a second PG-rated kiss.

When she broke the second kiss, her hand was still caressing his face. Gently he wrapped his hand around her wrist. They gazed at each other, neither speaking.

After a time, he groaned. "*Ano, ninjoh.*" Oh, what I want. "If only. . ."

"*Hai,*" she breathed.

The Diet Building was rushing close. Saitoh pulled her hand off his face. "It's time," he mouthed amid the rotor noise.

She looked down at his hand, then up into his eyes. Then she leaned forward. "Taijiroh-*san,*" she spoke into his ear, "your wife is a lucky woman."

Seconds later Saitoh pulled out his digital phone, and shouted a call as the helicopter descended for landing. As he put the phone back in his briefcase, he told Barbara, "Shohji has someone in his office, but his `telephone lady' doesn't know how long he intends to stay there. We must hurry."

The helicopter flew over the same Diet Central Porch where Barbara and Shohji had watched the demonstration two months earlier. Then the helicopter landed behind the Diet Building, in the parking lot for Shohji's office building. Barbara was out running as soon as the helicopter thumped ground, with Saitoh right behind her. People stared. The sprint for the door left her winded, and her healing abdominal muscles ached, but she had to hurry.

Saitoh vouched her through Security. She panted her goodbye to him as they made proper, but hasty, bows to each other.

She decided the elevators were too slow, so she raced up the emergency stairs to Shohji's floor.

That was a big mistake. Her healed arm and stomach muscles brought agony, her calves burned from the climbing, and her lungs felt scraped raw. "Jail has left me out. . .of shape," she gasped. "I'm sweating. This won't. . .impress Shohji at all."

She homed in on a rest room to fix her appearance and to catch her breath, her first pause since the helicopter's runners had hit pavement. She rushed to make herself presentable, then strode out the bathroom and to Shohji's door. Inside, she was ushered straight to Shohji's private office.

"Good evening, Mrs. Nakamura," Shohji said as he returned her bow. If he was surprised to see her, she couldn't tell. "Please, you remember Mister Iwata?"

A second later, as Barbara and Mister Iwata exchanged greetings and bows, she noted he had another big cardboard box at his feet. Through the open flaps, she saw signed petitions inside.

This meant trouble. But what truly alarmed her was the teapot and two teacups she saw. "If these two have bonded, `my back's to the water,'" Barbara muttered.

Shohji glanced at the teacups, then back to her. "I must warn you, Mister Iwata is convincing me. He's an interesting young man, and a fellow Tokyo U. alum.

Imagine, he and his team gathered over sixty-two hundred signatures.

"But I want to give you a fair hearing. So please, since Mister Iwata is hitting me with his new information, do you have anything new to tell me?"

"Oh boy, where do I start?" Barbara said, while she struggled to think.

"Then please, let's have a *bureiko*," etiquette-free time. "Both of you, for tonight please forget reserve, please disregard face."

"Excuse me?" Iwata said. He looked as confused as Barbara felt: Etiquette-free time occurred during informal after-hours bar-hopping, during end-of-year and New Year's parties, and during sporting events—*not* when discussing matters of state. Then Iwata rubbed his neck in his discomfort at arguing with a superior. He replied, "This is a little. . ."

Shohji nodded. "Yes, I understand. Time is gone, and tonight I can't afford to misunderstand you or to be kept ignorant of something vital. While Japan is rightly proud of our politeness, tonight `let's open our stomachs and talk' like Americans."

Barbara was aghast—Shohji wanted American frankness? That meant get as personal, be as insulting as you please. She hoped that nobody would exhume her failures with Matt, or with Mother. Especially with Mother, please Lord. "Yes, Shohji-*sensei*," she said, but her heart felt foreboding.

Iwata bowed and agreed, but the unease on his face couldn't be for the same reason as hers.

Shohji turned to her. "Mrs. Nakamura?"

The battle began, and ideas were the swords.

Barbara worried. *Do I dare say it? I might offend Shohji. But he needs to hear this.* "*Sensei*, I respectfully beg you: Please don't vote yes because Mister Iwata has questioned your manhood—"

"Excuse me," Iwata said, "I've never mentioned by name any specific person—"

"—For the man who doesn't dare be called a coward, proves himself afraid: of what people think."

Shohji gave her a look, then nodded thoughtfully. "Yes, it is so."

Great, I just zilched Mister Iwata's best argu—

Iwata glanced alarmed at Shohji. "Mrs. Nakamura, you call them manly, you imply they're brave, but Dietmen who vote against the treaty because of Article 32 remain cowards."

Shohji gave her another look. "Indeed."

She didn't dare argue with Shohji, but no way would she concede. "Stop, Mister Iwata. Many Dietmen are voting against the treaty for sound reasons."

"Perhaps, but why didn't you share any of those good reasons with *prefectural* Representatives?"

Shohji nodded. "Mister Iwata is correct."

Damn. Iwata had spiked *her* best argument. She echoed Yamamura's proven winner: "Japan cannot afford 36 hundred trillion yen. The California Treaty will destroy Japan."

Iwata turned to Shohji. "I hope not. But do we want the world to point at us, mocking us with 'Japan fears world leadership'?"

Shohji's answer was soft, patient: "A government can't afford indulging wounded pride, Mister Iwata. But do you feel Japan should grasp world leadership?"

"Yes, Shohji-*sensei*."

Barbara said, "As for America, are we to bow and step aside so Japan becomes number-one?"

Iwata looked uncomfortable, but he faced the question. "Yes. East of here, America's sun is setting."

"You're wrong. The United States has problems, yes—"

"America the bold, the home of Douglas MacArthur and Chester Nimitz, of Matthew Perry, and of William Clark. They were bold, but now your decision-makers are timid lawyers and accountants."

"Not true."

"America the hardworking, who defeated us because you rebuilt with shocking speed the fleet we sank. Now we see your voters, workers, and students demanding everything, without working for any of it."

"Not true!"

"America defeated Japan because your government was disciplined. Now your politicians in Washington vote appropriations to buy votes, with no thought of America's future."

"Not—"

"Hasn't your government said in essence, `We need sixty trillion dollars more than we need California'?"

"Yes, but sixty trillion dollars, it's a can't-say-no temptation."

"Still, now is Japan's time."

Easy, take it easy. "Japan can't defend itself; Japan's time will be short. In any case, does Japan deserve leadership? Remember how you treated Taiwan, Korea, the Philippines, and Manchuria."

Now it was Iwata squirming. "Those misdeeds are regrettable, certainly, but fading from memory."

"Japan is forgetting, yes. But Nanking will never forget."

"True."

Barbara used her momentary advantage and took initiative: "Shohji-*sensei,* if no other reason will persuade you, then please vote against the treaty because of the yakuza."

"Why them?" Shohji asked.

"The yakuza allied with Husband to frame me for gun-smuggling. Japan's criminals are eager for California to go Japanese."

"Why?"

"They plan to flood Japan with guns and drugs from California. When they do, they will destroy Japan."

Shohji's eyes widened. "Yes, I see it, buying California will energize the yakuza. Japan's enviously low crime rate will end."

He reasoned it out: Money that cash-drained Japan couldn't afford, would be spent anyway—diverted from productive areas to pay for customs agents, police, courts, private security, and insurance claims. ". . .Swelling crime rates will sink Japan."

"Yes, it is so," Barbara said.

Shohji looked at her. "This yakuza problem is more serious than it first appears. Mrs. Nakamura, you've shifted my whole viewpoint."

I've finally got it!

Iwata clearly agreed. He said, "Mrs. Nakamura, I'm so sorry I must ask you this: Your husband, perhaps he plotted with the yakuza because you cost him face?"

Damn, it finally turned personal. "He plotted against me because he betrayed California and I spoke up."

"Yes, he betrayed California, but it's also true that *you* betrayed *him*—"

"I've tried to stop him, not betray him."

"You betrayed him when you told family secrets to the whole world."

"How could I betray my husband? Matthew Nakamura has been the love of my life. Have you ever loved intensely, Mister Iwata?"

"Yes, I do," he said quietly. Then his voice returned to normal: "You betrayed your husband, you humiliated him. Why then should Shohji-*sensei* listen to you?"

Shohji, she noted, was paying keen attention. "Mister Iwata, goodness, I hardly know you. How can I answer such questions as only my mother asks?"

"Please, won't you answer? Perhaps *Sensei* also is curious."

Shohji remained silent, not disputing Iwata.

Touché, Barbara thought. "I didn't dishonor the house of Nakamura. Rather, I acted to remove Husband's dishonor, to clean away the stain on the house of Nakamura."

"Nobody else in your husband's family could speak out?"

"Nobody else knew."

"Neither did you. You humiliated your husband because of mere suspicion."

"Based on a quarter-century of marriage."

"Yet you had no proof. Please recall how awful you felt when he told TV that he suspected you were doing sex with another senator."

"Totally unrelated."

"Please excuse me for arguing, but your husband felt as terribly as that when you shamed him only because of suspicion."

Shohji turned to Iwata. "Her suspicion about her husband turned out to be correct."

"Yes." Iwata bowed to her as he recited, "I apologize if I've offended you."

She recited back, "It was a trifle, you needn't apologize." Now she could relax, she finally was safe.

But she wasn't safe at all. Iwata said, "You've mentioned your mother. Your relationship with her puzzles me—"

"Mister Iwata, we needn't discuss my mother. The California Treaty is what—"

"Mister Iwata," Shohji in turn said, "this relates?"

"Yes, Shohji-*sensei*. My father is an English teacher. He's said for years that Japan needs to push spoken-English ability as much as we require written-English skill. I believe that when Japanese people move to California, finally they'll see how correct my father is. Part of why I've labored for the treaty is to show my devotion to my father."

She said carefully, "Such *koh* you have."

"Thank you very much. What I don't understand: Your own filial-piety, where is it? Your mother fed you, clothed you, ensured you were educated. So why are you ignoring her known wishes?"

That topic was too painful. Barbara bowed low and most politely refused to answer. "Please forgive humble-me for not answering your question, but I fear that I would be clumsy in my words."

"Please reconsider. Might *Sensei* think you traitor to your family, as your husband is traitor to California?"

"I'm not a traitor to my mother, the same as I'm not a betrayer of my husband."

"Then please, explain to us."

She bowed again, to soften her reply: "Mister Iwata, please forgive my rude frankness: Humble-I don't want to discuss my mother."

Shohji broke silence: "I, too, respectfully ask you to reconsider. Your mother is Japanese, you're American. Is your conflict a portent of what will come? Or are you only a person of poor character?"

A request from the man deciding California's fate wasn't a request; she was subpoenaed. So she said, "My mother is my mother, but she's only one person. California is forty million."

Shohji asked, "Did the forty million feed you when you were an infant? Did they change you?"

"No, Shohji-*sensei*," she told the floor.

Iwata said, "I saw your mother say on TV that before you were school-age, she read you a Japanese story every morning and an American story every night."

"True," she whispered.

"She remained away from her country because of her husband and daughter. She didn't abandon you two to come home."

"Yes," Barbara said.

Shohji said, "Your obligation to her is heavy. Why do you not try to repay her now?"

Clearly the Mother-question was important to Shohji. If she answered wrong or evasively, then California was lost. But how could she answer "correctly" when she herself had doubts?

Both Shohji and Iwata fell silent. She was silent too, as she racked her brains for an answer. And the guilt she was feeling certainly wasn't helping her to think.

"Mrs. Nakamura? Please, we're waiting," Shohji said.

He's losing patience, she thought. *But when I answer, that answer must satisfy him.*

"Mrs. Nakamura?"

What do I tell him? How do I answer?

Seconds passed—too many seconds. She was about to forfeit.

And then she remembered Steve Leaird's words: *No private promise or obligation may come before my public duty.* "Leiard's rule, yes," she said aloud.

She raised her head and looked at Shohji. "*Sensei,* could you vote for a bad bill that you knew your mother favored? Would you then be fulfilling your *giri,*" duty, "to the voters?"

His face looked thoughtful. After several seconds he said, "No, I'd be betraying that *giri.*"

"Exactly. Here, Washington, Moscow, anywhere—any officeholder must look beyond family duty."

"True."

"Husband rejects the duties of a senator, so it's I who must fulfill them. It's I who bears the senator's dilemma. Even if my entire family would criticize me, I must fight for California. I know you understand."

"Yes. Hm, so I agree with you. I mean, about disregarding your mother's feelings for the sake of politics."

Okay, this time I really am safe.

"But she's not a senator, only a senator-pretender," Iwata said, his voice shaking. "And—and California still has another senator. She didn't need to ruin her relationship with her mother. Please forgive me for correcting high-you, *sensei,* but her pretty words misdirect you."

Shohji laughed. "I did ask you two to forget face," he said, before falling silent.

The silence grew.

"California's defense needed two senators' labors. One senator alone was not enough," Shohji said at last. "So Mrs. Nakamura behaved properly.

"Now, as for the treaty. . ." Shohji looked at Barbara and Iwata. "I've decided."

About which, the Variety-Show Host joked—

"Bomber" Nakamura and a Japanese gangster worked together to frame Barbara. I'm shocked—I was sure Japanese gangsters kept better company.

All airport baggage handlers envy "Bomber" and his gangster buddy Ebara. Those two managed to switch Barbara's bag <u>after</u> she'd left the airport.

Part IV
Sunset and Dawn

Hino toYoake

CHAPTER 18
Heisei 17-nen 8-gatsu 24-nichi, Suiyohbi (Wednesday, August 24, 2005)

It was Shohji's turn to vote. He climbed the steps in front of the Speaker and dropped his signed slip into the ballot box on the podium.

From the visitors' gallery, Barbara saw that the slip was blue. Shohji had voted no.

"Iwata-*kun*, I am deeply sorry for your frustration," Ryuuji said the next morning. Ryuuji was standing by Hiroshi's desk.

"Hey, it's not all bad," Hiroshi said, trying to laugh. The laugh sounded unnatural, because Hiroshi *felt* unnatural. "At least we don't need to spend long hours on our feet, getting either cooked or soaked outside the train station."

"Yes." Ryuuji shifted his feet, then recited, "I'm being rude, but please accept this poor trifle expressing how we share your disappointment." From behind his back, Ryuuji handed Hiroshi an envelope that was tied with black-and-white *mizuhiki* cord. Those colors said it was a sympathy gift.

Since a gift in Japan may not be opened in the presence of the giver, Ryuuji walked away. Or perhaps Ryuuji didn't know what else to say.

Inside the envelope was a *tanzaku* strip of decorated rice paper. Reiko had written calligraphically a haiku:

Yuki wa furu,
Shika wa furueru—
Hana no yume.

Snow falls in darkness,
The deer shivers in the wind—
A dream of flowers.

With the poem were two nearly square *shikishi* paper sheets, filled with everyone's names. Ryuuji's name was signed first, Reiko's name (and a tiny heart) were second, the names of Assembler Shinohara and Assembler Fukuda after that, Chairman Matsumoto's *inkan* stamp was fifth, and after that were signatures by almost everyone else at Matsumoto Robotics, including Section Manager Masumi and Section Manager Tsurumi.

Hiroshi managed a smile. *I don't have Japanese California—but I do have friends who care for me.*

At the airport two hours later, San Diego time was after 7:00 p.m. Wednesday. The Customs official asked, "Ms. Nakamura, do you have anything to declare?"

Barbara grinned. "Yes, it's great to be home!"

TV crews from throughout California filmed Barbara as she went through Customs. They kept filming as she cleared Customs. They filmed Ed and Carol throwing their arms around her.

"You did it, you did it! God, you're wonderful," Carol said.

"I'm very proud of you, Barbara," Ed told her as he hugged her again.

Takeko hung back, her face set impassive. Barbara hugged her mother briefly, but did not intrude into her mother's feelings.

Mom, one day I hope you understand.

"How do you feel?" Carol asked.

"Tired. Happy, but tired. I've been without sleep over twenty-four hours. But on the plane back I hardly slept, I was too overjoyed."

Takeko said nothing.

"Everyone ready to leave?" Ed asked. Then he eyed her tan carry-on bag and smiled. "Say, wasn't that blue when you left?"

"Funny, Dad," Barbara said, also smiling. To Carol she said, "Want to know what's weird? The woman in Customs who went through my bags—afterward she pulled out a notebook and asked for my autograph."

Carol smiled. "Get used to it, hero."

The camera crews followed as Barbara and her party headed out of San Diego International. This puzzled Barbara, until she left the building. Waiting outside was a high-school marching band, which played "America the Beautiful" and "I Love You, California." Barbara wept.

Minutes later, Ed was nearing Larry's house. Takeko had said little during the drive.

When the van actually pulled into Larry's driveway, Barbara saw Larry and Bobby standing in the front yard. Those two were grinning like idiots, pulling taut an enormous banner that was almost the width of the front yard. Lit from the west by the setting sun, the banner read, "WELCOME BACK BARBARA, YA DONE MEGA-GOOD!"

———————

At ten that evening, the party at Larry's house was in full swing. Barbara was dopey with jetlag, but still raised a glass at the champagne toast.

The cordless rang; Larry answered it. "Finleys' residence. . . .Yes, she's here. . . .*Who?*" He held out the phone, his voice sounding stunned: "Barbara, for you. White House operator."

Her hand reaching for the cordless was relaxed; her face, calm. She had beaten a knife-wielding assassin, and she had beaten Japan's criminal-justice system—she could face an angry president of the United States.

But Charlie Swensen wasn't calling to act the sore loser. "Barbara, maybe you didn't know this, but you committed a crime. *However*, I'm calling to assure you, I'm pardoning you."

"*What* crime?"

"Eighteen USC 953 bans carrying on any intercourse with a foreign government to defeat measures of our government. Anyway, you're pardoned; I'll tell the Justice Department and the press tomorrow."

"I don't know what to—that's so generous, thank you."

"I remember those campaign trips together—I know you're no criminal. Of course, I didn't think Matt was."

"I know the feeling." She needed to change the subject. "So what do you plan to do about the debt now, Charlie?"

The president's voice became a maniac's: "Levy more taxes, I will! This time I can't be voted out, hee hee hee!"

"I'm glad you can joke about this."

"Hey, we laugh else we die. But it was especially disappointing to lose in the Diet, which my experts predicted would be a slam-dunk despite you. After Matt's miracle in the Senate, I thought all my worries were over."

"'Miracle'? Before Matt jumped in, you didn't expect the treaty to survive the Senate?"

"Hell no, I was sure the treaty would be vaporized. But even so, it would give America the scare our country needed."

"*Scare*? The treaty was intended to be only a rubber snake?"

"Oh no, the treaty really is the debt problem's best solution. But before Matt spoke out, I had no illusions. I'm only the president, not God."

She smiled. "I know—I'm sure God can carry a tune. Anyway, what's next?"

"Go back to nursing the START III Treaty through the Senate. Then figure out how I'll pay for those Russian nukes without Japan's trillions."

"For this part, the Russian missiles, I'm sorry."

"Kind of you to say. Speaking of kindness: That was superb politicking you did in Tokyo."

"Why, yes it was," she said, surprised at the realization.

The next morning, Barbara consulted her divorce attorney. He reminded her to move back into her house if she wanted to win custody of it.

An hour later, she had rented a moving trailer, and was pulling stuff out of storage.

The fridge and pantry of her house were empty, so that afternoon Barbara drove to the supermarket. That's where she saw the latest *Union-Tribune*.

Splashed across the front page was a color photograph, three columns wide, of herself. She'd been beaming when she was photographed at the airport. Her picture was directly above the headline about Prime Minister Sasaki and his Cabinet resigning.

Friday morning, Barbara phoned Takeko. In her most formal Japanese Barbara said, "Please honor my humble house with a visit, Mother. I wish to show high-you something." *Here's where I try to heal our rift.*

Takeko's eyes widened when Barbara's door opened. Again, Barbara made her Japanese as polite as possible: "Thank you for honoring humble-me with a visit, Mother. `Please step up.'"

"You're wearing *hohmongi* (a matron's kimono)! And such a beautiful brocade sash."

"I bought these a few weeks ago. Do you like them?"

"Yes, *Baaba-chan*, they're beautiful. This is a surprise for me, your kimono." Mother didn't need to say more.

Barbara, kneeling by the front closet, offered her mother house slippers. "While in Tokyo, I got to know Grandfather and Aunt Makiko much better. They told me about you when you were young, and I felt so close to you as I listened to their stories. I bought the kimono to please you."

Takeko no longer sounded happy: "Perhaps I'm pleased enough to forget. Perhaps not."

"Please, don't be angry with me. Please, don't be bitter." Barbara bowed deeply until her back was nearly horizontal, and held it.

Takeko made a brief bow to acknowledge Barbara's, but then said, "*Baaba-chan*, please straighten up and look at me."

Barbara obeyed.

"*Baaba-chan*, I'm old, and I find myself yearning for the things of childhood. Not enough do I see *take*"—bamboo—"growing in California."

"True." *What is she trying to say?*

"I miss the tea ceremony, *koto* music, rice paddies, and temple drums."

"I'm sure." Barbara still couldn't guess Mother's point.

"With the treaty I could've had all those things here in California."

"But now you won't."

"All this could have happened, but my own daughter stopped it. Do you understand how much I ache? You shamed your husband. You shamed me, in Japan. You shamed my family—"

"Mother, please, Representative Shohji said—"

"Please don't interrupt. You've shamed my family in Japan, which you forget is *your* birthplace. Now you wear a new matron-kimono. But that isn't apology enough, not after you've denied me my greatest need. Daughter, you've dishonored me."

That evening in Washington, Matt was ambushed by a TV reporter as he was leaving his office.

It should be fun, Matt decided. Reporters whined that politicians weren't *honest*? Meet Matt, who had no reason to keep up appearances anymore.

The guy moved in too close, and needed breath mints. "Senator, the Senate Ethics Committee just started its investigation against you. It looks likely you'll be charged with soliciting a bribe, contempt of the Senate, and `conduct inconsistent with the trust and duty of a member.' Comments?"

"The committee began hearings yesterday. If you can read the future so well, play the stock market."

"And if the committee recommends those charges against you?"

"If the Senate agrees, I'll be censured or expelled, dimwit. I'll survive that."

"What's more, if the Senate doesn't expel you, it's rumored that Californians in the House—"

"Are eager to drop the impeachment bomb on me. If so, I'll survive that."

"Another rumor has you about to receive a federal indictment for—"

"For `bribery of public officials and witnesses.' Not worried at all."

"No? You could be banned from holding national office."

"No loss. And what's a few years in a minimum-security prison? I'll survive that."

"A third rumor has California about to indict you as an `accessory before the fact' to obstruction of justice, for felony solicitation, and for felony conspiracy. You're looking to rack up quite a lot of prison time."

"I'll get my lawyer to make all the sentences concurrent. Whatever California hits me with, I'll survive that."

"Really? Don't you think—"

"Listen, Hairspray Head, you are delaying my fun evening. This interview is over."

"But what about disbarment proceedings by the California—"

Matt, walking away, didn't hear the rest of the question.

Matt spent that fun evening at Stares and Strips Forever, watching strippers. None would go home with him, though—but he'd survive that.

Sometime after one, Matt drove his car into the garage. Parking the car was easier in the empty garage, now that Barbara's cartons had been shipped to San Diego. (All cartons but one; the rest of "kitchen and bedroom misc." had long ago left with the trash.)

Now in his kitchen, Matt opened the fridge while planning a sandwich. The floor creaked behind him. He turned around.

Facing him was a Japanese man in his twenties. The hand holding the pistol was missing half a pinky finger. This, the gunman's permed hair, plus the silencer on the pistol, all told Matt he was in trouble.

"You wasted our time, and you embarrassed us," the stranger said in Japanese.

———

It was Tuesday before Matt's body was discovered. Thursday afternoon, Barbara's former sister-in-law Marcia held Matt's funeral in Costa Mesa, California. Matt had left a will that not only disinherited Barbara, it denied her any say in his funeral.

But the will couldn't ban Barbara or her parents from attending. She was surprised how cordial to her were those few members of Matt's family who bothered to come. The Senate Sergeant at Arms attended, paying official respects. He clearly felt awkward, and Barbara felt sorry for him. He, and Joe Bob and Marilyn Saunders, were the only mourners from Washington.

When Barbara returned to her house in San Diego, the answering machine had a message: *Call Governor Dodson.* The governor needed to appoint a replacement senator; Barbara figured Dodson was calling for advice.

———————

Days later in Washington, a grinning Hector DeGarcia escorted Barbara down the Senate chamber's center aisle to the presiding officer's desk. It was Hank Collins who would administer the oath, one of his few perks as vice president. Hank was a little grayer-haired, with a few more wrinkles, since the Swensens, Collinses, and Nakamuras had ridden the campaign bus together in 2000.

Collins said, "Barbara Linda Nakamura, please raise your right hand."

She did so.

Hank Collins's face was serious. "Do you solemnly swear that you will support and defend the Constitution of the United States against all enemies, foreign and domestic; that you will bear true faith and allegiance to the same; that you take this obligation freely, without any mental reservation or purpose of evasion; and that you will well and faithfully discharge the duties of the office on which you are about to enter; so help you God?"

Barbara's face was serious as well. "I do."

The vice president's voice lost its stiffness. "Congratulations, Senator Nakamura—Senator *Barbara Linda* Nakamura!"

About which, the Variety-Show Host joked—

Remember how Barbara Nakamura won that knife-fight in Tokyo? Trust me, she'll find <u>this</u> skill useful in the Senate.

The End

End Matter
and
Alternate
Chapters

Parting Thought

. . .I have not accustomed myself to hang over the precipice of disunion, to see whether, with my short sight, I can fathom the depth of the abyss below; nor could I regard him as a safe counsellor in the affairs of this government, whose thoughts should be mainly bent on considering, not how the Union may be best preserved, but how tolerable might be the condition of the people when it should be broken up and destroyed. . . .When my eyes shall be turned to behold for the last time the sun in heaven, may I not see him shining on the broken and dishonored fragments of a once glorious Union; on states dissevered. . .Let their last feeble and lingering glance rather behold the gorgeous ensign of the republic, now known and honored throughout the earth, still full high advanced. . .not a stripe erased or polluted, nor a single star obscured, bearing for its motto, no such miserable interrogatory as "What is all this worth?". . .

—From Senator Daniel Webster's "Second Reply to Hayne" speech, January 26 and 27, 1830

APPENDIX 1
Treaty between Japan and the United States of America, on the Sale of California

Preamble.

The United States shall transfer sovereignty of California to Japan, in return for twenty annual payments of three trillion U.S. dollars.

After the United States and Japan each have ratified the treaty by the terms of their respective Constitutions, the treaty shall enter into force on the date that ratified copies of the treaty are exchanged. The first annual payment shall become due immediately upon the treaty's entry into force. The nineteen subsequent annual payments each shall become due on the anniversary of the date that the treaty entered into force.

At the time of the treaty's entry into force, the fifty-nine counties of the State of California shall immediately become prefectures of Japan, and a prefectural government for each California county shall immediately be established.

Article 1. What land is transferred.

Description of boundaries of region transferred: from the Pacific shore at 42°N latitude, east to 42°N 120°W; from 42°N 120°W south to 39°N 120°W; from 39°N 120°W southeast to the point that also is midway between the banks of the Colorado River; from that point southward, along a meandering line that is midway between the banks of the Colorado River, to the border with Mexico at 32°31′59.58″N; from that point west to the Pacific shore.

Japanese territorial waters shall extend west of the California coastline, and shall include all waters within two hundred nautical miles west of any part of the California coastline.

Article 2. Balance due.

Should Japan transfer sovereignty of all or part of California to a third country for any reason during the nineteen years that Japan is making annual payments, the balance of monies not yet paid becomes due to the United States immediately.

Article 3. State of California assets and liabilities.

Funds and financial assets of the State of California and local governments within it are ceded to Japan. Claims, by the United States government or by any government within the United States, against the State of California or its local governments, are extinguished, and Japan assumes no responsibility for these claims.

Article 4. Common waterways.

The Colorado River being divided in the middle between the two countries, and Topaz Lake, Lake

Havasu, Lake Tahoe, Lower Alkali Lake, and Goose Lake being divided as described in Article 1, the navigation of the listed waterways along the boundary areas shall be free and common to the vessels and citizens of both countries. Neither country shall, without the consent of the other, construct any work that may impede or interrupt, in whole or in part, the exercise of this right, not even for the purpose of favoring new methods of navigation. Nor shall any tax or contribution, under any denomination or title, be levied upon vessels or persons navigating these waterways, or upon merchandise or effects transported thereupon, except in the case of landing upon the other country's shores. If, for the purpose of making the said river and lakes navigable, or for maintaining them in such state, it should be necessary or advantageous to establish any tax or contribution, this shall not be done without the consent of both governments.

Article 5. Lawsuits against the State of California.

Lawsuits, whether pending, being argued at the time the treaty enters into force, or on appeal, against State of California state, county, city, town, or local governments shall be dropped.

Article 6. Automobiles and trucks.

After the treaty's entry into force, still in force in the California region are United States and California state motor-vehicle laws concerning exhaust emissions, air-conditioner coolant charging, car noise, fuel efficiency, car safety, alcohol safety, public-transit vehicle axle-load limits, commercial-vehicle length and width limits, and transporting hazardous materials; and California state and local traffic laws. Such laws shall continue in force until new traffic laws that are specific to the California region are passed by the Diet and are approved by referendum.

California state drivers' licenses, truck- and automobile-inspection stickers, and truck and automobile tags, if valid under California state law when the treaty enters into force, shall continue as valid until their stated expiration dates or until new driving-license, truck- and automobile-inspection, and truck- and automobile-tag laws specific to the California region are passed by the Diet and are approved by referendum. Drivers' licenses, truck- and automobile-inspection stickers, and truck and automobile tags renewed or else newly issued after the treaty enters into force, must meet applicable California state laws and regulations, such laws and regulations to be carried over, until new driving-license, truck- and automobile-inspection, and truck- and automobile-tag laws specific to the California region are passed by the Diet and are approved by referendum.

Until the time that the Diet passes new driving-license, truck-inspection and automobile-inspection, and truck-tag and automobile-tag laws that are specific to the California region and that are approved by referendum, the Motor Vehicles Department of the State of California shall remain in operation, at United States expense.

Article 7. Compacts between the State of California and other states of the USA.

Compacts made between the State of California and other states of the United States, in categories such as, but not limited to, what are listed in the following paragraph shall be binding on Japan until new treaties between Japan and the United States enter into force. United States laws requiring active cooperation of the State of California with other states of the United States, in categories such as, but not limited to, what are listed in the following paragraph shall be binding on Japan until new treaties between Japan and the United States enter into force. However, this Article does not apply for a given category when that category already is dealt with in a prior treaty between the United States and Japan.

The categories are: civil defense and natural disaster, corrections, criminal apprehension, education, fish and game, American-Indian tribes, juvenile justice, marine fisheries, multistate highway transportation, nuclear accident, oil and gas, oil-spill cleanup, paroles and probation, pest control, radioactive waste disposal, water use, and regional planning not elsewhere described above.

Article 8. Professional licensure, including the practice of law.

A license or permit for a particular individual to practice a particular profession, if valid under California state law when the treaty enters into force, shall continue as valid until the stated expiration date or until new laws licensing that profession and specific to the California region are passed by the Diet and are approved by referendum. Licenses or permits for a particular profession, renewed or else newly issued after the treaty enters into force, must meet applicable State of California laws and regulations, such laws and regulations to be carried over, until new laws licensing that profession and specific to the California region are passed by the Diet and are approved by referendum.

Until the time that the Diet passes new laws that concern licenses and permits for a given profession, that are specific to the California region and approved by referendum, the State of California agency charged with issuing that profession's licenses and permits shall remain in operation, at United States expense.

Attorneys previously licensed by the State of California, who reside and practice law in Japanese California, are initially exempt from the provisions of Japanese law that ban foreign attorneys from practicing Japanese law, and that ban foreign attorneys from entering into partnerships with Japanese attorneys. This exemption lasts for twelve years after the treaty's entry into force. After the twelve years, an attorney as described may continue to practice Japanese law and may continue partnership with Japanese attorneys if he has been granted a foreign attorney license by the Justice Ministry.

Article 9. Japanese gun laws.

California residents, regardless of citizenship or nationality, have six months after the treaty's entry into force to comply with Japanese gun laws.

Article 10. American permanent aliens in Japanese California.

American permanent aliens in Japanese California cannot be deported, nor their property seized, without due process.

Article 11. The U.S. Mint in San Francisco.

The San Francisco Mint remains the property of the United States while it is in use and for ninety days afterward, or for two years after the treaty's entry into force, whichever is less.

Article 12. Japanese California businesses essential for the USA's defense.

Businesses in California that are vital to the defense of the United States shall be considered as being on United States land and subject to United States laws for two years after the treaty's entry into force.

Article 13. Meshing the Japanese California and Japan school systems.

California schools shall immediately follow the Japanese school calendar, in terms of hours open in the day, and days open in the year. Children whose native language is not Japanese shall be phased into the Japanese school system over nine years. The Japanese part of the school day shall start at 10 percent, beginning the school year current when the treaty enters into force, and the Japanese part of the school day shall increase by 10 percent of the school day each following school year. Until the Japanese part of the California school day is 100 percent, an entrance test to earn admission into high school/upper-secondary school shall not be required of students whose native language is not Japanese.

Article 14. When no visa is required.

After the treaty's entry into force, people living in Japanese California may come fifty kilometers into the states of Oregon, Nevada, or Arizona without a visa, and residents of the United States may come fifty kilometers into Japanese California, for the purposes of tourism or trade.

Article 15. Japanese California regional government.

A regional government shall be established in Japanese California, whose function shall be analogous to the executive branch of the state government of the State of California. The duties of the regional government shall be to enforce United States and State of California laws and regulations elsewhere described as carried over after the treaty enters into force, and to fulfill obligations on the State of California elsewhere described as carried over afterward. The prefectures of Japanese California shall be subject to regulatory control by this regional government, and the regional government shall be subject to control by the Diet.

This regional government shall be headed by a governor and deputy governor appointed by the Diet. The regional government shall be denied a legislative component and the ability to make laws. The regional government shall be denied a judicial component, and no court within Japanese California shall be exclusively subject to the regional government.

Unless the Diet extends its existence through legislation, or unless a later proclaimed treaty extends its existence, the regional government shall be dissolved on January 1 following the tenth anniversary of this treaty's entry into force.

Article 16. Relations with Mexico.

The terms of any treaties between the United States and Mexico relating to the State of California, which had before been binding on the United States, shall be binding on Japan until such time as those terms shall be renegotiated between Mexico and Japan and such new Mexico-Japan treaties shall enter into force.

Article 17. Native-American reservations.

Japan shall respect the sovereignty of the California native-American reservations. Japan shall carry over United States and California state laws and regulations regarding the various native-American tribes and reservations in California, until new laws are passed by the Diet and are approved by referendum by the affected reservations.

The Chemehuevi, Colorado River, Fort Mohave, Fort Yuma, and Washoe reservations each cover parts of both California and other states of the United States. A native American whose home of residence now is on one of these reservations, on either the California side or the American side, shall be treated as any other United States citizen now residing in California, Arizona, or Nevada, except that he may travel without passport or visa to any part of his reservation. Laws or regulations made by the Diet under authority of the previous paragraph, by the regional government of Japanese California, by the United States government, by the government of the State of Arizona, or by the government of the State of Nevada, may not restrict this right of travel for residents of these reservations.

Article 18. USA nonmilitary government property in Japanese California.

National cemeteries remain United States property forever. Post offices, federal correctional facilities, and the San Francisco Mint remain United States property for a time, as described elsewhere, but rights of property in all other United States government non-military lands and buildings shall be transferred to Japan immediately, subject to restrictions in the next paragraph. Such United States government nonmilitary lands include the portion of Death Valley National Monument that is in California.

Everything on the land that is not a fixture, part of the building, or part of the grounds, on what were United States government nonmilitary lands, or in buildings that were United States government nonmilitary property, shall remain United States government property. Such may be removed as soon as practical without Japan's hindrance, and without Japan's levied tax or contribution.

Terms described in the previous paragraph relating to their moveable property also shall apply to United States post offices in California, to each federal correctional facility in California, and to the San Francisco Mint, when the post offices, correctional facilities, or mint are transferred to Japan.

Article 19. USA military bases in Japanese California.

All United States military bases in California shall be turned over to Japan's Self-Defense Forces one year after the treaty enters into force. Exempted from transfer to Japan are arms and military stores belonging to the United States armed forces. These exempted arms and military stores shall include anything marked as belonging to the United States, to the United States armed forces, or to a branch of the

United States armed forces. During the year that military bases in Japanese California remain under United States control, such weaponry or United States military property may be transported from these military bases by land, sea, or air, or by a combination thereof, without Japan's hindrance, inspection, or levied tax or contribution.

During the one-year transitional period, Japanese military forces may occupy and use some or all of the California bases, but only in accordance with any space limitations that the United States Department of Defense may place.

Once the California military bases are transferred to Japan, United States military forces may continue to use these bases under any space limitations that Japan may place, in keeping with prior treaties relating to the defense of Japan by the United States.

Article 20. State of California public records.

Papers and records of California state or local governments shall become the property of Japan, but authenticated copies may be received upon request by the United States or by American citizens.

Article 21. The owning of and the selling of property by American citizens in Japanese California.

Citizens of the United States in Japanese California can remain or move back to the United States, retaining their real property in Japanese California, or disposing thereof and taking the proceeds where they please. Furthermore, such people—prior residents of California who had owned real property at the time of the treaty's entry into force—may hold or sell without being charged with any extra tax, contribution, or charge. Furthermore, such people choosing to continue ownership, and their heirs, shall enjoy all privileges and protection under Japanese law as if these people were citizens of Japan.

The same shall hold true for interest in a mining or shipping business as for real property. Also protected, to the same degree is for citizens of Japan, is prior ownership of intellectual property: patents, trademarks, and copyrights.

Article 22. Owners in absentia of property in Japanese California.

In the region of Japanese California, real property that belongs to individuals or businesses who are established elsewhere shall be inviolably respected. The present owners and their heirs shall enjoy, with respect to the real property, guarantees equally ample as if the same belonged to citizens of Japan.

The same shall hold true for interest in a mining or shipping business as for real property.

Article 23. Stipulated ownership.

In the absence of prior legal proceedings initiated against an owner of real property within California at the time of the treaty's entry into force, the property owner's claim to his land shall be stipulated to be in good standing.

For married couples whose legal residence is California, assets acquired during the marriage and before the treaty's entry into force shall be stipulated as equally owned by husband and wife, or else owned as a prenuptial agreement directs.

Article 24. Church property.

Church property shall belong collectively to church members who also are residents of Japanese California, regardless of each church member's respective citizenship or nationality.

Article 25. Pensions and other ongoing claims against State of California governments.

The United States shall pay all valid ongoing prior claims, such as pensions or lottery winnings, against State of California local governments.

Article 26. Post office and telephone service.

United States post offices shall remain open for six months after the treaty's entry into force, at the expense of the United States. During the six months, for the purpose of determining Japanese and American postal rates, Japanese California shall be treated as if still part of the United States.

By six months after the treaty's entry into force, the telephone system in California must be made compatible both with the phone system in Japan and with the phone system in North America. Pacific Bell and other owners of telephone equipment in California are guaranteed the right to continue ownership beyond the six-month mark. Should these owners decide to sell equipment to Japanese telephone companies, these prior owners are entitled to receive payment at fair market value.

Article 27. Government services essential for public safety.

Fire departments, paramedic and beach-lifeguard units, and air-traffic control centers, as well as trash-removal departments, if funded by State of California local governments, shall be funded and maintained at United States expense for six months after the treaty's entry into force. The United States shall maintain in good condition the property of such fire departments, paramedic and beach-lifeguard units, air-traffic control centers, and trash-removal departments. Six months after the treaty's entry into force, the United States shall transfer such property to Japan.

Where air-traffic control towers are funded and maintained by State of California local governments but staffed by FAA (Federal Aviation Administration) air controllers, those control towers shall be funded, maintained, and staffed by the FAA during the six-month period.

Article 28. Nationality and citizenship for Americans in Japanese California.

Adult citizens of the United States remaining in Japanese California may remain United States citizens or else may choose Japanese nationality. They must declare their choice within one year from the treaty's entry into force. Those who remain after that year's expiration, without declaring a wish to become Japanese nationals, shall be presumed to wish to keep United States citizenship.

Residents of Japanese California whose nationality shall be switched from the United States to Japan, in the manner described above, shall be admitted to full rights and privileges of Japanese nationality at a time to be decided by the Diet. This time shall not exceed twelve years from the date of the treaty's entry into force. Until such time as they gain such nationality, these residents shall be maintained and protected in the free enjoyment of their liberty and property, and secured in the free exercise of their religion, without restriction; they also shall be granted permanent resident alien status immediately and automatically. These residents, once they have gained full Japanese nationality, shall enjoy all the rights of Japanese nationals according to the principles of the Constitution of Japan.

When California residents are granted Japanese nationality, household registers for them shall be established in accordance with Japanese law, and these California residents and their descendants shall be treated the same as island Japanese under the law.

United States citizens living in California and under the age of twenty when the treaty enters into force, who remain in Japanese California, may choose Japanese nationality between the ages of twenty and twenty-one. Without an explicit declaration, a child of a parent who has elected Japanese nationality shall be presumed to desire Japanese nationality himself; in the case of a child, both of whose parents or whose single parent retains United States citizenship, such child shall be presumed to desire retaining his own United States citizenship. Children who choose Japanese nationality, and children whose Japanese nationality is presumed, shall be granted such nationality in accordance with laws of the Diet, at the latest of: one week after their declaration, their twenty-first birthday, and the twelfth anniversary of the treaty's entry into force. When California children who choose or are presumed to choose Japanese nationality are given such nationality, the protections of the previous two paragraphs shall apply to them. California children who choose or are presumed to choose United States citizenship shall be stricken from the household registers, if applicable, and given permanent resident alien status.

A child born after the treaty's entry into force to an parent previously an American citizen, when the parent has chosen, or has been granted, Japanese nationality, shall be granted full Japanese nationality at birth.

Article 29. Legal name.

For people who are living in California at the time that the treaty enters into force, and who remain in California, their full legal name as recognized under United States and California state law, shall be their legal name under Japanese law. All given names, whether first, middle, baptismal, or maiden, if legally valid in the State of California, shall continue to be valid, and the current (non-Hepburn) spelling of such names shall continue to be valid.

This shall hold for any person remaining in Japanese California, whether that person chooses Japanese nationality as described in the previous article, or retains United States citizenship.

Article 30. Criminal courts, jails, and prisons.

California state and local criminal courts shall remain open as long as needed, at United States expense, to try cases involving prior violations of California state and local laws.

California state, county, and city correctional facilities immediately shall be transferred to the Corrections Bureau of the Ministry of Justice. Inmates in California state, county, or city correctional facilities shall serve out the remainder of their sentences at United States expense.

Inmates in United States federal correctional facilities in Boron, Lompoc, Los Angeles, Pleasanton, San Diego, and Terminal Island shall be transferred to federal correctional facilities in other states as quickly as possible. Until it is emptied, a given federal correctional facility in California shall be considered to be still part of the United States and to be subject to U.S. law. When each federal correctional facility in California is emptied, it shall be transferred to the Corrections Bureau of the Ministry of Justice.

Article 31. Enforcement of USA and State of California laws that are carried over.

United States laws and California state and local laws elsewhere described as being in force in Japanese California after the treaty's entry into force, and which cover neither the American-Indian reservations nor areas elsewhere described as still considered United States territory, shall be considered as Japanese laws. Violations of these laws shall be dealt with by the Japanese criminal justice system, in accordance with Japanese law.

Article 32. Apportioning seats for the House of Representatives and the House of Councillors in Japanese California and Japan.

Seats for Diet representation shall be created or reduced in such a manner as to create political representation equally proportional between Japan's population of 128 million and California's population of 40 million.

Sixty days after the treaty's entry into force, forty-eight single-member electoral districts for the House of Councillors shall be created in Japanese California. In addition, thirty-one seats for the House of Councillors shall be granted on the basis of party-proportional voting within the Japanese California region. Likewise, sixty days after the treaty's entry into force, ninety-four single-member electoral districts for the House of Representatives shall be created in Japanese California. In addition, three electoral regions shall be created in Japanese California for House of Representatives party-proportional seating, and fifty-seven party-proportional seats for the House of Representatives shall be divided among those three electoral regions.

The Diet law that establishes the single-member electoral districts in Japanese California for the House of Councillors also shall designate which half of the seventy-nine House of Councillors seats shall be marked for re-election at the next regular House of Councillors election.

One hundred one days after the treaty enters into force, the number of House of Representatives members in the Japanese archipelago shall be reduced by sixteen seats. Of those elected on the party-proportional basis in each of the eleven electoral regions of the Japan archipelago, at least one seat and no more than two seats shall be selected by lot for reduction. For the sixteen Representatives so selected, their term of office shall expire immediately, in accordance with Japanese law and House of Representatives rules.

In the tenth year after the treaty's entry into force, a census of population shall be taken in all parts of Japan, including Japanese California. Seats in both houses shall be reapportioned based on the census data. The total number of lower-house seats thereafter shall not be greater than the chamber capacity of 635.

Article 33. Candidates for public office in Japanese California.

For six months after the treaty's entry into force, only thirty days' residence is required of candidates for public (political) office in Japanese California.

For fifty years after the treaty's entry into force, candidates for any public office in Japanese California must demonstrate bilingual ability as follows: Candidates whose native language is Japanese must take or retake and pass, at five-year intervals, the English portion of the current upper-secondary entrance exam; candidates whose native language is not Japanese must take the Japanese Language Proficiency Test at five-year intervals, and must thereby demonstrate the ability to speak, read, and write Japanese at the sixth-grade level. Candidates claiming both Japanese and English as native languages must fulfill both requirements.

Candidates for any public office in Japanese California must be Japanese nationals, or have filed their intention to become such when Japanese nationality is not possible. Candidates must meet the age requirements as specified under Japanese law.

Article 34. Voting in Japanese California.

Between the time that prior residents of California who are United States citizens have declared their intent to become Japanese nationals in the manner described above, and the time that they are granted Japanese nationality, they shall be eligible to vote in elections in Japanese California, provided that they meet age and length-of-residency requirements.

Article 35. Special election in Japanese California.

Elections to both houses of the Diet, to elect a governor of every prefecture in Japanese California, and to elect other prefectural offices in Japanese California as determined by the Diet, shall be held in Japanese California 101 days after the treaty's entry into force. California residents who are United States citizens must have declared their intention to become Japanese nationals as described above, and prior Japanese nationals must have resided in California for thirty days prior to the day of the elections, to be tentatively eligible to vote. Requirements other than length of residency, and citizen/permanent-resident status, shall be determined by Japanese law. For purposes of Japanese law, the elections shall be considered as called for at sixty-one days after the treaty's entry into force. The elections shall be held in accordance with Japanese law, except that pre-election posters and mailed materials shall be trilingual, as described below; and that election ballots shall be trilingual, as described below. Those people elected to the Diet and to prefectural offices shall be installed immediately.

Article 36. Japanese California regionwide referenda.

Any legislation applying wholly or primarily to Japanese California, passed by the Diet after the treaty's entry into force but before the installation of Diet members from Japanese California, shall become law only after approval in a regionwide referendum in Japanese California, 101 days after the treaty's entry into force. Any legislation applying wholly or primarily to Japanese California that is passed after the installation of Diet members from Japanese California cannot become law without the consent of the majority of the voters in a regionwide referendum in Japanese California, such consent obtained in accordance with Japanese law except for the trilingual provision below.

Article 37. Trilingual requirements.

For fifty years after the treaty's entry into force, election and referendum ballots for voters in Japanese California shall be printed in Japanese, English, and Spanish. For fifty years after the treaty's entry into force, government forms given to persons in Japanese California, as well as the instructions on how to fill out these forms, shall be printed in Japanese, English, and Spanish. This shall apply to every level of government, whether the Japanese national government, the Japanese California regional government, and Japanese California prefectural and local governments. Forms and their instructions shall include, but not be limited to, applications and tests for driver's licenses, applications and tests for professional licenses, tax forms, postal forms, household registers, and forms for Public Employment, National Health Insurance, and National Pension Fund.

Article 38. Conflict resolution.

Japan and the United States agree that if they seriously disagree about interpreting some part of this treaty, they will submit to binding arbitration by the United Nations. Japan and the United States understand and expect that as conditions change, parts of this treaty will be clarified or renegotiated through diplomatic means.

APPENDIX 2
California v. Swensen
(Supreme Court Decision
on the California Treaty)
taken from Chapter 9

The Supreme Court already in 1828 (*American Insurance Company v. Canter*) had observed that ". . .[the United States government] possesses the power of acquiring territory, either by conquest or by treaty." The Court of 2005 found that being able to buy territory via treaty logically implied being able to sell.

Next, the majority opinion cited the 1845 joint resolution that incorporated Texas. That resolution added the Republic of Texas, a recognized foreign power, to the United States directly as a state. Washington's joint resolution was passed after the Republic of Texas legislature had passed its own resolution requesting annexation. The transfer was not done by treaty, because regional animosities in the Senate in 1845 would have prevented such a treaty from receiving a two-thirds vote. But the joint resolution was intended in 1845 to have the same effect as a treaty, and the Court in 2005 so treated it. From examining the inclusion of Texas, the Court in 2005 found that since the United States government could directly add a state via an agreement with a foreign power, it followed that the United States government directly could divest a state through an agreement with a foreign power.

Thus the California Treaty could be logically justified. But was it constitutionally sound?

Cited next, and most convincing to the Court, were two prior Supreme Court decisions. In the first decision, *Texas v. White,* the Court in 1868 had remarked of a state's joining the Union, "There was no place for reconsideration, or revocation, except through revolution, or through consent of the States." Thus the Court in 2005 found that a state could be sundered from the Union with the consent of the states as a whole. Next cited was *Edwards v. Carter,* in which the Court in 1978 had upheld a ruling that the prior consent of the House of Representatives wasn't required for treaties that ceded the Panama Canal Zone to have legal force. From *Edwards v. Carter,* the Court in 2005 concluded that the advice and consent of the Senate would be sufficient to give the consent of the states for one state's revocation. Thus the Court of 2005 found the right to cede part or all of a state by treaty to be an inherent power of the federal government, a result of the federal government's Constitution-enumerated treaty-making power.

The Supreme Court rejected California's first argument that, without a state Act declaring California's consent, the California Treaty was unconstitutional. California in its argument had cited Article Four, Section Three, that ". . .nothing in this Constitution shall be so construed as to Prejudice any Claims of the United States, or of any particular State"; and Article Five, that ". . .no State, without its Consent, shall be deprived of its Suffrage in the Senate."

California's argument, the Supreme Court declared, logically led to California's hypothetical Consent Act being supreme over the treaty. As this logical conclusion was in contradiction with Article Six of the

Constitution, and also as such a conclusion prejudiced the claim of the United States to make a treaty, California's argument was ruled invalid. The Supreme Court ruled that Article Four, Section Three applied to laws and constitutional amendments strictly domestic in effect, but didn't apply to treaties. The Court interpreted Article Five narrowly: Article Five applied only to constitutional amendments, whose effects would be domestic, rather than treaties, whose effects would be international.

The Court rejected California's second argument that, since the Constitution didn't specifically authorize the sundering from the Union of a state by treaty, the Tenth Amendment to the Constitution denied the federal government this power, even should California consent. The court's reply: Treaty-making was an enumerated federal power, so the Tenth Amendment didn't apply.

California's third argument was that the United States was required to actively "guarantee" California's remaining in the Union. This argument had cited Article Four, Section Four of the Constitution (". . .the United States shall guarantee to every State in this Union a Republican Form of Government.") The third argument also had cited a different part of the opinion of the Court in *Texas v. White.* (". . .By these [the Articles of Confederation in the 1780s], the Union was solemnly declared to 'be perpetual.' And when these Articles were found to be inadequate to the exigencies of the country, the Constitution was ordained 'to form a more perfect Union.' It is difficult to convey the idea of indissoluble unity more clearly than by these words. What can be indissoluble if a perpetual Union, made more perfect, is not?. . .It may be not unreasonably said that the preservation of the States, and the maintenance of their governments, are as much within the design and care of the Constitution as the preservation of the Union and the maintenance of the National government. The Constitution, in all its provisions, looks to an indestructible Union, composed of indestructible States.")

The Court rejected California's third argument. The Court ruled that Article Four, Section Four applied only to domestic insurrection or foreign invasion, not treaties negotiated freely in peacetime.

As for *Texas v. White*, the Court in 2005 understood this earlier opinion to apply only in the context of the question of secession or, as the Court in 1868 had phrased it at the start of its ruling, "the question whether the right of a state to withdraw from the Union for any cause, regarded by herself as sufficient, is consistent with the Constitution of the United States."

A state couldn't quit, the Court ruled, but a state could be fired.

APPENDIX 3
Barbara's Explanation to Carol of the Political Importance in Japan of the Reapportionment Treaty Article (California Treaty's Article 32) to understand Chapters 10-17

The *San Diego Union-Tribune* was paying for the international call, but the newspaper wasn't getting its money's worth. Carol growled, "What do you mean, `You can't print any of this'?"

Barbara replied, "My plan only works as long as it's unnoticed—by the Japanese government and by the Japanese media. And yours is hardly an unread, unnoticed, no-surprises paper these days."

"Yeah, I know for a fact that Japan's consulate in L.A. takes our paper now."

"So as I said in the beginning, I'll be glad to spell everything out for you, answer all your questions. But in print, you can't even *hint* about what you know, for right now. Still interested?"

Over the phone, Carol sighed. "Yeah—*someday* we can print this."

Then Carol adopted a businesslike tone. "You and your allies in the Diet are counting on treaty Article 32, which changes representation within the Diet itself. Please explain briefly the Diet's structure now, how Article 32 would change it, and how Article 32 aids you in fighting the treaty's passage in the Diet. And remember, I didn't take that class where you learned about the structure of the Diet."

"Sure, Carol. First, some geography: Japan is divided into forty-seven prefectures, each about the size of a California county. The Diet's lower house, the House of Representatives, has five hundred members right now. Of that five hundred, three hundred come from single-member election districts. Every prefecture has at least one district, and the candidate with the most votes in a district wins."

"Like a Congressional district."

"Right. Of the other two hundred seats, those seats aren't filled by voters in hundreds of districts, but by political parties in eleven regions. A region covers a number of prefectures. At the same time a voter in an electoral region is casting a vote for a candidate in a district candidate election, the voter is casting a second vote for a party in a regional party election."

"That's two different ways and two different votes that the same voter is voting in one election."

"Yes. Let me back up a bit: Before the election, each party in the region had submitted a list of its candidates for proportional-seating selection. The candidates on this list were ranked by preference. Now after the election, when the votes for parties are tabulated for a district, the party votes are pooled with the other districts of that electoral region. The number of seats then given to each party in a region is based on that party's portion of the total party votes for that region, and the number of total seats granted that region. Then the list for that party is read, and the top however-many candidates become Representatives."

"Can you give me an example?"

"If the Fuji Party wins one-fifth of the party votes in a fifteen-seat region, the Fuji Party would be assigned three seats. The Fuji Party's three most favorite candidates would be elected."

Carol said, "Let me try my own example: Say a region were granted twenty seats, and half the region's voters voted for the Liberal-Democratic Party, with the other half voting Social Democratic Party. Then the top ten men and women on the Liberal-Democratic Party list for the region, and the top ten on the Social Democrats' list, all would become Representatives."

"It wouldn't only be two parties receiving votes— currently it's six, plus the JCP makes seven—but yes, you understand. What I've just described is how proportional-representation seats are filled in the House of Representatives. It's important that you understand how these two hundred proportional Representatives get their seats, because these are the only people vulnerable under the treaty."

"Nobody else in the Diet needs to worry?"

"That's correct. The 300 prefectural Representatives, and all 252 members of the House of Councillors, are safe."

"Okay, tell me how Article 32 presents big problems to these two hundred Representatives."

"For them Article 32 creates *huge* problems. It would take from those two hundred proportional-representation seats, sixteen away."

"Why sixteen?"

"That's to make sure neither Japan nor California is underrepresented, and so that the total number of seats is 635."

"Why that number?"

"That's the seating capacity of the House of Representatives chamber. Right now in the House of Representatives, they have five hundred members, to represent 128 million Japanese. If only 135 more seats can go to represent forty million Californians, California becomes 14 percent underrepresented."

"Which wouldn't be fair."

"Right. The sixteen seats that the treaty transfers are what California needs so that Japan and California both have the same number of constituents for each Representative, whether that Representative is prefectural or proportional-representation. So the State Department negotiators insisted that sixteen seats be transferred, the Foreign Ministry agreed, and the Diet's lower house suffers the consequences."

"So Article 32 would change representation in the Diet. How does this divide the Conservative Coalition?"

"A majority of the two hundred seats at risk would be held by Conservatives."

Carol rustled paper over the phone. "Article 32's fourth paragraph says that, among proportional Representatives, who would keep his or her seat and who would lose it would be determined by lot. That must be pretty unnerving."

Barbara laughed. "To put it mildly." Then Barbara's face turned serious again. "So a proportional Representative, who is probably a Conservative, will worry that he might vote for the very treaty that will cost him his seat. If he'll lose his seat, he won't learn his sad fate until 101 days after California is transferred. By then, it'll be much too late for him to change his vote."

"No matter what the treaty's seeming merits, he'll think carefully before voting for it."

"He's eager to find reasons to vote no, so that back home afterward he can convince the voters and the local party bosses he voted wisely. Our strategy is to meet his desperate need and to teach him those good reasons no."

PROLOGUE-ALT
Wednesday, November 3, 2004

"Congratulations on your re-election," Ambassador Fujima said in the Oval Office. He was addressing Charles Arthur "Charlie" Swensen. The ambassador continued, "Japan looks forward to working with you for four more years."

The time was nine in the morning, and the president and the ambassador were alone. Behind his grand desk, Charlie Swensen smiled and replied, "Your Excellency, I thank you for your kind words." Then he frowned. "But I didn't ask you to come here to accept your congratulations. Now we have business to address, which I can't avoid anymore."

"Thank you for remembering your promise, that today you answer Japan's query."

"Japan's quite disturbing query: `Would the United States please sell us a state, preferably California?' Even after two months, I find the idea revolting."

The ambassador steeled himself, even as his face kept a fixed smile. "So what is your answer? Do our nations begin negotiations?"

"Yes. The U.S. needs the money." Swensen's face looked wretched, while the ambassador was trying hard not to look shocked. "I will sell you California, may God and Mr. Lincoln forgive me."

CHAPTER 18-ALT
Heisei 17-nen 8-gatsu 24-nichi, Suiyohbi (Wednesday, August 24, 2005)

It was Shohji's turn to vote. He climbed the steps in front of the Speaker and dropped his signed slip into the ballot box on the podium.

From the visitors' gallery, Barbara saw that the slip was white. Shohji had voted yes.

Hiroshi stood at Ryuuji's desk the next morning, and Hiroshi felt overwhelmed. "Kinoshita-*san*, I don't know what to say. *Sumimasen zo* to you and everyone." Hiroshi recited, "I apologize to everyone for the trouble I've caused."

Ryuuji returned the bow smiling. "It's the least we could do. You're the company hero, Iwata-*kun*."

A few minutes before, Ryuuji had surprised Hiroshi with a congratulations gift: an envelope that was tied closed with red-and-white *mizuhiki* cord, and a blue-wrapped gift that could only have been a book. The gifts' wrappings had told Hiroshi that these were auspicious gifts. Ryuuji, of course, had politely insisted that the gifts were inadequate, then Hiroshi politely had protested that he didn't deserve such fine gifts.

When Ryuuji had given Hiroshi the blue-wrapped book, Ryuuji had explained that it was from the petition team only. "We hope that soon you can use it."

The envelope, Hiroshi soon had learned, held tens of thousands of yen, and five pages of brief congratulatory wishes from everyone in the company.

Standing at Ryuuji's desk, Hiroshi hefted the now-unwrapped book, *The JAL Travel Guide to California.* "It's heavy."

"The evening news gave me the idea," Ryuuji replied. "In March, a typical bookstore sold about one copy a month. Now every bookstore sells two or three copies *a day.*"

"Wow."

"This travel guide is a bestseller now, they can't print copies fast enough. I had to visit *three* bookstores to find this one copy."

"Again, I am overwhelmed by the caring kind generosity of you and Miss Higashi, and Mister Shinohara and Mister Fukuda." With his voice choked up, Hiroshi added, *"Dohmo arigatoh gozaimashita."*

When Barbara dragged herself through Airport Customs two hours later, San Diego time was after 7:00 p.m. Wednesday. "Ms. Nakamura, do you have anything to declare?" The words were rote, but the Customs woman's eyes were sympathetic.

Barbara sighed. "Nothing to declare, you'll find no guns or drugs, but please check anyway." She could really learn to dislike going through Customs.

TV camera crews filmed Barbara as she went through Customs. They kept filming as she cleared

Customs. They filmed as Ed and Carol took turns hugging her.

"Please don't blame yourself, it wasn't your fault," Carol consoled.

Ed gave his daughter another hug, one-armed around her shoulders. "You did your best."

Tacky's face was set impassive, but she had a light in her eyes. Tacky gave Barbara a quick hug, then she as quickly stepped back. Her mother respected the fact that Barbara was exhausted and depressed.

When it was clear that Barbara and her party were about to leave the airport, the press moved in. Barbara wouldn't play, though. "Folks, I'm so tired I'm drunk. I'll take one—no, two—I'll answer two questions now. Please understand."

The TV and newspaper reporters conferred, and chose their first question: "What do you say to the people of California?"

"Californians must learn to 'endure the unendurable.' I'm sorry I let everyone down."

"Where will you go now, and what will you do?"

"Teach Japanese in San Diego, California, my home."

At ten that evening, the wake at Larry's house was going full blast. Carol had brought out snacks, but nobody except Bobby ate much. Barbara couldn't stop yawning when she wasn't falling sleep in her chair.

Larry was explaining, "Bank officers are really worried. The last few weeks, the number of account openings dropped sharply, and account closes shot way up. Nothing we couldn't handle, certainly not a bank panic, but cause for concern. But today, wow! It seemed that every person who walked in wanted to close their—"

The phone rang, Larry answered. A minute later, President Swensen was saying to Barbara over the phone, ". . .And neither my conscience nor Stephanie have quieted since."

"Again, thanks for pardoning me. I guess you're feeling generous—that treaty with Russia is a sure bet."

The next morning, Barbara consulted her divorce attorney. He told her an informant in Sacramento had called him to say Matt was hiding money in a Sacramento bank account.

The attorney also reminded Barbara to move back into her house, to keep custody of it. She immediately began taking furniture out of storage.

Sometime that afternoon, she'd gone to the supermarket and saw herself on the front page of the newspaper. She decided that the Barbara in the newspaper photo looked like someone whose chemotherapy wasn't working.

Below Barbara's ugly picture was a brief story about the Diet's House of Councillors. An extraordinary session of the Diet was to be convened next Monday, and at that time the House of Councillors would receive the treaty. Progressives were stronger in percentage in the upper house than in the lower, the newspaper article noted. Thus the treaty, the newspaper predicted, would be voted down if the treaty even reached a vote.

But as Barbara already knew, that didn't matter. The House of Representatives had approved the treaty, so by Articles Sixty and Sixty-One of Japan's Constitution, all the House of Councillors could do was delay the inevitable by thirty-five days. California's only theoretical rescue under Japan's law was that the House of Councillors would vote down the treaty, then in joint committee the House of Councillors would convince the House of Representatives to recant its approval vote.

In other words, California's only hope was that a body of politicians would admit they'd made a mistake. California had no hope at all.

The newspaper article, concluding likewise, predicted that soon the treaty would go to the prime minister for his signature and stamp. However, "sources close to the prime minister" believed he wasn't ready to proclaim the treaty as soon as he received it.

To the left of Barbara's picture was a one-column story. In the Senate the Committee on Foreign Relations had reported out favorably START III, the "Nickels-for-Nukes Treaty."

To the right of her picture was a matching one-column story. After a stormy meeting, the Senate leadership had decided not to hold disciplinary proceedings against Matt. Minority Leader Leaird's angry objections were quoted at length.

That night, with help from her parents and Carol's family, Barbara finished moving back into her house.

Barbara answered her doorbell the next morning. "Why hello, Mrs. Harper, how are you today?" Mrs. Harper was the elderly neighbor who'd witnessed Barbara's adventure with the Japanese tour bus.

Mrs. Harper's hands were playing with the handle of her handbag. "I'm fine, thank you. I came over to say goodbye. I'm moving to Louisiana."

"Uh-huh, I noticed that your house had sold. A Japanese buyer, I'd guess."

"Yes, his name is Mister Motonaga, and he seems nice."

"Oh?"

"He complimented me on my marigolds and red zinnias. He also offered a very good price for the house."

"That's good. Is it for him? Is he going to live there?"

"No, he told me he wasn't. I think he's an investor."

Barbara nodded. She'd been approached by several investors herself. "So you're moved out already?"

"My son and daughter-in-law arrived from Shreveport this morning. They're helping me move. Plus I hired that Alvarez boy down the street to help us."

"By tomorrow you'll be gone, then."

"The moving shouldn't take that long. I threw away or donated a lot when Gregory died."

"That's good, your move won't be too expensive."

"No, especially after my son reminded me to save my receipts, so the government pays me back for moving from California. He said it was the one good thing in the treaty."

"Yes, that's true."

"Oh dear, how thoughtless. I'm sure it bothers you, my talking about that awful treaty."

"I'm over it now." *Yeah, right.* "Good luck to you. You always had such beautiful flowers in your yard."

"Yes, I enjoyed many hours tending my flowers. But now it's time to say goodbye and move on."

That night at the Stares and Strips Forever, Matt was sitting alone, watching the strippers. Because he was alone, Matt also was tossing back the bourbons and working himself into a fury.

"Isn't *fair* how other senators are treating me," he told his glass. "Is not fair. Take Gibson, Nevada's *idiot* senator. This afternoon, he's talking to some Army three-star. Gibson wants a goddamn army border post off Interstate 15, so he's sweet-talking the general. I walk up, I try to ease into the conversation, and Ken ignores me as if I'm not even there.

"Damn it, Ken, *I'm* the one who showed you how you could spend that money. And remember, *I'm* the one who pointed out all the military bases you could bring in!"

"Sir? I must ask you to stop talking so loud. You're disturbing other clients."

She was tall and tan and young and lovely, and wearing a McGovern '72 straw hat. She was a cocktail waitress, but Matt's was not one of her assigned tables.

"Honey, you know who I am?"

"Everyone here knows who you are, Senator. You've been talking to yourself for ten minutes now. We ask you to please stop."

"Honey, you ever been sweaty with a senator?"

"No."

"Today's your lucky day."

"I have other plans tonight. Please be quiet and behave, or the bouncer will be sent over." She left.

A dancer in fuck-me shoes walked over. "Lap dance, Senator? Thirty bucks."

This dancer looked like a runway model, with a lingerie model's breasts grafted on. Matt smiled approvingly. "It's a deal, honey, if you go home with me tonight." He reached for her hairless thigh.

Her hand caught his wrist. "Sorry, gotta shampoo my kitten tonight. How about that lap dance anyway?"

"Like I said, come home with me, money's yours."

"Nobody needs thirty bucks *that* bad, Senator." She also walked away.

He glared at her retreating form. "First it's McGovern Bitch, and now Runway Queen here," he griped, quietly so as not to summon the human mountain in the blazer. "Dammit, I'm still a senator, and I'm almost single. All I want is a heart-stopping beauty to take me home and romp me 'til dawn. That isn't too much to ask, and until now getting her *wasn't* a problem."

It wasn't long before Matt again felt the need to stagger to the men's room. This time, the bathroom was empty. He yelled, "Where the fuck *are* everybody, they quit drinking? *Can't* be that the snooty cows in this dive are so great to watch."

Soon he was relieving himself in the urinal. Dizziness made him lean forward so that the cold porcelain top of the urinal pressed against his chest.

"All women are whores," he informed the urinal. "When a man's on top of the heap, *whole sororities* will hump him on the hood of his car. But down on his luck, all he hears is `Get lost.'"

Matt heard the rest-room door open and shut.

The man walked to the stalls at the end, then returned to stand quietly behind Matt.

Matt glanced back. "If you left something in one of the stalls, people here are thieves. Meanwhile, second pisser here is vacant."

"That's okay. I'll wait till you're done." Oddly, the man was removing his sport coat, which he then threw over the door of the nearest shitter.

Soon Matt was empty. He shook himself a few times, put everything away, and zipped himself up. "Mela, did you ever even *like* me?" he asked aloud. "All women are whores, mister," Matt called over his shoulder. "It's true, all women are whores."

Matt heard an odd rubbery sound, followed by a click close behind.

The stranger's mouth was right at Matt's ear. "Vince in L.A. sends a message—"

A muscular left arm snaked around Matt's throat. "You—"

Matt was jerked back, pulling him off-balance.

"Fucked—"

Matt caught a glance of a right hand shooting forward, then back—a hand wearing a surgical glove and holding a knife.

"Up—"

The knife blade flashed the overhead lights into Matt's wide eyes, just before the blade entered ribs.

"Senator."

Red, the urinal was turning red. . .

Three mornings later, Carol picked up Barbara at her house to take her to the spa. "So how was your trip to Costa Mesa?"

Barbara shook her head. "Very strange. Right when I accepted I'd soon be a divorcee, I became a widow. No surprise, I was disinherited."

"Puny crowd at the funeral." TV news had shown a telephoto shot of Barbara and the few other mourners at the gravesite.

"Mm-hmm, hardly any of Matt's relatives attended. Maybe they were ashamed of him in the end, I don't know. The only people at the funeral were Matt's father and sister, Marcia, her husband and two of her adult children, my parents and I, and Joe Bob and Marilyn

Saunders. And the Senate Sergeant at Arms, paying official respects. Eleven, that's all."

"Nobody from his law practice or time as a Congressman, nobody else from the Senate? His other relatives were ashamed of him, you say?"

"I know *I* was. Actually, I felt every emotion in the dictionary. Driving up there, I was pounding the steering wheel in rage. Yet when I viewed him laid out, I felt an ache because I'd never see him or hear him again. I was the only person who wept at his funeral."

"You still love him. Amazing. Especially after he worked so hard to become unpopular."

"Sure seems that way."

"And his toil paid off: He got himself murdered, and then only eleven people came to his funeral."

"Not counting the press people who, thank goodness, kept their distance—no offense. And two FBI agents, who questioned me for three hours. The FBI men went all the way back to Matt's law-school days."

"An earful they got, I'm sure."

Barbara rolled her shoulders, mentally changing the subject. "I wonder whom Jim Dodson will stick with the job of being Matt's replacement?"

"You haven't heard? Governor Dodson won't appoint another senator. He says it's a waste of everyone's time."

A few minutes later, on their way to the health club, Carol and Barbara passed an elementary school. Every window facing the street had a crayoned drawing of a flag, a California flag alternating with an American flag. The crayoned flags ran in one long unbroken strip, between the leftmost window of the school and the rightmost window.

The California flag challenged the children. All could master the red stripe at the bottom. The older half decently could draw the red star in the upper-left corner, and legibly could write "CALIFORNIA REPUBLIC" above the bottom stripe. Yet only the oldest children could draw and color anything in the middle that even remotely resembled a grizzly bear on a hill.

In the front seat, Barbara's upper body was twisted around in order to keep eyeing the flags. "Look at that!"

"Yeah, it's Governor Dodson's idea. Everyone's urged to fly their American or California flag if they have one. If you have neither, draw them and put them in your window. Display them every day, and don't stop until the handover, at the earliest."

"At the *earliest*? Defy Japan?"

"Yeah. It's not illegal, it doesn't hurt anybody, doesn't damage property, so Japan can't bitch, right? But it damn well makes our feelings clear."

Friday night a month later, Barbara had a California flag or an American flag in all her front windows. Supermarkets, drugstores, convenience stores, hardware stores—she could buy the self-adhesive paper flags anyplace. Some of her neighbors had flagpoles and were flying real flags from them. All her neighbors had paper flags in their front windows.

Except for Mrs. Harper's house, the Grahams' house, and the home of the Moore sisters, which all stood vacant.

Barbara was dressing for a date. His name was Walter Wheeler. She liked him, and they were well-matched. Walter was forty-nine years old and divorced two years, he jogged three kilometers a day, sold commercial real estate, and had two kids in college. He liked sports and country music (nobody's perfect).

Walter also was a student in one of the Japanese classes Barbara was now teaching.

While Barbara was finishing her hair, she had cable television on. ". . .Stay tuned for ASN Newsbreak, bringing you the top headlines from America and the world, after this *brief* message."

"Hello, this is a reminder from San Diego Cable. Once Japan takes over, San Diego's network-affiliate TV stations lose those affiliations. The only way for *your neighbors* to receive programs by ABC, NBC, Fox, CBS, or the rest will be through cable. Tell us who your cableless friends and neighbors are, and that might put *money* in your pocket! We'll credit your cable bill three hundred yen—about five dollars—for each name that you refer to us and we sign up. That's three hundred yen a name—no other San Diego cable company pays you more! Simply fill out the referral sheet that comes with your next cable bill, or else call us at 555-6354. Remember, we'll pay you for good referrals. So fill out the referral sheet, or else call 555-6354, *today!*"

"This is ASN Newsbreak, 10:00 p.m. Eastern time, Friday, September 9.

"The last obstacle to proclaiming the California Treaty will be gone soon: Japan now can borrow money to make its first payment on California. The Diet's House of Councillors, in extraordinary session, approved the California Bond Act. The Act authorizes the Japanese government to sell government securities to raise three trillion dollars. The California Treaty will be ratified, and California will be transferred to Japan's sovereignty, only after Japan has raised the money for the first three trillion dollar payment. The House of Councillors approved the lower-house version of the bill with no changes.

"The Emperor of Japan is urging all Japan to buy the California bonds. Following the House of Councillors vote, Prime Minister Sasaki and his cabinet met with Emperor Akihito at 7:00 p.m. Japan time, six this morning Eastern time. Emperor Akihito went on nationwide television an hour later. In his address, the Emperor urged all Japanese people and Japanese businesses to buy—"

The doorbell rang. She remoted-off the television and the cable box, slipped on her pumps, and went to the door.

Walter bowed to Barbara as he'd learned in class. "*Sensei, komban wa.*" Teacher, good afternoon. "*O-genki desu ka?*"

"*Genki desu, Uiraa-san.*" I'm fine, Mister Wheeler. "*Dohzo o-agari kudasai.*" Please enter.

He walked in and, just inside the door, bent down. "Shoes?" he asked, smiling.

"Keep them on, Walter. Class is not in session, and California is not yet Japanese."

Yokohama time was slightly after four in the afternoon on Friday, December 9, when Chairman Matsumoto used the public-address system. "I am Matsumoto. Everyone please go to the cafeteria now. I have an announcement to make."

Ten minutes later, the Matsumoto Robotics employees stood two or three deep along the four sides of the cafeteria. Everyone was there: line workers in white coveralls; clerks dressed in blue, white, and purple uniforms; engineers in white shirts and ties, with a few white blouses mixed in; and managers in suits. The chairman, sporting a Matsumoto Robotics lapel pin and dressed in a black suit to contrast with his gray hair, stood on a cafeteria seat.

"Everyone, I thank you for coming. I have very good news for you. I understand that in a few hours, the government will announce when we'll claim California. I hear California will be Japan's within a few days. I know you'll be glad to hear that."

The entire room burst into enthusiastic applause.

Mister Matsumoto added, "One among you will be *very* glad to hear that."

This evoked good-natured laughter, and people glanced in Hiroshi's direction.

"But that's not what I called you in here to tell you. Would Production Department Manager OHMAE Gempaku, Arm Design Section Manager Tsurumi Masayuki, and Sales Technical Support Engineer Iwata Hiroshi step forward, please?"

Seven minutes later, the chairman was saying, ". . .then in April, Section Manager Tsurumi and Engineer Iwata went to a conference in San Diego. The Section Manager saw for himself Engineer Iwata calm down an American so angry he intended to punch him in the nose. It's an exciting story—ask Deputy Division Manager Tsurumi before he leaves to tell it to you."

The room's applause was heartfelt.

Then the chairman shocked Hiroshi to the core. "For these reasons, Engineer Iwata also will go to Santa Clara and also will be marked for promotion. Engineer Iwata will be transferred to the Quality Control Analysis Section of Robby Robotics, and a year from now will be promoted to Deputy Section Manager. Congratulations, future Deputy Section Manager Iwata."

With only a few words, the chairman had slashed years off Hiroshi's first promotion. Hiroshi barely heard his coworkers' applause.

Five minutes later, Mister Matsumoto closed the meeting by announcing a company recreation day and farewell party to celebrate the promotions and transfers, about a month hence. The party would be right before Mister Ohmae, Mister Tsurumi, and Hiroshi (and whoever else was selected by then) would all leave for Robby Robotics and *Kariforunia*.

Hiroshi was overjoyed. *I'm going to Japanese California!* After *that* news, the promotion was just seaweed on the rice cracker.

Accepting everyone's congratulations meant Hiroshi took a while to return to his desk (not that anyone was complaining). As soon as he sat down, Hiroshi was summoned to Section Manager Masumi's desk.

"Iwata-*kun*, when you first came to us, I must tell you that I was concerned if you would learn enough robotics fast enough."

"I know."

"However, now you are a competent part of the Sales Technical Support team, and this is what I told the other section managers and department managers."

This was a total surprise. "I thank you very much, but I still have much to learn."

"In turn, Section Manager Tsurumi apparently told the chairman that your English is excellent, and that you calmed hostile Americans very well."

Hiroshi eyed the floor. "Deputy Division Manager Tsurumi exaggerates my poor abilities."

Mister Masumi let Hiroshi disclaim, but then continued, "When Section Manager Tsurumi was asked whom he wanted on his team, he urged we pick you. He argued vigorously that, for this unprecedented opportunity, we weigh other factors besides seniority."

"I see."

"You heard what the chairman thought of that Nissan write-up. I hear he also was quite impressed by the leadership you displayed in recruiting others here to join you at the train station. Soon-Division Manager Ohmae endorsed Section Manager Tsurumi's vision, and the Section Manager's candidate. I was asked by the other managers if I had any objections; I didn't object. Receivables Section Manager Kawazoe, he also spoke for you. We then quickly reached consensus to okay the new Deputy Division Manager's recommendation: you."

"Huh. I expected to wait five years to become a deputy section manager."

"Instead you've been marked as management material. Iwata-*san*, let me add my own congratulations and best wishes."

"Thank you very much, Section Manager. But I know so little. . ."

"That's why a yearlong wait, to season you. Now I'll tell you what your promotion means, besides a company-paid move to *Santa Kurara*." Mister Masumi spelled out job duties, pay, and perks.

A minute after a smiling Hiroshi bowed himself out of Mister Masumi's cubicle, Hiroshi was at Reiko's desk. Hiroshi gestured to a corner of the room that was empty except for a potted plant. "I need to talk to you," he whispered.

She walked with him to the plant. Her eyes shone, so she obviously knew what was coming. The two of them earned many knowing smiles from Reiko's coworkers, especially the young clerical women. *Everyone knows what I'm about to say, before I say it!*

Behind the potted plant, Hiroshi resumed his excited whisper. He repeated what he just had learned, about when he would leave Yokohama, his duties in Santa Clara, and finally, he told her what he would pocket from his promotion.

". . .So, Reiko-*san*, I can afford to be married, and I think we would make a good `love marriage.' Please marry me."

She showed reserve. She didn't throw her arms around him, in front of the office ladies and her other coworkers. Reiko didn't even touch him. But her smile was as bright as Fuji-*sama*'s five lakes reflecting the early morning sun.

In traditional Japan, since Mister Tsurumi had introduced Hiroshi and Reiko, Mister Tsurumi also would've done the proposing. Go-between Mister Tsurumi would've taken Hiroshi's proposal to Reiko, and would've carried Reiko's reply back to Hiroshi. Hiroshi and Reiko would've done all the negotiations for the wedding and marriage only through Mister Tsurumi as messenger.

But these were modern times. Mister Tsurumi didn't negotiate the young lovers' marriage, but he was the first one Hiroshi told after Reiko accepted his proposal. Mister Tsurumi smiled approvingly.

Hiroshi next stopped off by Ryuuji's desk, on the way back to his own. An hour later, Hiroshi looked up from his desk to see Mister Tsurumi standing there.

Mister Tsurumi smiled. "Higashi-*kun* just told me she gave notice, her last day being the recreation day next month."

"Yes, she doesn't want to create hardship by leaving earlier."

"Chairman Matsumoto wishes you two every happiness. He says she'll make you a great wife."

"How did the chairman—? Oh." That Ryuuji! To cover his embarrassment, Hiroshi remarked dryly, "It seems Kinoshita-*kun* enjoys talking about me."

"Yes, and what he tells everyone is that he admires your courage."

Saturday, December 17, 2005, was almost four months after Shohji's vote. In Barbara's house in San Diego, her cable-box clock showed 3:00 p.m. The changeover was scheduled for four o'clock, so California would be American for only one more hour.

San Diego was (mostly) defiant to the last.

Every streetside window on Barbara's house displayed a California flag, or the obsolete fifty-star American flag. It was the same in every San Diego neighborhood. And businesses of every kind (supermarkets, gas stations, fast-food restaurants, even adult bookstores) had American and California flags in all their streetside windows.

Hotels and motels displayed no paper flags. Those hotels and motels with flagpoles commonly flew the Japanese flag beneath the American and California flags. Almost all the motels and hotels that Barbara had seen had signs reading, "*Irasshaimase.*" (Welcome.)

But inside her house, Barbara was throwing a watch party. It was her way of coping with the fact of the handover.

Six of her Japanese-class students already had arrived for the party. Sprawled in front of the TV, three were watching American Satellite News:

". . .Sasaki hosted the Swensens at a state dinner at the Beverly Hills Hotel yesterday. Japan's consulate in Los Angeles made the arrangements, the consulate's last official act."

The picture showed the prime minister and the president, as well as their wives, drinking from box-shaped wooden cups. The men gulped the *sake*, the women sipped it.

The announcer again: "At the dinner, President Swensen announced `with relief' that the Treasury Department immediately was ending the issuing of deficit-covering bonds.

"Today the Senate okayed the START III treaty with Russia, the so-called `Nickels-for-Nukes Treaty.' Once he'd returned to Washington, President Swensen immediately ratified the START III treaty."

The picture showed Swensen in the Oval Office signing something, while Dave Fuller, Joe Bob Saunders, Dick Thompson, and Ambassador Borzov looked on.

The announcer continued, "That treaty now goes to Moscow for ratification, which is expected soon.

"California National Guard Colonel Scott Powers stated that the Los Angeles riot is mostly under control. However, the Oakland riot still is not under control, with incidents of shooting and looting. One fireman was killed and one wounded in a shooting incident, as emergency vehicles responded to a fire at an Oakland apartment complex."

The picture showed firemen and several fire engines. The firefighters were working to put out fires that raged simultaneously in several adjacent apartment buildings. The picture abruptly switched to a fireman, bare to the waist except for red-soaked bandages around his chest, an oxygen mask strapped to his blackened face. He lay on a stretcher being loaded into an ambulance.

The announcer continued, "Riot police from Japan's National Police Agency are now standing by, expecting to be called up in an hour." The television showed stock footage of riot police facing Japanese student demonstrators.

"Japanese California might face armed confrontation again in six months, this time with the Army of the Second California Republic. Today the ASCR vowed to fight `to the death' Japanese California's transition in six months to Japanese gun laws. The threat was made in a communiqué sent today by ASCR commander General Albert LeBlanc. LeBlanc wrote in part, `If you think Chinese Hong Kong is a powder keg, it's nothing next to Japanese California in six months.' Six months from now is the deadline for Californians to come into compliance with Japanese gun laws."

The television showed a fiftyish man with a trimmed gray beard and foreign-made camo fatigues, who was talking to a TV reporter.

———

By 3:14, Barbara's parents, Carol, Larry, and Bobby all had arrived at Barbara's house for the watch party.

A TV ad for microwave popcorn followed with the news anchor, looking solemn. "Folks, we have confirmation that the official plane now is landing at Sacramento International. We're switching you now to live pool coverage."

The television picture switched to an obviously telephoto-augmented shot of a passenger jet, only a few meters above the runway and descending.

A woman's voice narrated, "This is Sondra O'Dell, of Sacramento station KXTV. Besides carrying the three trillion dollars, the plane you're seeing is carrying Foreign Minister Masashi Irisawa and Governor Matsuzaka. The Honorable Tetsuya Matsuzaka will be the regional governor of Japanese California."

The pilot was good, the plane hardly bounced when it touched down.

O'Dell's voice resumed, "Slightly less than an hour from now, it is Foreign Minister Irisawa who formally will take possession of California, then Governor Matsuzaka will administer Japanese California."

Time: 3:21 p.m. On television, the plane had been met where it had stopped on its reserved runway. Once Foreign Minister Irisawa was down the runway stairs, he walked through a human corridor, a Japanese military honor guard on his left, and a multiservice U.S. military honor guard on his right. Two men followed behind Irisawa.

Reporter O'Dell commented, "The man behind Foreign Minister Irisawa, the one without the briefcase, is Governor Matsuzaka. You might recall that Matsuzaka was prime minister from 1999 to 2002. He campaigned hard in the Diet for the California Treaty, so regional governorship of Japanese California is his reward. The Japanese servicemen you see in the honor guard are in the Ground Self-Defense Force, which is Japan's army."

Past the honor guard, Foreign Minister Irisawa met Secretary of State Wendall Harland, who shook his hand. Then Harland and soon-Governor Matsuzaka shook hands.

When the dignitaries climbed into their limousines, reporter Ann Johnson in the KCRA News helicopter took over coverage.

Time: 3:34 p.m. On television, the limousines had dashed to Capitol Mall downtown, protected by a two-nation military escort (Humvees, Mitsubishi Jeeps, and a Blackhawk). Now as Harland and his aide, Irisawa and his aide, and Matsuzaka stepped out of their flagged limousines, reporter Johnson in the news helicopter handed off coverage to KOVR reporter Neal Lawson on the ground at Capitol Mall.

A wooden platform, seen now from ground level, had been constructed on the grass west of the Capitol Building. American and Japanese flags hung down from the front of the platform. Atop the platform were a speaking podium and a row of four chairs, with a second row of two chairs behind them. Banners resembling stretched American and Japanese flags ran lengthwise down the podium's front.

Harland, Irisawa, and Matsuzaka, followed by the two aides, mounted the stairs to the platform. Governor Jim Dodson already sat in the rightmost of the four chairs in the first row. Harland took the seat next to Dodson, Irisawa the seat next to that, and Matsuzaka

506 Tom H. Richardson

took the leftmost seat. The aides to Harland and to
Irisawa took seats in the second row, behind their
respective leaders.

The television camera quickly panned the audience,
who sat in front of the platform in neat rows of folding
chairs. All were well dressed; all but eleven of the
approximately hundred people were Japanese. Lydia
Dodson and her two teenage daughters sat in the front
row. Governor Dodson's family wore conspicuous
California-flag pins.

Time: 3:35 p.m. In Barbara's living room Carol
recalled for Ed and Tacky, "So Barbara had been in
Washington only a few months when I found out I was
pregnant. When I called to tell her, she went on and on
about the monuments, the restaurants, Smithsonian,
Library of Congress, all that. But by my baby shower,
she talking about how tourist buses in Washington
drive too slow, as if she a lifelong resident."

Ed nodded. "I think she's going through withdrawal.
She misses the excitement of the last sixteen years,
misses being close to the action."

Tacky also nodded. "She told me that now the
reporters not call her. Why she said that, unless she
wanted them call?"

Time: 3:35 p.m. On television, the four dignitaries
began giving speeches. Irisawa went to the podium
first. He spoke Japanese, but the voice of a translator
was what came out of the speaker (until Larry muted
the television).

Time: 3:50 p.m. On the screen, Harland and Matsuzaka had pantomimed their speeches. Now Governor Dodson took the podium.

From the kitchen doorway Barbara asked, "Would someone turn the sound back on, please? I want to hear Dodson."

". . .for the people of Japan, but a day of sadness for us of California. Feelings of sorrow, anger, and regret will stab us in the weeks ahead. Yet regret is pointless. So let us look no more to our golden past, but let us turn hopeful eyes to the future. . ."

Time: 3:55 p.m. Barbara thought, *Now's the time to announce it.*

Governor Dodson had just finished his speech. Standing in front of the TV, Barbara turned to Carol as she gestured to the TV. "I called Jim Dodson last night. The poor man, he was depressed but was trying not to show it."

Larry, who had been discussing with Walter and Ed how the takeover would affect San Diego pro sports, overheard. "Gee Barbara, you had Yamamura calling you, then the president, now you call the governor. Who will you chat with next, hm? Dimitrov? Al-Amin?"

As Carol gave him a wife-look, Barbara replied straight-faced, "Emperor Akihito—he often drops by for coffee. Unless I've been invited to Buckingham Palace again."

Then Barbara turned a serious face to Carol. "I told Dodson I was thinking of running for a Diet seat representing San Diego, two months from now when the treaty allows me to declare my candidacy. He begged me to run."

"You'd be perfect. I hope I'm the first journalist you've told, now that you're announcing your decision."

Barbara blinked in surprise. "You think I'd already decided to run."

"I *know* you did, girlfriend. You'll tell me and everyone else that you'll run for a Diet seat because Californians need Californians who can read and write Japanese to run for Diet seats."

"But that's true, Californians—"

"You'll add that too few Californians meet the sixth-grade Japanese-fluency rule."

"Which would be true. Those are excellent reasons for my running, Carol."

"But not the real reasons. Admit it: you told yourself, 'It's about time *my* name went on a ballot.'"

Barbara smiled. "You know me too well."

Time: 3:55 p.m. On television, when Dodson finished and sat down, Foreign Minister Irisawa beckoned to his aide. The aide opened the briefcase he was carrying and removed a large, flat envelope and a letter-size envelope. The letter-size envelope was tied with red-and-white cord. The aide passed the envelopes to Irisawa.

Irisawa gave the envelopes he held to Harland. Harland opened the envelopes, glanced at their contents, and nodded. Harland then gave the envelopes he'd received to his aide, who put the envelopes into his own briefcase.

The reporter Lawson was saying, ". . .gave to Secretary of State Harland was Japan's instrument of acceptance—the approved treaty—with Prime Minister Sasaki's signature, and perhaps some kind of Japanese government stamp or seal on it. Irisawa handed over the draft, or drafts, on the Bank of Japan as well. I have no way of confirming at this point, but an informed source told me that Swensen asked for ten drafts of three hundred billion dollars each, to ease the shock on the foreign-exchange markets. So this was how Irisawa supposedly made payment."

Time: 3:56 p.m. On television, the six men on the platform stood and faced the dome of the Capitol, as the USMC Marching Band began to play "The Star-Spangled Banner."

Neal Lawson on the ground switched the television coverage back to Ann Johnson in the KCRA News helicopter. The TV's picture switched to the Capitol dome and the flagpole atop the roof, now shot from the same height.

A door in the dome opened. Two Marine lieutenants and a sergeant, in full dress uniform, stepped out. They marched single file along a walkway to the flagpole atop the west wing of the Capitol. The flagpole flew three flags: the American flag, the California flag, and the black POW-MIA flag. The Marines saluted the flags, then they began to lower them.

The reporter Johnson pointed out the significance: "Except for normal replacement, these flags never came down. By California law, the POW-MIA flag only would've come down when all Americans missing in action in Southeast Asia were accounted for."

Time: 3:58 p.m. On television, the three flags were folded into three triangles. One Marine officer held a blue triangle, the other Marine officer held a white triangle, and the sergeant held a black triangle. Single file, blue triangle-white triangle-black triangle, they marched to the door by which they had come. They stepped through the Capitol-dome door, and the sergeant shut it.

Time: 4:00 p.m. On television, the three Marines, photographed from overhead, marched down the front steps of the Capitol. Camera coverage switched to the ground; the picture switched to the dignitaries' platform, again shot from the ground in front.

The three Marines climbed the stairs to the platform, as the men on the platform turned to face them. The sergeant handed the POW-MIA flag to the officer who carried the California flag. That officer presented both flags to Governor Dodson. The other Marine lieutenant presented the American flag to Secretary of State Harland.

Jim Dodson's chin and lower lip trembled, and he blinked often. Harland looked somber.

The three Marines saluted Dodson and Harland, did an about-face, and marched single-file from the platform. Every movement of every Marine was machine-precise.

Time: 4:01 p.m. On television, camera coverage passed again to the helicopter. Again the picture switched to the Capitol-dome door and the denuded flagpole, photographed at their level.

Two Japan Ground Self-Defense Force officers stepped out of the Capitol-dome door and marched single file to the flagpole. They hoisted the Rising Sun, then saluted it. They held their salute.

Back to the ground camera: the picture switched to a shot of the Capitol flagpole, from a ground perspective, flying Japan's flag.

A Japan Maritime Self-Defense Force military band began to play a song. According to the reporter Lawson, the song was "*Kimigayo*," Japan's national anthem.

Lawson added, "Behind the Capitol Building is Capitol Park. The garden you're seeing on your screen now is the California Vietnam Veterans Memorial at the east end of Capitol Park. An official with the Consulate of Japan in San Francisco informed me a minute ago that Governor Matsuzaka has directed that the Memorial's flagpole retain its American flag. This is out of respect for the dead of American war.

"Californians, treasure this flag. In two years United States post offices will be closed, the defense plants will be closed, the military bases will be given to Japan, and the San Francisco Mint will be torn down. In two years this flag, and the flags in the six national cemeteries within California, will be the only seven—I'm sorry, this is hard for me—will be the only seven American flags flying in California."

Time: 4:03 p.m. On television, Foreign Minister Irisawa walked to the podium. The podium, only a kilometer and a half away from the American River, amplified his words. "*Iza, kore ga Nihon no Kariforunia de aru to sengen suru.*"

I hereby proclaim, this is Japanese California.

After which, the Variety-Show Host was somber.

This is our last show here; starting Monday, we tape in Seattle. I've thought a long time about what to say now: an earthquake joke, or a crack about the Dodgers, or sumo humor. Instead, I'll say only—

God, but I'll miss California.

The (Alternate) End

www.ingramcontent.com/pod-product-compliance
Lightning Source LLC
Chambersburg PA
CBHW071336020726
47502CB00001B/116